Shadow Code

Mike Hawkes

First Edition

ISBN: 978-1-78926-211-7

To those that strive to support privacy, freedom and democracy.

Thanks to everyone that helped during my journey.

While the names, places and events are fictional, the core technology does exist; democracy depends on our ability to control it.

Mike: "Is it all Ok?"

Editor-in-Chief (AKA 'Mother'): "Yes, it's fine although I skipped through most of the technical bits"

Mike: "Oh, too much? Should I remove them?"

Editor-In-Chief: "No it's important and probably means something to someone."

1

The explosion ripped through the kitchen diner, the shockwave taking out the partition wall separating the diner from the living room. Windows shattered outwards as the pressure wave, debris and bits of scorched flesh burst through them. The air filled with the smell of acrid smoke and dust. Apart from the Honda's car alarm, the world around the house seemed eerily quiet.

As distant dogs started barking, two men walked towards the house, and then seeing matted blood and hair on the remains of the lawn, walked back and climbed into the rear seats of a waiting black BMW. Quietly, the doors closed and the car pulled away leaving a scene of carnage and destruction behind it.

Clive was having a bad day.

He was staying at a seedy hotel. It was clean enough, but had clearly seen better days. Built around the late 1970's, the rooms offered little in terms of creature comforts and lacked even basic Internet connectivity. This annoyed Clive - how could a modern hotel not provide even basic connectivity?

His mobile 'phone alarm went off. He silenced the alarm and turned the lights on before stumbling over to the shower, wishing he hadn't had quite so much to drink the night before.

Clive was due to give a presentation to Birmingham police on how to obtain data about people via social media and open Internet sources. He often lectured about 'online security', the 'perils of social media', and 'sharing too much information online'. On this occasion, his audience wanted to know how to obtain information from public sources - in other words, what could the police get for free, and without needing a warrant.

As he ran through his intended presentation, he thought of adding another twist. He preferred live demonstrations to 'death by powerpoint'. This additional section would demonstrate how easily hackers could build an automated 'profile crawler' by recursing through any publicly accessible data. He could use this to gather all the available data about randomly chosen 'victims', crawling through social media profiles to collect data about their location, friends, shopping habits, and pictures.

Due to the lack of Internet connectivity in the room, Clive decided to use his mobile as a wireless hotspot. He never trusted public wireless connections, so he used his own virtual private network to connect back to his computer at home. His home computer then acted as a gateway to the rest of the Internet. At least this way, he could provide a layer of protection for all his basic information - email accounts, usernames, passwords, and services used.

After a few minutes, the connection stabilised and he opened up a virtual desktop session. Virtual desktops allow you to see and control your desktop as if you were actually at the computer.

In keeping with the 'bad day' theme, the 'connecting' message appeared, but stayed on his screen. After a while, the virtual desktop manager threw a 'connection error' and exited. Clive, grumbling at the technology, tried to connect again, this time being advised that his virtual private network had failed to connect.

After several cups of coffee and much swearing, he finally gave up trying to connect to the computer back at home. It was either a network issue, or his home computer had failed to respond - perhaps it had crashed or there had been a power failure. Whichever way, he wasn't going to get his additional scripts.

In frustration, he slammed the top of the laptop closed and gathered his belongings to pack and leave for the presentation.

He turned to pick up his laptop, forgetting it was still connected to his mobile by its charging cable. Accidentally, he pulled his mobile off the desk and it fell onto the wooden floor with a sickening crack.

"Fuck!"

Clive bent down to pick up the shattered device. The screen had splintered and was displaying an interesting but entirely useless pattern. He turned it off. For the first time in many years, Clive was now 'off the grid'.

Swearing to himself, he packed the broken device into a pocket at the front of his bag.

He stomped to the hotel lobby, and from there to the conference room. After introducing himself to the event organisers, Clive made his way to the front of the room to look at the available presentation equipment. For an older venue, the kit wasn't too bad. He decided he could use the hotel's computer which would emphasise the use of 'normal' technology. The event host came and brought him another coffee and they chatted while the audience assembled itself.

Clive started off by demonstrating how people bridge different social network services. He searched for current posts from people close to the hotel and asked the audience to select a couple of entries – making them the target of the day's demonstrations. Being a predominantly male audience, they naturally chose two good looking women - the first being a woman with bright red hair called "Karen" - she had posted that she was currently "at Costa getting bored bored bored!".

"Who said sexism was dead?", he thought as he opened up a second browser window on the conference centre's computer. He wanted to make the point that the information gained from this session would be available to anyone using a standard browser on a standard computer. The fact that the venue had a good system made life easier - after all, had Clive used his own machine, the delegates might have thought he had specialised software to help him.

He called up a map showing Karen's current location - by chance, it was the building next door and it would take about 2 minutes to walk to her. From this along with the original selected post, Clive highlighted certain additional posts of interest and followed links to other social media sites while creating a network diagram showing: Karen's profile data; people she knew, locations, and their associated visiting times, and so on. Eventually he built up a complete profile including: her mother's maiden name, current address, telephone number, workplace information, colleagues, family members, children, and a reasonably comprehensive list of her friends. From the friend's profiles, he discovered more connections that showed links to past relationships, political leanings, holiday locations - even an argument with Barlcays Bank.

Clive was on a roll. The showman side of his personality came out and he suggested that, as she was virtually next door, he would ring 'Karen - aka the victim' and test the validity of the information gathered during the first part of the presentation.

'I have no idea if she'll agree to this, but it's worth a try', he said.

With that, he used the conference podium telephone to call the number gathered from the Internet search. After a few moments, Karen answered her 'phone.

'Hello - Karen?'

'Yes, who is this?', she replied.

'My name is Clive and I'm calling from the hotel conference centre next door to the Costa coffee where I believe you are sitting, getting bored, bored and bored, right now. I take it you are still in Costa?'

'Erm, yes', said Karen dubiously.

'Great! In that case I wondered if you could find a few moments for us to explain what we have been doing with your information from the Internet. It shouldn't take more than a few moments, we're right next door, I think you'll find it really interesting. After all – you did say you were bored - and from your profile, I bet you'd like to see a load of fit men in uniform on an otherwise boring wet Tuesday afternoon! - It's a Police conference and I'm showing what I can do with people's data that they share online. I'd really appreciate your help in letting me know whether I got everything right - and the only person that can do that is you …'

'Well … erm', Karen said hesitantly

As it wasn't an outright 'no', Clive came back immediately with 'Excellent - I'll send a couple of policemen to come and fetch you. And we'll even buy you another coffee afterwards for your trouble. See you in a moment.'

He hung up before Karen had a chance to reply.

'Could someone go and collect Karen from Costa please? Probably better if a couple of uniformed officers go - you know what she looks like', he asked, pointing to Karen's picture on the screen.

Two people stood up at the back of the room. Clive

thanked them - he thought they'd probably sneak a cigarette while they were out so he'd have a few minutes to kill. He filled the time by asking the audience to analyse the data collected and assist with the completion of 'Karen's network' diagram.

After about 10 minutes, a rather nervous Karen arrived, flanked by the two police officers. Clive went to meet her, shook her hand, and then brought her towards the front of the stage. He blacked out the screen.

'Hi Karen', he said, 'let me introduce you to my audience today. Karen - the audience, audience - Karen'

Karen smiled nervously as the audience gave her a somewhat muted round of applause.

Back in 'showman mode', Clive adopted his best 'Sherlock Holmes' pose.

'By the way you walked in, I would say that you're 38, probably with three children called Bethany, Carla and Kylie, you had your hair dyed again yesterday at the same place you always go, recently back from a holiday in Barcelona, new shoes that you really love - and you like Costa more than Starbucks ... how am I doing?'

Karen was visibly shocked.

'That's all right ...'

'Good - ok, next round ... I think you live at number 14 Tollgate Lane, you work at the Children's Centre on a part-time basis. Your children go to Central Academy although you think they're a little heavy-handed sometimes. Recently you found Mark and have loved the way he managed to get on with your kids ... still right?'

'How do you know all this?', asked Karen.

'Good question! We actually know a great deal more too - let me show you how we came to find out all this ...'

He walked back to the podium and turned the projector back on again.

'We chose you at random from people who were posting information locally. This', he said pointing to the initial comment, 'told me that you were in Costa, and bored. This ugly lot', he pointed the audience, 'wanted to know how much we could find out about a person using only the information they share.'

He called up the main browser again.

'From that initial post, we went to your main feed. Here, you can see most of the information about where you go regularly. Most evening and early morning posts such as this one …'

He pointed to a comment saying 'why do the kids take so long to get ready for school?'

'… And others like it, all come from the same location. Late night and early morning posts from the same place suggest that you must live there. Posts related to your job during working hours provide your work location - and that's before we go to your main profile page.'

He scrolled through a set of posts until he found some containing images.

'Most people don't know that mobile devices embed the location in the meta data for each photograph. This stuff shows us that you were in Barcelona - look', he pointed at the list of data shown by displaying the image meta data, 'it shows your location, the altitude, and the direction you faced. From this data, we can work out which room you stayed in - and if you look at these photo's'

He displayed a couple of pictures containing a shot of an hotel room.

'I think you stayed in this room … but …'

He showed another picture with a drinks on a balcony and a group of partying lads.

'You also seem to have spent some late nights and early mornings in this room.'

Karen looked visibly shaken. Clive, sensing her discomfort, backtracked to the main feed.

'Anyway, from here, you have shared links to your other profiles. It's always a bad idea to have all the social media services linked like this - you compromise one, you compromise all … here we can confirm your place of work, and you working hours … here we have pictures of the inside of your house and garden - along with confirmation of the location … here we see where and when you go shopping. And finally, for identity theft specialists, here's your birthday and off this one, a link to your mother's maiden name …'

Clive looked out at the audience.

'I always keep all my accounts separate. I never share information about my location until I leave somewhere, I strip all the metadata from pictures before I post them, and I always use a fake birth date for sites that really don't need to know it. Ladies and Gentlemen, this …'

He said, pointing to the browser windows.

'… Is what you can find online within a few clicks. It is all public data, so we don't need a warrant to look at it. However, please bear in mind that it might not be Karen - it could be someone impersonating Karen to create a fake online profile. Karen - thank you for coming over - I hope you found it educational?'

'Yes - very', replied Karen, 'Scary - never mind "educational" - I'm going to delete my profiles now …'

'No - no need - that's not what I'm saying', said Clive, 'perhaps just change the security settings to limit access to friends only, and post things that don't reveal as much about your personal life. Ladies and gentlemen, please show your appreciation to Karen …'

While the audience applauded, Clive went over to Karen and asked her to wait while he closed the presentation. There were a few questions and Clive finally finished off with his usual close: 'I hope you enjoyed today - please feel free to post comments or ask questions on my social media feeds - after all, I know where you are …'

After saying his farewells to the event organisers and answering a few questions from a few people who waited to speak to him, Clive took Karen back over to Costa and bought two coffees. They sat down and started chatting. They sat in an alcove with a television screen behind Karen on the wall. On mute, the TV was showing BBC News 24 with subtitles. Periodically, Clive would glance up at the screen as they discussed the presentation.

'I never realised you could get hold of so much information about me', said Karen, 'it's worrying!'

'Well, you put it out there', he replied with a broad grin, 'and it's your choice to publish or not to publish. I just hope you've seen what someone can do with your data - just imagine if I was a large corporate: I could work out how best to sell to you, and what will influence your decisions, your motivations and drivers … they make a fortune from selling all this data'.

'I bet! Are you a policeman then?'

'No, I'm an inventor - I invent stuff to secure people - I'm a big privacy advocate. I act as a consultant-cum-trainer as and when I can help!'

Clive glanced at the screen and froze.

Karen was saying something but he was transfixed on the TV behind her. While Karen carried on talking, Clive saw a picture of his house with fire-crews and police in attendance. The subtitles showing that at least one person had died in an explosion …

Clive went white and then grey. He was short of breath and his heart started pounding in his chest. He mumbled an apology and said he had to leave. Looking around him, he ran back to his hotel room and deadlocked the door.

Grabbing the TV remote, he skipped through the news channels. Waiting for news stories to cycle round was agony, but eventually the newsroom went live to his house again.

After showing the devastated house, debris and policemen taping off the area, the news reporter interviewed a Detective Chief Inspector Steve White - he stated that it was too early to determine the cause of the explosion, or how many people were in the house at the time - although he believed that at least one person had died at the scene. This was followed by an appeal for witnesses, along with a 'phone number.

Numb with shock, Clive picked up the hotel 'phone and dialled the number.

'Can I speak to Detective Chief Inspector Steve White please? I've seen my house on the TV and I think someone just tried to murder me …'

2

Bren dropped a document on Clive's desk.

'Look at this crap', he said.

'Ok - what is it?', asked Clive, picking it up and scanning the opening paragraph. 'Oh!'

'Yes', said Bren, 'what a waste of fucking time and effort. It's taken weeks and they come back with that crap!'

Clive and Bren were both founder directors of MKI, a company that developed and licensed security products for use on large networks. They had built extremely effective security products that would prevent people from intercepting or exploiting data sent over the Internet. Employing a team of specialist coders, MKI had defined and implemented a new set of security protocols that removed the need for much of the complex (and, frankly, broken) systems employed by most online services.

The UK is not a place in which to invent security products - the UK Government and banking communities rely on ageing and largely ineffective systems developed in the USA. With consultants employed by the big US firms (that make their money from these products and services) firmly ensconced within the national strategic areas of the Home Office and Cabinet Office, most of the UK security strategy exists merely as an extension of US policy. Small innovators have little - if any - chance of breaking in to the market.

To make things worse, for government or large corporates, security products must generally have some form of certification from CESG - the UK Government's Technical Authority for Information Assurance. MKI had employed a specialist consultancy firm to obtain the appropriate certification.

The report Bren had thrown on Clive's desk revealed that, MKI's products were new and didn't use any of the ageing US technologies. Thus, CESG didn't know how to categorise or assess MKI's products within its existing testing framework. Because they couldn't work out how to make the paperwork fit, they chose to bounce the whole thing - the final statement in the report stating:

"Unfortunately, CESG can only assess products in line with national strategic policy. This product does not utilise any of the standard technologies normally assessed, therefore CESG has no testing framework that would apply. If, however, a Government agency wishes to use this technology and has the available budget to allow CESG to assess the product, then CESG will extend its services to that Government agency in line with national policy and strategy."

'That's bollocks', said Clive emotionally, 'it means we need to get a Government agency to pay CESG to evaluate our stuff before they can use it - and if it doesn't pass the test, they'll waste their money. No project would engage on that basis - it's too risky', he sighed.

'We're going round in circles with it', agreed Bren, 'what do we do? We've spent fifty thousand on documentation, consultants, and assorted crap just to have the blasted door slammed in our faces.'

'I wouldn't mind if they had said the technology didn't work, or they'd found some form of compromise - but to bounce us on the basis that they don't have the right boxes on their forms …', Clive trailed off, '… how the hell does anything new get approved then?'

'It doesn't', replied Bren, 'perhaps we need to be a big American corporate.'

Clive handed the report back to Bren.

'We just keep our focus on Asia - perhaps once we've established ourselves out there CESG might play ball?'

MKI had spent some time out in Malaysia and Singapore working with a large communications network provider - NetTel. NetTel had opened numerous doors, and introduced MKI to the Ministry of Home Affairs in Singapore. After several meetings, the Ministry had invited MKI to work with them on the development of secured communications to a new breed of secured storage device.

Unlike the UK, Asia had an appetite to assess and develop new security solutions, and Clive had spent some considerable time getting MKI's products to work with the new devices. He often wished the UK had a similar entrepreneur-friendly framework and had raised the issue at several conferences since. In some ways, he felt he was working against the interests of his own country by making another country's technology more robust. However, the CESG report demonstrated the backward thinking and inability to innovate so often seen in the civil service.

'It's crazy', Clive continued, 'in Singapore, the MHA has engaged with this tin-pot inventor stroke company in a different part of the world, yet our own Government won't even get out of bed to look at it. Sorry - you say 'central heating' - hmm, how many fires does it need per household, how many logs per hour, what size bucket does it use? Automatic heat control, can't see that taking off …'

'Alright', said Bren, 'I'll get back on to Kenny and see what he recommends.'

Kenny Patterdale was a post-doctoral cryptography researcher for Imperial College. He acted as a consultant to MKI when required. Clive valued Kenny's word far more than any CESG official.

'I'm not sure Kenny will be able to do anything - other than burn some more money. See what he says, but I think we should stop spending now. It's cost more than enough already!'

'Ok', said Bren, 'I'll let Derek know - do you want to tell Lee?'

'Yeah - it'll please Lee: less for him to worry about. He can get on with the 1.3 build without this lot distracting him …'

Bren left the office. Clive called up Lee, MKI's Technical Director.

'Hi Lee, How're things?'

'Ok, thanks. What can I do for you?'

'Well', said Clive, 'I have good news and bad news …'

'Ok'

'Good news, you don't have to do anything else on the CESG certification stuff - bad news, we don't use SSL, so they haven't got any boxes to fit us in. To that end, they can't work out how to test us …'

'Damn!', replied Lee, 'So what now?'

'Well, to be honest, I thought it might end up here - they know how to test solutions using stock software. The second you have anything even vaguely new, they haven't got a clue. I wouldn't mind if they found some flaw in the protocol - but they haven't even lifted the covers to find out what we do. It's crap, but there we are!'

'Looks that way - is there an appeal process or something?', asked Lee.

'We're asking Kenny if there's anything he can think of - but I'd rather pay him for crypto-analysis than wasting any more time on some crappy government certification that actually means nothing!'

'Oh well', said Lee, 'I'll get on with 1.3 - it's a shame we can't hit everyone with a brick in the face - actually show them why the stuff they accredit doesn't work - and how easy it is to intercept everything …'

'Yeah', agreed Clive thoughtfully, 'anyway, I'll leave you to it'.

Clive hung up and thought for a few minutes. Perhaps Lee had something - a virtual brick in the face might just work.

He decided to contact a long-standing friend at MI5. David Harswell had been instrumental in getting MKI's technology adopted by the intelligence community. David had become Clive's unofficial link into covert and confidential policing - he had also effected a series of introductions into the FBI and CIA. Clive wasn't aware that David was actually monitoring the technology MKI was creating. The agency had uses for good-quality encryption systems and collected information from many research and development companies by befriending the founders or principal researchers.

'Hi David'

'Clive, what can I do for you?'

'Just letting you know that CESG don't know which questions to ask, so they can't validate our code. Any suggestions?'

'Not really my bag. As far as I'm concerned, you're probably better off without the publicity around common criteria or any other standards. Stay below the radar. It keeps you mysterious and unique ….'

'That doesn't help when we bid for projects. I don't suppose you could come up with some words that hint of approval?'

'MI5 can't endorse technologies. Even less shout about what we use. Look, let me see what I can do internally - perhaps we can find a tame project somewhere that might help with your product roadmap?'

'Thanks David - although I'm not sure a lot of the new stuff's really stable enough yet.'

'That's fine, I'm sure we can cope. In the meantime, keep shouting - someone has to listen eventually!'

'I'm thinking of creating an interceptor - something that shows just how risky electronic communications can be - what do you think?'

'Well, it's a thought - show that, then show how your stuff stops it. Just make sure you stay on the right side of the interception laws though. Always worth keeping public displays legal.'

3

The MKI team worked on sorting out the next release of the technology, generally referred to as 1.3. It added a whole raft new features to MKI's product suite. As the 1.3 build neared its conclusion, Bren and Clive sat in the pub discussing the business and the plan for the next few months.

The company had world-beating technology and were starting to make gradual inroads into the industry. Having spent a fortune on attempting to get CESG to certify the technology, it was a significant blow to the business when the agency decided not to give it anything more than a cursory glance.

Once again, the agency was a topic of conversation between the two directors. Clive was due to present at a major security conference on the 2nd December.

'You know, Bren, Lee said we should hit them between the eyes with a large brick … perhaps he's right.'

'What do you mean?'

'Well - if I build a fake hotspot, put all the hacking tools on it, and show the delegates just what a hacker can do with a network connection - perhaps if they see it for themselves, they might start understanding what we do and why we do it!'

'Build what though Clive?'

'How about something like a Raspberry Pi - it can run Linux, it's got two USB ports, HDMI, ethernet … everything I'd need to set up a fake hotspot - and it's only £20'.

'Is it legal?'

'Sure - I've been thinking about it. Set up a captive portal - force people to accept terms and conditions before we allow them to connect. Make sure the terms say we have the right to intercept communications for the purpose of demonstrating man-in-the-middle and other attacks. Make it specific, and give them a positive action that they have to agree to … ', Clive tailed off before continuing, 'we can show what comes through the network, and show what happens with our stuff.'

'Worth a try, I suppose', said Bren.

With that, the concept of FreeBee had been born.

Clive ordered a Raspberry Pi and a battery pack. This would give him a small, yet remarkably powerful, tiny computer. He could run the Pi off the battery for a few hours - certainly long enough to demonstrate the hacking tools. He also ordered a memory card big enough to hold a reasonable amount of data, along with the operating system and software required for FreeBee to work.

After looking around, he ordered two USB WiFi adaptors. The first WiFi adaptor would connect FreeBee to the Internet; the second becoming the 'public' side of FreeBee. People looking for a public hotspot would see 'FreeBee' in the list of available services. For purely dramatic effect, one of the adaptors had a large antenna - FreeBee had to look the part.

Finally, he ordered a small box in which to house FreeBee - this was a semi-transparent box about the size of a cigarette pack and allowed the audience to see the flashing light-emitting diodes that showed when FreeBee accessed storage or processed data. The network adaptors also flashed. This little box would look 'nice and technical' with all the flashing lights and its large antenna.

Clive looked around for 'penetration testing operating system images' for FreeBee. He thought that if he used one of the free network penetration toolkits as his starting point it would save him a huge amount of work. After some time searching online, he came across the H4CKFr33K distribution (HackFreek)- a complete set of hacking tools, all assembled on a single memory card image. Theory suggested that he should be able to transfer this image to his memory card and FreeBee would start up with all the hacking capabilities already installed and configured.

When the parts arrived, he assembled FeeBee and turned it on. Immediately, the box powered up and completed its self-test. Then the operating system booted up and, after a couple of minutes, presented Clive with a terminal prompt. It worked!

Clive unplugged FreeBee and took the memory card out. Having plugged the memory card into his Mac, he overwrote the standard operating system with the one downloaded from H4CKFr33K. It took about 20 minutes for Mac to write the new memory card. Once it finished, Clive removed the memory card from the Mac and put it back into FreeBee. Expecting it not to work, he was pleasantly surprised to find that the tiny computer not only booted, but connected to his Internet and downloaded updates to all the tools.

In all, the basic setup had taken about an hour. Clive then set about creating the FreeBee hotspot software.

Firstly, he installed tools to allow him to connect over the Internet as if he was using the TV and keyboard. Known as virtual desktop, the software took a few minutes to install. Clive rebooted connected to it over the network from his Mac.

At this point, Clive could unplug the keyboard and TV.

This would make FreeBee accessible from his tablet during the demonstration. It also allowed him to use the two free sockets for the WiFi adaptors.

Using the wired network to configure FreeBee's new WiFi devices, Clive created a system where any device could connect to the public-facing side of FreeBee. He then set up the other WiFi adaptor so that it attached itself to his mobile 'phone's hotspot. He needed to do this so that FreeBee could 'see' the Internet. In effect, FeeBee offered a free public wireless connection to the Internet via a hidden and locked hotspot provided by Clive's mobile 'phone.

Public users could see only FreeBee, and they could connect to it. Once users accepted the terms and conditions, FreeBee became transparent, and its users could access the Internet with FreeBee secretly recording everything.

He then set up a basic web-server to present the 'accept the terms and conditions' page. The page provided a big orange button saying "Yes, Yes, I Agree, Free My Bee", accompanied by a very small block of text saying "I agree to the terms and conditions". He created a link from this text, so that anyone clicking on the link would see an extremely long page of legal jargon.

To save time, Clive plagiarised the BT Internet terms and conditions, cut and pasting them them into FreeBee's website. He then set about modifying them, adding a little humour to the proceedings …

Firstly, FreeBee would offer an "unreliable and untrustworthy" link to the Internet and "may not work as expected". Later, Clive added a section authorising anyone using the service to intercept communications and collect user data. He had cleared this part of the text with MKI's lawyer - at least he could intercept communications without falling foul of the computer misuse act.

Finally, Clive wrote the code to remove the captive side of

the connection. When a user clicked on the 'agree' button, FreeBee would drop into the background, monitoring everything the newly connected devices did, while granting them access to the wider Internet.

Over the next couple of days, Clive took FreeBee everywhere. He was constantly tweaking it to make it more reliable - initially it died when his mobile 'phone connection died, then it would sometimes allow things to bypass the initial 'agree to terms and conditions' code. However, after he sorted these minor issues out, FreeBee was ready for its debut performance at the UK Money Summit in London.

4

Held in the Finance Conference Centre on the 23rd floor of a new office block in Canary Wharf, London, the UK Money Summit was one of the key finance technology conferences. Senior executives from the banking community, along with suppliers and journalists attended.

It would take a few hours for Clive to get to London, so he decided he would play with FreeBee on the way down. Would the public actually use FreeBee when other pay-per-use services existed?

He stuffed FreeBee into his backpack and set off for the station.

After boarding, he found a seat with a table and sat down. The train pulled off from the station and Clive removed FreeBee from his bag. While it booted up, he enabled data sharing on his mobile so that FreeBee could connect to the Internet. He put FreeBee on the table in front of him, half-expecting someone to ask what he was doing.

A few minutes later, FreeBee had finished booting up and had made itself available as a 'Free WiFi Hotspot' to anyone that was looking for a connection. Clive logged in to the FreeBee virtual desktop and fired up a protocol analyser - a program that can record, display and analyse everything travelling over FreeBee's network.

Almost immediately, someone made a connection to FreeBee. Clive jumped - he didn't really expect people would be stupid enough to use FreeBee. However, the person connected and agreed to the terms and conditions (without reading them) and started surfing.

Clive hit the 'start' button on the protocol analyser. It showed that the user's device connected to several social media sites, email services and a couple of games. Meanwhile, the device user started reading the Liverpool Echo. Clive could see everything coming over FreeBee's network connection - not only did FreeBee work, members of the public would actually connect to it!

Clive grabbed his mobile and took a couple of photographs of FreeBee and the tablet. He could add those to his presentation to show that people really did connect to something so clearly out on public display.

A few minutes later saw another device connect, and then another. By the end of the journey, Clive had 8 devices connected to FreeBee. He had stopped monitoring the traffic, but could have captured a massive amount of data that included device details, emails, user names, passwords - everything necessary to steal a user's identity.

Just before Milton Keynes, the train manager came through the carriage.

'Ticket please'

'Sure - I'll just get it for you', said Clive, deliberately delaying the inspector to see if he was going to challenge what Clive was doing with this flashing box of tricks on the train.

However, the train manager marked Clive's ticket and carried on to the next passenger.

Clive was amazed at just how blatant he had been. Here,

on the table, in front of the train manager, he was intercepting all the network traffic from passengers in the carriage. The train manager had seen the equipment, including the screen on the tablet, but said nothing.

Clive left FreeBee running and packed it into his bag as the train neared Euston. He travelled through the tube network and arrived at Canary Wharf. The protocol analyser now showed that another 21 people had used FreeBee.

Passing his bag through a security scanner at the venue, Clive was expecting the guards to challenge the device - but again he was waved through. Clearly a live FreeBee hotspot posed no risk according to the security staff at the conference!

He walked over to the lift and joined a group of delegates waiting for the lift to the 23rd floor. He walked out of the lift and went over to the registration desk.

'Hi - I'm Clive Knollys, I'm one of the speakers …', he said to the girl behind the desk.

'Ok, let me get your badge and I'll introduce you to Carla who can take you through.'

She turned round and scanned the list of name badges. Picking out Clive's 'Speaker Pass', she waved to another girl, presumably Carla, and then passed the badge to Clive.

'Carla's coming now …'

Clive stepped aside and smiled at the next in line for registration.

'Clive - I'm Carla, thanks for coming today. Let me take you through - would you like coffee or something?'

'Great, thanks - yes - I'm a techie, so coffee's always good!'

'Ok, let's get you settled first and then I'll sort that out for you …'

Carla led Clive through the delegates gathering around long tables offering coffee and 'breakfast nibbles'. It looked like the event was well attended.

Carla introduced Clive to the technical team who would

'mic Clive' just before he went on stage. They checked his tablet would connect to the event projectors, and made sure Clive's various devices didn't interfere with the audio signal.

In the meantime, Carla brought a coffee and a small assortment of biscuits. She introduced Clive to the event management team and then disappeared to meet and greet other delegates and speakers.

Clive had the graveyard presentation slot - the one immediately after lunch. During the course of the morning, he left FreeBee doing it's thing. Despite the venue offering free WiFi, another 30 people connected to, and used, FreeBee. Clive smiled to himself as he noted that not a single person had accessed the terms and conditions page.

He networked during lunch time - he hated these events as he didn't consider himself a salesman. Bren handled sales for MKI, Clive viewed himself as an inventor and not someone that should do all the sales activities. Nonetheless, he was here, so he was in best 'sales mode' for the day.

At the end of the lunch-break, Clive took a screen-shot that showed the number of connections FreeBee had established that morning. He decided to clear the logs and only allow his mobile to connect to FreeBee - after all, he didn't really want to expose delegates passwords or any confidential data to his audience.

With FreeBee locked down, Clive took to the podium.

'Good afternoon - firstly, I'd like to say thank you for taking part in my social experiment today. As with most social experiments, you probably weren't aware that you were involved … but you have been, and I have the results here …'

He walked to the centre of the stage.

'In this venue, we have several providers of free WiFi. The one with by far the cutest logo is FreeBee - but did any of you read the terms and conditions? Actually, no - I know that because I can see that despite some 59 people connecting, not one person even visited the T's&C's, let alone read them … but, let's see what they say'.

Clive deliberately started with the terms and conditions, it was a light-hearted way of introducing the whole topic of hacking. He connected to FreeBee with his every move echoed on the screen behind him'

'Ok, so I'm connecting to "FreeBee - the Free Public WiFi". As you can see, I'm now asking to go to Google in the browser - but wait - I'm here at a FreeBee page. I didn't ask to go here but it's asking me to agree to the terms and conditions before I can continue. In the trade, we call this a captive portal - regardless of what you try to do, you'll come back to this page until you agree to the terms. You'll see this type of thing used by hotels and coffee shops - it makes sure you've paid for accessing the network - even if the payment comes in the form of advertising or selling your browsing history!'

Clive clicked on the link.

'But let's read a few … as you can see, the legals go on for a bit - in fact, there are tons of these provisions. A few worth reading though …'

He scrolled to the start of the terms and read:

'The FreeBee WiFi is a resource from which we provide a variety of services to our customers. Our objectives for managing and operating the FreeBee WiFi are to provide low quality, unreliable services to our customers; disrespect the privacy of our customers …'

The audience giggled. Despite this being the graveyard shift, he had them.

'Now for the fun ones', he said scrolling down a bit further, 'Ok, part 10 … here we go .. "By using this FreeBee service, you authorise and permit FreeBee to: monitor all FreeBee WiFi network communications to demonstrate the weaknesses of using open public WiFi hotspots; Intercept any and all communications passing through the FreeBee WiFi for the purposes of demonstrating network security issues; and, impersonate FreeBee WiFi users to demonstrate man-in-the-middle attacks"'.

He scrolled to the next set of terms ….

'And, of course, there's this one: By using this FreeBee WiFi service, you agree to the sale of your best children (as long as they are healthy, well behaved and have good teeth); authorise FreeBee WiFi to empty all bank accounts (unless otherwise empty), and shoot your mother in law'.

He walked back to the podium and paused.

'Ladies and Gentlemen, I would like to introduce you to the star of today's show - please show your appreciation to …'

He held up FreeBee.

'FreeBee …'

A few people actually applauded at that point, while other simply laughed. Clive was enjoying himself.

'Ok, so while you thought you were connecting to something vaguely sensible, let's see what's actually going on behind the scenes.'

He called up FreeBee's desktop.

'Here's the sting in the Bee's tail … when you connect to it - this happens'

Clive pressed the 'Yes' button on his mobile. At that point a mass of data appeared on FreeBee's desktop.

'I am now recording every single bit of data coming to and from this device … look … here you can see a whole set of requests … there's a software update check, social media checks, email services, not sure what that one is, there's a diary request, contact list update … I have it all … I can capture the data in all its gory detail, or just screen-shot the interesting bits, like this' - he pressed a couple of keys and the device dutifully took a picture of the screen.

There were another couple of blocks of data on the screen that showed an unusual data pattern. Clive didn't recognise this data structure, and the protocol analyser highlighted it in red. He really wanted to explore this data further but had the rest of the presentation to consider. He took more screenshots so that he had a copy of the strange data. He carried on with his presentation.

Clive wanted to prove how he could intercept all the secure data to, so he called up the protocol analyser screen, 'worse than that, if you think it was protected by encryption, look here - this shows HTTPS - the thing that gives you a padlock in your browser. That merely means you have an encrypted link - however - you actually have an encrypted link to FreeBee, and then FreeBee has another encrypted link to your secure service. FreeBee sits in the middle of your connection and captures it before you can use it.

'If I was being clever about this, I wouldn't hack you myself. FreeBee costs about thirty quid to make, so I'd put a load of them in boxes printed with "alarm system: do not unplug", and put them in hotel linen closets. The cleaners wouldn't touch them - then I'd sell the live connections over the dark networks for a few untraceable bit coins - they hack your system, I merely sell them the live connections. I can afford to lose a few FreeBees because I'll make more than they cost by selling a single connection!'

As he had a few lawyers in the audience, Clive continued, 'and let's face it - what's happening to the burden of proof in all of this? If I managed to rip you off via FreeBee, but only took a small amount - would you be able to prove to your bank's fraud department that - yes, you were at Euston station two months ago - but didn't spend that £2.99 - I think you would struggle. In effect, we have created through mobile technology a reversal of common law: in this new world, you're guilty until you can prove yourself innocent. This is tantamount to printing a license to commit fraud.'

He called for the banking community to accept that the networks were fundamentally broken, and asked the assembled delegates to consider creating a cross-bank 'playground' where small companies such as MKI could demonstrate technologies that work, rather than relying on ancient legacy standards. Such an environment, he argued, could investigate new technologies and give the banks a fighting chance against hackers.

After a successful demonstration, he finished by demonstrating his own technology to show how it protected all the communications issues raised in the earlier part of the presentation.

All in all, he felt it had gone well, although at the back of his mind an alarm bell had sounded at the data he had captured, but couldn't read. He decided that he would look at that in more detail later. If his protocol analyser didn't recognise it then did MKI's systems protect against it?

5

Clive had received a few emails and messages while he was attending the summit. When he had managed to break free of the people wanting to get his card and talk about potential security threats, he sat at the back of the room.

A couple of the social media sites had lit up with messages like "Clive Knollys has hacked the UK Money Summit", and, "A brilliant and frankly terrifying presentation by Clive Knollys". A journalist at the event was already lining him up to speak to the technology editor of one of the leading financial magazines.

In amongst these Clive received an email from Harry Chambers. Harry was MKI's Sales Director for Asia. He asked how the presentation had gone - and whether FreeBee had the desired effect.

Clive fired up MKI's secure messenger application and chatted to Harry.

Harry: How did FreeBee go down?

Clive: I think I scared them a bit

Harry: Excellent!

Clive: I've been swamped with people asking to know more. Never know - it might prove useful as a tool.

Harry: Is it something I could plug into my Pi?

Clive: Sure - I'll send you the image. You'll need two WiFi ports but that's about it - the rest's all software - but I'll send the build stuff too, just in case!

Harry: Ok, I'll look forward to it

Clive thought about cleaning down the data, but thought it would give Harry something to show even if he couldn't get everything working. Clive called up the component sales page and copied the link over to Harry.

Clive: I frigged the network so you might want to get hold of these WiFi adaptors. At least that way I can guarantee it all working.

Harry: I'll order them. Thanks

Clive closed down the messenger and became a delegate for the rest of the summit.

Clive travelled back to Euston in the afternoon rush-hour. He hated the London tube network with its cramped smelly conditions and ageing stock. In the congested space, he started wondering about how many people had several devices - and how many connections he could steal within a single underground station. 'Shame I'm on the right side - I could make a fortune from this lot'.

He finally made it back to the train home. He ran through the presentation in his head - he always did that: it helped work out the best bits to reuse in future presentations. He was really pleased with how FreeBee had worked. It showed, in real time, real threats - much better than his old approach of merely telling people about these risks. FreeBee would definitely come out and play again!

Gazing out of the window at the dull grey buildings of inner London, his thoughts drifted to the data he couldn't immediately classify. With a few hours to kill, he thought he might just take a closer look.

He grabbed his tablet and looked up the screen-shot he'd

taken during the conference.

Sure enough, there were two blocks of data in the image. The screen-shot only showed the headers and the first few blocks of data. Headers describe the information - the source and destination network addresses, port numbers and so on. To read all of the data he'd need to fire up the protocol analyser in FreeBee. Even though he could only see the first few blocks of data, it was sufficient to tell him that two pieces of network data had been generated by his mobile handset, and that it had sent each piece to different servers.

The headers showed that both 'packets' of data had the same length - 2048 bytes worth of information - probably 1,500 characters or so, after all the header data gets stripped away.

Clive didn't want to set up FreeBee again, and anyway, the battery was probably on its last legs. Instead, he used his tablet and tried to trace the IP addresses - and therefore the services - that the data referenced. Both came back as unknown. In effect, both servers had ceased to exist as far as the tablet was concerned.

By the time the train arrived back at Crewe, Clive had exhausted all the standard ways of determining what the data packets actually contained. However, he was concerned that two blocks of data of the same length should be going from his mobile to unknown third parties - with servers that no longer existed.

Even without examining the content, the headers and fixed length data blocks suggested that some form of block encryption was in use - block encryption meaning that information gets broken into fixed length packets of data - if the data is naturally shorter than the block size, the software 'pads' out the remaining space to make every packet exactly the same length. This makes it much harder to determine what the encrypted data actually looks like.

He opened up MKI's secure messenger application and sent a broadcast message to all staff: "All - I may have acquired a virus on my mobile. Please check with me prior to opening any attachments and treat my communications as risky until I've had a chance to sort things out". Even though it would open him up to some friendly banter from the team, Clive preferred to err on the side of caution.

The following morning, Clive started updating and running antivirus tools. He backed up all his systems onto removable media - if someone was accessing his systems, perhaps they could lock him out of his own data and demand an 'unlock fee' from the company. An independent backup would prevent that from happening. While he was waiting for the various processes to finish, Clive copied FreeBee's SD card and sent the copy to Harry.

In the meantime, all the antivirus and anti-malware tools had finished. None reported anything anomalous - this made Clive even more curious.

He rang Kenny Patterdale, the cryptography researcher at Imperial College.

'Good morning Clive, how can I help', Kenny asked in his usual jovial tone.

'Hi Kenny - I thought you might be interested in something I came across yesterday. I was presenting at a conference where I was showing man-in-the-middle attacks …'

Clive went on to explain about FreeBee and the strange network packets it intercepted.

'Now I know it's only a couple of blocks, but AV's not picked up anything - it's got me intrigued. Fancy a look?'

'Sure', said Kenny, 'I'm not sure we'll see a great deal if it's encrypted, but I can give it a go'.

'Great, I'll send the protocol dumps later today - I'll use

our messenger, at least that way we know it's secure'

Kenny laughed, "Ok mate - I'll let you know what I find. See ya", and hung up.

Clive grabbed FreeBee from his bag and powered it up. Clive waited for it to finish booting up and then downloaded the protocol analysis logs to his tablet. Opening MKI's secure messenger, he sent the files to Kenny.

Bren called.

'Hi Clive - how did it all go yesterday?'

'Better than expected - I think it really struck a chord. I can't believe how different it was - I've been talking about this stuff for years, but actually showing them seemed to hit a nerve!'

'Excellent. Anything I need to follow up?'

'Possibly - I have a few cards and things I'll send over.'

MIK's impending software release consumed all of Clive's time for the next couple of days. It was a call from Kenny that brought his attention back to the unidentified data packets.

6

Clive's mobile rang. Seeing the name on the display, Clive answered it.

'Hi Kenny, how's life?'

'All good thanks, how are things in 1.3 heaven?'

'Slow, but all working - touch wood! What's up?'

'Nothing really - I just wanted to say I couldn't find anything in the data you sent through. Did you send the right logs?'

'What do you mean?'

'As I said - I can see standard stuff - HTTP, SSL, IMAP, POP3', he listed a host of other common network protocols, '… but nothing unusual … was I supposed to see something different?'

Clive paused. 'I'll send you the screen shot of the bit I was interested in', he said, 'although it should have been the last few packets in the log - I stopped it not long after I'd seen it go through. Pure fluke I saw it.'

'Hmm', said Kenny, 'perhaps I've missed it then. Send me the screen shots and I'll have another look'. He hung up.

Clive started up his computer and opened up the images folder. He scanned his way through assorted images and screen dumps. He cursed to himself as he trawled through them - he took screen-shots to capture all kinds of things - it was easier than making notes. The downside being that he had hundreds of images to sift through.

He sorted the images by the file time-stamp and looked for images captured on the 2nd December - the date of the summit. There were a few images there - and then there was the screen shot. He called it up and stared … it had changed. The data was all standard. Where the odd packets had been, he could see an email header and the first few blocks of data.

For a moment or two Clive just stared at the screen. Then, slowly, he reached for his tablet. Opening the images on his tablet, he could see the screen shot - but it too had changed to show standard email headers. Cloud synchronisation had worked perfectly - the images on his 'phone also showed email headers.

Clive unplugged the network cable from the back of his machine and fired up the computer's backup restoration tool. He sought out the file and looked through the backup revision history. There were no changes to the file as far as the revision history was concerned. This meant that the modified image had, as far as all the systems were concerned, never been modified - it appeared to be the original.

Clive fired up FreeBee and called up the network analysis toolkit. There was nothing in the logs at all. FreeBee had no data to analyse. He then went to his main computer and opened up the 'sent email' to extract the data he'd sent to Kenny.

The log files showed nothing unusual. Where Clive had seen the strange packets of data, he now saw a set of email headers - exactly as the image showed.

For a few moments, Clive wondered if he had gone completely mad - after all, the thought that someone had gone through his computer meant that this was no virus: it was someone working within MKI's network.

Clive wanted to speak to Bren. Firstly though, he wanted to call one of his better connected friends to see if anyone else had encountered a similar problem.

'David'

'Hi Clive, what can I do for you?'

David Harswell was an MI5 handler. He had worked on communication systems for nuclear submarines. Fluent in several languages and very technically capable, David was the ideal candidate when MI5 decided to bring in more technology specialists especially as it had to try to address the ever-increasing difficulty in monitoring encrypted communications.

David handled several industry specialists - those that were developing new technologies, or researching into methods to help defeat encryption systems. His job was to befriend them and to keep tabs on their activities to ensure that MI5 always had access to the latest thinking. Sometimes he used his influence to steer development in directions that could help the intelligence service. Behind the scenes, he used the knowledge gained from his industry 'down-stream' to help define national security strategy.

To a certain extent, Clive had become one of his better sources - he often called with information about new network attack tools or hacking approaches. By placing a few small orders with MKI, David had gained access to Clive's designs and future plans.

Of course, Clive had no idea that David - apparently a good friend - was anything more than his handler.

'Well', started Clive, 'I wondered if you'd seen anything new on image manipulation tools recently?'

'Such as?'

Clive went on to explain about the missing data, and the

fact that screen-shots had changed to match the text log-files on his FreeBee demonstrator.

'Sorry, Clive, I've not seen anything that can do that easily. That suggests a human touch somewhere - someone would have to look at that image, understand it, and then change it. That's a huge amount of work - and, sorry to say, most unlikely! Perhaps you simply misread it?'

'No - I didn't - I definitely captured something and it's been removed. It was made to look like something else.'

'Well Clive, the only thing I can suggest is that you look close to home. Is one of your team playing a prank on you? Someone must have access to MKI's internal systems to do that - so I'd have a look at your own team first. That's if you can ever find the missing data again! See if you can find any traces of anything inside your network - and if you do, I'd be interested in hearing about it.'

Clive hung up and then called Bren.

'Bren - I need to see you', Bren was working from home, 'how about we meet in an hour or so - this will sound weird, but I'll see you at the bandstand at the top of Queen's Park …'

Without giving Bren time to reply, Clive hung up and grabbed his coat.

Queen's Park in Crewe has an old bandstand. It was painted in black and white, although vandals had chosen to adorn it with their initials in bright day-glo colours. The park was reasonably well maintained, but in late December it was a cold grey place. A bitterly cold wind passed through leafless trees, however, Clive knew it was better to meet in an open place than to risk talking inside buildings.

Clive was trying (and failing) to blow 'ice rings' while sitting on the bandstand railings when he saw Bren walking towards him. Jumping down from the railings, he headed towards Bren.

'Thanks for coming over to the new MKI conference centre: we have a problem'.

They started walking towards the park's lake.

'What problem?', asked Bren.

'You remember I thought I had a virus on my mobile?', asked Clive

'Yes - I'm guessing it's not a virus then?'

'Correct! I took a screen-shot of the stuff I'd seen go through FreeBee. It recorded some outbound traffic - by the look of it encrypted and in small blocks. When I tried to trace where it ended up, the destinations didn't exist.'

'If it didn't exist, doesn't that mean nothing went out?'

'Not necessarily - something was trying to connect and send something to somewhere - but that somewhere could have changed its identity or gone off-line when I tried to find it again.'

'That's a lot of somethings and somewheres!', joked Bren.

Clive carried on, 'It annoyed me that I didn't know what my mobile was sending. If I hadn't actually seen it go through, I wouldn't have known. So here was something running on my mobile and communicating without my permission or knowledge.'

Bren rubbed his hands together. 'You know, it's pretty cold - can't we discuss this in the warmth?'

'No - you'll understand why in a minute or two. Bear with me!', said Clive, and then continued, 'I took a screenshot of the information FreeBee captured. But - it only showed the headers and a few bytes of the payload. When I got back, I took an extract from FreeBee's logs and sent them to Kenny, thinking he might be able to shed some light on them.'

'Right', said Bren, 'and …?'

'… And, when he looked at the data, there was nothing there', said Clive.

Bren stopped. 'So if there was nothing there, what's the problem?'

'The problem', said Clive, 'is that I mean there was NOTHING there. The logs had no record of the stuff I saw. Kenny found nothing …'

Bren looked a little confused. 'O … k …, where did it go then?'

'Precisely', said Clive, 'so - and this is where it gets really weird - the screen shots I took had been changed to match the data I sent to Kenny. It was as if those packets never existed.'

'But …', said Bren, '… how?'

'No idea! Absolutely no idea. I know what I saw. I know that data was captured in the logs and the screen-shot. For fuck's sake, I stared at it for hours on the train. I know it was there.'

'Ok', said Bren. He thought for a moment before continuing, 'What does that really mean?'

'Well', said Clive, 'it means that someone is in our network. I spoke with David Harswell at MI5 - he thinks the same thing. Someone's inside our network and has the right permissions to change things without us knowing. It means that we have a major compromise somewhere - what else have they hacked into - are our comms compromised, have they put back doors in our systems, have they frigged the software without us knowing?'

'Who do you think it is?", asked Bren.

'No idea - Chinese Government, Russian Mafia … David wondered if it's one of the team pranking us? I doubt it, but who knows?'

They started walking again. For a few minutes, they walked in silence though the cold. Bren thought they could be in a spy novel.

Clive carried on, 'I have wondered if it's Kenny. He's the only one who knew about the data, and he's the only external contractor we have. At least we know everyone else!'

Bren asked, 'What do we do?'

'Good question: I need to spend some time on this. I need to find out what's going on. Then work out who the hell's playing in our toy chest! If it is external, then we also have to consider how to close it down, and work out what damage they've done - if any. This could blow us out of the water - we're screwed if our customers get hold of this.'

'Shit', said Bren. 'Ok - do what you think's necessary. Who knows about this?'

'No-one apart from Kenny and David. Just in case, I'll send Kenny an email saying I must have been mistaken as I can't find it … give the appearance of letting it drop.'

'Ok', said Bren. 'What can I do?'

'Cover my ass - make sure people think I'm busy and keep them from bothering me. You will have to make it look like we're both up to our necks!'

'Not hard. I'm up to my nipples as it is!'

Clive laughed. 'On a serious note - I think we need a couple of simple codes - if I use Harry's 'Darling' in anything, then I need help; 'Brendan' rather than 'Bren' means I can't talk. I suggest we keep changing locations too - always outside, and always where we can see for a reasonable distance. So, next time we meet at Nantwich Garden Centre'

'All a bit extreme if you ask me'

'It's not - David said to look at people inside our own house first. If our computers and mobiles have been compromised, then let's start making it difficult for them - whoever they are - to find out what we know. For the time being, stay off email and messenger with this stuff. I'll invent a heart problem for Uncle Peter, then we can discuss his health and prognosis! Oh - and next time, leave your mobile at home. We'll get some burners.'

'Burners?'

'Yeah - 'phones bought with cash. Pre-pay. Extremely difficult to trace - use 'em throw 'em. Only for this stuff though - I'll keep my usual 'phone for day to day business.'

'Ok', said Bren, clearly not convinced, 'all very cloak-and-dagger. It's easy to become too paranoid you know - they keep saying that about me … the voices … Anyway, I guess we need to know what's going on. Good luck!'

'Thanks Bren, I'll keep you posted.'

They split up. As Clive walked he started structuring his approach to finding out who had invaded his network, and why. Clive thought Bren was right though: perhaps there was an element of paranoia - time to engage scientific principles and conduct some proper forensic research.

7

At about 3am, Clive awoke with a start. He was convinced that he'd heard something. He lay there for a few minutes before deciding to check the house.

He turned on the light and made a lot of noise getting out of bed - he'd prefer to scare someone away than confront them. He made his way through the upstairs of the house, and then checked the downstairs. Everything seemed in order, so he turned the lights off and went back to bed.

Clive was now awake though, and he started thinking about the work required to change a log file and its associated image. Someone needed to go to a lot of effort to recreate an image of the FreeBee Log. It sounds simple - but technically, it required access to FreeBee and Clive's personal 'cloud' - his Internet storage systems. Someone clearly wanted to remove all evidence of the additional packet data.

Suddenly he sat bolt upright. He'd made a copy of FreeBee without starting it up: Harry wanted a copy to demonstrate hacking techniques to his sales targets. If he hadn't started his version up, then the packet data might still exist.

Clive got out of bed and dressed. He went to the 'office' - actually the dining table in his kitchen-diner. He made a copy of the current FreeBee memory card - this could replace the one he had given to Harry. Clive made sure his laptop was charged - he wanted to copy Harry's card before plugging it back into FreeBee. He intended to build a 'clean-room' in which to analyse FreeBee's data. This would mean examining the data without actually executing a single line of FreeBee code.

A few cups of coffee and much preparation later, Clive put his laptop in the car and started driving. Harry worked out of the London office and it would take a few hours to drive down. Much though he hated the early morning rush-hour traffic, Clive wanted to secure that memory card as soon as he could.

Clive wondered if he was becoming paranoid - he knew that governments developed malware to spy on other countries. As a security systems inventor, he knew the processes required to create remote hacking tools - a non-trivial effort. Had they left the logs and images, or planted some malware with a detectable signature, then Clive would have kicked himself for letting his computer become infected; image modification, however, takes time and manual effort. Someone, rather than something, had tampered with data shared by his devices. Perhaps he was right to be paranoid.

When Clive got to about ten minutes from Harry's house, he stopped the car and rang him.

'Morning Darling', said Clive in an affected overly English accent, 'I'm on my way to a meeting from the banking summit, last minute thing, don't you know …'

Clive and Harry often bantered with each other. The affected English and 'Darling' originating from the BBC's Blackadder series - Harry was a huge fan.

'Marvellous', came the cheerful reply, 'how can I help?'

'Actually, I don't need help - well, none more than usual anyway: the FreeBee memory card you have won't work - I sent you the wrong set-up.'

'Oh, Ok - thanks for letting me know. I won't waste my time with it then.'

I realised last night', explained Clive, 'and given I'm passing by, I thought you might appreciate one that actually does something! If you're around, I can drop it off on the way through.'

'Marvellous Darling.'

A few minutes later, Clive arrived at Harry's house. He grabbed the new version of the FreeBee memory card, climbed out of the car, and knocked on the front door.

'Darling, I told you never to visit me like this', joked Harry, 'think of the neighbours.'

'Oh, I know, but I couldn't resist your charms for another minute.'

Clive handed over the new FreeBee card. 'Look, got to dash - have you got the other one around? I can reuse it.'

Harry went inside and returned with the envelope containing the original FreeBee image. Clive noticed the envelope was still intact. Perhaps the card might still contain the mystery data.

'Next time you send me naked pictures, I'm putting them online', Harry said as passed the envelope over.

'I charge for that usually - but as long as I get a share … anyway, got to dash. Any problems, give me a call. That one comes with a 10 second warranty from when you received it', he quipped, before walking back to the car.

'No worries', shouted Harry, 'good luck with the bankers.'

'Ooh, yes', replied Clive as he climbed into the car, 'I LOVE a good bank in the morning!'

Clive drove around the corner and plugged the memory card into his laptop. The timestamp on the memory card showed that it had not been accessed since he created it. He copied the memory card to the laptop hard-drive and put the original back in its envelope. Perhaps, just perhaps, he might have captured the data to prove his point.

It was a long drive back. Clive was tired and he really wanted to examine the contents of the memory card. However, the journey gave Clive the time to plan what to do with the card when he got back home. He would apply forensic techniques and examine it without allowing any software to run on the card itself. He had an old PC that had a removable network card - it was also running a very old operating system - Clive thought it unlikely that any modern hacking tools would have been installed on that machine.

Despite the morning traffic, Clive made good time. As soon as he got home, he grabbed the memory card and went inside. He went up into the attic and pulled out the old PC.

Setting the PC on the working top in his kitchen, Clive opened the case and removed its network card. Then, he attached a monitor, keyboard and mouse, and booted up the aged machine. With a strangled croak, the machine burst into life - Clive grinned to himself thinking that the speaker had probably suffered during its considerable time in 'storage'. After a few minutes, Clive was able to log into the computer and check the running processes - he wanted to make sure there was nothing unusual in the list of programs running.

He then went through the various startup and configuration scripts, changing them to stop the machine from all forms of network communication. He wanted the machine to run on its own, with no capability to link on to his home network or the Internet. Having removed the network card, and any associated network management software, Clive assumed the machine was now 'clean'.

He restarted the computer, and while it booted up, he made himself a cup of coffee.

Clive inserted the memory card into the computer, and typed in a command to dump the contents of it into a file on the computer. Then, he removed the FreeBee card, inserted a blank card and typed a command to write the newly created file onto the new memory card.

As he had created patents, and worked on numerous cases with the local police, Clive had a safe installed in the cupboard under the stairs. It was a floor-safe, underneath carpet, a wooden trap door, and usually a whole host of assorted junk: vacuum cleaner, shoes, boxes and so on. Clive removed the junk, lifted the trap-door and unlocked the safe. It had a heavy door and took some effort to open. Clive placed the FreeBee memory card into the safe, and then locked it. He put the junk back on top of the safe - making a mental note to tidy the cupboard out at some point: a note he had made to himself every time he needed to access the contents of the safe.

With a copy of the original FreeBee card in the safe, Clive could now start to analyse the copies without damaging the original. He returned to the old PC and typed in a couple of commands to load up the FreeBee 'image' he had saved to the hard disk of the computer. He mounted the image as 'read-only' so he couldn't inadvertently change the contents of the image. Not trusting the technology at his disposal, he also started making handwritten notes about the process in a small drawing pad he usually reserved for systems designs.

A couple of seconds later, Clive was delving into the image's filesystem and had located the log files created during the presentation. Being on an old machine, he had no access to any more advanced tools he would normally use to analyse the data. He set about writing a couple of scripts to scan the data and display anything matching specific patterns.

Each time he ran the scripts, he gradually whittled down the amount of data remaining to analyse. It was a case of stripping out all the 'standard' protocol data, leaving only the unknown packets behind. This process became completely absorbing to Clive: time flew by while he gradually improved the scripts.

When you have data captured from a network, you have large amounts of noise that actually has very little use after the task generating it completes - polling the network to find the identities of other devices sharing the network; scanning for printers; checking that some connections have remained 'alive'; checking that services can find an appropriate route to other services, and so on. Much of this data only persists for the duration of the task in hand - while useful to have the entire session captured, the sheer volume of data can overwhelm the inexperienced. Forensic data analysis is really the art of knowing which question to ask.

Clive, wasn't changing the original data files, he was merely creating more advanced search tools that gradually reduced the amount of data displayed. Working from the 'ground up' meant that Clive had access to the raw data without anything interfering with it or making assumptions on his behalf. However, it meant that Clive had to keep looking up protocol specification documentation to be able to rule out irrelevant data.

Over the next few days, Clive continued to work on his data analysis tools. With each iteration, he was eliminating 'valid' information: email or message service exchanges, web-site data and so on. He became obsessed with 'just another run', missing meal times and crashing for a few hours periodically to catch up on sleep.

On Friday morning, a worried Bren arrived at Clive's house. He had tried to call Clive several times over the past few days, without success. Getting no response from the doorbell, Bren walked around to the back of Clive's house where he could see Clive through the window tapping away at the aged PC.

Bren tapped loudly on the window and Clive jumped.

'Jesus! You startled me', said Clive as he opened the back door.

'You're a hard man to get hold of this week … fuck', said Bren, suddenly becoming aware of Clive's disheveled state, 'you look awful. Why didn't you answer the door or the 'phone?'

'Didn't hear you …', muttered Clive, and pointed to the 'phone, 'battery's dead'.

'Have you eaten, slept …. Anything sensible?'

'Erm, sort of.'

'That's a "no" then', said Bren, reaching for his 'phone. He called the local Domino's and ordered two large pizzas.

'God you look rough', said Bren, 'how's it going?'

'Slow', replied Clive, 'very slow. But getting there', he looked at the computer wishing that Bren would leave him to it, 'another couple of days or so …'

'Ok', said Bren, 'I've held off everyone back at the fort. Apart from someone to look after you, do you need anything?'

'Not really - just a bit of time to finish off the analysis. After that, we'll see what needs doing', Clive put the kettle on and opened the fridge door to get the milk.

'We shouldn't discuss this here anyway - let me finish this bit off, then we can meet as agreed. Coffee?'

'Please', replied Bren, 'but not with that cheese in it. Looks like you need a fucking nurse-maid at the moment.'

'A bit obsessed with this lot', said Clive. 'I just need to get this first bit done so we know what we're dealing with. How are things back at the office?'

Bren and Clive chatted for a while about the business. Part way through the discussion, the pizzas arrived. Bren passed them to Clive and told him to eat.

Having finished his coffee, Bren decided to leave Clive to

his analysis work.

'Look after yourself - what use will you be if you find something but need six months in hospital to recover from this lot. Eat!'

'Ok, Ok', replied Clive, 'go - the sooner you're out of my hair, the sooner normality will resume ...'

With that, Bren walked his car.

Clive returned to the cycle of writing scripts and assessing the data returned. Surely he'd see something soon.

8

In the early hours of Saturday morning, Clive had managed to remove most of FreeBee's data that he would expect to see during normal network activities. Finally, stripped of all the noise, Clive could see the two packets of data he had seen during the conference.

Clive did several things at this point: he made a long-hand copy of the data. Literally writing down the values that appeared on the screen; he then connected a printer and printed the screen, and printed out a copy of the program code so that he could have both independently examined, should the need arise. He put these in the safe and then went back to the PC.

He decided that he would save the two packets of data in its own file - that way, he could show them to other people. A quick addition to the code dumped the discovered packets to its own data file.

For some time, he sat and gazed at the screen. The proof he needed was here. Someone had attempted to hide the data from view. Now he needed to work out what the data contained, where it was going, and who wanted it.

By examining the data, Clive came to a few conclusions: the data was encrypted, each contained exactly 2048 bytes and looked like a random collection of values. They both went to different IP addresses - endpoints on the Internet. There were no acknowledgement packets - this suggested that both had been sent without caring whether the other end actually received the data, Clive wondered if there was another part to the data that he had yet to see.

He doodled for a while, trying to sort out what kind of structure might apply to the data. However, this proved difficult with only two packets available - he decided to catch more.

In the meantime, he'd have to let Bren know that he wasn't going mad. For the first time in over a week, he turned his mobile 'phone on. Within a few moments, email, voicemail and numerous other alerts appeared on the device.

He sent a message to Bren saying "Uncle Peter much worse. Will need to take more time off. How about meeting at 11 for coffee and a catch-up?"

A few minutes later, Bren responded with an "Ok".

Clive thought he should look at least vaguely presentable, otherwise Bren would only worry. He had a shower and got dressed in clean jeans and a sweatshirt. He shut the PC down, collected the printout of the screen, grabbed his coat and keys, then left to go to Nantwich Garden Centre - the place he and Bren had previously agreed to meet.

In what seemed a past life now, Clive had been a weapons systems designer. He had carried sensitive information around the world, and had been taught how to drive and observe properly - just in case he needed to get out of the odd tight spot or two. Military training gave him a 'mode switch' - no half measures: you observe, plan and act.

Had the data not changed on his computer, he mused, then he would have probably given up before now. The fact that someone had gained access to the company's internal network, and changed information of several devices at the same time meant that this was an extremely sophisticated and well targeted attack. If they had removed their own footprints in his systems, had they also gained access to (or worse, changed) the source code to his security systems.

Being the founder of an Internet security company, Clive knew he would probably end up as a target for hackers at some point. The sophistication of the attack suggested that someone was actively watching the information carried by MKI's network. The resources alone for this type of attack suggested to Clive that he was dealing with either large-scale organised crime networks, or a government. This went way beyond anything that a small hacking group could do.

As he drove to Nantwich, he watched every vehicle. He deliberately changed direction, varied speed, and (assuming someone might have used a GPS tracker) he parked in the Nantwich Park and Ride car-park, before walking to the garden centre, leaving his 'phone in the glove-box.

Nantwich garden centre was broken up into several zones: a general planting area, fish in tanks, exotic plants, and an open area for ponds and pools. It was a big centre and usually quite busy at the weekends. Ideal, thought Clive, for getting lost and being able to talk freely.

At exactly 11:00, Clive walked up to the front of the garden centre and looked for Bren. Bren was often late, and this usually annoyed Clive. Clive could be obsessive at times, but he was always obsessive about punctuality: he had been known to sit around the corner in the car for several hours to ensure he arrived at a meeting exactly on time.

Bren turned up at about 11:10, just long enough to annoy Clive. Bren had also parked at the garden centre - another 'black mark'.

'What's the point of meeting here, if you're going to park you damned car here?', asked Clive.

'Good morning Clive, good to see you too', replied Bren,

'coffee?'

'No, let's walk', said Clive, and walked to the large 'outdoor pool and pond' section of the centre. This was a landscaped area and was almost like walking around a park - indeed, had it not been for the price tags and signs everywhere, it could be a public park.

Towards the middle of this section, Clive noticed a few bench seats and guided Bren towards them.

'I was right Bren: I got hold of a copy of FreeBee's data before I connected it to our network. I ran a copy off for Harry just after the presentation - whoever changed the data couldn't get hold of that!

'Ok. What have you got?'

They reached the seats. Clive and Bren sat down. Looking almost as if they were planning a garden, Clive pulled the screen-shot out of his coat pocket.

'This is what I got', he said, showing Bren the paper. 'It's just two packets of data - both the same length, both full of apparently random data. So, we're talking a block cipher - an encryption system that works on chunks of data of a set size. In this case, 2K per block. They're being sent to different IP addresses, so we have at least two packets of encrypted data going to two different locations.'

'Ok … and?', asked Bren.

'AND! Someone didn't want us to see this. Someone went on to our network and removed this data from every device that connected to MKI's network. Someone's on the inside of our network. If they can change this stuff', Clive said waving the paper around, 'then they can change anything - what's changed in our source code - have we gained a back door in our code without us knowing?'

'How do you know it's someone, not just some malware?', asked Bren.

'The image', said Clive emphatically.

Bren looked at Clive with a blank expression.

'The image', said Clive again, 'it changed'.

Bren raised his eyebrows - he still hadn't got the significance of this news.

'Look - a computer can change data easily. An image, however, requires a huge amount of processing to sort out. What's in the image? A dog, your wife, your last holiday, some text or - in this case - an image of something that someone doesn't want us to see.

'That takes special processing - and I think it more likely that someone - not something - looked at it, realised what I had captured - and photoshopped it all out. Then they replaced the original with the photoshopped version and modified the system timestamps to make it look like it was the original. That's a lot of effort. That's a shit-load of effort, even for a human.'

Clive put the paper back in his pocket and continued, 'that's one sophisticated hack. I'm both impressed and terrified by it. It's too sophisticated for even a reasonably organised hacking group - we're talking mafia or government - it's big, and we're infected.'

'We'll have to let the rest of the board know', said Bren, 'and start implementing our own stuff on the development networks.'

MKI had built its own security technologies on standard commercial equipment. While the company demonstrated products externally, it had never upgraded the original development network to use its own products. Not a conscious choice, merely part of the natural evolution of the technology and company.

'No!', said Clive after a few moments, 'let me finish working out what's going on. I need more data before we tell the board. I'll build a network recorder and grab anything we don't recognise. We can, however, protect the development servers and administration systems. Do that, but don't say anything to the board. I'll do that when I have some answers - if we say something now, it'll spook them.'

'You sure?'

'Absolutely. This is between us for the time being. I'm serious - if we are under some kind of government surveillance or have an organised crime network on our case, we need to look after ourselves. The fewer know about this, the better - if it's Russia, China or the Mafia we could be in deep shit here. I'm off-grid as much as possible with this stuff. No tech! Phone's have GPS or cell identifiers, networks are obviously compromised, and God knows what they've installed on our computers. Time to get paranoid', said Clive as he stood up, 'time for me to find out what these bastards are doing on my network!'

9

Bren sent an email to the development and infrastructure team suggesting that as Clive's computer might have acquired a virus, it was probably time to implement MKI's security systems for internal communications. He asked Lee and Derek to work on a schedule to upgrade the development systems over the Christmas period, while most of the development team wouldn't need access to the servers.

He also set a daily alarm at 5PM saying 'Nursemaid' - a reminder to order food for Clive. If Clive was going to spend more time on the FreeBee Project as Bren now called it, then he would probably forget to look after himself.

In the meantime, Clive fired up his old PC again. The speaker had an annoying click, so he powered it down and opened up the case. He reached inside and pulled off the lead between the motherboard and speaker. 'Peace and quiet!', thought Clive.

He started building a new image for FreeBee. This image would strip everything down to real basics. He used the MKI network drivers and locked down all communications so that the new software could only read information running over the network.

After a while, he then created a set of filters that would

extract only the information that didn't match any of the standard protocols he would expect to see. In effect, taking the rules he had defined to find the unknown packets in the first place.

It took several days to get things working properly. Clive took a break only to buy a few 'essential' Christmas presents and delivered them on Christmas Eve.

He spent the rest of the Christmas period entirely focussed on building a dedicated network protocol capture and analysis tool. This device had no traceable fingerprint on the networks to which it connected. In effect, it simply captured packets of interest and stored them in a compressed and encrypted database on a memory card. Clive wanted it to be completely transparent to any other computers or networks, so he would need some way to see if he had captured anything.

He soldered a couple of LED's to the FreeBee connector strip - a line of prongs sticking out of the main board, usually used for connecting other hardware. Clive set up the software so that one LED would flash every time a new packet was intercepted and transferred to the internal database, and another for showing when the device was close to capacity.

Once Clive had the basic recorder running, he then revised the network drivers. He removed all the code that could write data to the network and recompiled the software. Now the recorder was hobbled to prevent anything compromising it - or allowing anything to write to the network. If it could only read data then, even if someone found a strange device through some kind of advanced network analysis, they couldn't do anything with it or understand what it was doing.

He also wanted to ensure that nothing could change the software he had written. As he had developed code for devices in the past, Clive had a couple of devices that 'burned' read-only-memory chips. The devices literally burned software into specialised chips - known as electrically programmable read-only-memory. He tested the software in hardware emulators, and seeing it did what it should, he then burned it.

With a small board attached to the other pins on the FreeBee connector strip, he had completed the build. After a very lonely Christmas and New Year period, Clive had built his network packet recorder and analyser.

Leaving the analyser in place would mean that Clive had lost the ability to demonstrate FreeBee and the MKI solutions. He ordered a new set of parts so he could build another FreeBee later.

On Saturday the 4th January at mid-day, Clive plugged his network analyser into his home network. When he turned it on, it took a few seconds to boot up and then the network traffic indicator started flashing quite happily. It was just a waiting game now - at some point, Clive hoped, the other indicators would light up, then he could start to work out what had cost him his Christmas and New Year.

Annoyingly, nothing happened. Clive took the recorder out of the network and tested it again. In test, it worked, however it received nothing when plugged into his home network.

Leaving it in situ, he decided to let things run its course. If anything came along, the protocol recorder would grab it. In the meantime, he needed to get back on to the day job.

Release 1.3 went live on 6th January. It was a massive milestone for the company and Clive was happy that everything seemed to work properly. The MKI team started rolling out the software to the customer base. Over the next few days, the release and management processes took most of the team's time.

Bren was pleased to see Clive back at work. Throughout

the protocol recorder development, Clive had become an almost total recluse. Apart from the occasional visit from Bren and a daily interruption as some form of take-away arrived at the door, Clive had devoted all his time and energy into building a totally invisible (to the network) device. Clive could plug it into any network and it would record anything that matched the data structure Clive had seen in the presentation.

Clive kept checking to see if either of the indicator LED's had come on - but nothing appeared. The incident had, however, given MKI the kick it needed to get its servers protected by its own technology. Clive modified the design slightly so that only encrypted data going to known end-points could exist on the network. He also upgraded the network routers to stop any unknown traffic 'leaking' from the internal systems.

The MKI team also built additional protection around its email and messaging platforms. In effect, MKI was in lockdown.

On the evening of Friday the 10th January, Clive received a call from Bren. For some reason, the mobile signal was terrible, so Clive suggested they switch to Skype. To do this, Clive needed to turn on the WiFi service on his mobile.

Bren and Clive connected via Skype and started talking. Clive stretched back in his chair and casually glanced down at the network recorder. The 'packet detected' LED was flashing.

10

'Brendan, I've just heard that Uncle Peter's taken a turn for the worse - I'll call you back', said Clive, hoping Bren would take the cue from his use of Bren's full name.

'Oh … anything I can do?', asked Bren

'No, thanks - I'll call you when I know how he is', said Clive and killed the call.

Clive closed Skype down on his mobile. The 'packet detection' LED carried on flashing. It appeared that Clive's mobile was the device generating these strange packets.

Clive turned his mobile off. The LED stopped flashing. He grabbed his laptop and opened it up. A few minutes later, he enabled the wireless network and immediately, the 'packet detected' LED started flashing again. Clive turned the wireless network off and plugged the laptop into the network. Again, the LED started flashing, indicating that the laptop was sending data whenever it found a network.

These simple tests told Clive that the devices could send data whenever connected to a network: wireless or physical. He surmised that even with wireless networks disabled, his mobile would probably send data via the cellular networks as these also provide Internet access.

Clive had had a computer attached to his home network

since he had plugged in the protocol recorder. Clearly, just having a computer attached to the network wasn't enough to trigger whatever system Clive now referred to as "Uncle Peter".

Clive devised a set of experiments to find out what triggered Uncle Peter. On his home computer, he wrote a small program file - something every software developer does when first checking out new languages or compiler installations - "Hello, World"; an extremely simple test that simply prints out "Hello, World", and then exits. After writing the code, he compiled it and ran the program. A few minutes later, he observed that the packet indicator LED's flashed. Either the source code, or the executable program, had caused Uncle Peter to wake up and send something over the network.

Then, he opened up a word processor and wrote a few lines of text, saving the document on his local hard disk. Again, the LED's flashed, suggesting that Uncle Peter had sent another message.

Clive spent some time playing with various file-types. It looked like anything that was written to his computer's file systems resulted in a subsequent set of messages via Uncle Peter. It would appear that Uncle Peter was spying on Clive's storage systems.

Interestingly, large downloads and program installations seemed to have little effect on Uncle Peter. Clive half-expected a new program or something large coming down over the Internet would get Uncle Peter very busy - but no, it looked like only locally generated material (material Clive created) ended up triggering the data transmissions. This could explain why Clive hadn't seen any activity from his network recorder - he hand't created anything unique on that computer.

Clive sent an email to Bren, "Hi Brendan, I'm having

problems with my email at the moment. Please will you let me know when you receive this? Thanks, Clive". He hoped the use of "Brendan" would let Bren know what was actually going on. As soon as he hit send, the LED's on the network recorder flashed - Uncle Peter obviously liked emails too!

Over the next few hours, Clive had noted that email, documents, images, and program code, all created network transmissions via Uncle Peter. Whatever service operated behind the scenes was obtaining any new data created by Clive.

Clive decided to play - he created a small application that would scan online patent databases, pull down the full patent document, and store it in a database. At each stage of writing the code, and getting the program to work, the LED's flashed.

Clive started up the program - he expected that Uncle Peter would get almost overwhelmed by the amount of data coming in to Clive's computer. Actually, the LED's flashed periodically, but it looked like Uncle Peter wasn't copying everything written to the database out to the network. It looked like the system was clever enough to capture only the new data. Either that, or Uncle Peter didn't like databases.

Over the next few days, Clive started to generate content: things that looked legitimate, but actually contained very little real substance. He wanted to keep Uncle Peter busy enough that he could analyse the data captured by the protocol recorder - however, that would require a reasonable amount of data. Also, by using a fake project, complete with a unique name, it might make deciphering any encrypted data easier.

Clive named the project "SeeZu" and created a series of documents that made it look like he was considering a patent application for a product allowing people to encrypt part of a communication 'on the fly'. In other words, a software switch that could allow a user to define particular sections of data that a service would encrypt. It sounded vaguely plausible as a concept, but made little commercial sense as a consumer application.

In order to make it look like a real project, Clive created conceptual designs and top-level system diagrams. Every time he saved information to his computer, he could see the data recorder LEDs flashing away. Uncle Peter was getting a lot of data that would eventually prove useless. Clive, however, was constructing a lot of data in known formats, and with key words and structures that would make it easier to crack encryption services: if he knew the format, structure, and content of the files, perhaps he could use that to work out how Uncle Peter encoded it.

Once again, Clive lost track of time - and once again, Bren started sending food on a regular basis. Clive found the interruptions annoying, but eating gave him more time to consider his fake project, and to build in additional data types. After all, part of this phase of the analysis was to work out just what Uncle Peter considered interesting enough to capture.

Finally, on the 18th January, the 'memory full' indicator LED came on. Clive had managed to fill the protocol recorder with data sent to Uncle Peter. Clive wanted to jump in and analyse the data, but having experienced Uncle Peter's apparent ability to delete traces of any network transmissions, Clive set about things in a more forensic way.

Firstly, he disconnected the protocol recorder and then copied its contents to a new memory card. He put this memory card in the safe, alongside the original FreeBee memory image. Then, he plugged the protocol recorder into his old PC: the one not connected to the network. He copied the data from the protocol recorder and then created another copy so that he had something to fall back to should anything happen to the original copy.

Then Clive reset the memory within the protocol recorder and plugged it back in. He was determined to capture as much information as he could. The protocol recorder went back to work, while Clive started to delve into the data captured so far.

11

Clive listed out all the files he had created as part of the fake 'SeeZu' project. The listing contained each file name, the time it was created or modified, and the size of each file. Clive wanted to see if he could correlate the SeeZu data and that sent to Uncle Peter.

Because he had the time stamps for when his computer stored each part of the fake project, he expected each data storage time stamp to align completely with transmissions to Uncle Peter. In reality, however, it seemed that Uncle Peter received data after a random delay - sometimes up to 10 minutes - after Clive had created the original file. This delay was sufficiently long to have made it almost impossible to see this traffic amongst all the noise generated by other network data.

Clive had established that he would create or update a file then, after the delay, Uncle Peter would encrypt the file contents, split it into small chunks, and then send these chunks of data to several different destinations. Sometimes it would send the same block several times, but to different destinations. Periodically, Uncle Peter changed the destination addresses - presumably this was why Clive couldn't contact the addresses he captured during the presentation: they must only last for a short time.

Over the next few days Clive managed to work out an approximate structure: a system identifier that was somehow tied to the destination computer - perhaps, a way of identifying which computer was sending information and validating where it ended up; a constant number - 6.8 - Clive thought this might be a version number of some kind; then a block of encrypted data that Clive couldn't yet decipher; finally, a checksum - a way of ensuring that the information sent hadn't been tampered with during transit.

There were several other segments of data that he couldn't work out. They had the same structure of data, but the content was different - and they went to a separate destination to all the other data. Clive worked on these for a couple of days, but couldn't find anything to relate this information to any other.

The whole time he worked on understanding Uncle Peter's protocols, Clive made copious notes. However, the biggest problem remained the encryption processes. He needed to see the contents of the encrypted bits of the data. Without that, he had no idea what Uncle Peter actually received.

He also came to the conclusion that he could only see one side of the communication: a bit like only listening to one side of a telephone call, it's far too easy to misunderstand or jump to conclusions. In order to communicate with another computer, each system needs to agree on things like data formats, encryption standards, what to do in case of network problems or power-cuts, and so on. These communication protocols usually have some form of control mechanism - at it's simplest a confirmation that information was received properly. Most protocols also include specific mechanisms to re-send data lost in transmission. Clive wanted to obtain this 'control data' in addition to that already captured.

Somewhere in the original FreeBee data set, he had to have

'the other side' of the communication. He had to have recorded the control data Uncle Peter was using to gather the information that went through FreeBee during the presentation.

Clive went back to the original data FreeBee had captured. Applying his new-found knowledge to the original data, he hoped to find something coming in that matched the data sent out. However, after many hours wading through network data, he found nothing unusual. He was missing something: he knew he was missing something, but didn't know what to look for.

In one of several late-night conversations with Kenny Patterdale, Clive had discussed the concept of 'deep packet' searches: the ability to search for information inside an encrypted container, but without actually being able to decipher the container. In other words, the ability to search through secret data without breaking the encryption - something of great interest to covert and intelligence units. Kenny had mentioned open-source research that would allow you to enter a keyword and software would then give a reasonable degree of confidence that a particular word or phrase existed within the data. While you still couldn't read the contents of the data without encrypting it first, you could come back with a probability that the chosen word existed inside the encrypted data.

He fired up his laptop and found the project Kenny had mentioned. He downloaded the source code and read the associated installation notes. He transferred the source code he'd downloaded to the old PC and while it compiled, Clive had a shower.

Much refreshed and in better spirits, he started learning how to use the deep-packet inspection tools. The tools could only inspect certain types of files, so Clive needed to extract the protocol data from the database and create a set of compatible files. This work took him a couple of hours to complete, then he ran the search tool.

"Search for:", the tool asked.

"SeeZu", typed Clive and hit return.

The tool responded with "Searching …"

Clive made a coffee and waited impatiently. On this old machine it was taking a lot longer than he expected.

Finally the computer came back with "8 instance(s) found with probability of higher than 0.9". Even though Clive couldn't see it, the software thought it almost certain that some of the data contained the name of his fake project. Uncle Peter, it seemed, was stealing Clive's intellectual property.

12

'So what now?', asked Bren as they walked on yet another of Clive's outdoor rambles.

'Dunno! I know we're leaking data and there's a high probability it's being split between several systems, but I have no idea how it's controlled or what we've lost already.'

It was snowing and Bren shivered.

'How far have you got?', asked Bren.

Clive shrugged, 'Nowhere near far enough. This is clever - I still don't know what's generating the traffic. I can't find a single process running that I wouldn't expect to see. The next thing's to run a system inside a virtual machine and see what we can pick up from that. It's driving me nuts!'

Bren sighed. He knew Clive was right in trying to resolve the problem but wondered if this was the time to pass it on to the police or someone with more resources to throw at it.

Clive rejected the suggestion that they involve the police: 'at this stage we don't know for certain that it's something illegal - it's only a reasonably high probability that someone's getting hold of our data. I think we need a little more proof before we can go to the police, or anyone else for that matter', Clive sighed, 'and anyway, they're more strapped for resources than us. They'd probably ask us to quantify the loss in monetary terms so that they can allocate resources.'

Bren thought for a moment or two, 'have you thought about just killing it like you would malware. Remove the communication code and we're done - just keep an eye on it to make sure it doesn't come back?'

It was a sensible suggestion.

Bren carried on, 'or contact one of the antivirus companies and see if they can do something. This is costing us nearly all of your time - we have a business to run, we're missing you!'

Clive frowned and then replied.

'Look, I don't want to do this any more than you want me to - I needed to understand whether we actually had a problem. I'd at least like to know what we're losing. If I can find the process generating the traffic then I can go to the AV companies with something sensible - I can't even give them a copy of the data as none of it makes sense without the files and everything associated with it.'

Clive paced up and down, deep in thought.

'I'll create a virtual machine and see if I can trap anything there - if I can, I'll pass the whole thing over to one of the AV companies or the police - or anyone that might take an interest!'

'You've got BlackHack in a couple of weeks', said Bren, 'perhaps you could find someone there to take a look?'

BlackHack was the biggest annual hacking convention. Held in San Jose, it brought the best of the hackers together in one venue. Clive never missed a visit to these - the BlackHack events offered presentations on current threats and new ways to exploit computer systems. As a security specialist, he found these events incredibly useful.

'Possibly', said Clive, 'I'll see if I can work out what's sending this stuff in the meantime - if not, then I'll contact the police and see what I can do, if anything'.

'Ok Clive, but we really can't afford to keep you out of the company for much longer. At least let the others know - perhaps split the work between a few of us - that way we get some of your time back.'

'We can't let the others know yet. If we tell the board then they'll insist on us informing the investors - duty of disclosure and all that - and we don't know if this lot's down to one of our team either. It could be internal …'

'Bollocks! It's not one us. Do what you must on the lead up to BlackHack - but after the conference we need to think very seriously about MKI's future.'

Bren was right, but nonetheless, Clive didn't want to hear it. Clive wanted to find out what process was leaking data - he knew what Uncle Peter data looked like, and had a reasonable degree of confidence that he could find out what created it.

He set about installing a virtual machine - a software emulation of a computer. Commonly used by large Internet companies, it allows one physical computer to create several 'software only' versions of computers. Most computers only consume a small percentage of their processor's power for the majority of the time - a virtual machine allows several 'virtual computers' to share one physical computer. The software running inside the virtual machine generally thinks it's running inside a 'normal' computer.

Hackers and software testing companies also use virtual computers - it lets developers freeze a machine and inspect everything that's going on inside it. Clive wanted to use this feature of his virtual machine to see what was being received and sent via the software versions of network interface cards.

He installed the software and then created a virtual computer. Inside the virtual computer, he installed the operating system and a set of developer tools. Once he had these running, he transferred a few of the files from his

'SeeZu' fake project into the virtual computer. At this point, he saved the entire computer image - this meant he could just copy the image and start from this point again, should he need to.

With the network protocol recorder working, Clive created a few files in the new virtual machine. Each time he created new source code, the protocol recorder flashed. Uncle Peter was getting a copy of everything.

With a virtual machine in place, Clive could enable a set of debugging utilities that run outside of the system under test - anything running inside the virtual computer wouldn't be aware of this logging activity.

He enabled the network logs - the software running the virtual computer would now copy anything coming in to, or leaving, the virtual computer to a set of log files.

Clive set about modifying the SeeZu project files. He created a few files, moved them between the virtual computer and the real computer - he wanted to ensure that Uncle Peter had a lot of data. Unfortunately, the protocol recorder showed that the installation of the virtual machine software and all the tools within it had no effect on the network.

It had taken the best part of a day to set everything up and get it working properly. Clive had, however, confirmed that Uncle Peter was only interested in new material. As he transferred the old SeeZu files from the real computer to the virtual computer, the protocol recorder remained inactive, but as soon as he edited a file and saved it, the data recorded LED's flashed. Uncle Peter was choosy!

At this point, Clive pressed 'Pause' on the virtual machine. He copied the log files it had generated onto a memory card. He then transferred the memory card to his old PC and ran the network analysis tools. He expected to see many packets of data heading out to Uncle Peter - instead, the analysis tool came back with nothing. The virtual machine logs hadn't recorded any of the traffic Clive knew had gone to Uncle Peter.

'Twats!', said Clive, exasperatedly - but impressed at the same time - Uncle Peter was one step ahead again. He had already seen data go missing from log files: clearly the virtual machine logs would be useless. Clive would have to get inventive.

13

Clive never stayed at the hotel hosting BlackHack - the annual hacker's conference. Too many people wanted to demonstrate their skills at hacking everyone else, or breaking the venue's security systems. He also turned off his mobile 'phone: far too easy a target.

Instead, Clive had checked himself into the local Holiday Inn - cheap and cheerful. He had copied the virtual machine onto his laptop so he could continue playing - and he had the protocol recorder with him - he wanted to keep capturing what Uncle Peter saw, even if the encryption stopped him from decoding it.

This year's BlackHack conference had a few interesting demonstrations. One showing how to hack the hotel TV's infra-red remote control system - it sounded innocent enough, until the speaker showed a list of all the people registered at the hotel, along with their credit-card numbers. The TV system needed to carry this data to enable its pay-per-view and room service charging mechanisms to work.

Another presentation explored the weaknesses in wireless communication systems. With some highly specialised equipment, the presenters went through everything from exploiting the standard cellular networks, to more advanced attacks against the radio signals used to monitor people's movements in airports.

Clive really enjoyed the presentations highlighting the ways to exploit credit-card contactless payment and chip-and-PIN systems. Clive objected to the way banks had introduced a contactless payment mechanism without asking customers to accept the change in risk profiles, or giving them any option about using standard cards instead. He saw the presenters reading card details from several rows of seats in the auditorium - 'so much for a few millimetres' thought Clive as the presenters then discussed the ability to charge a few dollars to every passing card in an airport or tube station.

Clive attended as few of the track presentations as he could - particularly those discussing the latest trends in malware. He wanted to hear more about the new techniques for deploying, controlling and hiding malware in systems and these generally happened in the smaller conference rooms. Perhaps one of these presentations would mention the system infecting MKI's network.

By the end of the first day Clive, had seen several useful presentations but nothing that would help solve his immediate problem. He headed over the hotel's bar and ordered a beer.

'Clive, how are you?'

Clive spun round and recognising the owner of the voice beamed back, 'Whiteman, I didn't think you attended events that might actually teach you something useful!', and held out his hand.

Whiteman grinned and shook Clive's hand. 'Bastard!', he said good naturedly, 'I just saw you at the bar and thought I'd get a free drink, even if I have to suffer a few insults to get it …'

Clive ordered another beer and the two walked to an unoccupied table at the rear of the bar. They sat down.

Phil Whiteman generally just known as Whiteman in the hacking community, was an FBI agent. Clive had met Whiteman after a session at the Royal United Services Institute in London. They hit it off as soon as Clive had raised a fundamental problem with the security arrangements for that session - under the Chatham House Rule, none of the attendees should attribute what was said to any particular individual within the session. To that end, the security staff had taken mobile 'phones off everyone - but not the tablets or laptops. Clive made a point of recording part of the session and playing it back to the organisers. Future strategy sessions should be either technology-free, or with all devices allowed argued Clive.

Over the couple of years since that session, Clive and Whiteman had shared a reasonable amount of information about security issues and new hacker technologies. Clive had also helped resolve a couple of technical issues regarding mobile device security for the FBI. Bizarrely few people made the link that Phil Whiteman was the hacker Whiteman, or that he ran several of the dark-net honey-pots: sites offering illegal services paid for by untraceable Internet currencies. The FBI had actively run several major dark-markets for many years to compile data about those using the networks, and help trace criminals operating inside the USA.

Clive had provided MKI's technology to the FBI in order to secure the servers used to run Whiteman's dark market services. With the networks secured properly behind the scenes, the FBI had managed to create a widely respected (within the criminal world) dark market - with the FBI's data capturing systems and covert intelligence units able to monitor activities without being seen themselves.

The FBI's systems had proven so successful that they actually hosted several of the dark market sites on behalf of criminal groups - drug dealers and paedophile rings mainly, but also a few messaging platforms used by mafia and larger organised criminal networks. Between the NSA and FBI, the US had managed to develop several 'secure' messaging platforms and make them available to various application stores around the world. Users had security, but with the NSA monitoring all the data going through these platforms. Whiteman was the 'sales' side of these services, popularising secure frameworks within the hacking community and offering to host them.

'Seen anything interesting?', asked Clive

'I enjoyed the video-camera snooping session, genuinely impressive stuff for covert monitoring'

'What do you mean?'

'Really impressive stuff: set up a high-speed camera to record foliage, paper, even the curtains …', Whiteman took a large swig of his beer, 'run the video through some software and it can recover the sound from the room by analysing the vibrations in the video content. Too small and fast for the human eye, but relatively straight-forward for this tech - they showed it working though glass, and using consumer video cameras - really cool tech - we could have fun explaining that to a court room.'

'Yes, but how long does it take to process the video?', asked Clive

'Trust you - they didn't say. I'm guessing it's not realtime though.'

Like many FBI field officers, Whiteman liked his drink - he could happily drink most people under the table on a night out and carry on well into the following morning. However, despite the alcohol, he somehow managed to keep things together and rarely overstepped the mark.

After several beers, Whiteman asked how things were going with MKI.

'No idea!', exclaimed Clive, 'Someone's in our network.

I've been trying to work out what's going on but it's a real challenge. Whatever's behind it is good - really good.'

'Oh?', asked Whiteman, 'Can I help?'

'I'd appreciate the assistance, but not formally. I'd prefer to keep it under the radar for a bit - work out what's happening and then close it down. But I want to know what's behind it all first.'

Whiteman looked at Clive, 'Ok', Whiteman said, 'I'll have a look - off the radar', and then in an extremely bad Italian accent, 'I know nothing … I need more beer'.

Clive ordered another couple of beers, and started explaining his thoughts.

'I was doing a presentation on man-in-the-middle so I built a fake hotspot. As part of the demo, I recorded a few minutes of data and showed people what was travelling through the network - standard stuff: email, web, chat histories and so on - but I also captured a couple of packets of data I didn't recognise', said Clive, taking another swig of beer.

'Ok', said Whiteman.

'Well', continued Clive, 'I screen-shotted the data and grabbed a copy of it. The day after, both had gone - actually', Clive paused, 'the screen-shot image changed to show normal traffic. The evidence had gone.'

'Shit! That's a person instead of a machine then!'

'My thoughts exactly. I thought I was going mad for a bit - but, by sheer fluke, I'd got the original recording on another memory card so I took it offline and built a protocol analyser …'.

'As you do', replied Whiteman.

'So …', said Clive and then continued in his best Texan impression, 'I got me a whole posse of bad data.'

'Really?'

'Yeah. But it's all encrypted and I haven't got a cat in hell's chance of breaking it without knowing where it's coming from. All I know is that if I create anything new, it gets split into several segments, encrypted, and sent over to loads of different endpoints - each of which disappears after a few minutes.'

'Sophisticated setup', said Whiteman, 'that's organised crime or government standard by the look of it.'

'Too big for organised crime. I wasn't going to mention it, but you might just have an angle I don't - someone's very interested in what we do. I'm keeping the data off-grid for the time being.'

Clive went on to discuss the protocol recorder and the tools he built to capture data. 'It's taken weeks so far', he complained, 'I'm only getting one side of the story. I'm seeing what's going out, but there has to be something coming in and I can't see it.'

'Alright', said Whiteman, 'you got me interested - let's see if two brains can solve this little ol' mystery.'

'Well Dang Ma Diddlies if that aint a plan', joked Clive. This had been a standing joke between Whiteman and Clive - the first time they'd met, Whiteman had taken Clive to a local bar where they'd drunk themselves into a slurring mess. At the end of the night, Whiteman asked what Clive thought of California, Clive jokied 'it's all good apart from no-one speaks proper American'

'What d'ya mean, proper American'

'Well, you know, American'

'Like?'

'Well, "Dang ma diddlies"'

'Dang ma WHAT?', asked Whiteman.

'Diddlies'.

The following day, Clive had rung through for Whiteman and got his secretary, who immediately said 'Well dang ma diddlies if it aint the Englishman … hold on, I'll put you through'.

14

Clive woke up to the sound of his mobile 'phone ringing. His head hurt - and he felt sick. He rarely allowed himself to drink enough to get a hang-over, but after all the beer the previous evening, he was definitely ill.

'Clive', said a familiar voice at the other end. After a few moments, Clive realised it was Whiteman.

'Jesus, Whiteman, what the hell were we drinking last night? My mouth feels like Ghandi's Flipflop!'

'Bloody Europeans can't take a night on the tiles huh?'

Clive gazed at the clock. It was 8AM.

'How are you even functioning at this time in the morning?', asked Clive, 'You drank more than me.'

'Pah!', said Whiteman, 'You should come out when we go for a real drink. In the meantime, get your shit together - I want to take a look at that network data you promised me. You're flying back this week, so let's make the most of the time we have together.'

'I need a shower and coffee first.'

'Well, I'm waiting downstairs in Starbucks, so any time you're ready', replied Whiteman.

Clive stumbled into the shower and, despite the effects of the hangover, managed to make himself vaguely respectable.

He grabbed his 'technology bag' and took the lift to the ground floor. A few minutes later, having located Starbucks, he saw Whiteman standing outside holding a couple of large drinks.

'Here', said Whiteman, 'it looks like you need it!.'

'Thanks', said Clive, 'I think I need a new head.'

'You can always get head in this town', replied Whiteman, 'but let's do some work first. I'm parked round the corner.'

They walked round the block and to the multi-storey car-park. Whiteman climbed into a BMW and Clive put his bag in the back before getting into the passenger seat.

'Are you fit to drive?', asked Clive.

'As fit as I always was'

'That's no recommendation', mumbled Clive as Whiteman floored the accelerator.

After about 20 minutes or so, they arrived at the office block where Whiteman worked. The building looked like any typical mid-70's office on any typical industrial estate. It had a name plaque on the building suggesting that the company inside was called "Field Services Inc". Clearly it wasn't advertised as an FBI Field Office.

He signed Clive into the building at the front desk, and then led Clive through a set of security gates akin to those found at airports, and then to another set of doors. Beyond these doors was a much stronger set of security gates with metal interlocked cubicles: enter the first part, and when the door closes behind you the other opens. Whiteman went through first and then held his card over the 'visitor' gate sensor. When the green light came on, Clive pushed through the visitor lane and into the main office.

'Interesting design', said Clive.

'It used to be an old CIA place, built in the 70's', said Whiteman, 'it's actually a building within a building. From the outside it looks like a normal office block, but all of this lot's actually invisible from outside - it's a complete faraday cage, so we don't even leak radio signals from the back of the computer kit. Ideal for us now - although your mobile won't work, of course.'

He led Clive through a series of open plan areas before heading towards an office at the far end of the building.

'Underneath here', he continued, 'they put an anechoic chamber - it's still there. Must have cost a fortune and we haven't had the heart to take it out yet. No idea what the CIA wants with an anechoic chamber, but hey, it's interesting. I'll take you down there later if you want a surreal experience?'

'Sure, thanks', replied Clive, following Whiteman to his office.

Whiteman had an impressive office. Large flat-panel monitors filled one wall, in front of the monitors was a two sofas, a coffee table, and a couple of arm-chairs. Whiteman walked over to very large and imposing desk and motioned that Clive sit down.

'Make yourself comfortable', he said before pressing a button on his desk 'phone, 'Paul', he barked into it, 'can you grab us a couple of coffees and come join us in my office? Thanks.'

A few minutes later, Paul appeared with three mugs of coffee balanced on top of his laptop. He set the coffee down on the table and wiped the top of the laptop case with his hand. Paul nodded at Whiteman and then at Clive. Clive offered his hand and Paul shook it briefly before putting his hands tight against his legs.

Paul Davis was an extremely thin and very tall man. He had thick-rimmed glasses, a shock of black curly hair and a sharp expression. He gave the appearance of planning every move before making it. 'Overly methodical', thought Clive, and wondered if he had Aspergers.

Whiteman did the introductions: 'Paul, Clive - Clive, this is

Paul. He looks after all the protocol analysis stuff in the office. If there's something in the data you've brought, Paul will probably see it before anyone else.'

'Great', said Clive, 'Good to meet you Paul. I'll show you what I've got.'

With that, Clive went through the history of the 'investigation' up to that point. He emphasised again about the data going missing or being modified within images, and then explained about the protocol recorder build and the clean-room environment necessary to keep everything off the networks. Then, he discussed the honey-pot he had created using SeeZu as the code word.

Finally, Clive mentioned about the virtual computer, and the fact that the logs never recorded traffic going to Uncle Peter.

'So', said Whiteman, 'we want to know what data goes to Uncle Peter, right?'

'Actually', said Clive, 'I want to confirm that data is actually going to Uncle Peter. It only looks like it is - I can't say for certain.'

'Yeah yeah', said Whiteman, 'but assuming it is, we want to know what's going, and where it ends up …'

'That would do for starters', said Clive, 'then perhaps we have a chance of stopping this thing.'

Paul had remained silent until now. He chipped in with 'Before we do anything, I would like to understand the tools you've created. How do we know we're not looking at a network backup or something benign?'

Clive opened his bag and pulled out his laptop and the protocol recorder. I'll show you what I've got. Clive fired up the virtual computer on his laptop. Whiteman passed Clive the end of a long lead going to a cabinet in the corner of the room.

'Let's see it on the big-screen', he said.

Clive plugged the lead into his computer and one of the large wall monitors came on. He started by presenting the original data set captured from FreeBee off a memory card, and then went through his process of elimination to find the data sent to Uncle Peter. Then, Clive walked the others through the scripts he'd written and then the code that ran on the protocol recorder.

Finally, Clive copied the contents of the protocol analyser over to the virtual machine so that Paul and Whiteman could see the most recently captured data.

Paul reached over and took Clive's laptop. Whiteman looked at Clive and smiled.

'Coffee time', he said quietly.

Whiteman motioned to Clive to come with him and they left the room. When out of earshot, Whiteman said, 'he comes over a bit antisocial at times, but if anyone can find a pattern, he can. At least he's not blown your stuff out of the water yet - you've lasted a lot longer than some of the CIA geeks we get in here.'

Clive went to the bathroom to relieve himself. He was starting to feel a little more human - the coffee and concentration had stopped him dwelling on his hangover.

By the time he emerged, Whiteman had made another round of coffees. They carried them back to the office where Paul was still paging through the data.

'This is really interesting', Paul said, 'it's a simple protocol but we're only seeing part of it.'

'I thought that', said Clive, 'there's no control side.'

'More than that', replied Paul, 'it looks like we have a device identifier, but how does the transmission control and assembly work? We're missing quite a lot.'

'What do you mean?', asked Whiteman.

'Well', said Paul, 'let's assume this is sending a copy of a file for a moment. It's sending lots of parts of it to lots of different computers. It looks like it works the same way as a file-sharing network does - no one computer has a copy of all of the data while it's on the network - nice and secure, tricky to intercept, and almost impossible to crack unless you've got all the parts or can capture things at the very start.'

He looked up from the screen and continued, 'However, some of these parts will get lost or might arrive out of order - part 1, then part 2, then part 5, then part 4 … so how does this know whether part 3 has been lost in transmission. If it has to send part 3 again, then how does it deal with two copies of part 3 in the event that the original part 3 was just delayed? Somewhere, there's something assembling these parts and controlling how they arrive, where they go, to which servers and so on … that way we end up with parts 1,2,3,4 and 5 - exactly one of each, in the right order, so we can re-assemble the parts and make sense of it. We're missing transmission control data and probably a set of commands coming in from somewhere telling this thing what to send.'

'Ok', said Whiteman, 'I take it you think Clive's onto something?'

'Oh yes. Undoubtedly', replied Paul, 'But I think we're only seeing one third - or less - of the traffic. Where's the transmission control data, and where's the command and control stuff? If we can find those, we might stand more of a chance of finding out what's going on.'

15

'So', started Paul, 'we know something's leaving your machines, and we know that it looks something like this'

Paul was standing in front of Whiteman's monitors. Clive was secretly envious: the geek in him wanted the same kind of set-up at home or at least in his office.

Paul pointed to a network diagram on one of the displays.

'I want to set up a fake network and hook up Clive's laptop - as the data source - we know that's already compromised, so we should be able to get it to generate something of interest to Uncle Peter. I'll set it up on a dedicated network segment so it looks like it's on a local hotel or something'.

'Ok', agreed Whiteman, 'Clive, you're good to generate more content for your honey-pot?', he asked, referring to the fake SeeZu project Clive had already created.

Clive, feeling like he was one of Whiteman's FBI employees, nodded.

'Good', said Whiteman.

'I've already set up the network recording tools - let's grab everything: it's transparent to the honey-pot network, so we should be able to see Uncle Peter's dark side!', said Paul, grinning.

'Great', said Whiteman, 'I'll let you two get on with that then. Just shout if you need anything', he added, looking at Paul.

'Sure', replied Paul.

Dismissed from Whiteman's office, Clive and Paul went into Paul's lab - it held a huge array of equipment and could easily have been the control room for some kind of major industrial plant. In the middle of the room was a large cabinet containing a rack of computer equipment. Brightly coloured cables ran between the various boxes in the cabinet and up into the artificial ceiling.

The room was air-conditioned, just a little too cool for comfort. Clive noticed how quiet this room was, compared to most computer rooms.

Around the edges, he could see a mix of technologies - some old, some new, but all running. He wondered if Paul had turned everything on for his benefit, or whether they always kept the equipment running.

Clive whistled softly. 'Wow - this is some kit!'

'Nah - the real kit's downstairs in the basement. They get to play with everything from Quantum prototypes to massively parallel toys down there - I just get the mundane.'

Paul walked over to the far side of the room and cleared some space for Clive's laptop.

'You Ok with connecting to our tracing tools? They'll capture everything so you might want to dump anything confidential off the machine.'

'No need, I won't access anything critical. We keep all the sensitive stuff in encrypted vaults, so as long as I don't access them, I'll be fine'

He grinned and put the laptop on the newly cleared space. 'Besides, there's nothing that interesting in the browser history anyway!'

'Right - let's get going then'

Clive hit the power button on his laptop. Paul made out some FBI paperwork.

'You'll need to sign this - it just covers us for accessing personal information over the network - keeps the lawyers happy', said Paul, passing the form to Clive to sign.

Clive signed the form, 'Welcome to litigation central!', he joked as he passed the completed form back.

'You're in America, have you met my lawyer? Actually, it's more for forensics, chain of evidence and all that crap', acknowledged Paul.

'Yeah, I know - been there, done that'

By now Clive's laptop had booted up and was asking for his user name and password. Clive put these in and waited for the desktop icons to appear.

'All the networking's off at the moment - do you want my protocol analyser in-circuit?'

'Yeah. I'll sort out a couple of network leads.'

Paul walked over to a cupboard in the corner of the room. It was locked with a combination lock. Paul unlocked the cupboard and swung open an obviously heavy door. Hanging off the inside of the door were assorted cables. Briefly, Clive could see the equipment inside the cupboard - most of it in forensic bags marked 'FBI -Evidence'. Paul grabbed a couple of bright red leads and swung the door shut again. It locked itself with a loud clunk.

'Right: let's get this show on the road ...'

Paul inserted one of the network plugs into a socket mounted on the bench next to Clive's laptop.

'This is a monitoring port, it's off at the moment. We'll get everything wired up, then I'll enable the port'

'Ok - want to pass me the other end of that lead?'

Paul gave Clive the tail end of the network lead, along with the other lead from the cupboard. Clive plugged in his protocol recorder and then connected this to his laptop. Then he started up the protocol recorder and waited for it's 'ready' LED to illuminate.

Meanwhile, Paul had moved over to a computer with an extremely large display. He was running some network administration tools.

'I'll set it up to look like you're at an hotel downtown. I've already got a load of configurations from sniffing them in the past and it'll save creating a new one'

Clive wondered how many hotel network profiles the FBI had. Paul was obviously creating an emulation of a real network setup so that the laptop (and, presumably, Uncle Peter) would think it was connected to that network instead of one of the FBI's technology centres.

Over the next few minutes, Paul loaded a network profile and tested the connections to ensure that everything looked 'normal'. Once he was satisfied with the result, he clicked on a 'record' button and then enabled the network port next to Clive's laptop.

'Now we wait!'

'Actually, I might be able to trigger something. Uncle Peter likes new content, he only gets excited when he sees something original …'

'Ok. Go for it'

It was Clive's turn to tap away on a keyboard. He started creating a document that defined another imaginary piece of SeeZu. He came up with a series of formulae that looked vaguely sensible.

'It's a Merkel Hash - but I've changed the variables so it'll look like I'm working on a variant', Clive explained.

'Cool'

'I want to create something we can trace. It might give us a fighting chance against the encryption if we know what we're looking for!'

'Yeah. Don't hold your breath though. If it's good enough

crypto then we won't crack it - we're better off working out what's sending it'

'Tried that! Couldn't find anything unusual'

'You don't have our toy box - we do this for a living.'

Clive hit the save button and a few moments later, the protocol recorder LED lit to show that Uncle Peter had received another few packets of data.

'Told you!', Clive said.

'Consistent: that helps'

'Took me a while to work out what floats his boat', said Clive with a grin, 'but I got him hooked in the end.'

'Ok, I'll leave it online for a while and see what we get. Keep going with the honey pot content and I'll check back in a few.'

Paul left Clive and walked round the corner. Clive assumed he had gone to tell Whiteman that they had managed to capture something.

Feeling more like an FBI employee, Clive started creating a whole series of viable encryption services. He was creating documents that mimicked his usual creative process but in reality regurgitated principles already known. By creating the material in his own way, however, Clive was ensuring that whomever read the material would have to have a significant amount of knowledge about ciphers and encryption technologies. He wasn't about to make life easy for Uncle Peter. Clive also made a couple of changes to the honey-pot data to make it look like he was exploring variants to established principles.

Clive consoled himself with the thought that Uncle Peter would have a headache trying to understand this lot. As he worked, the LED continued to flash.

16

'Come on, let's eat - it's late'.

Whiteman's voice brought Clive and Paul out of their technical 'trance'.

'We're struggling to capture anything new', said Paul to Whiteman's unasked question.

'Really?'

'Yeah, we can see packets going out alright, but still nothing coming in.'

'Ok, can you leave it running while we go and eat?'

Whiteman was hungry. He'd deliberately left the two geeks working together for the day.

In discussions with Clive, he mentioned that he was concerned about his department's internal systems and that they might have been compromised. He wanted to understand the risk to his department's activities. Clive's activities could take Whiteman beyond his remit but he would argue the case when he knew all the facts.

Whiteman said he held a strange position in the agency: he created honey-pots on dark networks to monitor organised crime and determine how best to engage. His work sometimes involved other agencies and he maintained the name "Whiteman" to everyone who worked with him. It was easier if everyone adopted the same name for him as it meant he would respond more automatically if compromised. Rarely operating legally, this was work that he couldn't usually discuss - Clive was one of the very few people taken into his confidence, and Whiteman used a lot of Clive's technologies in his department: if Clive's equipment had issues then so did Whiteman.

He went on to explain that this part of the agency didn't formally exist: it was part of a confidential network with a remit to gather intelligence. He collected information on people and used the department's supercomputing facility to help search through the data collected.

It was then up to other agencies to work out how to use the information gathered. Quite often, Whiteman had to work out ways of 'leaking' information to the police so that prosecutors had a formal evidence trail for court use. As the head of a confidential and intelligence unit, Whiteman also assessed FBI staff to look for data breaches or hacking attacks within the agency itself. He assumed that somewhere someone was watching him watch others. It was that kind of a job.

If anyone heard about data leakage within his area, it could prove devastating to current investigations. To that end, he had spent the day tidying up documentation and preparing to brief his director.

Being cautious, however, he wanted to establish all the facts before taking things any further. He needed to give Paul and Clive both the time and resources required to see if they could work out what was behind Uncle Peter. More importantly, he wanted Clive's protocol recorder to detect if any communications left his department.

Whiteman wanted to retain absolute control over the work that the two geeks that were doing in the lab. If nothing came of it, he would act responsibly and pass the information up the chain of command so someone else could make the call on how important it was; if they discovered something, then he could raise the alarm and propose a suitable solution. Whichever way, he would come out of it well. For the time being, he just needed to keep the team happy - food usually did the trick.

'Guys - come on - food!', said Whiteman.

'You've been at it all day and a few minutes to eat and rest will do you both the power of good'

'Ok, ok', grumbled Paul, 'leave it going and we can check the logs when we get back.'

They left the lab and Clive suddenly became aware of how cold he had been.

'Jesus! It's like a freezer in there. I hadn't realised how cold I was.'

The warm air in the main office made Clive shudder.

'I'm thinking that we need to image my laptop', said Clive as they walked out of the office, 'that way you can carry on after I leave - assuming you want to'

'Good idea', agreed Paul.

'Is there any point in checking any of our internal systems?', asked Whiteman.

'We know what we're looking for now', said Clive, 'but I think we need to concentrate on one system at a time.'

'Yeah', agreed Paul, 'I want to find the command and control side. Once we've got both bits then we can sort out how it works - until then we're just gathering data. At least we know what we've got on Clive's laptop. Adding more systems might just swamp us with crap.'

'Ok'

'But we will look at that when we know what's happening. I guess we have to.'

They climbed into Whiteman's car and he drove with his usual lack of care to a local Diner.

'I've been coming here since I was a kid', said Whiteman, 'go for any of the burgers, they're the best in California'.

The diner was an interesting place. It was a common meeting place for business angels and entrepreneurs. Whiteman talked about the various deals that the place laid claim to hosting while Clive looked at the walls and ceiling.

Virtually every inch of available space contained something - photographs of tech gurus, original technology posters, old core storage systems, sections of circuits and so on. Models of aircraft and all kinds of assorted junk hung down from the ceiling. This was, without doubt, a technology-centric diner.

'It's amazing what you can pick up here just by listening to the punters', said Whiteman, 'you could sell books about it'.

A young waitress came over and took their drink orders while everyone scanned the menus. In the end, they all took Whiteman's advice and ordered the tech-burger. They chatted about the items on show in the diner with Whiteman highlighting certain objects around the room.

'That was the first proper mouse … and that the original core store prototype … worth a fortune now … passed to the owners here as junk at the time', said Whiteman between bites of food, 'at least that's what they say - could all be crap bought from computer breakers of course, but it's a good story'.

Paul's 'phone beeped and he pulled it out from his jeans pocket. He looked at the screen and then across to Clive.

'Got one', he said

'One what?', asked Whiteman.

'I set up an alarm. Simple stuff - every time we generated something, Uncle Peter got a copy. Can't understand why we didn't see anything coming back in'.

The 'phone beeped again.

'So, I set up an alarm', said Paul, and tucked into his

burger.

'An alarm … for …?', asked Whiteman.

'Oh yeah, sorry, when stuff comes in to the system, it doesn't usually trigger anything from Uncle Peter. So I set up something that looks for anything coming in but only alerts me if something goes out to Uncle Peter straight afterwards.

'It means we have seen data coming in to the laptop and then something going out to Uncle Peter. It has been coming in, we just didn't know what to look for. No idea what it is yet, but it's the first time we've seen something coming in that seems to have something going out in response.'

'This is really important', said Clive, 'but it could be a false positive. We just know we've seen something in and then something going out. Hopefully, we can find out more when we get back to the office.'

'I'm done', said Paul in response to another set of beeps from his 'phone, 'ready when you are.'

17

Whiteman turned over and silenced the alarm clock. The red glow of the numbers showing 06:30.

He climbed out of bed gently, trying not to wake Janet, his wife. She muttered something sleepily, but he was already closing the door to the en-suite and missed what she said.

Whiteman's house was a split-level affair, built into a steep sloping plot. A driveway ran from the road to the front of a double garage. Steps went up and along the side of the house leading to a veranda with a balcony above the garage. With the accommodation above the garage, the house commanded a reasonable view - nothing spectacular, but enough to warrant sitting out on the balcony on summer nights.

He liked the house; it was quirky. The biggest advantage was that the bedrooms were at the back of the place, making it easier for him to come and go without disturbing Janet. While they had been together for 28 years, they both ran their own lives and understood when the other had to work late - Whiteman considered himself lucky as it seemed that domestic stability was a rare thing for most active agents.

While he showered, he wondered if Clive and Paul had actually noticed he'd gone home. He left them looking at screen after screen of data, trying to work out what they had captured - and what had triggered Paul's 'phone alarm at the diner.

He finished his shower and walked through the house to the kitchen wearing a white bathrobe with a 'Hilton' logo on the left hand pocket. He pulled a coffee filter bag from its packaging and tipped a rough approximation of a measure of coffee into it. As always, this probably amounted to more than healthy, but it was early and he wanted the caffeine hit. Filling the water container, he yawned and flicked the switch on the coffee maker.

As the coffee percolated through the filter, he fetched his 'phone and checked for emails or messages. Reading a few of the overnight email deliveries, he poured himself a coffee and then went to get dressed.

He took an envelope containing a Valentine's card out of his bag and propped it on the mantlepiece. Janet would see that when she got up.

'You old romantic', he thought, before collecting his coat from the back of the chair where he'd thrown it the night before. Gently closing the door, he went down a set of steps from the balcony above the garage, and opened the car door. The garage was full of junk, so the car stayed on the drive at the front of the house. He climbed inside and started it up.

Calling for some donuts and coffee on the way to the office, Whiteman arrived slightly later than he planned. It didn't matter, Paul and Clive were still discussing the data they captured.

'Morning guys, how's it going?'

'Good, thanks', replied Clive.

Paul looked up at Whiteman.

'We've got something. Give us a few more minutes to get it all together and we'll come through'

'Ok - should I worry, or is it something for the malware guys to pick up?', asked Whiteman.

'Worry! Worry a lot. This is big - possibly multi-state stuff. We'll need a team on this soon, and probably need some cross-agency support', replied Paul, 'but we need a little more time to distil what we've found.'

'Right - well, there's coffee and donuts here. Eat, drink, enjoy …'

Whiteman walked back to his office thinking. "Multi-state" suggested that Clive and Paul had found something that included components from several different countries. One of the problems with open-source projects is that some people use them to create malware toolkits. People didn't need to be expert hackers any more - instead, they could create their own services by using simple wrappers around existing code libraries.

These kits contained everything necessary to deploy malware to unsuspecting users - indeed, Whiteman had showcased a set of 'self-updating' hacking tools at a recent workshop: 'Press a button to deploy the latest malware builds to any device on any operating system.

'This stuff works out what it needs to deploy and installs the right stuff on the right computer - as soon as one mechanism gets closed down, the odds are that the hacking community has already found another 3 or 4 ways to infect any given device, and automatically update the development toolkits.

'It's simply a case of trying to stay as up to date with these hacking libraries as you can - but you'll always find yourself one step behind the bad guys …'

Whiteman hoped it wasn't as bad as Paul had made out a few moments ago. Nonetheless, he trusted Paul's judgement - if Whiteman was going to need a team, he would need approval from the departmental Director.

Whiteman picked up his desk 'phone and hit a button. 'Too early in the morning to speak to the Ops Director', he thought so he left a voice-mail: 'Derek, just a heads up - we might have a problem. One of our UK security vendors has discovered what they think is a new multi-state attack vector. This might give us a problem at a national level. He doesn't know much about it yet - or how serious it is - but we might need to raise the profile on this one. I'll keep you posted.'

The downside to passing this up the chain was that Whiteman may well have to hand over the investigation to other agencies. Whiteman had a job to do, and while malware observation formed part of that, he was more concerned with creating and maintaining environments to monitor or control criminal activity. Other department and agencies usually dealt with the complexities of malware and any impact it might have on critical national infrastructure.

Whiteman went to his computer and hit one of the shift keys to bring it out of 'sleep'. Then he paused. He had intended to start writing a report, but if his computer was also compromised …

He picked up the 'phone again and hit the Ops Director's call button again.

'Oh, and I suggest you stay off email for this one - I'm not sure we have anything locked down properly at the moment.'

He hung up again. His last message would probably alarm Derek, but Whiteman was playing safe.

Without a computer to work on, Whiteman grabbed a sheaf of paper from the printer and started writing out his report in long-hand. At least he was doing something while he waited.

About an hour later, Paul and Clive arrived at Whiteman's office.

'Come in guys, what have you got?'

Whiteman motioned for Paul and Clive to sit down.

'It's big and it's sophisticated', said Paul.

Whiteman resisted the opportunity to come back with an

innuendo, 'go on.'

Paul continued, 'It looks like we have some kind of data harvester. It grabs anything new and distributes it through to multiple endpoints. We think it sends the original file when its created and then only delta changes thereafter.'

Paul looked at Whiteman, 'Databases look a little different - we think it sends a small amount of data when you create a new one, I'm assuming its only sending the schema: the structure of the database rather than the actual data. Presumably there's some back door process somewhere to extract data when required, but we haven't seen that yet.

'The data gets split so no single end-point has all of it. I don't know where it's assembled because I can't trace the real end-points. It goes through something like the onion router (a dark network, used to hide user activity and mask real identities). It seems that it automatically sends everything Clive generates.

'Last night, we found another side to it. The reason Clive couldn't see any command and control data was that it wasn't where we thought it was. We'd left the machine and then saw software update checks going out while the machine was idle. In response, Uncle Peter hijacked these updates to contain instructions and changes to the end-points.'

'I'm not with you', replied Whiteman.

'When the machine's not in use, it issues what appears to be a software update check, only it's not just a check for software updates - it looks like it gets any commands from Uncle Peter. At the same time, this process changes all the network end-points, so that any subsequent data transmissions go elsewhere in the dark net'.

'So this is a software update hack?', asked Whiteman.

'More than that - much more than that', replied Clive, 'that's just one channel. We think we have found others. It's compromising the operating system itself and we think that someone looks at what's valid with this stuff.'

'What do you mean by "someone looks at what's valid"?'

Clive responded, 'We created a couple of dummy files last night. They got distributed out like everything else, however, one contained a link to a non-existent project. We looked at the device search history and found several references to that project immediately after we saw an inbound update request.

'Someone had looked at the data and wanted to know what was in the document we referenced. It took them a while to realise it didn't exist, and that was long enough for us to see them looking for it. Whoever it was subsequently deleted the search history entries.'

Paul picked up the conversation, 'it looks like we have real people on the other end of this. And enough intelligence to realise what to look for. I don't think it was a robot trolling through the directories. I think someone was issuing remote commands to Clive's machine.'

Derek Groban came into the office in a good mood - although that would change through the course of the day. A relatively short and slightly-built man, he had worked his way up through the agency before becoming its Director of Special Operations within its Digital Resources section.

'Digital Resources' was a general title to mask the real activities of the unit: to use virtually any means possible to track serious and organised crime. More often than not he would cite 'encryption' as the single biggest problem in attacking organised criminals. When criminals employ good encryption systems, it could add months or even years to an investigation. In some cases, it was simpler to resort to 'old fashioned' policing techniques.

During the early 2000's, the US Naval Research Laboratory created technologies to be able to share information amongst defence contractors via the Internet. The US government spun this project as an ecosystem to help people 'regain and reclaim autonomy' – a method to enable freedom of access and expression on the Internet while theoretically keeping users in control of their own privacy.

This system - known as The Onion Router, or Tor - provided a level of anonymity that led to its rapid adoption by those with less idealistic values than its inventors. It led to the creation of online criminal communities using Tor as a dark network through which they exchange information about hacking, scams, exploitation of personal data, drugs, weapons, and so on. The development of online anonymous currencies provided the dark network with a way to commercialise criminal activities on a global scale.

It became apparent very soon after the release of the network that defence and policing agencies would need to consider the use of dark networks themselves in order to infiltrate organised crime networks, and provide a reasonable response to criminal activities enabled through the use of these technologies. The FBI, like many international agencies, decided to create a series of entry points on the dark network – in effect, providing a monitored front door to allow them to determine who used dark networks, and for what purpose.

Although hotly denied, the FBI also created numerous honey-pots: services on the dark networks that allowed criminals to promote and exchange information – all under the watchful eye of the FBI's newly formed Digital Resources team. These honey-pots became vast repositories of extremely useful information to law enforcement agencies; however, the FBI could never admit that they were supporting criminality (or turning a blind eye to crime).

As the information within the repositories grew, it became more important to ensure that criminals never knew that the FBI ran some of the largest dark-network services on the planet. Criminals had to remain confident that these networks protected their anonymity and the FBI (along with many other international agencies) had to use any information gained from the dark-networks with extreme care. In many cases, agents would have to find another way to get hold of a more public version of the information originally found via FBI-hosted dark-networks – a process known as dual-sourcing.

The FBI's digital resources department was formed to collect data, create dark networks, encourage the formation of so-called 'anonymous communities' and encourage their development. This work required specialist knowledge and absolute secrecy.

Derek had created several teams, each with specialist subject-matter knowledge – some covering drugs, others weapons, another section dealing with fraud. Whiteman's section assessed new technologies that could assist in maintaining the anonymity of the FBI's covert services, investigate anything that could compromise activities, or enhance the capabilities of the Digital Resources section.

'What have you got?'

Whiteman jumped at Derek's question. He hadn't heard Derek approach.

'Don't know yet - but there's definitely something, I'll grab the team and let them brief you properly.'

Whiteman picked up the desk-'phone and called though to Paul while Derek made himself comfortable in Whiteman's office.

'Paul - can you both come through. I want to bring Derek up to speed and it's better coming from you guys directly. Ok. Thanks.'

A few minutes later, Clive and Paul arrived.

'Come in - make yourselves comfortable. Clive, I think you've met Derek before.'

Clive and Derek shook hands and they all sat.

'Right', started Whiteman, 'By way of background, Clive saw some unusual data left his systems while presenting at a conference - potentially indicating theft of information. He has built a gadget to detect whenever this occurs. As everything was encrypted, he was struggling to find out where the data ended up, but suspected organised crime or state-sponsored acquisition of intellectual property. We met last week and I thought the department should take a look at it. Clive has kindly joined us to provide his input prior to returning to the UK.'

Derek looked at Clive and then back at Whiteman, his expression asking whether it was appropriate to involve Clive further.

'Clive's ex-UK military and a real expert in security. We're using his company's kit to secure our comms, so we need his expertise in this matter. We had him go through developed vetting so he could advise and supply.' Whiteman grinned, 'he's almost one of us now!'

'Ok, go on'

'I think Paul or Clive should carry on …', said Whiteman.

Paul jumped in, eager to impress the Director, 'We have established that this system targets intellectual property. It has an active process that collates and disseminates new material via dark network connections in encrypted form. It sends the entirety of new documents and then appears to send only delta-changes thereafter. In other words, something assembles and maintains the state of these new documents at the backend.

'It would appear that whoever's behind this has the ability to understand documents written in English, and that a physical team or individual assesses the content of these documents in order to send command and control instructions to the compromised computer. In this case,

Clive's laptop.

'Clive created a honey-pot and filled it with documents. All the documents appear to have been uploaded to a person or persons unknown.'

Clive smiled at the use of 'person or persons unknown'.

Paul continued, 'We believe that someone had to assess and act on the information provided in the documents, suggesting that Clive's documentation was read by a human being, not a computer system. This human being then instigated search proceedings to look for non-existent material Clive referenced in his documentation. We have subsequently seen numerous attempts by the third party to locate this information.

'All transmission and search activity disappears from system logs. Some never even makes it to the logs. The attack seems to cover numerous operating systems and hardware profiles, so I believe we have a state-sponsored attack as very few organisations will have sufficient resources to assess this data. I think the level of sophistication shown in the ability to compromise these different systems also points to state sponsorship rather than organised crime.'

'Who?', asked Derek, 'Chinks? Arabs? Russia?'

'We don't know yet.', Clive responded, keen to get a word in, 'Data gets split up and sent via many different routes simultaneously. All end up somewhere in the Tor - sorry - the dark net. We don't know where it really goes yet. And, we're still working out how it does it, the code's buried deep in the operating system somewhere. It's very well written - hat's off to the developers.'

'What about our systems?', asked Derek.

'We haven't had a chance to check our systems yet', said Whiteman, 'until yesterday, we weren't really sure we had anything. These guys have worked overnight to find out what's going on. I thought you'd need to know as soon as …'

'Ok - how soon before we can check it out?'

'Well, we can use Clive's detector, if he'll allow ...'

Whiteman looked over at Clive, who nodded.

'Sure'

'Thank you. Let me know as soon as you can.'

With that, Derek headed back to his own office, leaving Whiteman, Paul and Clive to work out how to test the department's own systems.

Clive looked at Whiteman.

'I have a suggestion that might also see how sophisticated these guys are ...'

'Go on'

'Why don't we create the document referred to by my SeeZu project. Transfer it to the FBI systems and then see if they stop looking for it on my laptop - assuming, of course, that they are in the FBI's network too.'

'Why?'

'Well, let's see if they have any context for the stuff they're grabbing - if Uncle Peter grabs everything and keeps searching on my laptop, then there's no bridge between the various documents and grabs - it's a dumb "grab everything" - but if it then stops my laptop being searched for the document, then it shows a potential link between us - and that's a very different proposition to just grabbing everything.'

'Not sure that'll prove anything', replied Whiteman, 'there must be thousands of documents with the same name. Perhaps more interesting to see if a copy uploaded from here also gets uploaded from your laptop in due course. Do they grab the full document again or do they have some way of knowing that they already have that document, so they only upload the first copy?'

'Good point - still - worth doing', said Clive.

18

Milo's was a special place for Janet and Whiteman. It seemed almost a lifetime ago since they had their first 'proper date' there.

They checked themselves in and one of the 'meet-and-greet' team led them to a couple of small sofas where they could relax before being led to their table. They ordered drinks and started looking through the menu,

'Scallops for me, followed by the Steak', said Janet, smiling.

'The usual, then?'

'Well, why not?'

The two made small-talk while they waited to be shown through to their table. Whiteman's mobile 'pinged' several times to announce the receipt of a message. He wanted to ignore it, but with Clive due to head back to the UK soon, he thought he should check the device.

The message was short and simple - but it knocked the wind out of Whiteman's sails:

"Bad news: Uncle Peter worse than discussed. Potentially terminal".

Reading the message several times, Whiteman made his apologies and stepped outside. He rang Paul.

'What's up?'

'It's tracking everything. We plugged Clive's analyser into the primary network and its a wonder it hasn't burned out. I think it's on every machine in here …'

'Shit. I'll come back.'

'No need', said Paul, 'a few minutes won't make a massive difference, eat your meal first and then come over. We've still got to work out the full extent - so we'll crack on with that and document it so that you have all you need for Derek.'

'You're a life-saver, I'll get over as soon as I'm done.'

While Whiteman went back to join his wife (and to break the news that he was needed back in the office afterwards), Clive and Paul were analysing the data captured.

Janet dropped Whiteman off at the office and went home. It was the first time that Whiteman had been called back to the office in years. She thought it must be a seriously important matter for Whiteman to allow his team to call him back in on Valentine's night of all nights.

Whiteman strode into the lab.

'Right, what have we got guys?'

'Well', replied a pale and drawn Paul, 'it looks like everything here's compromised. Everything!'

Whiteman looked over to Clive who was tapping away at a machine in the corner.

'Clive?'

'Oh yeah - this is really clever. We've got to respect what they've done. I'm still trying to work out how the damned thing hangs together, but it's probably got everything you're doing here. Most likely right across the agency too …'

'Shit!'

Whiteman picked up his mobile and called Derek.

Clive was impressed with the speed at which Derek called the team together and laid out a strategy for protecting data assets within the unit.

While it was a fair assumption that Uncle Peter had already received most of the data stored within the unit, it made little sense to take those offline. He called in the unit's protocol specialists to help Clive and Paul understand the data captured by Clive's protocol analyser.

'Can we use the analyser to block traffic?', he asked Clive and Paul

'Not yet', replied Clive, 'we can recognise outgoing data, but at the moment we only know we received something from the command-and-control side when we see a response going out when we haven't made changes to anything.'

'Yeah', added Paul, 'the problem is that if we stop the outgoing side without knocking out the command-and-control stuff, they could update their code behind the scenes and then we have to start again. At the moment we know what we're looking for, so it's a little easier to work out what's going on.'

Clive nodded in agreement.

'Really, we need to keep both sides active for a while - if we close one side, they'll know they're rumbled!'

Through the course of the night and early morning, more people started arriving in the lab. Clive and Paul were asked to present their findings to the senior management team.

Just before the presentation, Derek asked Clive, Paul and Whiteman to come his office. Derek introduced them to Bill Price, the Director of Digital Intelligence.

'Gentlemen', Derek started, 'Bill's here to take ownership of this problem. As you're aware, we have a specific remit in this department and we're starting to go beyond our boundaries or areas of expertise here. Bill has the budget and resources to throw at this, so I'm going to ask that you brief Bill and his team and then step back to allow him to do his job.

'Our friends in MI5 asked that Clive return to the UK - they already know of this problem and I briefed them again earlier. With the full agreement of our friends in London, we intend to take control of the investigation at this point, so we need the team here carrying on as if nothing has happened. We ask that anyone involved now steps out of this space to let us to do our job. We need to minimise the risk of someone outside the agency tipping this 'Uncle Peter' off, therefore, my department now owns this case in its entirely. Please surrender any information you have that could help with the investigation but then leave us to it.'

Paul wanted to object, but had suspected this might happen from the moment he realised that Uncle Peter had been controlling data within some of the FBI's own internal systems. Whiteman was monitoring criminal activity, Uncle Peter was far too elegant to be a mere criminal tool.

The main systems would remain online but, advised Bill, could be subject to interruption at any point. As the systems were already compromised, all existing data would be considered in that light. New projects would now be handled more carefully to ensure that nothing essential leaked, however it made sense to keep things running as normally as possible to avoid spooking those behind Uncle Peter.

Bill and Derek returned to Derek's office to talk. Some time later, they asked Clive to join them.

'Clive', started Derek, 'So you're heading back to the UK tomorrow?'

'Well, I can postpone if it helps', replied Clive.

'No', said Bill, 'we have to handle this ourselves now. Although I would appreciate it if we could borrow your protocol analyser for a few days - we'll create our own and get yours back to you of course, but it will save us a few days'

'Ok', said Clive, not really hiding his disappointment, 'I was rather hoping to stay engaged here - I want to clear this from my systems too.'

'I can understand that, but this is a federal investigation into state assets now. Recent changes in our laws mean we now view things like this as potential terrorism or an act of aggression against the USA. While we appreciate your assistance, it's time to hand it over to professional investigators with state resources. Anything you do now could compromise our work, so we thank you for bringing it to our attention.'

19

The aircraft bucked from side to side. Even the flight assistants strapped themselves back into their seats.

Clive usually slept through the flight back from the US. It seemed that this time the aircraft and turbulence were working in concert to prevent him from sleeping. At least with his headphones on, he could listen to something a little more appealing than the noise of the engines.

He removed his shoes and stretched out as far as the cramped conditions would allow. Then he wiggled his toes tapped his feet in time with the music - under the pretence of deep-vein thrombosis prevention.

He was officially bored.

When Clive got bored he usually started designing things. In his youth, he had invented an entire 'systems description language' that looked vaguely math-like. While nothing was recognisable to anyone other than Clive, it allowed him to work though processes and computer algorithms - and get ideas down on paper.

He went to the bathroom. On the way back, he grabbed a pen and pad from his bag in the overhead locker. Sitting back down, he immersed himself in his own world of abstract pictures, terms, and system designs.

By the time the aircraft was on its final approach to Manchester, Clive had worked out how he would design an Uncle Peter clone. Based on the knowledge he had at the moment, he also worked out how he thought Uncle Peter operated.

He was annoyed with Bill and Derek. They had, in effect, confiscated his toys and sent him packing. He, not the so-called "professional investigators", had discovered Uncle Peter - and he was now determined to beat the FBI in solving the problem.

Bill had specifically asked Clive to resist the temptation to do any further investigations, suggesting that if Clive triggered a change to the protocols then the FBI (and Clive) could potentially alert Uncle Peter to the fact that the system had been discovered, causing the whole system to change or disappear. Clive had felt under pressure to agree to Bill's request, and had Bill kept Clive on the team, Clive would have been happy. Instead, Clive was annoyed and the petulant side kicked in: he would get to Uncle Peter first.

The flight arrived at Manchester at 7:30am. Clive turned his mobile on as soon as the aircraft taxied off the runway. As he disembarked, a few messages came through.

The first message confirmed that Bren would collect Clive from Manchester Airport and wished him a safe flight. The other messages came via MKI's secure chat service - these messages came directly to Clive in encrypted form. MKI was licensed to use military-grade encryption within its product suite, so Clive was able to communicate with the likes of the FBI within an untraceable and encrypted environment.

Message from Paul: "Hey Clive. I'm off the case - no really! Like fuck. Do you have another image of the recorder? They took yours."

To Clive, it looked like Bill had taken the entire case on. He was slightly amused that they'd allowed the lab to get back to normal. He would have kept the whole place locked down until they knew what was happening.

He replied to Paul: "Thanks. They made me promise to stay off it too. So, I guess we're both not exchanging any more information. Therefore, don't look at the MKI SyncShare in a couple of hours in case I accidentally leave a copy there. I suggest staying away from it - but if you do come over it, perhaps you could delete it so I know it's gone?"

MKI's SyncShare allowed people to share specific files or folders in complete secrecy. It left virtually no trace of its existence on the Internet, sending lots of extremely small encrypted packets of data through a vast number of systems around the world. Clive had sold it into both the FBI and UK Intelligence service. It was so secure that MKI had to acquire export licenses for it - and the technology was subject to strict restrictions that largely prohibited its use by the general public. The state likes encryption, but only if it can see what's encrypted!

Clive collected his baggage and found Bren.

'Morning!'

'Morning Clive, how was the flight'

'Ok, thanks - didn't sleep much, so I'm wrecked.'

'Well, it's the weekend, so you can grab some sleep when you get back in'

'Nahh - I want to stay awake for as long as I can - need to get back to a sensible timezone'.

They walked to Bren's car.

'How was Blackhack?'

'Interesting - actually really interesting. Well worth the effort.'

'And our friends in the FBI?'

'Less so! They agree that I have found something significant. But, it's gone into counter-terrorism or homeland security or a similar domain. So, they've taken it in-house -

and they took my analyser. Bastards!'

'Really?'

'Yeah - well, I let them have it to save some of the effort on their part. I'm not sure they'll share anything back the other way, but here's hoping.'

Leaving the key with Bren had been a good thing for Clive. All the mail from his time away was neatly stacked on a pile on his desk. Bren and his wife had spring-cleaned the whole place from top to bottom. Clive made a mental note to send them some flowers as a 'thank you' for their trouble.

After dumping his bags and making a coffee, Clive set about creating a new image of the analyser for Paul - being anal about remote backup meant he had the latest version of the software used by the FBI.

Clive wanted to make the analyser slightly more flexible, so he decided to build in a few enhancements that could allow him to do further work later, should the need arise.

He fetched the papers he had completed on the plane and pinned them to a cork board positioned above his old computer. Having read through them again, he started making a few modifications to the base source code for his analyser.

Clive finished just as fatigue started hitting him. He compiled the code to create an 'image' of the software for Paul. He then compressed and encrypted the image before transferring it to a secure memory stick.

Clive opened up his laptop and inserted the memory stick. He typed in the password when prompted do so, and then fired up MKI's SyncShare tools. He used Paul's MKI messenger ID so that it would never show in the FBI's audit logs. Clive smiled to himself, thinking 'a little inside knowledge is all it takes …'

The transfer started up, Paul must have been at his

machine. Clive watched it start to trickle through the network. He instructed the SyncShare tools to dismount the memory stick when it had finished sending the data.

Clive then sent a message to Paul via the secure messaging application: "Revised image on its way. Pw: DangMyD1ddl1es"

From Paul: "LOL. Thanks. Will let you know how I get on"

Clive sat on the sofa to finish his coffee. Within a couple of minutes he was asleep. His coffee went cold.

20

At 2PM, Clive awoke and tried to move. Everything ached. He felt like he was 104 years old. He had fallen asleep on the sofa, and his neck was suffering for it.

He walked through to the kitchen and filled the coffee machine water tank. Having checked it had beans in it, he turned it on and then hit the 'double cup' button to give him an extra-strong caffeine kick.

While he waited for the machine to finish brewing his coffee, he checked the laptop and saw that the transfer had completed in the early hours.

Collecting his coffee, he went back to the living room. He wanted to finish his coffee and then freshen up.

He picked up his mobile and saw that Paul had sent a secure message.

Paul: "Thanks for the image. It's in and working. Loving the addition of rules and pattern matching combo. Will make things a lot easier"

The additional sections of the analyser were actually direct copies of a rules engine Clive had created years earlier. He always kept code and designs, even if he didn't use them there and then, there was always the potential to use them later.

The pattern and rules components had always been at the centre of the analyser, but Clive hadn't made the configuration of these components available to anything outside of the code itself. Now, Paul could update some text in a file and the engine would update itself and obey the new rules.

Clive figured it might prove useful to create rules that could effectively block Uncle Peter from receiving any packets. If the FBI kicked their heels for too long, Clive fully intended to prevent Uncle Peter from accessing data on MKI's systems. Firstly, though, he wanted to understand how Uncle Peter's command and control systems worked.

Somewhere in the infected machines, a piece of software had to listen out for Uncle Peter's instructions and then act on them. In order to trace what was actually happening, Clive needed to be able to trace data through a system - perhaps even stopping a computer mid-process so that he could see what the processor was doing at any given moment. To do this in hardware would require a very specialised piece of equipment, so Clive decided to create a virtual machine instead.

He had already created virtual machines to trap traffic within the SeeZu project, but hadn't seen anything significant. Perhaps running everything in debug mode would allow him to see additional information.

Clive installed the virtual machine control software onto his laptop. While it downloaded, he built his own protocol analyser. As he completed both tasks he thought, 'who said men can't multi-task?'.

By early evening, Clive had a working analyser and a fresh virtual machine running in debug mode. He made a copy of the virtual machine so that he could restore it to this running state at any time - one of the benefits of having a computer emulated in software - you can copy, share, or restore it with everything intact.

'Now', thought Clive, 'for the test.'

He created a set of documents called "SeeZu Prototype Thoughts" and saved them. Nothing happened on the protocol analyser.

Clive made a coffee and waited. Perhaps it would take a few minutes to sort itself out. It was, after all, a new virtual machine - to anyone outside of Clive's diner/office, it would look like a Clive had a new computer, with no way of telling if it was real or not.

Just as Clive was getting bored, the protocol analyser LED flashed. Uncle Peter had taken the bait.

Clive leapt into action. He had created a set of rules for the analyser that, as soon as it detected a packet of data destined for Uncle Peter, would pause the virtual computer. This would stall the transmission of data to Uncle Peter, but would give Clive a complete image of the entire computer at that time. Clive could then drill down into the image to find out what was active.

With the new rule in place, Clive edited the SeeZu document. Almost as soon as he closed it, the machine paused. The analyser had done it's job: in theory, Clive should have a copy of the entire machine, mid-way through sending its data to Uncle Peter.

Clive made a copy of the image and then let the original run again - he didn't want Uncle Peter getting suspicious. Then he closed down the virtual computer and assembled all the various debug logs to start working out what had happened.

The debug tools had logged every interaction with all the virtual components: virtual network card, virtual keyboard, virtual mouse, and so on. In theory, Clive should be able to replay every single action and step through them to find out what had piqued Uncle Peter's interest.

Clive disconnected the laptop from the network, compressed the log files and transferred them to his old PC. He wanted to make sure that Uncle Peter didn't get a copy of the log files, or have any opportunity to modify them. He then did a secure delete of the logs off the laptop - effectively removing any history of their existence. A normal delete simply removes the name from the list of files and marks the space as usable by the operating system - a secure delete overwrites the files with junk before marking them as deleted.

After a few hours of reading through the system log files, Clive came across a series of entries that looked like software update requests. These were the only real events occurring around the time that Uncle Peter was active. Interestingly, a few seconds before and after the update, there seemed to be a massive increase in the amount of network traffic. The software update itself was the only thing that went beyond the local network - Uncle Peter, it appeared, was trying to hide itself in some artificially generated network 'noise'.

Clive sent an encrypted copy of the relevant traffic logs to Paul via MKI's SyncShare. He then sent Paul the password to decode the data along with "It looks like it's camped on to the software update mechanism. Can't see anything odd in there though. Perhaps you can?"

With that, Clive went to bed.

Paul received the files and message from Clive during the afternoon of the 17th February.

Using the software update mechanisms certainly made sense. It wasn't a new way of attacking systems, though a little less than imaginative to Paul's mind.

Technically, he was off the case now, so he decided to leave 'playing' until after 5PM. That way, he could look at the information on his own time. The lab had significant computer resources to crack online payment ciphers and the like. Paul decided that he would approach the systems management team to see if he could book some time for researching the protocol data within Clive's debug log.

Luckily, he was good friends with the systems manager at the facility so he called him up.

'Chris, I could do with a favour - part work related, part personal'

'Ok', replied Chris, 'how can I help'

'This case we had to hand over to special ops has popped up on my desk again. Now before I send it in their direction, I want to make sure the information I have received makes sense. No point in sending crap through and it'd only make us look bad …'

'Right', said Chris, hesitatingly.

'… So, I have a set of log files here and would like to run them through the facility this evening. But I could do with the accounting for this coming from yesterday, before they took the case off us. No problem with forwarding the data as a result - it'll just look like we were waiting for the results and forwarded them when we got them.'

'I could make it look like it was a deferred job request, I suppose?'

'A what?'

Chris explained the procedures for booking the system.

'Sorry - everything comes in as a job request, when we're busy we defer those without a priority associated with them. So, perhaps you could fill in the paperwork but without an entry for "priority". I'll send you log-in details and set up a virtual partition so you can do what you like inside it.

'Remember though, you submit the paperwork without a priority, I'll say I only got round to it now if anyone asks. You run your job as normal - we can't modify the timestamps on the system, but the accounts will show a request coming in last week, if that's all you need.

'Thanks. I owe you one!', said Paul, 'I only need it to look like it was done as part of the investigation last week. I can just say I carried on because the time became available - and I'll probably moan about the inefficiency of paper systems to book computing resources!'

'Okay man. Consider it done. You should have the login details now. Valid for one week.'

Paul's phone beeped. Chris had sent him an SMS with an additional code to use for logging in. The mobile networks don't redirect SMS messages, so this provided an easy way to ensure that supercomputer resources were only assigned to someone with access to both an authorised terminal and a 'phone provided by the FBI.

After his 'day job', Paul logged into the supercomputer facility. The system had phenomenal computing abilities and could analyse data faster than anything else available in the world. Each user was assigned a 'processing priority' for any given job - the higher the priority, the more processing grunt was available. Given the enormous cost of running the facility, any user had to request access and was charged for the machine time used - a throwback to older computing models perhaps, but it meant that several departments could access a valuable resource on a sporadic basis. Paul smiled as he noticed he was allocated resources as a high-priority user. He was one of the top classes of user, so he would have some serious kit available for his use. The top class was reserved for active terrorism or national security threats. Users at this level could claim all the computer resources if necessary. To date, only 9/11 had triggered that kind of action as every ounce of power was required to analyse the entire US Internet traffic.

Paul uncompressed the files Clive had sent and transferred them into a filtering toolkit on the supercomputer. Clive's

SyncShare tools showed the number of bytes (the size of the file) in the description of the file shared.

Paul was surprised that the file size on the supercomputer was smaller than the image within SyncShare. He tried the transfer again. Once again, the file ending up in the supercomputer was smaller than the header suggested.

Concerned that he was doing something wrong, Paul grabbed his laptop and disconnected it from the network. He copied the file over to it and checked the file size. This time, it was the same as that on SyncShare.

He checked the file size on the supercomputer and them checked again on the laptop. By this time, the laptop had changed and now showed the smaller file size.

This confused Paul. But then he wondered if the laptop, being an old machine, simply hadn't had the time to delete the information from the log. Once it got round to looking at the file, it had removed it. The supercomputer was so fast that it had done it without Paul being able to track its progress.

Paul sat back in his chair. This meant that the supercomputer was also compromised. Uncle Peter had access to the most secret information in the world.

Paul came up with a plan. He compressed the new version of the file and then submitted both versions in their compressed form. Sure enough, both files landed in the supercomputer intact. Uncle Peter obviously didn't bother looking at compressed files.

'Strike 1', muttered Paul.

He ran a comparison between the two files and came back with several blocks of data that were different. Then, he wrote a series of search utilities to expand and reverse the 'Uncle Peter' data within the compressed file. This meant that he could expand the file to its natural size, but the bits of interest were different: Uncle Peter wouldn't recognise them.

By about 10PM, Paul had extracted data and (by looking at

the data in reverse) could determine what it looked like. At last they had a break.

21

Paul worked through until the early hours of the morning. He captured more packets of data and then worked them through to see what information he could extract. Gradually, he worked out how Uncle Peter operated. While he hadn't traced through to any program code, he was beginning to define the communication protocols, and this would eventually lead him to the code. To a certain extent, Paul didn't worry to much about the coding side of things: once he understood the protocols, he could find out where the stolen data landed - and then block Uncle Peter once and for all.

When given a problem, Paul had to resolve it - it was a fundamental part of his make up. The whole principle of giving incomplete work to a different department (that seemed to lack any real understanding of communication systems) really grated. Somehow, Clive had managed to get through Paul's usual communication barrier. Paul and Clive got on incredibly well and seemed to share the same need to see Uncle Peter identified and stopped.

Whiteman had often wondered whether Paul was Autistic, or suffered from Asperger's. Paul could become so fixated on a particular problem that he simply had to resolve it - he could obsess for days on end before finally collapsing from exhaustion, and then repeating the cycle. Having said that, Paul was able to detect patterns and analyse data better than anyone Whiteman had ever seen. Despite his slightly odd behaviour and general lack of communication with the rest of his team, Paul was Whiteman's best asset.

For once, the time difference between California and the UK helped keep things moving. Paul sent a series of secure messages to Clive and then SyncShared the data he had managed to capture. When Clive awoke, he was confronted with Paul's comments and a significant amount of data.

Clive called Paul so that they could split the work.

'You're up late!', said Clive as soon as Paul answered his mobile.

'Yeah. I don't think Bill's Digi-Intel team will sort this out anytime soon. Can't let the amateurs trample all over our party!'

Clive laughed. 'Yeah - I know what you mean. They seemed a little slow on the uptake. Anyway, what's all this data you sent through?'

Paul explained how he managed to extract the information from Uncle Peter's data. He then shared the method required to save and then view it so that Uncle Peter didn't delete anything before they could get a proper look at it.

'At this point, Clive, I still can't read the data payload. But I'm working on the header format. Once I understand that, we can get on with cracking the payload, but I think that might take a little more time than we're comfortable with, so any suggestions or tools you have are most welcome ...', he tailed off.

'I'll modify the protocol recorder so it transforms the data on the way in. That should capture more stuff and save that work at least. I'll do that while you keep on the headers, if that's Ok?'

'Fine. I can't ship the code I've used - it's written for our supercomputer, so unless you've got one knocking about …'

'Hah! I wish. No worries, it's easy enough now we know what we're looking for!'

'Hello stranger', said Bren.

'Hello - what are you having?', replied Clive as they walked into Costa and joined the short queue.

'Green Tea, thanks'

'Ok. How's Deb?'

'She's fine - we're going to have another baby you know?'

'WHAT?', asked Clive.

'Not really - just checking you were listening. You seem to be on a different planet these days.'

'Yeah, well, sorry - Uncle Peter's definitely a complex thing. I'm just hoping it's not something we've introduced through our kit.'

'What do you mean?'

'Why do you think I'm so worried about it? Think for a minute - every system that's connected to our network seems to be infected. Perhaps we're the point of infection. The last thing I want to do is go to some of our intelligence friends and tell them we've introduced a massive back door into all their systems. It'll finish us!', Clive was speaking so quietly that Bren was struggling to hear him over the noise of the shop.

Clive continued once they had collected their drinks, 'I have to see this through. Blocking it isn't enough. We have to stop it from infecting anything else - sorry, mate, I have to do this. Anyway, I'll tell you more once we're out of here - what do you need from me to keep the MKI team going?'

For the next couple of hours Clive and Bren huddled over Bren's laptop and went through a series of issues, plans and strategies. MKI took a reasonable amount of time to manage, but as a team, Clive and Bren could resolve things relatively quickly. Bren missed Clive's input, but understood both the urgency and need to resolve the "Uncle Peter" problem. For the time being, it was better that Clive worked through the problem than leaving it to the FBI.

After their coffee, Clive and Bren went for their now customary walk to discuss progress on Uncle Peter.

'Paul has managed to grab the incoming messages properly now. While we can't read them, we understand the trigger mechanisms and hopefully we can start to align the incoming and outgoing messages.

'I've modified the protocol analyser/recorder that I built to incorporate a set of rules and between us, gradually these will allow us to define the whole system. Once we've got the incoming and outgoing messages aligned, we can then start to trace the code internally.'

'Can't we just block it?', asked Bren.

'No - at the moment we don't understand enough to block it. If they change the format slightly, we'll lose the ability to trace the messages.'

'Why?'

'Because … at the moment we know the pattern. It's a very specific pattern. If they change the pattern, even slightly, then we lose sight of it and have to start again. If we understand the way it works, we can stop it regardless of the pattern it uses.'

'Are you any closer to finding out where the stolen data ends up?'

'Not yet', Clive sighed, 'Paul's working on decoding the header format, hopefully that should allow us to sort that out.'

'Header format?'

'Yeah - all network transmissions need a few things to work: a piece of information up-front that says where it's going from, and where it's headed. This information is a bit like a self-addressed envelope. The envelope wraps around the stuff inside it. Now, in order to get from me to you, we would need to use a standard way of addressing the envelope - you can't encrypt the name, address and postal code because the delivery system can't read it.

'So, Paul's looking at that information and trying to work out what we can gain by looking at the envelope. It's a bit like a kid shaking a parcel to guess what he's got for his birthday present.'

'If you know where it's headed, can't you simply block anything going there?', asked Bren.

'That's one of the problems: instead of it being one envelope, addressed to one person, this system uses several envelopes, each wrapping the next. And instead of sending all the information inside that one envelope, Uncle Peter splits up everything into lots of small envelopes.

'Back to the birthday present analogy: I could send a deck of cards as a birthday present. Anyone stealing that one present, gets everything.

'So, I put each card in its own envelope, addressed to the real recipient, along with my name and address - after all, I want a thank you note back.

'Then I put each of those envelopes inside another envelope and address it to a go-between, put that in another envelope with another go-between and so on.

'Each go-between opens its envelope and then sends the package on to the address on the newly exposed envelope.'

'You can only ever see where the outermost envelope came from and where it's going - because you can't open the envelopes, you can't work out where the playing cards really end up, or where they came from originally.

'Unless you happen to have my list of go-betweens, you also don't know where all these tiny packets will end up or where they've been.

'Because it's the post office and it might lose the odd envelope here and there, we also have a method that says 'here's package 1 of 52' and some way of assembling them into the right order at the other end. The system also has to deal with delays - so if it doesn't get all of them, say it's missing card number '3' - it has to ask for package number '3' again. Because it's just a delay, it might now get two copies of card number '3', in which case we can discard the duplicate.

'So, in order to work out who's behind Uncle Peter, we need to get to the address on the innermost envelope. To work out what's in the envelope, well, we need to see inside it. But to do that, we have to play a massive game of pass-the-parcel between a few thousand computer systems all the way around the world.'

'Got it', said Bren.

'Good - Paul's now working on the envelope structure - and the information on the label: how big it is, what it looks like, does it rattle when you shake it - all that kind of stuff. He's also trying to work out where the Uncle Peter gets his initial list of go-betweens and the way of encrypting each envelope so that you can only ever see the layer you're authorised to see.

'By creating a fake project, we've effectively sneaked something into the envelope that rattles, and when we shake the envelope, we can hear it. That's how we know it's taking our stuff - we hear the rattle.

Paul looked at the capture data again.

'Strike 2', he shouted and picked up his 'phone.

'Clive', he shouted, 'I think I've got the initialisation sequence - and I can repeat it!'.

'Jesus Paul', said Clive, 'what time is it there?'

Clive had just gone to bed. He was still suffering from the effects of jet-lag.

'I don't know - 8am'

'You've been on this all night?'

'Yeah - but listen - I created a new virtual machine and used your method of pausing the machine as soon as it received anything from Uncle Peter.'

'Ok'.

'Well, the first message on a new virtual machine went out almost immediately. Uncle Peter responded. So I did it again. Completely new instance but of the same virtual machine, same thing - same message out, different message in.'

'Same message out?'

'Yes - so I tried again. Same thing. Then I did it with a different instance of a virtual machine, a new build. The first message was different, but if I stopped it as soon as it received Uncle Peter's message and started again, I got the same thing each time!'

'Slow down a bit, I'm not with you', said Clive.

'New machine. First message out is obviously a 'hello' message. The 'hello' back from Uncle Peter must contain the first real key for communicating thereafter. It's "Hello", "Oh, hello, here's your key". I think we've got a way to capture the first key exchange.'

Clive sat bolt upright.

The most difficult bit of any encryption system is 'boot-strapping' it. Somehow, both parties have to authenticate themselves and exchange some information to allow them to encrypt information. It looked like Paul had captured the initial exchange from a new computer. The fact that he could repeat it meant that the two could start to work on decoding this part of the encryption process.

'Wow!', said Clive, 'can you send me the capture logs and rule-set you used?'

'Already have', replied Paul.

Naked, Clive went downstairs and looked at his laptop. He

clicked 'accept file' on the MKI SyncShare software, and downloaded Paul's data.

'Got it, thanks. I'll take a look.'

Paul rang off and then made a copy of the data and then rang through to Whiteman. Whiteman in suggested that Paul contact Derek so that he could pass the information over to the Digital Intelligence team.

Within a few minutes, Derek stormed into the lab.

'Paul. Stop with this fucking case. Digital Intelligence has the lead on this. What the hell were you playing at, and who gave you the authority to use the supercomputing facility?'

Paul stammered, 'It … it … I had already booked it, but my slot didn't come up until last night, so I thought I may as well use it … we were going to get charged for it whether we used it or not …'

'I'm not bothered about the fucking accounts', Paul shouted, 'This is an intelligence matter. You were taken off the case. This entire lab was taken off the case.'

He slowed down, emphasising each word, 'Digital Intelligence own this case. We do not get involved. Who else knows about this?'

'No-one', lied Paul.

'Good. If they need our help, they'll ask for it. In the meantime back off. Ok?'

'Ok', replied a visibly shaking Paul.

Derek stomped out of the lab, heading towards Whiteman's office. Presumably, Whiteman would receive the same instruction.

Paul picked up his 'phone and called Chris, the supercomputer administrator.

'Chris - head's up, I've been pulled off the case. I said what we agreed - that the slot had been delayed and I only got access last night so thought I'd use it.'

'Yeah, I know', replied Chris, 'Derek's already told me that any requests for systems access from you will have to be cleared by him personally.'

'Really?', asked Paul, 'You know your facility's compromised by this thing too, right?'

'Yep', said Chris and added at a much quieter level, 'and that's why you can use any spare slots you want. Let me know if you need access and I'll sort it.'

22

'Joining me on the 'phone is Clive Knollys, our regular online security specialist. Can you explain just how this problem affects us, and what we can do to protect our personal information?'

Clive had been called by the local radio station. Researchers had uncovered a massive security flaw in one of the components used by most web-servers globally. This, in effect, left most web-servers open to attack.

He paused. 'If they think this one's big, wait until they know about the one I've found', he thought.

'Basically, this is a problem that affects web servers and the computers that control them.'

'A web-server being …?'

"Sorry, a web server is the thing that generates any Internet web-sites you visit. It literally serves you with the information you need. Security consultants have discovered that open-source web-servers and routers, the ones used by most of the really big services, have a security hole - and this hole allows hackers to extract the encryption keys used to protect your information between your computer and, for example, your bank.'

'What use are these encryption keys? What can I do with

them?'

'Well, most encryption systems need some form of shared secret. Otherwise I can encrypt something, but you can't read it - unless you know the secret. Modern web services usually split this secret into two parts, a private key kept by the service, and a public key that it shares with your computer. Your computer also has a private key which it keeps, and a public key that it shares with the service. The idea being that you both exchange the public keys, and can then use the combination of private and shared public keys to encode and decode data.

In practice, it means that you can share public keys without any real risk, but you must keep the private keys private. This hole allows me to extract private keys. So, if I know the secret for your bank, I can pretend to be your bank and fool your browser into thinking I'm the real thing. Basically, it opens up all of your personal data, but most importantly, it opens up your username and password, along with any other data you might share online.'

'It's obviously a very technical issue, but what does this mean to me as an Internet user?'

'It is technical, and you need to know what you're doing to exploit this hole. You can imagine that most systems administrators are panicking to close this hole down. As a user, you have to assume that if the service uses an open-source web-server, then you risk your data being accessed by hackers. They need to fix this, and fast. Then systems administrators need to patch their systems, so this could take a few days or even weeks to resolve. In the meantime, you have to assume that your network connection has no security at all. Once they've fixed it, and believe me, they're working hard to fix it because it's so critical, I suggest that you change all of your passwords on all of your online accounts.'

Open source software usually works better than

proprietary code: it receives more scrutiny from the software community and many self-appointed programmers tune and tweak the source code over many years. As anyone can download and use open source software, it has grown into a huge body of code with many millions of developers creating and tuning it continuously.

It was, therefore, surprising to find a major hole in the security of the most commonly deployed web-servers. Even more surprising was the ease with which hackers could exploit the hole to recover vast numbers of private keys and some of the associated authentication data.

The media had already called the network security issue 'Hackageddon', and it was making headlines globally. The team that originally created the web-server code was working on a fix, but fixing anything in a cryptographically sound way takes considerable effort followed by comprehensive testing.

Whiteman's department was offline. Every dark service ran on open-source web servers. Hackageddon meant that it was safer to take the systems offline than risk exposure. If the dark market users discovered that they were monitored by the FBI they would leave in their droves. It made more sense to put 'holding' pages in place saying that normal service will resume once the Hackaggedon problem had been solved.

Whiteman and Paul were having a coffee.

'When did you last sleep, you look like shit?', asked Whiteman.

'Dunno - I got interested in Clive's case', replied Paul sheepishly.

'Where did you get to?'

'We're off the case, remember?'

'I know - just humour me, we've got nothing else to do - and we're just talking right? Where did we get to?'

'Alright - we've seen a new machine sending a unique identifier and some other encrypted data, and then receiving what looks like a replacement key. It then sends an acknowledgement and some more encrypted data. All of this masquerading as a normal software activation or update request.'

'Where does the initial request go?', asked Whiteman.

'It looks like it goes to the usual software update servers … there's obviously something wrong there, it must be diverted somewhere else, but it appears to terminate at genuine software update services.'

Whiteman raised an eyebrow, and asked, 'Do you think they're in the same boat as us?'

'What do you mean?'

'Hackageddon?'

'Shit!', exclaimed Paul, 'Great idea.'

'We're off the case though, remember!', shouted Whiteman to the back of the rapidly moving Paul.

Paul turned, grinned, and said, 'What case?', then ran to the lab.

'Chris, I need some time now, if you can sort it?'

Paul had collected a vast amount of data in a relatively short time. He needed the advanced processing capabilities of the supercomputer to help process it all.

'Ok, you got it. I'm sending you the access code now - it's coming off an investigation into the offshore platform oil leak last year. It's a long-running process where they use loads of fluid dynamics calcs. They never keep track of usage and have a virtual carte blanche on their resources - you can tell that the lawyers have gotten the oil industry to pay for it. No idea how you got the access codes though, ok?'

'No idea what you're talking about', replied Paul, 'Thanks Chris.'

'Go get 'em', replied Chris hitting 'send' on the code generator system.

While Paul waited for the lab to boot up and reconfigure itself as a Hackageddon attacker, he rewrote a few of the rules within Clive's protocol recorder. He sent Clive a message saying he was testing for Hackageddon.

Clive had already seen the Hackageddon profile data - he knew what an attack looked like, so he shipped some code to Paul that would exploit the bug.

The first message sent to Uncle Peter appeared to go to one of a small number of servers. The initial connection was clearly the most open to attack.

Between the two of them, Paul and Clive sent a series of messages that mimicked a new machine set-up. Once they had established which servers to attack, Paul launched his Hackageddon service.

Within a few minutes, the supercomputer had determined that the servers were running the most common web-servers in the world - and that they were the compromised open source versions.

A few minutes later and the supercomputer's serious computing power had opened the remote servers key-stores and extracted all the keys, along with a substantial amount of other data.

'Strike 3!', shouted Paul. Then realising he'd been a little too loud, ducked back behind a monitor.

Paul started up MKI's SyncShare and sent the collected data to Clive. Then, he walked into Whiteman's office.

'We found Uncle Peter's server farm', Paul said gleefully.

'I thought I told you not to continue with this case.'

Paul froze. He hadn't noticed Derek sitting in the far corner of Whiteman's office.

Derek stood up and walked out of Whiteman's office. At the doorway, he reminded both Whiteman and Paul that they were in breach of direct orders from the Digital Intelligence director.

'I'll let Bill know what you've done. In the meantime, you both keep this to yourselves. You stop discussing this, you stop working on it. For fuck's sake JUST STOP.'

'Sorry', said Paul to Whiteman after Derek had disappeared.

'Go shut it down in case Digital Intelligence want to tear another piece off us', replied Whiteman, 'why do I feel like a naughty schoolboy?'

Paul reconfigured the lab. Putting it all back to how it was took a couple of hours - and it was now going dark outside. He yawned, satisfied he had covered his tracks and put the lab back in its previous state, he decided to go home.

He climbed into his car and started it up. It started raining.

'Great', he muttered under his breath. He hated driving in the dark, even more so when it was raining.

He drove back towards his house. As he pulled off the freeway and onto the quiet road that dropped down towards his house, he came across an accident.

It had obviously only just occurred: a woman was crouched down holding her head in her hands. To Paul, it looked like she had spun out.

He stopped to make sure she was Ok. Grabbing his mobile 'phone, he approached the lady.

'Are you Ok?', he asked.

'I lost control in the rain', she said bleakly.

'Can I help you up, are you hurt?', asked Paul, and reached out to her.

Quickly, the woman spun round and Paul felt a sudden sharp pain in his leg. The woman pushed the end of the syringe now lodged firmly in Paul's leg, delivering its fatal payload.

Paul just stood there. Shock had taken over. With a

questioning expression on his face, his vision clouded over. He collapsed onto the wet road and took his last few stuttered and painful breaths.

23

Whiteman was surprised to see the grim faces of Bill and Derek waiting in his office as he arrived. He put his jacket on the hanger in the corner.

'Morning gentlemen.'

'Whiteman', began Derek, 'this morning I was advised that Paul Davis died in a road traffic collision on his way home last night.'

Whiteman sat heavily on the nearest chair.

'Jesus!', he looked at the two Directors, 'How?'

'First indications suggest that he fell asleep at the wheel - although the police have said they're waiting for the autopsy report. It looks like he was nearly home and skidded off the embankment. A woman motorist travelling in the opposite direction called it in.'

Bill continued.

'It does, of course, bring in to question the work he was doing immediately prior to his death. It raised questions around the research into this "Uncle Peter" system, and whether that put him at risk. I need to protect my team, and we want to ensure that nothing untoward occurred.

'I am assuming the worst-case, and to that end, we're going to assign a couple of internal affairs agents to piece together his last few days. We will need your assistance in this matter.

'Further, we need to look at any and all communications between Paul, you and any other parties working on all of his active cases. I'll need to see copies of your reports, and will also ask my agents to interview you.'

Derek started again.

'We also need to address the issue of you continuing with intelligence activities when expressly ordered to stop. I may have to consider whether the agency has any liabilities here - either from putting Paul in danger from hostiles, or from you lacking the management skills necessary to ensure his well-being.'

'Wait … what do you mean, liabilities? Are you holding me responsible for Paul's death?', asked Whiteman.

'Not directly. But we need to ensure that we have covered all the bases. You allowed him to work here for days and nights at a stretch. You also allowed him to go home knowing that he was exhausted, instead of arranging transport.'

'For fuck's sake, the man's not even in the ground and you're closing ranks on me.', shouted Whiteman.

'Calm down', replied Bill, 'we're not saying anything yet. We need to ensure that the agency has no liabilities here - we intend to look at every aspect of it.'

Derek sighed heavily. 'I have to take the decision to suspend you from duty temporarily. This allows us to go through all communications between you and Paul, look at any systems he accessed and follow due process with you too.

'Hopefully, we find that it's nothing more than the poor guy losing control on his way home. In the meantime, we have an agent who died while working illegally on an intelligence case, with your approval, contrary to agency orders. You understand that we have to investigate this matter internally.'

Bill carried on.

'We will need your mobile, laptop, tablet - and the passwords to access these and any other systems you use. If you could leave those on the desk and then go home. We'll be in touch - my team will need to talk to you, so please stay in the area.'

A text message from an unknown US mobile arrived for Clive: "Clive am on a burner. Need to talk on this number. Urgent. W."

Clive called back.

'Hello', said a familiar voice at the other end: it was Whiteman.

'Whiteman? What's up?'

'We need to talk securely. Can you set something up?'

'Sure - give me a couple of minutes - this number?', asked Clive.

'No, I have another here - it's another burner.'

'Ok, what's the make and model? I'll send you a link to get the secure messenger stuff.'

By using 'burners' - disposable pay-as-you-go mobiles, Whiteman could call anonymously. It would make tracing any calls more difficult. Clive could use the MKI communications platform to make anonymous and encrypted calls, but that required Whiteman to download a piece of software.

Clive logged on to the MKI server and registered Whiteman's burner. After the initial configuration, MKI's system generated random identities for each subsequent connection. Clive used the configuration usually reserved for military encryption - this anonymised all parties in any communication, and encrypted everything. It was virtually untraceable. After telling the platform what type of device to configure, he hit the 'deploy' button and waited until Whiteman installed the messenger application. As soon as he saw the device register on MKI's system, Clive sent a secured message to Whiteman.

Clive: "Call when convenient. Use the dialler in this app and it will set up an anonymous encrypted session over ToR".

Whiteman: "Ok to call now?"

Clive: "Sure"

Whiteman hit the dial button. A few seconds later, he was through to Clive.

'Hi Clive'

'Whiteman! This is very cloak-and-dagger. Proper spy stuff already! Before we go any further, what's the word showing on your screen?'

Whiteman looked at his burner. It had the word "Fumble" on the display.

'Fumble'

'Good - same here. For information, any time you use the voice channel, we share a code-word set up between the devices. If we have different words, someone's in the middle. We're secure. Now, how can I help?'

Whiteman paused.

'Paul's dead.'

'What?'

'You heard. He went off the road last night. They think he fell asleep at the wheel.'

'Fuck!'

'That's one way of putting it. Listen - the police are doing their thing, but Bill's been in and they've suspended me over it.'

'Why?'

'He was working on this Uncle Peter stuff and intel has taken over. They're lining me up as a scapegoat - saying it's fatigue from me overworking him; or … well, it's also possible that he uncovered something and got hit.'

'Hit - like for real?'

'It's intelligence, and you both thought it was state operated. Perhaps the Russians or Chinese got wind of what was happening. You never know.'

'What do we do?', asked Clive, now nervous.

'Well, for starters, I think it best to keep schtum about all the stuff you've been working on. You might even want to back off Uncle Peter you know?'

'No way', said Clive, 'I'm going to see it through. I can't ignore it because it'll finish the business if anyone finds out we knew about a breach - especially given the circles that use this stuff. Anyhow, Paul would want us to carry on.'

'I thought you'd say that. Where did you and Paul finish off?'

'He shipped me a load of captures. He had worked out that Uncle Peter initialises itself by a fake software update call right at the start of things. It looks like it has a system-generated key to kick things off.'

'System-generated key?'

'Yeah - something that it can recognise when it starts up. A one-time thing - used when the machine starts up for the first time. Once it's made contact, the identifiers change.'

'After that, everything seems to change along with the identity, keys … the lot. What Paul did though, was to find out that he could use the initial identifier and repeat the requests to Uncle Peter - as long as he stopped the machine before the machine could acknowledge the change.'

'So a bit like me saying "use 123 as the new key" - but if you don't say "ok", I'll happily give you a key for the old identifier again …? Something like that?'

'That's right. This means that we have a way of working out what the exchange means. It's the start of the process.'

'Hmm. Ok.'

'So I used that information to create a new set of rules - something to trap where the initialisation stuff went … and then Hackageddon hit.'

'Did that stop you?'

'Oh no - quite the opposite. We worked on modifying the protocol recorder to back-trace all the requests, Paul found a few consistent links and targeted them with the Hackageddon exploit.'

'Impressed!', exclaimed Whiteman, 'and …?'

'Paul recovered a set of root certificates, end points and other data I haven't had a chance to analyse yet … he found Uncle Peter!'

'Fuck!'

'Luckily, he sent everything over to me, so I can carry on using the data he obtained.'

'What kind of trail has this left? Anything to let them know you have this? Anything left on the lab's computers?'

'No. He sent it over MKI's SyncShare - there's no trace at this end - presumably he was careful at this end too. Anyway, I'll disable all his MKI device services from this end. That will remove any evidence that we even had a way of communicating securely.'

'Ok. Well, unless I say anything different, I suggest you know nothing at all. You came back to the UK and have done nothing on this since. I bet Derek or Bill will arrange for MI5 to find out what you and Paul were up to!'

'Can't I just tell them?'

'Not at the moment. It's probably better to keep quiet. Technically Paul was in breach of his orders. If they find out he'd sent stuff to you, they'll assume I knew and approved of that - it'll backfire on me and probably land me in something like a treason case: allowing US intelligence data to go overseas and all that crap.'

'Ok. Can I do anything to help?'

'Just do what you do - but watch your back. We can talk via this, but I'm otherwise off the grid for a while.'

24

After the initial shock of Paul's demise, Clive made several copies of the data. He knew he'd never have the ability to get it again, and wanted to ensure he could always go back to it in the event that Uncle Peter managed to modify or delete his working copy. His safe was getting more use than ever before.

As Clive now knew how to kick-start communications with Uncle Peter, he decided to examine the digital certificates and key data Paul had managed to obtain.

Paul's notes on the header data also came in useful. Before long, Clive was starting to understand the structure of the data contained within the requests coming in and going out of Uncle Peter's system.

Clive became a virtual recluse during this time. Bren started having food delivered to Clive again. Periodically, Bren and Clive would meet up to discuss progress and to cover the important issues for MKI.

Clive used his old PC to build a new version of the protocol recorder. This version also allowed him to mimic Uncle Peter – or at least as much that Clive knew of the system at that time. Periodically, Clive would transfer the working code to the new version of FreeBee so that he could test whether the software on his compromised virtual machine would respond as if it was talking to the real Uncle Peter.

It took him over a week to get the virtual machine to respond properly, and to send additional information to the protocol recorder. This small breakthrough meant that Clive could start to work on the rest of the protocol – he wanted to work out how the encryption system worked so that he could decode information coming from and going out to Uncle Peter.

In amongst the noise, Paul had obtained some critical data: Clive managed to use it decode the initial exchanges between the virtual machine and Uncle Peter's systems.

Pleased with himself, Clive sat back and started to define a series of rules that would trap traffic travelling between any compromised machine and Uncle Peter. Now that he had the structure of the data, he was in a position to expand SeeZu – the honey pot containing information that he had already leaked and shared with the FBI.

Then he set about processing the rest of the data. Paul had certainly managed to amass a fair quantity to analyse. He set the computer processing and arranged to meet Bren. The break from the intense and solitary work he had undertaken would do him good. They met at a local beauty spot – a disused railway line that ran alongside Rudyard Lake.

'I'll be glad when you get back to normal work – it's becoming increasingly tricky to field questions from the rest of the board', said Bren, 'any idea how much longer you will need?'

'I'm getting closer. I'm starting to understand the data structure and how they transfer information.'

'You still haven't said how long this is going to take.'

'The problem is I don't know yet.'

'I'm going to have to say something to the board soon - this has been running for months now. Isn't it something of material importance to the company?'

'I think it's more than material to everyone. This fundamentally breaks every form of encryption that it touches. No-one's safe.

'It looks like the something buried deep – very deep – perhaps even into the lower levels of the operating system itself. If it is, then our systems can provide some level of protection for data in transit by restricting the communication endpoints to known services, but if those end services suffer from this problem then we may as well not exist. Uncle Peter will get his data from those systems - either end, it doesn't matter. We're back to security being only as strong as its weakest component.'

'Won't a firewall stop it?', asked Bren, hopefully.

'I don't think so - it uses standard protocols, and looks like it's doing a software update. The thing that surprises me is that it really does look like an absolutely standard software update check - something somewhere in the network must be recognising the traffic and getting to it before it gets to the software company.'

'Should we work on a statement for the next board meeting?'

'Not yet. Let me keep working on it for a while longer - I want to give an accurate statement - there's nothing worse than not having answers - especially the obvious ones like "can we stop it", "what are the implications for us", "have we wasted the past few years on developing something that doesn't work" .. And so on.'

'We will have to say something at some stage'

'Yes I know, Bren, but not yet – let me establish the facts and then we will work out what to say to the board.'

They had reached the end of the lake so they turned round and started walk back towards the cars. It was surprisingly warm in the winter sun and both Clive and Ben benefited from the tranquil environment around them.

As they walked back, they caught up on a combination of team news, Bren's forthcoming holiday and general MKI business. Bren also commented that the team was missing Clive's input.

'Well, if necessary, I can always join one of the development calls - it'll show I'm still alive, at least!'

'No, no need yet', replied Bren, 'Thanks for the offer, but you need to keep going. The faster it's sorted the better.'

25

'I'll have another pint'

'I think you've had enough mate'

Jason tried to look the bartender in the eye, but as he could see several versions of the bartender, it was difficult to locate an eye to lock on to.

'Aww. Come on mate. Jus' another one and then I'll go.'

'Nope. I think we're done for the night anyway. Good night.'

Jason Haggely was a very beautiful young man. He had blue eyes, short ash-blonde hair, a slight tan from working outside, and a well defined body. While being beautiful was a bonus, the fact he knew he was irresistible was somewhat less attractive. He had a habit of sleeping with anyone that could provide a roof over his head, food in his belly and a few drinks to wash it down.

His biggest problem was that he fell in love with each of his bed partners and when that love wasn't reciprocated he would get hurt and angry. Arguments would follow, sometimes revealing a totally unnecessary vindictive streak in his personality.

Jealousy could also come in to play: he had a son from one of his drunken encounters and he had found himself in the cells for a night after attacking the mother's new boyfriend - he'd turned up worse for wear and ended up hitting the boyfriend for denying Jason access to his son while in his drunken state.

When not drunk or high, Jason could be extremely loving. He worked long hours - taking on all kinds of cash-in-hand labouring jobs. Employers would normally exploit his loyalty and hard-working nature in return for providing alcohol or turning a blind eye to late starts and drinking on the job. Whatever money he earned never lasted long as he simply converted it into drink or drugs. While he had largely managed to stop the drugs, alcohol proved to be a more difficult mistress to avoid.

Jason had been drinking all day and was now virtually falling off the bar-stool. He'd drunk most of his earnings for the week. He had no problem with justifying his current state - he was in trouble, and alcohol provided a temporary reprieve from worry.

Clive came back from his walk with Bren to a machine still processing data. The house was a mess, so he tidied up. Then he hit the shower.

He stood with the water hitting the back of his neck. He swayed gently from side to side letting it massage his shoulders and neck. Thoughts drifted back to Paul and the time spent with the FBI in California. Sometimes the 'big corporate' or government roles appealed - he came to the conclusion that the perception of security and continuity was just that however - a perception. Whiteman had lost the ability to keep control of the case and was fast becoming a scapegoat for what happened to Paul.

A loud bang brought Clive from his thoughts. A couple of seconds later another louder set of bangs came from downstairs.

With his heart pounding, Clive leaped from the shower pausing only to grab his dressing-gown that he had draped over the bathroom towel-rack to warm through. He ran down the stairs and saw a shadowy figure at behind the frosted glass of the front door.

'Jesus!', Clive said, and opened the door, 'Jason, you scared the shit out of me.'

'Sorry', replied Jason making a good attempt at a suitably sorry face.

'I'm in the shit.'

'Come in - it's fucking freezing.'

'Yeah I know, I've just walked here from The Ship, bastards chucked me out.'

Jason tottered past Clive and flopped down on to the sofa in the living room. Clive closed the door behind Jason.

'I'm not surprised - you're wrecked.'

'Nah, I'm good. I only had a couple …'

'A couple of what, gallons? I take it you're wanting to sleep it off here?'

'Yeah', said Jason, already beginning to fall asleep.

Clive shook his head in disbelief and went to fetch a duvet to cover Jason. There was no way he could get the drunk lad upstairs in that state. Jason was already snoring by the time Clive came back with the duvet.'

'Let's get these boots off eh?', Clive said as much to himself as to Jason. He didn't want muddy boots ruining the bedding.

He pulled one boot off and then the other. The odour of sweaty socks filled the room. There was nothing for it - it was either wash Jason's clothes or suffer a malodorous night and have the house stinking in the morning.

Clive set about removing Jason's clothing. Jason was so drunk he didn't wake up during the process - Clive wondered if this was how it felt to be an undertaker.

After covering the sleeping Jason and throwing all the dirty clothing in the washer-drier, Clive sat back down at the PC and looked at the data being generated by his system.

Paul had made a few notes about the structure of the data being processed. Clive re-read them and started looking at the data with Paul's insight. As he stared at the data coming out of the analysis scripts, he noticed a distinct pattern.

He grabbed his pen and started drawing out what he saw: time-stamps; source and destination addresses; mac addresses (the supposedly unique identifier for each device connecting to the network, although hackers frequently mask or modify these); some form of consistent code - probably a system identifier; another constant number - perhaps the protocol version number; and, the encrypted payload along with a check-sum - basically a number representing a hash of all the data within the current block.

Before long, Clive had seen the same pattern again and again. He was beginning to understand the top-level protocol properly. Now he could use the certificate and key data Paul had stolen by using the Hackageddon exploits.

Loud snoring broke Clive's concentration. He looked at his watch - it was 3AM. He'd been gazing at this data for hours.

With a massive yawn and a stretch, Clive turned the lights off in the kitchen/diner, checked the doors were properly locked, and headed for bed. He would let his 'night brain' process everything he'd just seen and attack the encrypted data in the morning.

26

Clive awoke to the sound of the shower running. At least, he thought, Jason was still alive. He hopped out of bed and dressed himself.

Jason always left the bathroom door open, so Clive grabbed his bath-robe and threw it over the towel-rack in the bathroom.

'Morning - you'll need that.'

'How did I get here?', shouted Jason over the noise of the shower.

'On your magic drunken carpet … either that or you walked. Coffee?'

'Oh God yeah - my mouth feels like a nun's crotch.'

Clive went downstairs and made a couple of large strong mugs of coffee. He contemplated making breakfast and then realised he didn't have anything in for breakfast: he'd need to go shopping.

He walked over to the computers whirring in the corner and moved the mouse to bring the screen back to life. Sleep had helped - Clive could see the pattern in the data on the screen. If he could see it, then he could modify the various tools he'd built and finally work out what was happening.

Jason interrupted Clive's thoughts by walking through to

the kitchen, the front of Clive's dressing gown open.

'You've got no shame', said Clive, 'what if my neighbours saw you wandering through the house like that?'

'Ha! They'd only be jealous - and anyway, if they're looking in here then that's their problem for being nosey. Got any tins in?'

'You're not drinking at this time in the morning - haven't you got to go to work?'

'Ahh', said Jason looking somewhat sheepish, 'might have a problem going back there'

'Why? What's happened?', asked Clive walking through to the lounge. He moved the duvet and pillows aside and sat down on the sofa.

Jason followed and flopped down into the seat opposite.

'Pass me my fags …', he said.

Clive didn't like Jason smoking in the house, but once every now and then he'd make an exception to the rule.

'Here'

Clive picked up the packet and Jason's lighter from the floor by the sofa and chucked them over.

'Where are my clothes?'

'No idea, you turned up naked …'

'Fuck off!'

'No, seriously - you turned up naked as the day you were born'

'I might have been pissed, but not that pissed!'

'They're in the washer - you stank and I didn't want my bedding messed up'

'Sorry about that - it's been a tough few days.'

'Come on then, what's happened?'

'Well', started Jason lighting a cigarette and inhaling deeply, 'God, that's better … well, you know Mark Poole?'

'Nasty piece of work!'

'Yeah - but he's been wanting some plastering doing, and I

owed him for some skunk so I said I'd do it to settle up'

'You don't want to be owing the Pooles for anything - they're evil bastards'

'Meh! Met worse.' Replied Jason, 'Anyway, he said I could shack up at his while I was working so I stayed up in the granny flat in his house.'

Jason stopped and took another large drag on the cigarette, and then a swig of coffee.

'And?'

'Well, we went out for a few. When we got back, he passed out and Julie wanted some, so she sneaked into the flat.'

'You shagged his wife?'

'Well, she came to me …'

'And you, of course resisted knowing he's an evil bastard?'

'Fuck that - I was pissed. Any port in a storm!'

Clive sighed loudly. 'Did he catch you?'

'Nope. Not then …'

'Oh, so it's happened more than once then?'

'Yep. She called it rent for the flat.'

'Nice. Classy!', replied Clive, standing up and fetching a saucer from the kitchen for Jason to use as an ashtray.

'Anyway, she and Mark got pissed up and were arguing. I think she told him. Next thing I'm getting text messages telling me I'm dead and to watch my back … usual crap!'

'Might be usual for you. So what now?'

'I'll give him some time: he'll get over it. It's not the first time - and he shags around anyway.'

'He'll kill you.'

'Nah. He'll come round eventually - I can't help it if I'm a better shag than him, can I? Anyway, she asked me, I didn't do anything wrong!'

'You could have said "no".'

'What, and get kicked out of the house?'

'You're out of the house anyway, or hadn't you noticed?'

Jason laughed and stretched.

'Yeah - bit of a twat that. Fancy a shag?'

'No, but thanks for the offer!'

'Just thought I'd ask. Another coffee?'

'I'll make them, you finish your fag.'

Clive collected the mugs, went into the kitchen and made another round of coffee. Jason followed Clive and started looking at the assembled bits and pieces of computer equipment that littered the dining area.

'What's all this?', asked Jason.

'Oh - I've had a few problems of my own. There's someone grabbing all our software, designs, data - the lot - a digital thief, if you want to call it anything. This lot's all stuff I've built to try and work out who's behind it all, and see what they're doing.'

'Can't you just stop them?'

'Not that easy - if I stop them, they might just come back with another way of stealing from us. I'm trying to work out how they do it, then I can look at where it all ends up, and either prosecute them or find a way of stopping it permanently.'

'Any guesses who's doing it?'

'I think it's a big group … could even be a government thing. Whatever it is, it's very well put together. It even tried to hide its tracks - but we have a few tricks of our own.'

'We?'

'Yeah - you were lucky to find me here - I was working with the FBI in America. They're looking at it too - but they've moved it up into part of the agency that doesn't like working with businesses - especially foreign ones. So I'm doing my own thing for a while. See if I can sort it before they do.

'Anyway, this stuff managed to trap a load of the data going out. Now I'm working on something that can sit in between an infected computer and them: a man in the middle attack on their system. Once I'm in there, I can see what's happening, what they go for, and how they do it. It's just taken a while to get this far.'

'I bet Bren's happy about all this …'

'Bren has no choice - I've got to sort it. Whoever it is seems to be stealing our software and ideas. We've got to stop it or we could lose the business.'

'Fuck! Rather you than me.'

'Rather anyone than me, to be honest. I've got much better things to be doing than chasing this lot. It's a good mental work-out though.'

Jason walked back into the living room and lit another cigarette.

'Sure you don't want a shag?', he asked again, clearly bored with the technology.

'Positive, thank you', replied Clive.

'Any chance I could stay here again?', asked Jason, 'Just until the dust settles?'

Clive had expected the question.

'As long as it's not a permanent thing!'

'Thanks - I'll do a few odd jobs around the place too. Grass needs cutting!'

'For God's sake Jason, if you're going to stand in the window, at least fasten up!'

27

'Hey up Mother, how're you doing?', asked Jason affectionately as he answered the door.

'Jason!', exclaimed Bren, 'You're back again then?'

'Yeah, I thought he needed the company. Someone's got to look after him. Come in'

Bren stepped inside and walked through to see Clive once again buried in amongst his computer equipment.

'I see you've got a visitor - is he staying?'

Bren and Jason didn't really see eye to eye. Bren considered Jason nothing but a wastrel, and Jason thought Bren fussed far too much over Clive - hence calling him "Mother". Nonetheless, Bren was relieved that someone was around Clive while he was so involved in resolving the "Uncle Peter Problem". At least Jason would make sure Clive would eat and generally look after himself. The house certainly looked tidier.

'Yeah', said Clive, hardly looking up from the screen, 'he's shagged the boss's wife, so he's in hiding from the boss for a few days. Nothing changes.'

'I thought for a moment that you two were back together ...', Bren trailed off.

'Nope', replied Jason, walking into the kitchen, 'although

there's only one bed made up!', he winked at Bren as he walked past, 'coffee?'

'No need!', said Clive, grinning at Bren's embarrassment.

'I guess I can stop with the food parcels for a while then?', asked Bren, changing the subject, 'How's Uncle Peter going?'

'Getting there now: I've managed to get few responses back and forth between my responder and the PC. The PC's beginning to think it's talking to Uncle Peter. Give me another day or two and I should be able to plug it into the net and capture everything. We'll know what's really going on then.'

Jason passed Bren and Clive coffees and left them to their conversation.

'I'm starting to get a few questions from the rest of the board', said Bren, 'I'm struggling to find excuses ...'

'Don't worry - I'll be clear of this lot soon enough. Once I've got this live, I should be able to talk to the board properly. I'm thinking we could use it as a positive thing.'

'How?'

'Well, I've got a new tool in the fight against the hackers - something that allows us to evaluate low-level communication threats - and resolve them. If I can get it all working, I can demonstrate it to the board as a tool that virtually every company in the world will want to employ at some level.'

Bren looked surprised.

'I hadn't thought about it like that.'

'I need to position the commercials a bit better - but I'm thinking that we could demonstrate this kit, and then come up with a method to update the rules side remotely. We can build the rules and license them. Annual recurring licence - that should keep the investors happy.

'Potentially let other people generate rules too - offer license payments for anyone coming up with sensible proven rules to prevent future attacks of this nature. That could make the product much more marketable - perhaps get Staffs Uni involved …'

'You know, I was beginning to worry about this being entirely negative for us', said Bren, 'but this opens up a whole new market.'

'Exactly', replied Clive, 'and we already have the FBI using the prototype version of it - even if they didn't know it was a prototype at the time.'

'Good point', replied Bren thoughtfully, 'can I say you're working on something new?'

'Only if you really need to - I'd suggest I get this working properly first. Once I've got it up and running, we can talk to the others. Then I'll let our friends in the police and MI5 know about it too. Until I've cracked the next bit, it's all a little subjective - as soon as I can see all the traffic, then I can talk about it. Until then, it's all "could be", "might be", and will probably scare the pants off our glorious investors. Something stealing from us will scare them - something preventing people from stealing from everyone globally will probably excite them. We need to position it very carefully.'

'True'

'If you have to say something then just mention that I'm looking at an extension to our portfolio and need some time to assess it properly.'

'Ok'

'But … if you say that, I'll get calls every five minutes from them all asking what I'm working on, and at the moment I have nothing …'

'Yeah, yeah', said Bren nodding, 'I understand. Only if strictly necessary. I'll give the commercials some thought. It's possibly the break the business needs. We night get sensible money to manufacture and sell these … we need a name for it.'

'Now you're thinking about it properly.'

'How long have you had this in mind?'

'When I first started - it seems sensible to have a hacker-prevention tool, something updated by the online community - sort of cloud-sourced anti-hacker tools. It needs a proper gateway though, and this box here …', he pointed to the jumble of wires and circuits, '… might just do the job.'

'Were you going to let me know, or just keep me worrying?'

'Ahh, worrying's what you do best! Anyway, if I'd told you earlier then you'd have already told the board and they'd be on my back asking when I intended to finish the new prototype. You know what they're like!

'Once I've cracked this, I also need to do some work on making some kind of user-interface to create the rules. It's all pretty ugly at the moment.'

'That's the value-add for the annual licence', said Bren.

'In what way?'

'We put the rules in and maintain them for the installed user-base … if they want to create their own, then we charge them for the tool to do it.'

'Ahh, with you. Yes, although I'd want others involved in that, otherwise we end up doing nothing more that defining rules for the rest of our lives - boring!'

'Fair enough', laughed Bren, and then continued a little more quietly, '… and Jason?'

'We're fine. You know he'll shag anything that walks. He's welcome to stay as long as he likes - as long as he doesn't bring trouble back here.'

'Ok. Just checking.'

'Thanks for your concern, but we really are fine.'

'Fair enough - well, I shall leave you to it. If you need anything, give me a call.'

'Ok, thanks. I'll let you know how I get on.'

Jason saw Bren to the door, leaving Clive tapping away on

the computer keyboard.

'Keep an eye on him please - if you need anything, just shout. You have my mobile number, right?', asked Bren.

Jason raised an eyebrow.

'You know I will. He'll be fine - if I'd known he was this busy, I'd have looked in to make sure he was Ok anyway.'

'Thanks', said Bren then grinned before adding, 'and don't distract him too much - I need him back in the office once he's finished this lot.'

'Don't worry, I've fitted a timer on the bedroom door!'

Bren laughed and walked back to the car. As he opened the door to get in Jason shouted loudly across the street, 'Thanks for the sex. It was great. Same time next week …', then closed the front door.

28

Clive's mobile buzzed.

Sleepily, Clive kissed the back of Jason's neck and gently broke the sleeping cuddle.

'God I've missed you', whispered Clive to the apparently sleeping Jason.

Clive eased out of the bed and picked up the mobile before it buzzed again. He picked up his jeans and a t-shirt and went to the bathroom to relieve himself. En route, he opened up the secure messenger application and saw a message from Whiteman.

Whiteman: "Hey Clive. Wanted to let you know that I'm off the unit now. They did some bullshit trick to blame me for letting Paul work too hard. Bad management etc."

Clive wrote back: "That's too bad. Are you out of the FBI too?"

Whiteman: "No. Pen-pushing for a while. Bored. Wondered how Uncle Peter's doing?"

Clive: "Progressing - have managed to get some responses back from my emulator. Want to talk, easier than typing?"

Whiteman: "Sure. Give me 5 and I'll get out of the office."

Clive went downstairs and put the coffee percolator on.

His 'phone rang - it was a secured call from Whiteman's

burner.

'Hey Clive'

'Whiteman … good to hear from you. Sorry to hear about the shit'

Clive pulled the jug out from under the percolator and filled a mug with the extremely strong coffee. He put the jug back so that the machine would continue to brew the remaining coffee.

'Yeah, I think Bill Price has wanted to get his grubby little fingers on my department ever since it started getting real results. It's the only thing that gives him real intelligence these days. Every criminal worth his salt know's to encrypt everything and use the dark net, so they're buggered without our insider data.'

'Dog eat dog in the FBI! That could be a comedy movie plot', joked Clive.

'Yeah - inter-departmental conflict. More of a tragedy than a comedy.'

'So what have they got you doing?'

'Crap. Crap and more crap. I'm looking at some old drugs cases and trying to work out if there's a pattern in the gang's cellphone use. Cold-case heaven!'

'What a waste!'

'Yeah - I'm bored out of my tree.'

'Did you find out what happened to Paul?'

'Yeah. Seems he fell asleep at the wheel. Crashed off the edge of the coast-road into some trees. Smashed up his legs pretty badly and that caused him to bleed out and have a heart attack. He was dead before anyone got to him.

'Some woman saw the crash and called it in. Said he'd just drifted off the road. She thought he was drunk or something.'

'Here's hoping he didn't know anything about it', said Clive.

'Yeah - indeed', agreed Whiteman, 'I guess we've all got to

go sometime though.'

'I thought he was always working ridiculous hours?'

'Yeah, he was', agreed Whiteman, 'he rarely needed more than four hours sleep. I've known him go for days on end when he's involved in something.'

'I thought he was autistic - an absolute focus on one topic to the exclusion of everything else. If he hadn't been a reasonably good communicator, I'd have put him well and truly in the autism camp. Anyway, I'm no doctor!'

'Hmm', replied Whiteman, 'Well, they're holding me partially responsible. I can't argue - I did let him work. Between you and me, I encouraged it - you were heading home, so I wanted to get as much of your joint brain-power as I could.

'Talking of which - how's it going with Uncle Peter?', asked Whiteman.

'Good', replied Clive, taking a large swig of coffee, 'really good. Paul worked out that Uncle Peter was also compromised by the Hackageddon server problem. He managed to get a load of data from some of the servers at the back-end.

'I've been able to get my virtual machine talking to my fake version of Uncle Peter for the past couple of days. I want to get it responding fully, and then I'm going to put it in the middle of the real network connection and see if I can intercept traffic moving in both directions.'

'All sounds great - what then?'

'Well, I'll know exactly what's going to and from Uncle Peter. After that - I either block it, or find out what else it's doing.'

'Don't you want to know who's behind it?'

'I'm not sure we'll ever know for sure. I need to get on with business at this end. If I can get to the point where I know how it works and what it does, then I can block it - and I've built tools to allow us to analyse future attacks and prevent them too. I think it'll end up being someone overseas, in which case I've got virtually no chance of anyone doing anything about it.'

'Intelligence might have a different view on that', said Whiteman.

'They might - and I'll forward all the evidence when I have it. I'm getting pressure from my board to get back to the day job. Having said that, if I still think it's a foreign government behind this, then I will raise it with contacts over here - and possibly send something to you - or Derek or Bill or whomever you suggest might like to hear from me ….'

'Yeah, probably Bill now. You'll really piss him off if you get to it first. I've heard absolutely nothing since I was kicked off the project, so I have no idea how they're getting on with it. I doubt they're doing as well as you though.'

'Well, without Paul's data, I couldn't have built my responder kit. I don't think he shared that with anyone in Bill's team. Should I send it over?'

'Hell no. Let them struggle. They'll happily shaft you, so you might as well get some commercial gain out of it.'

'So much for the greater good!', said Clive, laughing.

'Send it if you want …'

'No - only joking. I'm nearly there with it all. I'll let them know when I have the MHI toolkit to solve the problem. Who knows, I might even throw a little bonus your way for helping out!'

'Please don't', said Whiteman, 'I'd never be able to explain why I'm getting strange payments from a company making money from selling into the federal government. It doesn't look good on the CV.'

'Well, if you get bored, I could do with someone on that side of the pond to head things up …'

'Thanks Clive. I'm nearly pissed off enough to take you up

on that.'

'Seriously, the offer's there, if you want it. I should be able to convince the board that it's a good idea.'

'Thanks. I'll bear it in mind - anyway, I've got to get back to the office. I'd appreciate any updates on Uncle Peter. Purely academic interest.'

'No worries. I'll keep you in the loop. Bye for now.'

Clive hung up. A pair of hands came round his chest from behind him and a naked Jason kissed the back of Clive's neck and said, 'I've missed you too'.

29

From his research, Clive knew that Uncle Peter, when it started up, changed all the information required to authenticate a computer and encrypt its data over the network. This meant that, at some point, he would have to connect one of the virtual machines to the real Internet. If he got things wrong, as soon as the computer and Uncle Peter changed encryption details, he would risk losing that machine - and he only had a limited set of keys Paul had captured for these virtual computer images.

Because of the risk of losing opportunities to communicate with Uncle Peter, Clive set up everything so he could not only capture everything, but pause the machine at every stage during its communication with the Internet. He wanted to stop the machine right at the point where it would send some form of acknowledgement back to Uncle Peter that it had received the new encryption data - in theory, if Uncle Peter never received this acknowledgement, then it would try to use the old credentials again. Hopefully, Clive surmised, this would allow him to capture how the update mechanism worked, and then capture the update so that he could then sit in the middle of the ongoing communication.

Throughout the day, Clive set about creating a new virtual

machine and capturing the startup identify and associated information he had seen sent to Uncle Peter in the past. His fake version of Uncle Peter proved invaluable in allowing Clive to confirm that he had set everything up properly.

Around mid-afternoon, he finally connected the virtual machine to the Internet via the latest version of his protocol analyser. Within a couple of seconds of it starting, the virtual machine paused.

'Well that was an anti-climax', said Jason, who had witnessed the virtual machine boot up.

'What were you expecting?', asked Clive.

'I dunno. But something more than that!'

'Look - I've got a flashing light - it captured something.'

'A flashing light - whoop de doo!'.

Jason went to the fridge and grabbed a can of lager.

'Want one?'

'No thanks', replied Clive. He wanted to get on with analysing the result of the startup sequence. It might have been short, but the protocol analyser had captured a large amount of information. To prevent anything inside any of the other computers from destroying the data, Clive had modified the protocol recorder to write a copy to an external memory card at the same time as its internal storage. Everything was compressed and reversed to prevent Uncle Peter from working out that the information exchanged with the computer had been captured.

Clive transferred the memory card to his old PC and waded through the vast amount of data captured. He started running the filters to remove all the 'normal' exchanges a new machine makes, gradually stripping everything that was known, leaving only the data exchanged with Uncle Peter.

Through the course of the evening and into the early hours, Clive battled with the data, trying to work out exactly what he had captured. Eventually, he had drawn out a complete set of exchanges and was confident enough to start reprogramming his protocol analyser.

Over the next few days, things started to become strangely routine. Clive programmed and tested out various builds of his protocol analyser, each grabbing more data than the last; Jason kept Clive fed and provided far more coffee than was good for either of them; and after each full day, Jason made sure Clive went to sleep physically tired out too.

Clive was actually more relaxed and happier than he had ever been. For once, he was enjoying solving a problem that could otherwise derail the company.

He was also enjoying having Jason around - it was good to have some who had no technical knowledge: Clive could explain what he was doing and Jason would ask all the 'stupid questions' that forced Clive to justify why he was approaching things in a particular way.

Late on Sunday evening, Clive decided that he had enough proof that his method was sound. He made a backup of everything: the virtual machine image before and after it had initialised; the memory card images from the protocol recorder; the modified software and rules; and, the data he had captured on each run of the system so far. He put the backup in the safe before announcing that he was finally ready to start chasing Uncle Peter for real.

'About time too', said Jason, looking up from a programme he was watching on the TV.

'Well, here goes nothing …'

Clive pushed the 'start' button on the protocol recorder, and then started up the virtual machine - this time letting it go through a complete cycle with Uncle Peter. Clive then created a series of folders and started transferring information into the virtual machine about the SeeZu project.

Within a few minutes, the LEDs were flashing wildly on the protocol recorder. Clive let it all run for a few minutes and then closed everything down.

He took the memory card out of the protocol analyser and made a copy of it before putting it into the old PC. He ran the modified software over the data captured and started reading the contents.

Sure enough, he had managed to capture and decode the initial data exchanges. He could see a whole series of updates to the virtual computer's encryption keys. Using these new keys, Clive could then read the incoming and outgoing requests. At last he could see what was going on - with the keys that unlocked the data, he could simply record everything in the knowledge that he had the tools at his disposal to read through it later.

Clive picked up his mobile and opened up the secure messaging application. He sent a message to Whiteman.

Clive: "Cracked it. Have live captures - working now to understand the internal structure. Captured key exchanges and updates. Will keep you posted."

Whiteman responded almost immediately: "Well done. If you need anything tracing from this end, I might be able to help. Limited resources but still have channels available."

Clive: "Thanks. Will let you know."

Clive also sent a message to Bren to let him know that he was a major step closer to getting Uncle Peter out of MHI's systems once and for all.

Bren responded with: "Great stuff - remember the security convention on Tuesday - they're expecting you."

Clive: "Yeah, I know - Jason's going to run me to the station in case he needs anything while I'm away."

That night, in the heat of passion, Clive looked at Jason and rubbed his hands down his back.

'Would you like to move in properly?'

'I'm in already, slack Alice!', replied Jason.

'No, you daft sod. I know that. I'm serious - move in

permanently. Live with me.'

Monday morning started with all the various parties going about their business unaware of how momentous the next few days would be.

Clive wanted to make sure he had everything necessary for the presentation the following morning, and also wanted a copy of the data on his laptop so he could go through it in the hotel that night.

Jason packed Clive's clothes and was working out how best to collect his own few belongings that were scattered amongst his various ex's.

Bren briefed the board on a series of topics before being pressed into revealing that Clive had been working on a new concept - and that he had finally managed to get it working. Something, he promised, that would interest companies around the world as it provided a new way of protecting networks. He assured the board the Clive would demonstrate it all in person at the next board meeting.

In California, Whiteman slept as Jason dropped Clive off at the station and then headed for his new home.

After Clive settled in the hotel, he opened his laptop and started reading through the captured data. He drank from a bottle of Bacardi that Jason had hidden in his packing, then smiled ironically as he read line after line of (now unencrypted) information that had been sent out about a project called "SeeZu".

'Yeah', he whispered to himself, 'now I sees you, now I's going to get you.'

30

Detective Chief Inspector Steve White assembled his major incident team to give the first official briefing in relation to a massive explosion on a residential estate. Early indications led him to believe that at least one person had died in the blast, and it was now up to him and his team to work out what had happened.

Steve had a good reputation and was well respected by most who knew him. He had little time for politics but could navigate his way through the extremely volatile senior management 'landscape' - funding cuts and changes imposed by a newly elected Commissioner meant that he was constantly fighting for resources. However, despite these annoyances, he had led several murder investigations to successful prosecution.

Most of the officers under his command assumed that he would soon climb another rung in the police ranks: Steve's immediate superior, Detective Superintendent Howard Ellis had retired and it looked very likely that Steve would step into his shoes. However, recent cuts in budgets meant that promotion would have to wait for the time being.

Bespectacled and at around 6' tall, with greying short hair, Steve was quite an imposing character. He had blue/grey eyes that gave him an intense 'policeman's stare' - that gaze that could penetrate through someone, giving the impression that he could see far more than language alone could convey.

He stood in front of a series of boards and looked over his newly assembled team. The room was shabby: an office block built in the 1960's and last painted in the 1980's. Old desks were already starting to collect paper and dust - always a common problem for any major investigation. Steve wondered how many vital clues had been left buried in paperwork over the years.

Steve had a relatively informal approach to managing his team. He encouraged communication between team members and invited ideas that would help move things forward. During his time on the force, he had spent enough time working for 'old-school' detectives to know how to keep the team focussed while giving the impression of being relaxed and open.

He knew most of the faces in the room, although he had a couple of new people on his team. He wanted to move quickly as, with each passing hour, any evidence would start to decay or disappear. He didn't need just to consider the fire damage - smoke and water would add to the forensic difficulties in determining exactly what had happened. The immediate and more pressing difficulty with this case was that the fire service had yet to declare the scene safe. Steve wanted to ensure that the crime scene team had everything necessary to begin the second after the fire service crew had completed their work.

In the meantime, he intended to kick-off house-to-house enquiries and start working out who had been in the house at the time of the explosion. All the background work could start without needing access to the scene.

'Ladies and Gentlemen, let's begin', he shouted over the general conversation and hubbub. The noise in the room faded out.

'Thank you. I think most of us know each other, but I shall ask everyone to introduce themselves so we can all put a face to the names … I'll start, I'm DCI Steve White, Senior Investigating Officer for this case. My door's always open and if you think there's something major that can't go through the normal reporting channels, or if you come across something that could affect the case in a broader sense, then please contact me directly. I've put my mobile number on the top of this board … I'll ask that everyone else does the same - and check your contact details on the board to correct anything on there. Communication between us all is key, so if in doubt, talk to each other. Ok?

'Perhaps we introduce ourselves by going clockwise round the room, starting with you, Alan.?'

'Hi DS Alan West, Deputy SIO for this case - if you can't find Steve, find me.'

'Pat Langton, office manager. Here to help you with logistic support and general, well, filing, I suppose. I've also created all the HOLMES stuff …'

'Hasn't that just blown up', said one of the officers in the room.

'Funny! HOLMES - Home Office Large Major Enquiry System - I've created all the main entries to start off with.'

'Mark Lockhurst, Senior Analyst - here to help with data, comms, analysis of evidence - particularly computers, phones, vehicle traces - anything along those lines. All I ask is that you co-ordinate any communications or computer requests through me so that we avoid duplicating effort or requests to any of the utility or telecoms companies, ta.'

'DS Steve Bates - investigator, I guess - unless Steve says otherwise!'

'DC Anna Hibbert, Hi'

'Hi, Oliver Wickes, scientific support manager. Any

forensic evidence, trace etc. Please send my way. Er - if I may remind people … Please observe chain of evidence precautions, I'll log and receipt everything - if you don't get a receipt, it doesn't exist in court. Thanks.'

'DS Theresa Higgins, search and house-to-house co-ordinator.'

'Dr Gregory Jones - Greg, behavioural investigative adviser.'

'DC Richard Duff, family liaison'

'Bill Sheppard, Press Officer - if anyone feels the need to speak to the media, then please run it past me first. It's key that we maintain a consistent public story, so treat me as the single point of contact for all media communications - please take a card so you have my details handy in case anyone asks. We'll have a press schedule on the board in due course: it keeps the press off our backs as they'll know when they'll get updates. I suggest you keep an eye on these schedules so if anyone from the press collars you, then refer them to the press office, me, or the next scheduled press update. Also, to state the obvious, make a note of who's asked you for information - just in case it turns out to be a person of interest merely wanting to find out what we know.'

'DC George Kerr, CTU - er - counter terrorism unit. I'm not expecting to stay around unless SOCO find evidence linking the explosion to terrorist activities …', he shrugged, '… but you never know!'

'DC Eric Butler'

'And last but by no means least …', said Steve looking at the last person in the room.

'DC Phil Bateman, Sir'.

'Ok, thanks everyone', said Steve, 'you are all part of the core investigation team. I've arranged for a mobile field office and we have the offices here at our disposal. With two offices, it's imperative that we ensure that everything and everyone keeps up to date. To that end, I want to have a meeting here, every morning at 9AM sharp. You only miss these briefings by getting permission off myself or Alan. Ok? Any questions?'

Steve left a few seconds in case anyone wanted to ask anything. Then continued.

'So, at the moment we know that we received several triple nine calls at 08:32 this morning, reports suggested an explosion occurred at 136 Sheringham Drive. We have ascertained that an explosion did indeed occur, most likely in the kitchen area, and that at least one person received fatal injuries at the scene.

'Fire and rescue are still making the environment safe and have concluded their initial searches to ensure that there's no-one else in the building. Once fire and rescue conclude their assessment of the fire, they will let us know about the probable cause. However, we have a fatality and, at the moment, we have to ensure that we are ready to react in the event that this wasn't something as simple as a gas leak.

A telephone started ringing at the back of the office. Steve Bates rushed over to pick it up - it's almost part of a policeman's DNA to never ignore a ringing 'phone.

Steve started allocating tasks to the various members of the team. He really wanted to gain access to the explosion site, but in the meantime he started defining background investigations into the house owner, family connections, and anything unusual.

Steve Bates had answered the 'phone and was taking down details. He hung up and waited for Steve White to finish off allocating a block of tasks before approaching.

'Sir, that was the home owner - a Mr Clive Knollys - he's at the Black Boar - it's an hotel near Birmingham, he says he thought someone tried to kill him. He was presenting at a police conference today and wasn't at home this morning …'

'Ok - in that case, take Richard and go and pick him up. Let's find out what he knows. Get his mobile, computers and anything else he might have as soon as you get there. Get the local force to guard the room in the meantime. Theresa, can you secure and search the hotel room after we've got him out?

'Everyone - listen up - it looks like the home owner's on the way in, so as soon as we gain site access, we'll have to determine who was in the house at the time of the explosion. At this time, we need to treat the home owner as a significant witness, possibly in need of protection, possibly vulnerable. If anyone asks about Clive Knollys then defer to me and log all details about the person asking.'

Steve approached Mark Lockhurst, the senior analyst. 'Mark, I need to you look at finances for Clive Knollys, local CCTV, ANPR - phone records, everything and anything related to him and his recent activities. Grab anyone you need for the time being, but let me know if you're going to spend anything significant.'

Before Mark could reply, Steve looked over to Alan West, his deputy.

'Alan - can you also talk to our friends at the NCA's protected persons service - if he was the intended victim, then we need to look after him.'

Steve strode into the interview room. He looked at Clive, who was clearly in shock. There was a pad and pens and a paper cup containing black coffee on the interview table.

Steve wanted to capture the initial 'core' facts as soon as possible and the visibly shaking and pale Clive had insisted on only speaking to the officer in charge of the investigation.

'Hello', he said offering his hand to a now standing Clive, 'I'm DCI Steve White and I'm heading up the investigation into the explosion at your house. I heard you wanted to speak to me and me alone …'

'Yes', said Clive, 'was anyone in there when it happened?'

'Firstly, what do you think happened?', asked Steve.

'I have no idea - it looks like someone blew the house up - I've only seen the news. Was anyone in there?'

'Should someone have been? Who do you think would have been in there when it happened?', asked Steve gently.

'Jason might have been - er, Jason Haggely'

Steve started making notes as they talked.

'And who's Jason - a friend, relative?'

'Partner', said Clive, 'was he there?'

'We don't have access to the site yet', said Steve, 'we're waiting for the fire service to finish making it safe. Then we can have a look. Was anyone else other than Jason likely to be at the house?'

'No', replied Clive. Tears started welling up in his eyes.

'He'd only just moved in … God, what a mess.'

'What else can you tell me about Jason? His date of birth, next of kin ... Sorry to ask, but if he was in the house, then we'll need to look into him too.'

'Yeah. January 6th 1994. Him mum lives over in Brown Edge, Stoke, somewhere - I don't have the address, sorry.'

Steve jotted down the details as Clive spoke.

He looked up and continued, 'Ok, now, you said you thought someone might have tried to kill you - why would you think that?'

'I run a specialist digital security company and I've discovered something - it's probably a foreign government or organised crime syndicate - they're stealing information - most likely state secrets, and I've been working on ways to stop them.'

'They?', asked Steve, 'Who are they?'

'I don't know. That's what we've been trying to work out for the past few months.'

'We?', asked Steve.

'Both MI5 and the FBI - I just came back from the FBI's special operations and digital intelligence department in America where we've been trying to work out how it worked …'

Steve raised an eyebrow. He wasn't sure if the distraught character in front of him had some kind of mental health issue or was telling the truth. It was different, if nothing else!

'Ok - and who would you be dealing with in these agencies?'

'MI5 is David Harswell and it's Whiteman in the FBI - sorry, his real name's Paul Whiteman, he worked in the special operations department until …', Clive's pupils dilated and his breathing started increasing.

'Until?'

'His colleague died a few weeks ago, working on this same project; in a car accident. We'd been working on this together. I need to warn Whiteman …', Clive was becoming agitated.

Steve lifted both hands to calm Clive down. 'You just need to leave things like that to us', said Steve, wondering if he would need to arrange a mental health assessment. He switched back to Jason for a moment.

'This', he looked at his notes, 'Jason Haggely - what can you tell me about him?'

Clive ignored the question and responded with 'Whiteman might be in danger. Look, if they're after me, they might be after him too - we have to warn him. I need my laptop so I can warn him. Can I have my laptop please?'

'I already said we'll take care of that for you. I'm trying to establish what's gone on …'

Clive cut Steve off, 'We HAVE to warn Whiteman. If they've killed Paul Davis and tried to kill me, then he must be on the list. I can warn him but need my laptop to get on to my secure messenger. I haven't got his mobile number any more.'

'Why?'

'Because the FBI moved him off the case. They blamed him for Davis' death. Corporate neglect or something similar - all bull'.

'Right, I'll look into it. Leave that with me. I just want to clear some of the basics first: as I said we have yet to gain access to your house - the fire service are still finishing up. Apart from Jason, would anyone else have cause to be in the property at the time?'

'Why, what have you found?'

'Just answer the question please? I want to make sure we don't miss anything.'

Clive thought for a moment and shook his head.

'No', replied Clive with tears now freely running down his face, 'I think there's only Jason. Unless he managed to get out.'

Steve watched Clive for a few seconds, trying to work out how best to proceed. If there was an intelligence link of any form, then he would need to approach things very differently. Steve thought he would have to give Clive the benefit of the doubt for the time being, but it all seemed a little too far fetched to make sense. To Clive, those few seconds under Steve's steely gaze seemed to go on for hours.

Steve stood up.

'Look - I'm going to need to interview you properly within the next few days. If MI5 are involved, It might well end up being someone from the agency that wants to talk to you - but right now - we need to get you safe while we look into the possibility that someone could have come after you. I'll get in touch with our contacts here about the FBI and MI5 stuff. Perhaps you can understand that it all seems a little - well - over the top at the moment, so I need to do some digging.'

'Can I contact my family and the company so that they know I'm Ok?'

'Not at the moment. If someone wanted you dead, then perhaps it's better you are - for the time being, at least. I shall, however, ask our family liaison officers to get in touch with them. In the meantime, I have arranged for my colleagues within the protected persons service to help you. They're specialists in looking after people - as soon as they arrive, I'll send them in.'

He pointed to a pad and pen. He'd found a simple yet effective way to capture information was to let a victim work out how best to represent a shocking event - just leaving them with a pen, paper, and their own thoughts for a while often yielded very good results.'

'If you want to do something, then can I ask you to jot down your movements over the past few days, and anything you think we might find useful.'

Steve went back through the investigation room and to his office. He walked over to the windows and gazed out over the town. If Clive was telling the truth, then the case was suddenly much more complicated.

He picked up the 'phone and called his immediate boss, Superintendent Dennis Keeling.

'Sir - I wondered if you could spare a few minutes?'

After a relatively brief meeting with his superiors, Steve called in his deputy.

'Alan, I am going to split this case into three main lines. Firstly, let's look into this Jason Haggely character - he could be the real victim, or there's a suggestion that he could be collateral in a hit against Clive Knollys. In parallel, we want to keep looking into Knollys and his business affairs because he also claims that he was the real target.'

'Oh? So it's a botched murder attempt?'

'Possibly - Knollys claims he's been working on some techno-spy-crap with the FBI and MI5.'

Alan looked surprised and slightly amused.

'Really?', he asked.

'Furthermore, he says that one of the FBI guys also working on the project died in suspicious circumstances a few weeks ago. Now he's either barking mad, or … well, there could be something in it.

'I've already asked Dennis for an opinion and he's suggesting we inform the confidential unit and get them to liaise with MI5. At least we can check that bit of his story out reasonably quickly.

'If, however, there is some truth in it, then we might need to split out part of the team to work just that section. I need you to concentrate on that bit - get someone else doing the background checks on Knollys and Haggely, start Mark off on looking at Knollys' laptop and 'phone as soon as.

'For the time being, I think we keep the cloak and dagger conspiracy out of general circulation. We might need to take a view on this, or hand the case on to the confidential unit in due course, so we need to ensure we're better than good on documentation, logging and reporting. Ok?'

'Yes, fine', replied Alan.

'If it turns out that Knollys is having a fantasy trip, then we might need to give him vulnerable witness status. In the meantime, I've got the PPS looking after him. If you want to talk to him then you'll have to arrange for the PPS to bring him in. Bear in mind that they will have frozen all his assets by now, so be aware that he won't exist as Knollys after today.'

'Ok', said Alan, 'I'll dig out my poisoned umbrella and invisible ink too - what's the pass-phrase again?'

'Yeah, I know', laughed Steve, 'reminds me of the self-styled diplomat we picked up for having no MoT on his 20-year old Morris Marina when I was in traffic!'

'Sir', interrupted Anna, 'we've just had a call from fire and rescue - they're about to release the scene.'

31

'Good morning everyone. Can we start please?', shouted Steve across the room.

Once the noise had abated, Steve stood in front of the boards and started with his executive summary.

'136 Sheringham Drive was largely demolished by what appears to have been, at first glance, a gas leak in the kitchen. At the moment, SOCO believes that a single victim died at the scene, although we will have to wait for DNA to confirm that. We have no other way to identify the person or persons involved at this time due to the damage caused by the explosion. It does, however, suggest than the victim or victims were in extremely close proximity to the source of the blast.

'The home owner, one Clive Knollys', Steve pointed to a photograph of Clive, 'was presenting at a police conference on digital forensics, thus was in an hotel near to the conference centre from the night before the explosion, until we picked him up yesterday. As a significant witness, I have placed him in the care of our friends at the protected person service pending clarification of some claims he made around being a potential target. Ensure that we log any queries made about Knollys during the course of the investigation.

'I have asked for CCTV examination to confirm his journey times and stay at the hotel, but currently see no reason to doubt his whereabouts at the time.

'Knollys has provided a potential identification for the victim - one Jason Haggely, Knollys' partner. We can't rule out homophobic attack, but I think it unlikely - however, keep your eyes open, just in case.

'What else do we have - George?'

'Well Sir, we've worked very closely with SOCO and the fire and rescue service to identify the source of the explosion. The explosion and subsequent fire started from around the gas entry point for the premises - and must have been a substantial leak for an explosion of this size. Fire and rescue will conclude their investigation either by close of play today, or sometime tomorrow. I have obtained an original floor plan of the house and have marked up the key points - it's on the board.

From a counter-terrorism perspective, we have picked up traces of materials that could be used to start or exacerbate an explosion. However, the home owner had a large collection of computer boards, PC's and other paraphernalia that has made it difficult for us to say conclusively whether this was an attack of some form, or just a gas explosion. I'm hoping that the fire service report will clarify this for me, when I should be able to conclude my part in this investigation.

'To summarise though, without compelling evidence to the contrary, I'm leaning more towards a gas fault than any form of incendiary device.'

'Thank you - Anna?'

Anna, stood up.

'As requested, we completed a search of Knollys' hotel room. We bagged everything belonging to or used by him and have subsequently released the room. We also got CCTV footage from the hotel, the conference centre, and have requested the footage from the council too.

'With respect to the house - it took a while for fire and rescue to release the scene as some of the structure needed support to prevent it collapsing on us. SOCO is still working the scene Sir. It's a mess and it will take some time to go through everything. We've had gentle rain overnight but put tents up to protect as much as we can. Also, we've had a huge number of people trampling through the scene - from fire and rescue, the gas company, structural engineers - and a few builders to shore things up. We've taken a lot of photographs and I'm working with the coroner to identify and collect as many parts of the victim as quickly as possible. I'm sure we'll have issues with rodents unless we can clear the remains. We're working from the source outwards, but have created initial distribution maps and have the initial fire reports too.'

As she went to sit down, she checked her notes.

'Oh - sorry, Sir, nearly forgot - the fire investigators thought it was possible that accelerants were there - but again, weren't sure - it could have been cleaning fluid or alcohol. We'll know more when we've had a chance to look at more of the lower-levels of debris.'

'Ok, thanks. Theresa - how's the house to house going?'

'Mixed - most people were either leaving for work, in the process of dropping kids off, or generally preparing for work.

'We had a couple of reports of a dark car - blue or black, possibly a Mercedes or BMW with two to four occupants. No index for it. One of the neighbours mentioned a utilities sales effort in the area, so we're not sure how important the car is yet.

'Those nearest to the blast were the ones calling triple nine. It would appear that no-one saw anything, but all report a single large bang, consistent with a gas explosion.

'Generally, Knollys kept himself to himself. A couple of the neighbours commented about him being obsessive about noise - he complained a lot when kids played outside his house, apparently. He didn't join in with any of the local neighbourhood initiatives, or the neighbourhood watch scheme.

'Neighbours either side suggested that, until very recently, he didn't maintain the house or grounds particularly well, however, it looked like the lawns had been cut pretty recently and there were efforts to make the gardens respectable.'

'Ok, thanks Theresa. Mark, Can we check CCTV and ANPR cameras in the area and see if we can trace the car? I know it's the middle of the rush-hour and an extremely vague description, but do your best.'

Steve looked over to Steve Bates, the investigative team leader.

'Steve?'

'Ok, limited background data on Haggely at the moment - seems he's had a few run-ins with the police. He was fined for committing an assault while drunk and disorderly, and then caught driving a vehicle without insurance, license, tax or MoT. Banned from driving for 12 months and a £900 fine. He hasn't paid anything off the fine despite making arrangements with the Court. The court was in the process of raising a warrant and had issued final warnings to Haggely to explain himself.

'Apart from being a Disco driver, he seems to live something of a cash-in-hand nomadic lifestyle - so we're still working out his movements over the past few days. Bear with us Sir, this is proving to be something of a challenge.

'Knollys, however, is a much easier case. He's an inventor of some seriously clever network security systems - he's sold stuff into virtually every friendly nation to protect military and government communications. A lot of secret stuff - nuclear defence through to police and intelligence support. He's something of an expert and has even trained our local force in digital forensics, mobile communications, and network analysis. He's written books, appeared on radio and TV - he's the "go to" guy for media questions on Internet fraud and mobile communications. If you ask around here, the odds are someone will have heard of him. He's the chairman of a few trade associations and heads up mobile futures for a couple of local universities. Heavyweight and technically competent guy.

'His company seems to be doing reasonably well, with a few financial constraints, but nothing majorly wrong there. In keeping with PPS requests, we have merely said that we have no sharable information about Knollys at this stage and that we'll keep the company posted.

'I spoke to all the board members except the Chief Exec who's in a conference over in Barcelona - I was assured by the other board members that he'll contact us when he returns and I have also left messages to that effect.

'As far as we can tell, Knollys has no major debts - even paid off his car loan, so nothing strange there. A few thousand in the bank, so not broke - but not excessively wealthy either. Pretty average guy.

'We're still contacting friends - but it seems he is generally quite popular - gay, but never shouted about it. Nothing really exceptional or out of the ordinary. That's about it at the moment - we'll have more once we have done a formal interview.'

'Good work, thanks Steve. Technical - Mark?'

'We've started off all the usual enquiries - we're waiting back from the mobile operators, contacted ANPR and CCTV ops, we've also started imaging the computer and telecoms equipment - but have nothing substantial yet. There's a fair bit of kit at the house too, so we've asked SOCO to send it over as soon as they can extract it from the scene.

'Social media has been relatively quiet about this - just the usual chatter and banter, so we've seen nothing unusual there either. We're watching this for a few days, but will stop pretty soon unless something interesting comes up.

'We're looking into the banks and insurance companies for both Knollys and Haggely, but we've only just sent the requests out, so I'm not expecting anything for a few days yet. In the meantime PPS has frozen all Knollys' known assets so that he can't do anything that would raise his head above the trenches.

'Finally, we're yet to see Haggely's 'phone. We could do with this as a priority - if you come across it, please get it to me soonest - I'd prefer to get hold of it while the battery's still alive.'

'Thanks Mark, I'm guessing it's a little early for any scientific input?', the question aimed at Oliver Wickes.

'So - so', said Oliver, 'we're gathering all kinds of evidence at the moment. And we'll need a good few days before we can work out the full scenario. Suffice to say that the explosion, fire, water, and cold temperatures are doing little to preserve evidence. For us, it's a race against time to gather as much as we can.

'There's a lot of circuitry and computer kit in varying states of repair. I have photographs of it all and would like to get Mark involved in working out what's what - it might save us some time, if that's Ok?'

Steve looked at Mark, who nodded.

'Ok - we could ask Knollys to have a look too?', suggested Mark.

'Perhaps', said Steve, 'see how you both get on first.'

Oliver continued, 'Thanks. I've made a few opening comments and sketches - they're on the board. These largely agree with the statements made previously. We think there's only one body, but can't absolutely confirm that yet. I will let you know if we come across anything further.'

'Thanks Oliver - anything from the family, Richard?'

'We've not really had a great deal of time to talk to them. We're also hampered a little by the PPS - Knollys' family want to know what's happened. I've arranged to take formal statements over the next few days, once the shock has eased off a little. Initial questions suggest a pretty normal family unit - they don't live in each other's pockets, so they weren't aware of anyone living with Knollys, and only have very limited knowledge of Haggely.

'With Haggely, we have yet to make contact with the mother - it appears she's the only living relative - well the only known living relative. So, currently no further information available on him.'

Steve looked around the room.

'Anything from the press side?'

'Nothing coming in - we have a press conference scheduled for 16:00 so that we can share anything relevant. The local press covered it as did regional news last night. So far, they're saying it's most likely a gas explosion. At this point I'm merely covering the essentials - not determined the cause yet, still working the scene, at least one person dead, not yet in a position to confirm any details but will release information to the press through the usual channels.

'If anyone needs media support or needs something released, please clear it with Steve and we'll help with wording, presentation, and distribution of course.'

'Thanks', said Steve, 'We might have a couple of visitors here today - we've asked the confidential unit to assist us with looking into Knollys. Given the nature of the work he does, we want to make sure we haven't missed anything. Please give them any information they need but I'd appreciate feedback from anyone speaking to them - I need to know what they're asking so that I can make sure we're all aligned. Carry on folks. We'll do this again at the same time tomorrow morning. Good work everyone.'

'Gentlemen, please come in', said Steve. He moved a couple of chairs closer to a circular table, luckily clear of paperwork.

'Could you ask Alan to come and join us?', he asked Pat, the office manager. She had chaperoned the two 'men from MI5'.

'Of course - can I get you gentlemen tea or coffee?', she asked.

'Yeah - that'd be good: coffee - black, thanks', then to Steve, 'I'm David Harswell, and this is John Fitzpatrick'. He held out his hand while John asked for a coffee too.

Steve assessed the two men. David Harswell was a tall bespectacled man who had all the presence of a senior officer in the forces. He carried himself well and Steve thought he looked around 45-50 years old. His greying hair and steel blue eyes seemed to enhance what was obviously a very fit physique under a white shirt, blue/grey suit, and matching blue tie.

John, on the other hand was slightly scruffier. He was bald, perhaps 35 or a little older. He was wearing a brown leather jacket and could almost have stepped out of a civil protest group.

'Please - sit down', said Steve, 'once we've got drinks sorted and Alan - my deputy - joins us, then we can start'.

After a couple of minutes of pleasantries about the weather and the standard of the office, Alan joined them and closed the door. He sat down.

'Right', said Steve, 'we might be wasting your time here - but I have to check things out. I've got a potential victim that says he could have been the target behind an explosion that occurred at his house. He says that he was working on something to do with data theft and that he was involved with both the FBI - and MI5 …'

'Clive Knollys', said David.

'You know him?'

'Oh yes. And if he thinks he was the target, then I wouldn't rule it out', David spoke clearly and with precision.

John started making notes.

'Really?', replied Steve, 'I thought he was some kind of nut?'

'Quite the contrary. Some of our networks use his technology. He told me, in confidence, that he had discovered something that had the potential to defeat existing security measures. The FBI also use his systems and, as he was in the USA, one of the field offices offered resources to assist him find out whether it was a real threat or not. With our current financial constraints, I was happy for him to work with the FBI on this matter. I contacted a Bill Price, the director of digital intelligence to thank him - and to ask formally to be kept up to date with any developments - I wanted the real risk profile.

'While I trust Clive, he has a vested interest in keeping things contained - it could do some serious damage to his business if this defeats his technology too. It's either supremely good for his business, or extremely bad. Basically, it could make or break him - at least I'd get an unbiased opinion from the FBI team.'

'Well', said Alan, 'that certainly puts a different spin on things.'

'Indeed', replied Steve and then looked at David.

'Did you know about the death of one of the FBI agents?'

For a fraction of a second, the MI5 men exchanged a surprised glance.

'Who died?', asked David, regaining his composure.

'Hold on …', said Steve as he thumbed back through his notes, 'Do you have any idea who might target Clive, if he was targeted?'

David and John ignored the question, leaving an awkward silence until Steve found the notes he took during Clive's initial interview.

'Ok - here it is - one Paul Davis: he died in a car crash, according to my notes. We haven't checked this out - I thought it outside of the remit for this case.'

'I'll see if the FBI have anything useful to contribute on the matter', said David.

'Thanks for that', said Steve.

'Can we talk to Clive?', asked David.

'We'll have to arrange that - I'll ask PPS to get him here tomorrow. We want to interview him too - I've only had the chance to do a preliminary ...'

'You said someone died at Clive's house', said David, 'what else do you know?'

'Not a lot yet', replied Steve, 'we think it was probably one person, possibly a Jason Haggely. We're getting more information all the time - still nothing certain about the cause of the explosion - inconclusive results from CTU and SOCO so far. Forensics still working the scene, so it'll be a while before we've got enough to say for sure.'

'Hmm. Ok. I'll come back tomorrow to meet up with Clive. If you need anything else from us, please let me know. In the meantime, I'd like to ask a favour ...', said David.

'Go on'

'I'd like you to keep the FBI and MI5's involvement reasonably low-key for the time being. I'll ask the office to do some background work here, but some parts of this could compromise the integrity of some of our activities. I'd prefer it if we could keep the content of this discussion on a need to know basis.'

Steve nodded. 'Ok.'

'Thank you. Also, I could do with John attending the team briefings for the next few days - just so that we can stay up to date without bothering you.'

Before Steve could answer, David and John both closed their notebooks and prepared to leave.

David passed a business card over to Steve.

'If you could let me know when you expect Clive here, I'll pop over. I'd appreciate speaking to him before you interview him, and either myself or John attending each time you speak to him. Thanks once again for your co-operation.'

With that, the MI5 men left.

'Thanks once again for your co-operation', mimicked Steve.

'They didn't know about the FBI guy', said Alan, 'did you see the expression?'

'Yeah, I noticed that too. You know, I might have to change my opinion of Knollys. For a while, I thought he was a nutter - then today, I thought they'd take the case off me - now, however, it looks like he might actually BE a target. I've never worked an espionage case before!'

'Me neither - but I am getting myself a brown briefcase - oh, and stay well away from umbrellas with pointy ends …'

32

Steve had to attend a meeting with Superintendent Keeling, so Alan headed up the morning briefing.

'Thanks everyone, we've got a couple of new faces in the room today - John, welcome. Also, we have DS Terry Bosson from the drug unit to give us some background information on Jason Haggely. Perhaps we could start with Haggely this morning, Steve, what do we have?'

Steve Bates stood up and walked over to the boards. He pointed to a picture of Jason.

'Jason Haggely, a 20 year old male, seen here after being arrested having given a false name. He was stopped for driving a vehicle without a full license, tax, MoT, or insurance. He's had a few run-ins over the years, mostly for alcohol related incidents. Currently no outstanding warrants, although one could be coming his way as he has yet to make good on commitments made to the court to pay his fines.

'He was a bit of a jack-the-lad character: it seems that he took cash-in-hand jobs and drank whatever he earned. It looks like he latched on to anyone that took an interest in him - got them into bed as long as they could provide a roof over his head, at least until he finds someone else more interesting, or who hasn't previously thrown him out.

'From information received, it would appear that he has done a reasonable amount of building work for the Poole family, where we are led to believe Haggely stayed for a few days before coming to Knollys. Perhaps this is where I should ask DS Bosson from the drug unit for his input.'

DS Bosson stood up and took his position next to Steve Bates.

'Thanks Steve. We've been watching the 'Poole Family' for some time. They call themselves either 'The Pooles', or 'The Family', depending on where the are, and who they're with at the time. Something of a self-styled mafia group by all accounts. We think the family is running quite a substantial operation under the guise of property rental businesses, fast food outlets and most likely using local taxi drivers as runners. They also rent out two pizza outlets in the vicinity, and we think they use this as the front of house for drug distribution. Rented so that Poole can claim that he has no control over the activities of his tenants - something he did at one of his houses that had been converted into a cannabis farm.

'Mark Poole, pictured here, gets seriously nasty when upset - and he has the right connections to make life extremely nasty for anyone crossing him.

'We understand that Haggely, prior to his death, had been renovating property for Mark Poole and that he stayed with Poole while doing this work. An as yet unsubstantiated rumour has it that Haggely slept with Julie Poole while Mark Poole was asleep and then Haggely did a runner - possibly the most sensible thing he could do in that situation.

'We know Haggely had a substantial amount to drink, bragged about his conquest in the village local, and then disappeared - probably that's when he arrived at Knollys' place. The landlord thought Haggely was in hiding from the Pooles.

'We're currently running an extensive operation centred around the Poole family and have seen nothing yet to link this investigation to ours. However, we can't rule out the possibility that Poole discovered where Haggely was staying and wanted to set an example - regardless of anything else, if Haggely was the victim, we'll struggle to find a direct link back to Poole. He's not stupid.

'We will, however, provide access to the 'phone records and activity logs during the run up to the explosion, and would appreciate being kept informed about anything that can link this explosion to Poole.

'In all honesty, it wouldn't surprise me if Poole hadn't arranged this - it's certainly dramatic enough. I would, however, have expected one of our team to have heard him bragging about it to warn off others - and we've heard nothing to that effect.'

While Terry walked back to his seat, Steve Bates continued with the rest of his report.

'We hope to get to interview Knollys formally today. We've asked Mark to attend part of the interview as we think there may be some technical aspects to the case and we'd welcome his insight.'

He checked his notes, 'And that's me done, Sir'.

'Ok, thanks - Anna - what do you have from the scene?'

Steve sat down and Anna moved to position herself in front a board now covered with pictures from the house ruins.

'We have now identified, photographed, and removed what we believe to be all of the remains of the person in the house at the time of the explosion. We're still collecting evidence from the scene - this was a substantial explosion and we are having difficulties in keeping the scene free from environmental contamination.

'Having said that, we have now recovered - as requested -

most of the computer equipment and that has all gone to the lab. There's probably another couple of days work to do before we can complete our analysis of the scene and I'll give everyone a full update when we have done that.'

'George', said Alan, inviting the Counter-Terrorism officer to speak next.

'Not a lot for me to do here. I'm happy that this doesn't appear to be a terrorist-related incident so I intend to step out of the enquiry today. If anyone thinks there's something that indicates terrorist involvement, then please let me know and I'll come back over. But currently, I have seen nothing to indicate that CTU need to remain engaged with this case.'

He looked directly at Alan.

'I'll finish our paperwork today and get it to you by close of play.'

'Great', replied Alan, 'thanks for your help. Theresa?'

'We've had a few conflicting reports from the house-to-house enquiries. Some people are suggesting that there were two unusual vehicles in the vicinity at the time: potentially a black BMW and a black Mercedes. A couple of the houses on the estate have CCTV and we have asked for copies of their footage to see if there's anything we can get from it. We'll go through it as soon as we get it.

'There are a few shops just off the estate. We have already asked for copies of any CCTV material they have and we'll have a look through that too.'

'Ok, thanks. It's worth seeing if we can cross reference with traffic to see what vehicles match the descriptions - we may end up with 50 or so vague matches, but it's worth pursuing.

'Anyone else?'

The PPS Officer and Clive sat in the hotel room watching two angry youths on TV arguing about who had done what, and who really was the baby's father. Although it was on the TV,

Clive wasn't really watching it - it was noise: something that distracted the officer enough to prevent Clive having to make small-talk.

Clive had brought the pad and pen from police station. It was now largely filled with a mass of tiny diagrams and process descriptions written in Clive's own design 'language'. Every waking moment was spent on working out how Uncle Peter operated - it was the only thing that kept Clive from thinking about Jason. His designs had become the container for his grief.

At exactly 11:00, there was a knock on the door. The PPS officer leapt up and looked through the peep-hole in the hotel door. With the door-chain still in place, he unlocked the door and opened it a fraction.

'I don't know what good the chain will do - if I wanted to come in, I'd be in by now', said a familiar voice from the other side of the door.

The officer closed the door, unlatched the chain and the opened it.

Clive recognised David Harswell and started looking round for the TV remote.

'I firmly believe that if you watch too much daytime TV you'll end up on it at some point - and not in a good way!', exclaimed David as he strode into the room, 'I thought I'd gatecrash the police investigation and have a chat with you first.'

David looked at the PPS officer.

'So, thank you in advance for leaving us to chat alone for a few minutes. Perhaps you would be as good as to go and wait for DCI White in the lobby. I'll stay with Clive until he arrives.'

Summarily dismissed, the PPS officer left the room and the door closed behind him with a reassuring clunk.

Clive sighed.

'Thank God for that! I can't breathe with those idiots around all the time - I know they're doing their jobs but I have nothing in common with them at all.'

David grinned. 'A necessary evil at the moment. You seem to have ruffled a few feathers so either you were on the right track, someone was after this Jason chappie, or you were just unlucky. Which do you think it is?'

'Jason might have been a dickhead at times, but I can't see anyone wanting to blow my fucking house up to get to him. No - I think I found something - and whoever's behind it doesn't want it leaking out.'

David sat down.

'What are we dealing with here - I mean it's not a trivial thing to blow someone up - much easier and less attention-grabbing to have you crash you car, shoot you or have you killed in an apparent robbery surely?'

'That's what makes me think it is someone out to kill me and get all the equipment I had. They would need to destroy everything there - if someone else gets hold of that kit, then the secret's out. Much easier to blow the lot up, with me in there.'

'Still - it's a spectacular way to go …'

'Look - if I had been in there, I'd be dead. As it was, the second I connected from my hotel room to my virtual desktop, the house blows up. No-one would have known what I was working on and it would probably end up being classed as a gas fault or something similar. The media's already hinting at that.'

'Back to the core question then - what are we dealing with?'

'It's big. It's too big for a crime syndicate - even with the computing resources available to the Russian or Chinese Mafia, I think there's too much data for them to worry about. I think it starts out as a general phishing exercise - cast out a line and see what comes in. But I think there are people behind it - they see what comes in and they target specifics - and quickly too.

'I built a honeypot and it only took a few hours before I saw requests coming back in to search through it. That's intelligence beyond a computer's capabilities right now - that took a human level of contextual understanding. It's way too complex a set up to just grab bank account numbers or for identity theft. This is serious computing with a serious amount of manpower behind it.'

David looked very intently at Clive. 'So you're thinking state-level resources?'

'Yep. I'm almost certain of it.'

Clive paused for a moment. 'And a big state at that - we'd struggle to find the manpower to pull this off.'

'So who?'

'It can only be the big three - the US, China, or Russia - perhaps any two of the three. Realistically, I think it more likely to be China or Russia - after all, the FBI's thrown a fair amount of resources at this too. Why would they spend so much investigating their own?'

'Talking of which', Clive continued, 'has anyone warned Whiteman yet? He's in real danger if this was an attack against me!'

'I tried - I got hold of Bill Price and he thanked me for the warning but said that Whiteman was officially out of the unit and off the case now.'

'Whiteman isn't though', said Clive, 'he was helping me behind the scenes.'

'Oh?'

'He has a burner and our secure communicator - we were exchanging ideas right up until the night before the explosion.'

'Can you get hold of him? It might be useful to get his view on things too?'

'Get me a machine with our software on it and I can get hold of him.'

'Can anyone trace it back - I mean it might prove useful to leave you dead for a while yet?'

'No - I used fully anonymous mode - they can trace encrypted packets back to an encrypted device. They won't find who's using the device, or what it's doing. There's nothing usable over the air - if you can get me a burner too - something I can use and throw away, ideally getting someone else to get it for you with cash …'

'Yeah yeah', said David, 'I know. Ok, We'll do that - let's see what Whiteman can add.'

'Well, it's pointless having me sit around waiting for someone to work out they missed me? They'll get me eventually - especially if these muppets put any information on a compromised machine.'

'Give me a shopping list', said David, 'then I can get you everything you need in one go'.

Clive stood up and walked to the table. He had already made a list of all the things he thought he might need.

'Physical death's easy - it takes a real expert to create digital death. If they've gained access to the case computers - like HOLMES or the internal PPS systems - anything that mentions I'm still around, then they'll already be looking for me. I really need to go dark - completely dark, and for that I need this lot.'

He handed the list to David, and continued, 'Along with some cash, my stuff from the safe, and I need to get away from the care of the PPS: they're a digital liability.'

A knock on the door was followed immediately by 'Hi - it's Steve, I hope you two are decent in there'.

David opened the door to admit Steve, accompanied by

Alan West.

'Sorry for the informality - it looks like housekeeping are on the corridor', said Steve, and looked at David.

'Are you …', he started.

'Yes. I'd like to stay here, please. I need to hear everything first-hand.'

'Ok', said Steve, putting a folder down on the desk, 'it's all a bit cosy, isn't it?'

With Clive sitting on the bed, Alan set up a video camera on a tripod and pointed it towards Clive.

'It's easier than writing everything down', explained Alan as he set up the equipment.

David moved out of camera-shot.

'There may be a few details about Clive's work that could be considered sensitive information. I appreciate you have a job to do, but I might suggest you keep focussed on the case, not on the technical background to Clive's work.'

'Ok', said Steve, 'but this is potentially a murder enquiry. I'll need answers to a few questions to ensure I can check things out. If there's something you're not happy with, then we can stop the interview and talk about it off the record, if that helps?'

'Thank you', replied David.

Alan had finished setting up and he sat down in the other chair.

'Right', said Steve, 'let's begin. With me, Detective Inspector Steve White, I have Detective Sergeant Alan West, David Harswell, and Michael Knollys. What can you tell me about the explosion at around 8:30 AM on the 11th March 2014 at 136 Sheringham Drive?'

'Very little', replied Clive, 'I was presenting at a police training conference and saw a news report in the coffee shop after I finished. I went back to my hotel room and rang you.'

'Ok. You said you thought someone was trying to kill you.

Who would that be, do you think?'

'I don't know - I've been working on something ...', Clive looked at David, '... it's a technical problem - someone's stealing information from computer systems. We think it's gathering information from systems inside some of the agencies - we saw it grabbing data from my own computer and FBI systems, so there's a chance it's also doing it to your computers too.'

'What, like a virus?', asked Steve.

'Sort of - but much more intelligent. It hides its tracks.'

'And why would that make you a target for this type of attack, do you think?'

'I think someone found out that we had discovered it.'

'We?'

'Yes, I was working with the FBI's Special Operations department - I only flew back a couple of weeks ago. Derek Groban's the director of the department, then there's Paul Whiteman, and then there was Paul Davis. Paul died in a car accident the day after we cracked the encryption.'

David raised his hand.

'Recording stopped at 11:52', said Steve as he stopped the video recorder.

'I'm dealing the FBI side of things', said David, 'I can confirm that a Paul Davis died in a road traffic collision. At this time, the FBI has left the investigation to the US Police, who suggest that Paul Davis may have fallen asleep at the wheel while driving home. The FBI has no intention of taking it any further.'

'Ok', thanks said Steve, 'can we carry on?'

'Please do.'

Steve restarted the video recorder.

'Interview resumed at 11:54'.

Steve used what he thought was a gentler tone. 'Now, with respect to Jason Haggely - how did you know him?'

'I've known Jason for years - first met him at a pub in Leek. He was drunk and had been thrown out of his mother's house for something - arguing, I think. Anyway, he was going to sleep in a friend's car - but this was January, and a cold one at that.

'I couldn't see him sleeping in a car in that weather when I had a perfectly good spare bed!'

'Do you make a habit of picking up homeless men?', asked Steve.

'No', laughed Clive, 'he'd only been thrown out that night. I thought a roof over his head might help him out - on a very temporary basis, until he'd found somewhere more permanent.

'Anyway, he went up for a shower and came down prancing around naked. Needless to say, he slept with me that night - and for the next three months or so. He went to Manchester to work, and ended up staying there - arrived back, drunk, naturally - and stayed with me again. A pattern he's repeated a few times. He travels for work, spends what he earns and ends up penniless back at mine when the work dries up.

'This time, though, he'd been shagging some woman that was either married or attached in some way to a local mafia guy, by the sound of it. He'd been found out and had come to me so he could lay low for a while.

'To be honest, it suited me - I love his company. We actually agreed to make a go of it - so he'd just moved in permanently.'

'Ahh', said Steve.

Clive carried on, 'Well, if you can call a bin liner with a few clothes moving in! Comes to something when you can carry all you own in a bin liner.'

Clive sighed. He was resisting the urge to cry, but he was clearly upset.

'What can you tell me about the woman or mafia guy?'

'Nothing - I don't know them. In fact, I have never even seen them. Sorry.'

'That's Ok. Can you recall anything Jason said about them?'

'Only that they were scary - but he'd probably be able to bring them back round again. He can do that - he has a way of disarming people. Somehow, he can just turn on the charm and get away with pretty much anything.'

Clive felt tears running down his cheek.

'But not this time', he whispered more to himself than anyone else in the room.

After spending some time going through Clive's history, his family, and MKI, Steve called Mark Lockhurst and asked him to bring some of the site photographs with him.

Mark was the force's senior analyst. Clive thought that Mark looked exactly as a senior analyst should - tall, bespectacled, suited. Mark had worked for the police as a civilian for most of his career. He had transformed the process of data analysis - and brought the force, kicking and screaming, into the right century at least.

Having worked through numerous confidential and intelligence cases, Mark had a huge amount of experience of dealing with data relating to cases involving the mafia, extortion, fraud, and terrorists. Mark had also developed several analysis tools to improve how police officers could visualise crime scene data. To most people around him, Mark was an extremely valuable and competent, if somewhat geeky, resource.

'Ok', said Mark in his broad Yorkshire accent, 'we took some photographs just after fire and rescue cleared the area. I'm only showing you a few of the pictures because I'm only interested in the technology. I'm trying to work out what should be in the picture - and if there's anything there that shouldn't be, if that makes sense?'

'Yeah, perfect sense', replied Clive, who managed to surprise himself - he actually wanted to see the damage done.

'It's a bit of a mess', said Mark, half apologetically.

Mark opened a mauve folder and started to lay out a selection of A4 prints on the table.

'These', he said, pointing to the first couple of pictures, 'seem to be close to the main blast site. The others move further away for the epicentre.'

Clive stood up and looked at the pictures.

'Geez! What a mess.'

'Sorry, I guess it's a bit brutal', said Mark.

'It's ok - I hadn't expected it to be quite that bad …', said Clive.

Steve, Alan, and David also stood and looked at the pictures. Actually, Alan and Steve were watching Clive more than looking at the pictures: Clive's body language could give them huge amount of information.

'Ok?', asked Mark.

"Yes', said Clive, looking at each picture in turn. 'I'm struggling to work out where everything is - pass me the pad and I'll draw out where everything was, then we can look at these again …'

Clive quickly sketched out a plan of the kitchen/diner and the position of all the equipment that had been there when he left the house.

'So', he said, 'if we go back to the pictures …'

Mark handed Clive a pack of highlighter pens and they started highlighting obvious parts of each piece of equipment all colour keyed back to the sketch.

After about half an hour or so, Clive stepped back.

'Right', he said, 'we're missing the protocol analyser and the router. I also think there's a drive missing from my PC.

Can you tell if it had its case on at the time of the blast? Look', he said pointing the one of the photographs, 'this is the chassis - and I would have thought the case would have protected it - or would still have been around the chassis.'

'What else did you say?', asked Mark.

'A protocol analyser and my router: the protocol analyser's only small, so it could be under something - it's in a plastic case and looks like this …', Clive sketched out a rough-and-ready picture of the analyser.

'Do you have anything showing the wall above this lot?', he asked, 'because it looks like my system design has gone too …'

'Sure', said Mark and fetched his tablet. He called up a series of scene photo's trying to shield the gory scene from Clive as much as possible. 'Here.'

Clive looked and then nodded.

'Yes - there should be a system design on the wall here', he said, pointing to an area clearly marked with scorch patterns. You know, that's weird …'

'What?', asked Steve immediately.

'Well, I would have thought that the wall would have been at least a little protected from the paper stuck to it - I mean, if that burned after, I would have expected to have seen where it was … it looks like the rest of the wall … just weird.'

'I can ask our fire experts about that', said Steve, 'I take it you're suggesting it was removed before the explosion?'

'Possibly', replied Clive, and sat back down on the bed. He suddenly felt overwhelmed again.

'We'll call it a day', said Steve, although we'll probably need to speak to you again over the next few days.'

'Yeah, sure', replied Clive.

'By the way - was the safe intact?'

'Safe?', asked Steve.

'Yes - it's under the stairs. It's a fire safe so it might have survived. I had it fitted when I was tendering for projects with these guys', said Clive, looking at David.

'I've got the keys here …'

Clive walked over to his coat and pulled a set of keys out of the right hand pocket. After a few minutes of working on the keyring, he passed the key to Mark.

'There are a few memory cards and pieces of kit in there amongst my notes. I strongly suggest you copy anything on a non-networked machine before doing anything with the content of those cards. They hold the only proof that I have - and a working copy of the protocol analyser software. Please take great care of it.'

David held his hand out to Mark.

'It might be more appropriate for me to look after that. We'll make sure you get a copy of anything you need.'

Mark and raised a questioning eyebrow towards Steve. Steve nodded, so Mark handed the key over to David.

'Yes of course', said Clive to David, 'Sorry - I hadn't thought that the safe might contain sensitive material. I'm not thinking properly.'

Steve, Alan, and Mark left the room and advised Clive that they'd send the PPS officer back up when they got back to the hotel lobby.

'Interesting', said Steve to Alan as they walked down the corridor, 'seems our intelligence friends are taking this guy seriously. I wonder how long we'll have the case …'

At that moment, Steve's 'phone rang.

'DCI White, hello'

'Hello Sir', said a voice, 'it's DS Bates. We've just had a call from traffic. They've picked up a young man driving a black Mercedes. He and the car are on their way to the station now so I'll go down and meet them because the driver says his name's Jason Haggely.'

'What?', exclaimed Steve, 'If Haggely's alive then who the

hell was in that house?'

33

'Haggely certainly adds a new twist alright', said Dennis Keeling, Steve's immediate boss, 'what happened to him?'

'Well, Sir', replied Steve, 'it turns out that Brendan Burke, MKI's CEO had turned up to talk to Haggely. I think it's a case of checking that Haggely wasn't about to run off with Knollys and the crown jewels! Haggely wanted to get some cigarettes and milk, I gather. Burke's car was blocking the drive so, according to Haggely, Burke told him to take the Merc. When Haggely came back, the house was gone and police were coming from all directions. Thinking he had warrant out for his arrest, and being in Burke's car, he turned round and disappeared.

'He says he was bringing the car to the police when traffic stopped him. Not sure I'm entirely convinced, shall we say?'

'So this puts this Burke chap in the house at the time of the explosion - have we confirmed that yet?'

'Not yet - information to date suggested that Burke had gone to Barcelona to attend a conference. The rest of the Burke family are on holiday, and I think Brendan Burke intended to join them after the conference. We're checking up on all of that now.'

'How do you want to handle it now then?', asked Dennis,

standing up and walking towards the large windows at the end of his office.

Steve squinted slightly as he looked towards the silhouette of his immediate superior. Dennis was in his late fifties, in good shape for his age. He had short grey hair. The police had been his sole career - in fact, it had been his entire life. He had moved through the ranks relatively quickly before stagnating at the rank of Superintendent.

With the introduction of Police Commissioners and the extreme pressure on funding, he thought it unlikely he would progress any further in the force, so he wanted to work his last few years and then retire on a good pension. Something of a political animal, he had a reputation of getting his own way, even if it meant treading on a few toes along the way.

However, Dennis looked after those he considered worked well, and Steve had never really encountered any problems with his management style. Steve was obviously on the 'working well list'.

'Well, Sir', replied Steve, 'I think we need to split this case into three strands: we have Knollys and his MI5/FBI friends - God knows where that will take us; then we've got Haggely and, at the moment, he claims he could have been the target thanks to a tete-a-tete with the Pooles; then we've got Burke and the company side of things - we've done very little on this side at the moment as we're pretty much saturated …'

'Alright, I think we need to bring in another deputy SIO to help out on the Burke line - a couple of DC's to do the legwork. But let's try and keep away from trips out to Barcelona!'

Dennis turned back round to look at Steve.

'What's happening with the cloak-and-dagger-clan?', he asked, referring to David Harswell.

'You know those guys', replied Steve, 'they've got their guy installed in the investigation so they're getting everything we know. We, of course, see nothing coming back the other way - yet.

'They wanted to speak to Knollys before and after the formal interview. But I don't know what's going on there at the moment.'

'Hmm', replied Dennis, 'not entirely unexpected. All a bit unlikely if you ask me - anyway, if you think they know something that could close that line of enquiry, let me know and I'll make some noise on your behalf.'

'Listen up everyone …', shouted Steve, '… let's get started.'

The noise in the team conference area subsided.

'Right - you've probably already seen that Haggely is no longer the poor unfortunate soul in the house. It looks like that honour now belongs to one Brendan Burke, MKI's Chief Exec. We had believed that he was en-route to Barcelona attending a conference before joining his family on annual leave.

'We know it's not Haggely, because we picked him up yesterday, driving Burke's black Mercedes. That, at least, tallies with some of the witness statements about a black car being seen in the area around the time of the explosion.

'However, Haggely has confirmed that he was playing the field with Julie Poole, of the Poole Family fame. It's not beyond reason to assume that Mark Poole could have wanted harm to come to Haggely - we've brought Poole in to investigate that line of enquiry.'

Steve paused for a moment, and then continued, 'Scenario two looks like Knollys and Burke were either collective or individual targets. Who knew Burke was at the Knollys house? Was there something going on at MKI that could warrant the removal of Burke and/or Knollys? The list goes on.

'So, we need to dig a lot more in Burke's background, and

do a complete investigation into MKI. To that end, I have asked for extra support. I think you've probably all met DS Gary Collier …'

Gary stood up, nodded to the assembled team, and then sat down again.

'… And I'd also like to extend a welcome to DC Kevin Chauhan and DC Sara Lawson.'

Both officers waved to the rest of the team as they heard their names.

'DS Collier is acting as a second Deputy Senior Investigating Officer, and concentrating on Burke and MKI. After this meeting, please arrange to run through anything you have with respect to these two areas of the investigation only.

'This then leaves us with the other lines of enquiry, so where are we up to? Let's being with the technology - Mark.'

Mark Lockhurst stood up and walked towards the board.

'We have had a couple of responses back from the mobile operators. But we're still waiting for the others. We have determined that Knollys' mobile was only active from the area of the hotel and conference centre. So his 'phone was where he said he was prior to, and at the time of, the explosion.

'The forensic recovery of computer equipment continues. As you can imagine, it's proving difficult to determine what's what. However, Knollys yesterday suggested that some equipment had disappeared from the scene.

'I've asked SOCO to look for equipment looking like these items here and here', he said pointing to sketches Clive had provided the day before.

'We're also missing a technical drawing. To a certain extent, we're lucky because Knollys says he photographed it using his mobile. We have yet to go through all of the data on his handset as it's a 64GB device: it's a huge amount of data to trawl through!

'So, if we can't find these items, then we could be looking at intellectual property theft - but it means someone knew what they were looking for. This is, after all, pretty specialised knowledge.

'We are now in receipt of data from Burke's Mercedes. We are now checking with Tracker and the on-board satnav, along with the CCTV archives to validate Haggely's statements and whereabouts at the time of the explosion.

'We only received Haggely's 'phone last night, so we have yet to look at it. It's pretty high-up on the priority list though. But, just to set expectations, it might take a few days to get anything useful from the network operators. I would expect to start getting that back at the beginning of next week, so nothing usable until mid-next week.

'Finally, we've seen nothing on any of Knollys' bank accounts since the explosion. Knollys had a current account and two savings accounts: we've seen nothing strange going on in any of these accounts. I can't find any other accounts tied to Knollys.

'Haggely only has a savings account and a cash-card. Not entirely surprising that - I doubt he has a usable credit history. Again, nothing of consequence to report there.

'We're still processing the computer systems recovered, prioritising Knollys' laptop. As the search teams provide more technology, we'll look at it. If you need anything prioritising, then please let me know and I'll see what I can do.'

Mark sat down while Steve continued.

'Thanks Mark. We're formally saying 'thanks and goodbye' to George Kerr today - George, we appreciate the support and assistance from the counter-terrorism department. Richard?'

Richard Duff, the family liaison officer stood up.

'Well, we've started enquiries to find Burke's family over in

Spain. I'll pass over all the information to date to DS Collier and his team.

'We've been proceeding on the basis that Haggely was missing but potentially the victim, and will now go back to the Haggely family members to formally advise them that he is alive …'

'Not yet, please', interrupted Steve, 'first it's worth checking whether he'll be at risk from the Poole Family or anyone else for that matter.'

'Ok, Sir', replied Richard, then continued.

'Other than that, we're getting assistance in sorting out familial background profiles. Nothing significant to report - a typically dysfunctional family unit - father disappeared; mother working to support the kids, one disabled, couldn't also find the time for Jason or his drinking, so ended up chucking him out. She doesn't see a lot of him at all, when she does, it's usually him arriving drunk begging for a bed for the night or some cash.'

'Knollys has a much more standard family - brother, sister, both parents alive and well. All friendly enough - although understandably concerned. At the request of the PPS, we have provided very little information about his current status.'

Richard sat down.

'Thanks Richard - anything new from forensics?', asked Steve.

'Still processing', replied Oliver Wickes, the scientific support officer, 'we still can't determine the cause of the explosion for sure. We can't find any unusual chemical signatures - although that doesn't rule out things made from domestic ingredients. It does appear to have been an extremely powerful explosion, however.

'We're still analysing tissue samples and beyond saying we only have one body so far, I can only say that we should have initial findings on these samples soon. I was hoping to have more for you by now, but it's a massive scene to process. Sorry it's not more yet.'

'Ok', said Steve, 'I appreciate that it's a lot of work - just keep me posted.'

Steve looked around the room.

'Where's Greg?'

'I'm over here …'.

'Oh, good. Today we're going to bring Haggely and Knollys back together, and let Knollys know about the likelihood, pending confirmation, that Burke was in the house. I'd rather he hears it from us than Haggely. Therefore, I'd like you to come with us. Also, Richard, we could do with you too. I've sent the request over to PPS, so they'll find somewhere for us all to meet up - hopefully a little bigger than yesterday's hotel room!'

Greg Jones, a behavioural investigative advisor had been involved in the team meetings, but had not really had much to do until now. With MI5 all over Clive's interviews, Steve hadn't wanted to go in 'mob-handed' and overwhelm Clive emotionally. Because of David Harswell's request not to release information about the hacking investigation, Greg hadn't even seen the video recordings of Clive's interview.

The PPS had arranged for everyone to meet up in a hired meeting room at the Crewe Arms Hotel - a large hotel immediately opposite the station in Crewe.

'At least this time', thought Clive, 'we won't all end up sitting on a bed together.'

David came into the room pulling a medium-sized black suitcase on wheels. He looked at the PPS officer and asked for a few moments with Clive alone - before the investigation team arrvied.

'Here you go', said David, opening the suitcase. Inside was

a collection of equipment, all neatly placed within a customised foam structure.

'I was expecting a carrier bag', said Clive, moving towards the suitcase.

'Well, you know us. I mentioned you're somewhat mobile at the moment, so they want to protect their investment. Give it back to me if you don't need it.'

'No, no. It's good - actually, it's very good. They keep moving me around, so it's handy to have something to keep all this lot safe.'

David handed Clive a manilla envelope.

'Here's some cash and the memory cards from your safe. They're copies - we had to hand the originals over to the police to protect the chain of evidence. Currently, we have them under an embargo directive, so they won't look at them unless they can convince us that they need to.'

'Thanks', said Clive, 'doing nothing's been driving me mad! Any news from the outside world?'

'Beyond the case, no. Obviously I can't discuss the police investigation with you at the moment, so all I'll say is that we're keeping a watching brief on the investigation - and doing a little of our own.'

'Fair enough - it's the first time I've been on this side of the fence.'

'I'm assuming you're not going to use any existing online identities?', asked David.

'How stupid do you think I am?'

'Yeah - sorry. I get to ask all the stupid questions.'

David asked Clive to sign a receipt for the equipment and bag. Just as Clive had handed the signed document back, there was a knock on the door.

'Hello, it's Steve'

Clive closed the suitcase and put it on the floor, while David opened the door.

Steve walked in to the room, accompanied by Alan West and Greg Jones.

'Hello Clive', said Steve, 'you've already met detective sergeant Alan West, today I have brought Dr Gregory Jones who is assisting with the investigation.'

After shaking hands, the group sat around a large conference table, set with paper pads and pens. Steve opened one of the water bottles and poured himself a glass of water before passing the bottle around the table.

'We have some additional news - and I'm afraid it's a bit mixed - good and bad. But before we get to that, we could do with asking a couple of questions about the relationship between yourself and Brendan Burke.'

'Bren?', asked Clive looking surprised, 'Why - do you think he had something to do with this?'

'Not in that sense - were you on good terms with Bren?'

'Absolutely - we've been friends for years. He's been covering for me while I worked on Uncle Peter ...'

'Uncle Peter?', asked Steve.

'Sorry, yes - Uncle Peter - I called the computer project Uncle Peter: it gave me an easy way to send messages to Bren to let him know what we were dealing with: Uncle Peter's got a lot worse or Uncle Peter seems to be communicating - that kind of thing. Easier to do that if there's a proper name for it.

'Anyway, we didn't want to worry the rest of the board about Uncle Peter's activities. After all, MKI provides security and privacy protection systems - if something breaches that lot, then we have a very real problem. Something like that could close the business, or severely reduce its value. Our investors would probably run a mile too. We had to keep it largely secret.'

'But you told your customers? MI5, the FBI?'

'I had to - it's national security', said Clive and looked towards David, 'I've been involved in a couple of projects over the past few years - even from the little I've seen, this could seriously compromise what they're doing.'

'So you tell your customers but not your own board?'

'I told Bren. Then I told two customers - those I considered had a need to know. I told them in confidence and started working with them to ensure that we still provided protection. The rest of the board are also investors - I have a duty to protect the company and this would seriously worry them, especially as I hadn't proved anything beyond a suspicion.

'If I can work out how to stop this thing, and provide a detector for it, then I have a new product for MKI. The equipment I was making could analyse and stop Uncle Peter - along with anything similar. The protocol analyser/recorder was taking shape nicely - a dedicated piece of equipment that would be capable of updating itself from a central repository of known attacks, automatically blocking this type of thing out - but at a network level. There's a consumer market, there's the opportunity to embed what I was creating in every domestic router, in every company, in every network … it's potentially huge!'

'Ok', said Steve, 'daft question then - do you think a competitor would want to do this to you?'

'Come on', said Clive, 'competitors are all bigger than us. They can buy us - it's a company, buy a license, buy our products or buy the entire company - they wouldn't need to take me out, I'd sell for any reasonable price!'

'Did the rest of the board share this opinion? Did Bren?'

'Yes! We set the company up to sell it. Prove the design, build a prototype, and then put the whole thing up for sale - we only created products to prove the concept and give us revenue - all to add value before we sold out. It was the plan from the beginning.'

'How would you describe your relationship with Bren?'

'Odd question!', said Clive, 'Good.'

'Were you …', asked Steve - a little unsure how best to phrase his question.

'Lovers?', said Clive with a broad grin, ' Hell no! He joined a company we set up a few years ago. He sort of gave me the concept for this company and we set it up together when the last one was acquired. He's a happily - or at least I think it's happy - he's married. And yes, I get on with Deb, Bren's wife too - although I don't see a lot of her or the rest of the family. It's pretty much a work relationship, but we've become good friends through working together.'

'That makes this all the harder', said Steve.

'What does?'

'Last night, we picked up Jason Haggely - he's been in hiding since the explosion at your house. At this stage', said Steve choosing his words very carefully, 'we have reason to believe that Bren was in the house at the time of the explosion. I will, however, say that we have yet to complete forensic tests to prove this either way. Jason has, however, suggested that Bren had lent him his car to go to and buy cigarettes a few minutes before the explosion.'

Clive was stunned. He started shaking and the colour drained from his face. Steve thought Clive would pass out and poured a glass of water, passing it to Clive over the table.

'Here', he said gently, 'drink.'

Clive picked up the glass with shaking hands and sipped from the glass.

'This is fucked up!', he said.

Steve carried on.

'Listen to me - at this stage, we have not confirmed that Bren was in the house. As we found Jason, we know for sure it's not him - Jason said he left Bren to go and buy cigarettes, but until we have completed that part of the investigation, we can't say for sure.'

'You've spoken to Jason? He's Ok?'

'Yes, he's fine. He's been sleeping in Bren's car since the explosion - I think he thought there was a warrant for his arrest for non-payment of some fine or other ... did you know anything about that?'

'Yes', replied Clive, 'but I'd paid it off for him. I was going to tell him when I got back - it was only a couple of hundred ...'

'Ok', said Steve, 'now we still have a couple of lines of enquiry to pursue that involve Jason, but I'm happy to add him to the protection order, if you want him here with you at this time.'

'Yes!', exclaimed Clive.

'Before you say that - bear in mind that if you want him to join you under the arrangements of the protected person service, then you are effectively both in this together for the time being - I can't have Jason dropping in and out of protection. It could be a long-term arrangement ...'

'If Jason's Ok with that, then it's what I wanted anyway.'

Clive's emotions were all over the place: part of him wanted to scream and shout with joy because Jason was safe, the other part wanting to burst into tears at the loss of Bren. Yet another part was already questioning the viability of MKI without Bren - he hadn't really thought about the fact that if he was under the protection of the PPS then MKI would have to fend for itself anyway.

'What will happen to MKI? What does the board know?', asked Clive.

'At the moment, we haven't really said anything - we need to be sure of our facts first. We're telling you because Jason will tell you anyway - it's better that you hear it from us first.'

'When can I see Jason?', asked Clive.

'Now, if you'd like?'

Clive looked up and nodded.

'Please.'

Steve pulled his 'phone out of his jacket pocket.

'Hi Richard?', he said into the device after placing the call, 'will you bring Jason here, thanks.'

The silence in the room was deafening to Clive. Every second seemed to go on for hours. Clive felt he was on a stage with everyone watching him while they waited. No-one really wanted to break the silence.

A knock on the door made Clive jump. Alan stood up and opened the door.

Clive stood up and, seeing Jason, immediately burst into tears. The little remaining colour drained from Clive's face and he looked like he was going to fall. Jason ran over to him and caught Clive in his arms.

'Hey, hey, hey', he said softly, 'it's ok. It's ok'.

Clive just sobbed and sobbed against Jason. With a soft click the door closed and Jason realised that he and Clive were alone in the room together.

'What the hell do you think you're doing?', shouted Steve to David Harswell and John, 'we've got Knollys under PPS and you're giving him computers and communications equipment! How the hell can I protect him if he goes online?'

'There's a potential national security issue here and that has to take priority.'

David closed Steve's office door.

'Clive's not stupid - he won't use any existing accounts or anything traceable. You have to bear in mind he's one of 'the hidden': the people that can work invisibly on the Internet. He leaves absolutely nothing behind him - you hear of digital fingerprinting: I'd challenge you to find a single ridge!'

Steve looked unconvinced. David carried on.

'He's run training courses on this stuff - even this police force has used his techniques for forensic analysis. If he wants to go dark, then he will - and there's nothing we can do to stop it. We may as well embrace, monitor, and control it - as much as we can.

'I'll level with you: he's either a solution to a problem, he's part of the problem, or he's created the problem - tactically, we want to see which camp he falls into.'

'What do you mean?', asked Steve, calming down a little.

'Has he created this problem to demonstrate technical skill? Is this merely a guise sell more equipment - scaremongering, if you will? Is he part of an organisation that intends to do damage by revealing weaknesses in national security, making him part of a techterror network? At the other end of the scale, is he a legitimate target and, therefore, at risk?'

David looked very intently at Steve.

'Right now, it helps to keep him partially isolated, focussed on this stuff, and away from distractions. I'm his handler for now and I want to see where he goes with this Uncle Peter technology.'

'You're his handler?'

'And have been for some time.'

'So he's MI5 too?'

'He just doesn't know it. The most valuable assets are those that don't know they are assets.'

'That brings a new dimension to the case - anything else you haven't told me?', asked Steve.

'Only that our friends in the FBI thought Clive was on to something significant. So much so that they were positioning to keep him on US soil. We forced the issue and pulled him back here before they got their talons in too deep - or 'disappeared him' - Clive, of course, knows nothing about that.

'I need to know if this was a hit. If it was a hit, then I also need to know if it was down to this pratt Haggely, something to do with MKI, a crime syndicate targeting Clive, or something else. Tactically, it makes sense for you to run the case publicly - do what you do. If you uncover something that puts it back in our camp, then John will let me know and we can go from there.'

David stretched.

'We have to let your investigation run so we know which it is.'

Steve noted the "let your investigation run" and felt a little deflated. Perhaps, he was just a pawn in a much bigger game.

'If it falls into the 'something else' category what do you want me to do?', he asked.

'We'll cross that bridge if and when we get to it.'

34

Jason kissed the back of Clive's neck gently and ran his hands down Clive's chest. Clive had been awake for a while but didn't want to leave Jason alone for a moment.

Clive turned his head.

'Morning', he said.

'Morning', said Jason and moved closer, pulling Clive's naked body closer towards him.

'I've been thinking', said Clive, 'can you go shopping for me?'

'Shopping?'

'Yes. I could do with a new 'phone - I've got cash. It has to be a cash deal with no questions asked. And it's got to be a smartphone - I want to jailbreak it.'

'Can't you?'

'No - I don't want anyone to know I've got it and I doubt the PPS will leave me alone.'

'Ok, I'll go for some cigarettes or something.'

'They'll want to come with you', said Clive, referring to the PPS officers. He continued, 'They'll want to make sure you're not out on your own.'

'I'll use my best sweet and innocent smile, it always works.'

'Sweet and innocent, you?', joked Clive.

'Works on you', replied Jason with a thrust forward.

'Are you saying I'm easy?'

'Easy - I wouldn't even go that far - desperate more like.'

'Cheeky bugger'

'Talking of buggery …'

Jason wrapped his arms and legs around Clive with obvious intentions.

'No', whispered Clive, 'we can't - not with them outside.'

'Fuck that!', said Jason, 'Let's give them something to talk about.'

'The problem with this lot', said Mark Lockhurst, 'is that we don't know what's on the laptop.'

'What do you mean?', asked Steve.

'Well, we know the hard-drive is encrypted and password protected. I got the password to it from Clive. The problem then is that I don't know what I'm looking at without doing a huge amount of work.

'Take this, for example', he said, showing a file listing, 'here's a list of files in Clive's documents folder. I can work out that some of them are secure vaults - I don't have the password for these - but I'm having to look at all the files on the system to work out whether we're missing additional vaults - or whether we're even looking at the right ones …'

'Surely you can just start with those you've already found?'

'Again - the type of encryption used here allows you to support two different modes at the same time. With one password, it reads from the front of the file and goes towards the back, as you'd expect; enter a different password and it reads from the back of the file towards the front. He has to have one password - the one that accesses the vault normally, but we have no idea if the other one exists, it gives him what's called plausible deniability. He can give us a password, we access his secure data, and everyone's happy - him especially so because he's only given us access to the softer data. He can keep the other password entirely to himself and we'll be none the wiser.

'This is robust encryption. There is no way of knowing if he's used the dual or hidden file-system mechanism or not. It's really not simple - Clive uses a whole series of management tools to categorise and file his data - I've never seen anything like it.'

'So what do you want to do?', asked Steve.

'Well', said Mark, 'it's a little unorthodox, but, I'd like to ask Clive to go through this stuff with me. Or at least explain the methods used, if he will. It'll save a huge amount of time and effort.'

'Can we work off copies to keep the evidential chain intact?'

'Absolutely. I'd imagine Clive wouldn't want my size 12's trampling all over his data anyway!'

'Ok. Let me talk to the PPS and I'll get you and Clive together. The odds are that you'll have one of our friends from the confidential team with you - either John or David. I'd suggest you keep them up to date - but after you tell me. I get to know everything first, ok?'

Jason stood next to the bedroom door in the hallway, facing the open door to the flat's living room. He was naked, sweating slightly, his face and chest blushing from his exertions in the bedroom.

'Hey - have you got any ciggies?', he asked the PPS officer who was sat watching the TV.

'Jesus! Put some clothes on for fuck's sake'.

'Chuck me a ciggie, come on.'

'I don't smoke.'

'Oh - in that case I'll pop down and get some then. Ok?'

The PPS officer cursed under his breath.

'Look I'm on my own for another couple of hours - you shouldn't leave here. I'll see if I can get some delivered …'

'Well, if you're getting deliveries, there's a chemist on the corner too - can you get me some Nair or Veet - he's let himself go a bit and there's nothing worse than pubes in your mouth - oh, and some lube - he might not be able to walk properly if we keep doing it dry …'

'STOP! Too much information!', exclaimed the poor PPS officer.

'Go - get what you need, but please use your hoodie and be back as quick as you can. If you're more than 30 minutes, we'll be gone.'

Jason gave a broad grin.

'Thanks - I'll be so quick you won't even know I was gone.'

He bounded back into the bedroom and pulled on a pair of grey tracksuit pants and his hoodie. Pulling on socks and trainers, he glanced over at Clive. Clive climbed out of bed and grabbed some cash from his MI5-supplied stash.

'Did you have to?', Clive asked.

Jason kissed him passionately and loudly, then said quietly, 'he won't want to be buying our sex toys - best way I could get out on my own. Wait until I ask for a vibrator to use on you!'

Clive grinned, and said, 'No - just no.'

'And besides', continued Jason, 'you were nearly sporting some stubble down there - it's murder on my face!'

Clive aimed a good-humoured slap in Jason's general direction. Jason dodged the slap and ran out of the flat, slamming the door behind him.

Clive put a dressing gown on and somewhat sheepishly headed towards the living room.

'Sorry about Jason - he's a bit of a handful sometimes.'

'It's Ok - my job's to look after you pair - but I'm going to need counselling if that kind of trauma continues. I'll put the kettle on - drink?'

'Yeah, coffee please', replied Clive as he sat down, he wanted to keep the PPS officer busy while Jason shopped for him.

'I must apologise - I've been a bit antisocial over the past few days.'

'No worries mate', said the PPS officer from the kitchen, 'you've been through a lot.'

For the next few minutes they drank their coffees and talked about anything other than the case. The TV carried on chattering away in the background, somehow the noise helped break the occasional silences while the two talked.

The PPS officer stood up quickly as Jason slipped his key into the flat's front door. Jason closed and then deadlocked the door, before walking into the living room.

'Everything Ok?', asked the PPS officer.

'Yep!', said Jason cheerfully. He threw a small carrier bag to Clive and then

noisily grabbed his own crotch through the tracksuit pants.

'Go and prepare yourself - I might need to inspect you've done everywhere properly!'

Clive caught the bag, blushed, and headed towards the bathroom.

Jason looked at the PPS officer, sat down, and said, 'What? I've been on my own for a few days - my balls are still full.'

The crotch-grabbing distraction had done its job and kept the PPS officer's attention away from the carrier bag. The PPS officer beat a hasty retreat into the kitchen to make Jason and himself a drink.

Clive closed the bathroom door and looked inside the bag. Jason had bought a reasonable 'phone along with a couple of top-up vouchers. He'd also put a couple of tubes of Nair in the bag - the wait after the cream's application would give Clive enough time to set up the 'phone so he could make it look like it was part of the equipment given to him by MI5. He assembled the various components, put the device back into the carrier bag, and then started the shower.

'Morning everyone', said Steve.

'Things are starting to become a little clearer - let's begin with Mr Wickes and the scientific community.'

Oliver stood up.

'Good morning - we have finally managed to confirm that the remains belonged to Brendan Burke. It's taken a lot longer because of the force of the explosion. It looks like Burke's lungs exploded as well as the environment around him. We think he had inhaled a reasonable amount of the gas and within the confined space, it literally blew him apart.

'DNA matches samples taken from Burke's family, so we have a positive identity.

'Unfortunately, we have not been able to confirm the full reason behind the explosion. It certainly started at, or near to, the gas meter. However, it was so comprehensively destroyed that we still haven't pieced it all together. We have asked the manufacturer to assist us in this regard.

'The explosion was intense and extremely hot. It did a huge amount of damage to the property - the explosion, fire, and subsequent actions to control the fire really have left us very little to be more definitive. To date, we have not found an accelerant - petrol, alcohol etc.

'We have received a lot of electronic equipment via the SOCO team and continue to try and piece it all together. Knolly's map of his kit has really helped us in that regard.

'I am surprised by the intensity of the explosion, but have no evidence to suggest the use of conventional explosives either. Basically, we have nothing to support anything other than a gas explosion - other than its intensity. It also seems odd that, with such an amount of gas in the building, Burke remained in the premises. He must have been able to smell it!'

'Ok, thanks - Anna.'

Anna Hibbert stood up and walked towards the board while Oliver sat down.

'My scene of crime team has now mapped out the entire site. We have 3D models available on the network - so please let me know if you need access to them.

'We are now in a position to move some of the debris and have brought in local contractors to work with us to keep everything safe from a structural perspective while we strip things down - we're basically skimming a thin layer off, then going through a documentation and recovery process and repeating. It will take us another 2 or 3 days before we finish.

'I've also posted up all the photographs taken to date on the shared drive. Internally, I've marked them up so you will know what to expect before looking at the images.

'Here', she said pointing to the board, 'you'll see a few large-format shots, showing the scene as we've been working through it. With all the photographs, I've marked up on the house plan where we were, direction of shot etc. This should help orient you when looking at shots - on the computer, you can click on the house plan to see all images related to that particular location.

'The advice from the structural engineers is that the house will have to come down. For that reason, we're taking the approach of documenting and bagging everything, because once we clear the scene, they'll demolish the remaining structure.

'We also had the offer to take a few arial shots via the structural engineer's drone. It wouldn't distract us too much and might help, so I accepted the offer. As a result, we have both video and stills from above. These shots really show how big an explosion this was. The shots give us a much better view of the debris field - again, the projectile path points towards the gas meter - however, it would appear that there was some computer equipment near to the source too - as Oliver mentioned in his report, we passed that over to him and his team for further analysis.'

'Thanks Anna', said Steve, 'I'm getting that we still can't pin down the actual source of the explosion yet - or what caused it?'

'Correct sir', replied Anna, 'Personally, I'm leaning more towards a gas explosion, triggered by a spark from the computer equipment - but that's conjecture and our friends in the lab need to answer that for sure.'

'Ok, Richard', said Steve.

'Things have been busy with the Burke family', replied Richard Duff, the family liaison officer.

'We managed to contact them in Spain, with help from our Spanish colleagues. Deborah Burke, Brendan's wife, and their son Liam are flying back today and we have arranged to meet them. Clearly we need to handle the news about Knollys and Haggely sensitively, so I am intending to say that I don't have information regarding their current whereabouts - unless you'd prefer me to say anything different sir?'

'No, that's fine.'

'Ok, thank you.

'Yesterday, we put Haggely and Knollys back together - I think it'll help Knollys come to terms with Burke's demise - and it means he's not facing everything alone. They're now considered a family unit under PPS protection, so you'll need to go through DCI White if you need to talk to them and arrange an interview.'

'Indeed', replied Steve, 'anything from the other families - Knollys and Haggely?'

'Nothing significant sir.'

'Ok, in that case, moving on, Steve.'

Steve Bates, the investigative team leader, walked to the board and looked at the central section where he had posted a series of diagrams linking Haggely to the Poole Family, the local wannabe 'Mafia' group.

'I'll begin with Haggely: he has seriously upset Mark Poole, the self-styled head of the Poole Family. With the assistance of DS Bosson and the drugs team, we interviewed Poole to ask for information about his relationship with Haggely.

'He did, of course, deny having anything to do with the explosion. He claimed he didn't know where Haggely was hiding - and he used the term hiding - but admitted putting out a warning that Haggely would be in trouble if he ever approached the family again.

'He claimed that Haggely, in a drug and drink induced state, had sexually assaulted Julie Poole, causing Haggely to disappear.

'When asked why he didn't report it to the police, he replied that he preferred to handle things himself, and that it wouldn't have resulted in anything happening anyway. When we asked what he meant by "handling it himself", he said he would give Haggely "a strong talking to" - to make sure he understood he'd crossed the line and would never do it again. He suggested it was just a case of "putting the frighteners" on Haggely.

'We also spoke to Julie Poole and she refused to comment, merely saying she knew Haggely and that he had stayed with them while doing some building work in the house. She admitted to having a drink with him, but declined to provide any additional information.

'When confronted with the suggestion that he had sexually assaulted her, she declined to comment and said that "it was nothing" and that Mark had misread the situation. She also claimed to have tried calming things down between Haggely and the family.

'In and around the area, we have heard numerous reports of Poole looking for Haggely, and one person also admitted to a reward being offered for giving up his location. Another, we believe, was subjected to a more physical interrogation. It looks like Poole was serious about getting hold of Haggely, presumably to save face as much as anything. It's perhaps a good thing he's under protection at the moment.

'DS Bosson has asked that he be allowed to talk to Haggely if we've cleared him from our part of the investigation - he believes it may help provide the drugs team with more information about the inner workings of the Poole family. I said I'd pass that request on to you, sir.

'We have also confirmed that Haggely went to the local tobacconist - we have CCTV showing him in store with Burke's car outside at the time of the explosion. So he wasn't anywhere near the house at that time.

'Moving on to Knollys. We are uncovering more information by the day. We've imaged all of the MKI servers, prioritising the email and messaging platforms - these are with digital forensics now. It looks like Burke and Knollys pretty much ran the company and were pretty solid in progressing things for the business.

'Over the past few months, however, Knollys had dropped out of the company to look after a sick family member - and Burke had picked up most of the work, occasionally meeting Knollys and getting him to respond to urgent issues. Most of the staff seemed to think that pressure was beginning to build between Burke and Knollys, but none thought it extreme enough for one to want the other harmed.

'The story behind Knollys and Haggely seems to stack up - they've been seen together repeatedly over the years. The neighbours said they know when he's around because the garden gets tidier and all the odd-jobs get done.'

Next, Steve invited Dr Jones to talk.

'I was present at the reunion yesterday between Knollys and Haggely. All I can say is that the behaviours were exactly as I would expect. I think both of them are in varying levels of shock.

'You could argue that Haggely's behaviour was odd, given that he simply drove off - but I countered that with the potential for him believing he would be arrested and in the middle of something obviously much bigger.

'I'm not sure he was driving to surrender Burke's car - and I'm not entirely sure why he didn't just dump it. Perhaps it was the only place he had left to go - particularly if the Pooles were after him.

'Generally, though, I'm happy that both Haggely and Knollys are telling the truth, as far as we can tell. There are, of course, sections of the interviews I haven't been granted access to see …'

'Ok', countered Steve, 'we still have a few areas of the investigation that we need to manage directly. Moving on', said Steve and addressed his new SIO, DS Gary Collier, 'anything from MKI that we should know?'

Jason kept the PPS entertained to allow Clive to concentrate on getting his mobile, and the MI5-supplied equipment up and running.

Firstly, Clive plugged in the new burner 'phone that Jason had bought. Clive downloaded a network driver that would allow him to connect to hidden servers anonymously. Then, he entered the service encryption key into the device - immediately, he was prompted for his user name and password so that he could log in to the remote service.

Clive had wanted to protect MKI from most forms of

network attack. As he was a leading security and privacy advocate, he was often targeted by some idiot trying to take MKI offline, or score points off Clive directly. In order to counter this, Clive had created a dark-net copy of MKI's servers.

Without any in MKI knowing, he had created a reflection service that would silently copy MKI's server contents and distribute it over several hidden servers around the world. No single server carried all the information - so the loss of a single server wouldn't matter. Also, the only way to access the information on the server was by knowing the service key, and establishing a connection to a hidden service using that key.

The original covert network system was built in case someone managed to compromise MKI - perhaps even encrypting all data within the organisation and demanding payment to decrypt it - or one of the employees fell out with the company and decided to wreak havoc. This secret network was his baby, and he made sure it used all the latest techniques to stay hidden.

Clive started up a software delivery service and made a mental note of the service address - this changed every time the service started, so Clive would need to know this address to download MKI's software to his 'phone.

He then entered the address into the 'phone's browser and downloaded MKI's secure browser. After entering the relevant keys into the newly installed secure browser, he then accessed the hidden version of MKI's file system, and downloaded all the latest tools. Then he stopped the download service on the hidden network - he never left it running for longer than it was actually needed.

Clive installed the software he had just downloaded and restarted the 'phone. The 'phone hunted for a signal and then connected - Clive's software meant that the 'phone assumed a different identity every few minutes and tagged on to other people's data connections. In effect, Clive's 'phone appeared to the mobile networks like several random people, accessing secured services via encrypted channels. Because the data was encrypted and split between different operators, user accounts and networks, none of the networks or anyone monitoring communications would have access to all the information. Clive now had a covert handset and was completely anonymous.

Rather than allow information to leak out onto other networks, Clive connected to his dark-net service again and started up a distributed private network. This network ran across his hidden international servers and would allow Clive to lock down all communications so that only the traffic he authorised directly could get onto the open Internet - and even then, through a series of connections that would make it impossible to trace back to MKI's systems, or Clive.

Another 'phone restart later, Clive's handset displayed a secure network icon. Clive smiled - it had taken about 20 minutes to set everything up. 'Not bad', he thought to himself, given that this was the first time he'd used the entire system in anger.

Clive opened up the MKI communication suite and entered Whiteman's encryption key: a seemingly random set of letters and numbers that would allow the MKI network to connect with Whiteman's handset. As Whiteman would see a new device asking for permission to communicate, Clive added a phrase so that Whiteman would know it was Clive calling: "Dang Ma Diddlies if it aint the Englishman".

A few minutes later, just as Clive was beginning to wonder if the system was actually running properly, his handset responded with a connection confirmation message. Both handsets had established a secure channel through which Clive and Whiteman could exchange encrypted messages.

Clive: "Thank God you're still alive. Someone tried to kill me. Watch your back."

Whiteman: "WTF?"

Clive: "House blew up. They got Bren instead. I'm a protected person now."

Whiteman: "Sorry to hear that. A hit?"

Clive: "Thinking Paul - car accident. Me - gas explosion at my house - analyser and router taken. You - next?"

Clive: "MI5 all over me too. Provided me with replacement kit to keep working while in protection. Seems they want me to keep going."

Whiteman: "Strings attached? Bet all in a nice holdall.'

Clive: "Yes"

Whiteman: "They got you tagged man! It's what I'd do."

Clive hadn't thought about the bag being bugged. 'Damn', he thought, 'it's a nice case too.'

Whiteman: "I got booted off the case - said nothing. Wondered why you'd gone quiet."

Clive: "Police and 5 all over my kit. Analyser/router went missing in the explosion."

Whiteman: "Yes, saw that."

Clive: "Did you get message from me via MI5, warning you?"

Whiteman: "No"

Clive: "Some support network you've got."

Whiteman: "Not surprised. Told you I'm off the case. Head down."

Clive: "Keep it that way!"

Whiteman: "Got to go. Will contact you later. You might need cc - use one off the platform - Corporate Visa 5529 4203 5061 5465 Ex: 12/24 CCV: 002 name Summers Inc., 4470 Mission Blvd, San Diego, CA, 92109. Bitcoin-backed with $10K limit, no trace. Can top it up if necessary."

Clive made a note of the credit card details. As soon as the chat session closed, the data would disappear.

Clive: "Thanks! I wasn't expecting that. I'll pay you back as soon as I can"

Whiteman: "It's out of flexible funds - we need them sometimes to get into an organisation. Comes from running dark-nets. Officially I'm tracking a new Silk Road and need to fund 3rd party purchase of kit for it - can always bluff it out. There in case of emergency only."

Clive: "Understood. Thanks again."

Whiteman: "Bye for now. Talk later."

The messenger session closed.

Clive and Jason walked into the hotel conference room.

'Another day, another conference room', said Clive.

Mark Lockhurst was already in the room, along with Clive's laptop and a few remnants from the house.

'Hi Clive. Thanks for coming over', he said, extending a hand.

Clive shook Mark's hand.

'Glad to help - gives me another view of the outside world!'

Jason busied himself with the coffee pots in the corner.

'Coffee?', he asked Mark.

'Thanks', Mark replied and motioned for Clive to sit down at the conference table, 'please take a seat.

'I wanted to go through a few things with you. Mainly around access to the technology, but also Steve's asked me to get a better understanding of what you think you found - mainly because I don't think he understands the implications of it - I think I do, but am not really sure. Better to ask, if that's ok?'

'Sure', replied Clive.

While they waited for the coffee, Mark and Clive went quickly through the equipment recovered from the house and identified most of it.

'Thanks for that', said Mark as Jason put coffees down on the table, 'I wondered if you could take me through the missing equipment as well?'

'There are two main things missing: the first is a protocol recorder, the second being a modified router.'

'Modified to do what?'

Clive took Mark through a very high-level overview of the way that Uncle Peter worked. During the course of the conversation, Mark started asking questions that paralleled points that Paul Davis had raised. Clive began to warm to Mark and dropped into a lower-level of detail.

Jason lay down along the seats on the outside of the wall and started thumbing through one of the magazines provided by the hotel.

Clive took a sip of coffee and started to explain the FBI's stance on Uncle Peter.

'Once we confirmed that there was something real going on, Whiteman flagged it to the agency. Then there was some kind of political in-fighting about who should own this because it didn't fall into Whiteman's remit. We were all told in no uncertain terms to bugger off and leave it to the FBI experts!

'However, Paul's a bit like me - once he's got the bit between the teeth, he wasn't letting go. He also had some time booked on the supercomputer so he used that to crack some of Uncle Peter's protocols. Secretly, Paul sent me a set of encryption certificates. No-one knows I have them. Paul died on the same night he sent me the certificates and, following the explosion at my house, I think someone wants any knowledge of this lot to die with me.'

'Ok', said Mark, 'can't they just update the certificates?'

'I know the protocol thanks to Paul's work. Changing the certificates won't stop me from trapping the start-up process.

So, the cat's out of the bag - it's a massive system and I suspect we're talking state-level (as in government) compromise: it's clever, and I think it uses human resources behind the scenes.'

'And', said Mark thoughtfully, 'the missing hardware you mentioned …'

'That was my prototype and could identify the traffic and record it. I had another that would allow me to block data from the system, although I was still working on that. From the photographs you showed me, it looks like they'd also taken my system design off the wall.'

'Ouch!', said Mark sympathetically.

'No - it's Ok', grinned Clive, 'I have most of it in my head anyway. The one on the wall's wrong as I never updated it with the information from Paul.'

'Might be a good thing.'

'Yep. But that should explain why I'm saying you need to take care if you still want to look at my machine. Uncle Peter will change data behind the scenes, it did it to me. If you're connected to a network, then your entire machine's wide open.'

'That could raise evidential integrity questions - luckily we keep things offline when we check out machines. However, it could make some cases more difficult to prosecute if this thing is that capable!'

'It makes everything difficult - that's why I'm so keen to stop it. But if I simply stop it in its current form, then they'll morph it into something else, and it's then a game of catch-up. If I can work out who's behind it, and locate the core code, then we might be able to work out how it does it and seriously compromise any ability to re-infect machines. With any luck, we can kill it permanently.'

'Of course, that's useful for MKI too', suggested Mark, looking up from making notes.

'Naturally - it's a new product for us - but if I'm right then this compromises everyone's stuff. Everything in the security landscape, including us and all the big guys - well, we all end up being useless.'

'Scary!', said Mark, 'of course I need to go through the various machines as part of the investigation, so thanks for the warning. I'll keep off the net as much as possible. I would appreciate some help though: device and vault passwords, if you don't mind?'

'Of course', replied Clive, 'pass me the pad and pen.'

Clive wrote down a list of passwords and details of a few vaults stored on his machines - password protected and encrypted files containing sensitive information.

'Thanks', said Mark, 'much appreciated. I might need to come back, if that's ok?'

'Of course', replied Clive, 'I'll happily take you through anything on there.'

'I'd also be interested to see how you get on - I'm a geek at heart, and could possibly add a little analyst insight, if that helps.'

Clive appreciated the offer.

'I might just take you up on that, but only once I know it won't get you bumped off too!'

Mark packed up and left the room.

Jason looked at Clive and said, 'You gave him all your passwords?'

'No, of course not', replied Clive, 'only the ones I wanted him to have.'

'Won't he know he's missing a few?'

'No - I've given him the passwords to the data he can see. The stuff he can't is very well hidden. It doesn't exist unless you know how to find it.'

Back at the apartment, Clive set about re-creating his

development environment. In some ways, it was good to get something done: it kept his mind off Bren and concerns about what was going to happen in the future - after all, if he had to permanently 'disappear', he would need to find an entirely new career.

He had given a slightly 'tongue-in-cheek' list to David Harswell, exaggerating the storage and processing requirements for the equipment required to continue his research. However, David had provided the equipment exactly per Clive's specification.

Clive took the back off the new laptop and located the device's various antennae, then disconnected them. It was a simple yet effective way of preventing the machine from communicating covertly - he didn't trust the software on/off switch any more and with the wireless communication systems disabled, the machine could only connect to the Internet via a cable, putting it entirely in Clive's control. Besides, reasoned Clive, it would only take a couple of minutes to re-connect the antennae.

A few minutes later and he started restoring backups from the memory cards. Overall, this process took about four hours, but finally he had a working development environment.

Clive then assembled two kit computers connected them to a small network switch, and then powered them up. He was relieved to see that his rigorous backup regime had worked - he had managed to rebuild his protocol analyser and Uncle Peter 'blocker'. At last he was back in business.

'How long will it take to move this lot?', asked the PPS officer, interrupting Clive's flow.

'Why?'

'Well, we might need to vacate the premises reasonably quickly, so we generally recommend keeping everything in a state where you can move it at the drop of a hat.'

'Oh', said Clive, 'well - I can set it up in the bag, that way I only need to unplug it and run!'

'Might be wise - hopefully we don't need to go anywhere, but you never know. Coffee?'

'You can never have too much coffee', replied Clive and set about laying out the equipment in the bag. He would need to keep an eye on the equipment temperature, but other than that, he quite liked the idea of a completely mobile development machine - it made him think that he was becoming 'Q' in a Bond film.

For the rest of the day, Clive worked to rebuild the other parts of his computing environment. The final piece of the build involved using the two remaining kit-computers to create a new machine that he could use as bait for Uncle Peter.

Clive decided to create a user profile that made it look like the police were looking through Clive's assorted projects, including the fake SeeZu designs, as part of their investigation.

To anyone at the other end of a network connection, it should look like someone had simply turned on Clive's original laptop. Clive was actually interested to see what Uncle Peter would do when what looked like Clive's laptop came back online, if anything.

Finally, Clive connected a wireless network adaptor to the rig and the powered everything up. The various machines booted up, and then the laptop image came online. The protocol analyser LED's didn't light up. Clearly, there nothing going out to Uncle Peter.

Clive checked all the connections and, happy that he had a working rig, waited for Uncle Peter to come knocking.

35

Clive and Jason slept in a little as it was Sunday morning. Jason seemed to want to make a point about personal space, so he ensured that they were both indisposed for the entire duration of the PPS officer's shift-change.

'Shh', said Clive.

'No way! Look it's the only way we get any privacy. As long as my kit's off they leave us to it. Anyway, it's fun watching you blush.'

Jason slapped Clive's backside and said, 'now where were we?'

Once they'd finished, Jason walked towards the bathroom.

Clive sat up when he heard Jason speak.

'Oh, hello, you're new!'

'Erm', replied the voice, 'I'm, er, I've just been assigned to you two - do you need clothes?'

'Nah', replied Jason, 'I was just grabbing a ciggie and then going to have a shower.'

Clive scrabbled around for his pants and sweatshirt. Pulling them on, he walked out of the bedroom.

'Sorry about that - go and get dressed, Jason.'

Jason grinned, clearly enjoying the embarrassment he had created.

'In a minute - I'll just finish this', he said as he lit his cigarette.

'What's all this', asked the new PPS officer, trying to divert things and looking at the computer equipment in the case.

'It's my pet project', replied Clive, 'it's the thing that got me in this mess in the first place.'

Clive walked over to the equipment. Uncle Peter had still not visited Clive's laptop simulation.

'I need to keep working on it', Clive continued and then yawned, 'but first, I need a coffee! Anyone else?'

"Please', said the PPS officer.

'Thought you'd never ask!', replied Jason.

'You can have yours when you've had your shower and got dressed - go on, go and get decent.'

'If you've got it, flaunt it', replied Jason, stubbing out his cigarette in the ashtray, then yawning and stretching loudly. He left the room.

'Sorry', said Clive, 'I think it's his hormones.'

"It's Ok', replied the PPS officer, 'I've seen worse.'

'I can still hear you!', shouted Jason from the bathroom.

'Stop listening in to other people's conversations - you'll never hear anything complimentary', Clive shouted back and busied himself making coffee.

As Clive waited for the kettle to start boiling, his mind drifted.

Suddenly, he exclaimed 'Of course - stupid me!'

'What?', asked the PPS officer.

'I haven't changed anything. Why should Uncle Peter visit if I've not changed anything?'

'What?', the PPS officer asked again.

'Sorry - ignore me. It'll make no sense at all to you - can you finish the coffees, I just want to try something?'

'Did you say someone was visiting?', asked the PPS officer, somewhat concerned.

'No - I was talking figuratively', said Clive, 'sorry - ignore me, I just need to try something.'

Clive went over to the computer equipment and logged in to the virtual laptop (actually running on one of the kit-computers). He went to the SeeZu project and listed the files contained in the project, sending the output of the 'list files' command into a new file. He ran that command as it was something a sloppy forensic analyst might do.

Within a few minutes the protocol analyser LEDs illuminated. Uncle Peter had a new file to examine.

'Yes', said Clive triumphantly, 'gotcha!'.

'Right, listen up everyone', shouted Steve above the background noise.

'Today marks the last day working on the house with everything in place. I'm told we have everything we need in terms of photographs, scans, and assorted samples. If anyone thinks they need anything else from the scene, please contact myself, Alan or Anna so that we can sort things out quickly.

'Oliver - perhaps you can bring us all up to date with the scientific support activities?'

Oliver Wickes stood up and started to give his commentary.

'We've taken everything we need from the site now. We have also retained samples from the site so that we can release the scene now.

'However, we're still unable to confirm the exact cause of the explosion at the moment; while things point to it having the potential of being a gas leak, the heat and ferocity of the blast seem somewhat more severe than gas alone. The feedback from the labs being that they can't rule out gas alone, but can't find anything else at this stage. In all likelihood, I think we have probably found as much as we can - we may well have to file this under 'inconclusive', sorry.'

Steve frowned.

'Ok. Thank you', he said, 'where are we with the technology? Mark?'

It was Mark Lockhurst's turn to talk. He used a series of slides to support his presentation.

'Ok, so we have confirmed a few details from the mobile operators and device forensics.

'Firstly, it appears that Knollys used his mobile to establish a data connection at 08:32. The explosion occurred at roughly that time, so the data connection didn't complete - according to Knollys, he attempted to connect to his computer at home, it initially established a link but almost immediately died.

'Cellular data also puts Burke in, or very close to the house - it looks like he had travelled there early in the morning.'

'Do we know why he was at the house at that time?', interjected Steve.

Richard Duff, chipped in with 'Yes, Sir, it would appear that he wanted to ensure that Knollys actually went to the conference. Knollys can get a little too involved in projects and miss things. Burke wanted to get there in good time to be able to take Knollys to the conference.'

'Ok, thanks', replied Steve. Then to Mark, 'Sorry, you were saying?'

'No worries. Erm - yes, the cellular hits also show some movement by Haggely, suggesting that he did go out as per previous statements.

'We're still awaiting the information on the Poole clan. We have been asked to share that data with DS Bossons as part of their ongoing drugs work - the drug squad have said that they think Poole was probably after Haggely as they have heard of several requests from Poole with respect to Haggely's whereabouts.'

Steve looked at Mark.

'Go easy with that sort of statement please', he said, 'keep everything to facts - I can't work with unsubstantiated rumours, make sure we've got a evidentially sound source for everything, thanks.'

'Indeed', continued Mark, 'I'm independently checking everything or at least dual-sourcing it.

'We now have the passcodes for Knollys' machines and vaults. So, we're working our way through those now - there's a lot of data in there - I think Knollys has kept every email and message he's ever received.'

'All very interesting', said Steve, 'but is there anything that the case management team need to know?', in a less-than-subtle way of keeping things moving on.

'Nothing more at the moment', replied Mark.

'Ok', said Steve, 'DS Collier, how are things progressing with Burke and MKI?'

Gary stood up and read from his notes.

'MKI seems in a reasonable state - nothing remarkable about the company or its performance. We've spoken to most of the staff and the remaining board members. Of course, the remaining two directors are desperate for information regarding Knollys, given that we have now advised them of Burke's unfortunate demise. I have, at this stage, given no information about Knollys, although I suspect we may have to reasonably soon as it could materially affect the state of the company.

'At this stage, the FD and acting CEO has asked that we do not speak to any of the investors until we have clarified the situation with Knollys in particular. He was one of the founders and his departure would potentially cause investors to panic. Until we see something to indicate that we should pursue a line of enquiry with respect to the investors, we shall, for the time being at least, respect that request.'

'Stuff that', said Steve, 'it's a murder investigation. Talk to them. They'll have to know at some point anyway.'

'Ok, Sir. We've also started looking at the data from the company's servers: email, messages and the like. The tech-team are pretty saturated at the moment because there's a lot in there - but we're working on it. If there's anything interesting to report, I'll let you know immediately.'

36

Clive had set out the equipment on the hotel-room table. He had asked to see David Harswell and the PPS had arranged for them to meet at the Crewe Arms Hotel and they had a conference room on the ground-floor with windows looking out over the car-park and Crewe Station, opposite.

'You see - this here', he said pointing to an LED on the side of the analyser, 'flashes whenever data goes to or from Uncle Peter. It's capturing everything from my mini-network here.'

'Now', he moved to his laptop, 'I'm going to start up the honey-pot, AKA the SeeZu project.'

'SeeZu?'

'Yeah, now I sees-you, now I'sa goin'a'get you', Clive replied, 'Sorry - geek humour'.

'Nothing's happening', said David, looking at the LED's.

'It won't - until I change something. Now, watch.'

Clive opened one of the files in the SeeZu project and made a small change. A few minutes later, David looked at Clive.

'It flashed!', he said.

'Yep. As I said - it only captures new stuff. And sometimes very specific new stuff.'

'So what did it send?'

'According to Paul, before he died, he thought there was a

high probability that it contained all new data created on the machine. We're still working on the encryption side of things to work out what actually goes backwards and forwards.

'I managed, thanks to Paul, to work out the initial handshakes - the things that start up the whole system, and I'm hoping that - with a lot more work - I can work out the entire protocol. Once I've done that, I can work out how to stop it.'

'Can't your equipment here stop it?'

'It can at the moment. But - if Uncle Peter changes anything significant, I'm screwed - I want to work out what drives all of this, then I can stop it at source.'

While Clive was talking, the protocol analyser had flashed a few more times.

'It's still flashing', said David.

'Yes - they're sending instructions to the compromised computer now - I also need to work out how these instructions work - that way we can prevent that working too. Paul had gone some way into working out the basic structure, I think - but that information's gone with him.'

Clive turned his attention to the analyser and logged into it.

'Now, this has captured all the traffic and immediately compressed and encrypted it - it needs to in case Uncle Peter sees a capture pattern. It's intelligent enough to remove any trace of itself from network and system logs.'

'Neat', replied David.

'It is - and it's the level of integration that gets me', said Clive, 'I mean it's buried really deeply into the operating system itself. Not just one operating system either, it seems to work across all the machines here - with the exception of my hand-built kernel in the analyser. This is why it's got to be a state-sponsored development.'

'Which state?'

'No idea. Still working on that. But, it's too complex and takes too much human effort at the other end to be anything other than a state-level system.'

Clive felt his mobile 'phone buzz in his pocket. He talked loudly to cover the sound.

'So that's where I'm up to - I've captured the network traffic and can see it going between the compromised machine and Uncle Peter. Thanks to Paul, I have been able to capture and decrypt all the start-up messages. Now I want to expand on that to work out the rest of the protocol and trace the path to its final destination. That's a lot of work to do, but it's starting to make sense now.'

'Ok', said David, 'I'll get in touch with the Joint Intelligence group at GCHQ. They might have some resources available to help you out.'

'Not sure that would help a great deal at this point', replied Clive, 'I'm nearly there with the rest of the protocol. Perhaps they could come in to help trace the traffic once I've sorted this bit out.'

'Alright, I'll prime them so that they know something's coming their way. In the meantime, we'll keep you under protection, just in case. Although I'm getting some pressure from the police about who's paying for it! My problem, though.'

David and Clive finished talking and David left the room. Before the PPS officer returned, Clive grabbed his mobile from his pocket. He had received a secure message from Whiteman.

Quickly, Clive entered his credentials and looked at the message. He went pale and started shaking.

'What's up?', asked Jason.

Clive showed his 'phone screen to Jason.

Whiteman: "GET OUT. THEY HAVE FOUND YOU. POLICE COMPROMISED TOO. GET OUT NOW!"

* * *

Dennis Keeling had called in Steve White, Alan West, and Gary Collier.

'Ok, chaps, what do we think?'

'Well, Sir', replied Steve, 'we're in the frustrating phase now - waiting for information from the labs and tech teams. We can wind down the house to house, behavioural analysis, and scene of crime teams.

'At the moment, we're not sure about the cause - still leaning towards it being a gas explosion unless proven otherwise. Obviously, we want to check out Knollys' claims, the potential that Haggely was subjected to a hit from the Poole clan, and anything from the company side.

'Mark Lockhurst seems to think that Knollys was on to something - but - I've never heard of anyone dying from a computer virus before.'

'Indeed', replied Dennis, 'I would have thought the MKI board would have passed on the information to one of the big anti-virus companies and moved on.'

'Possibly', said Gary, 'but it looks like no-one other than Burke and Knollys knew what was going on. Knollys had taken the view that this could finish MKI, so he wanted to be the one to fix it.'

'Yes', chipped in Steve, 'and Mark Lockhurst seems to think that there's some commercial viability behind the detector/suppressor kit, or whatever he calls it. I think Knollys was working on it as a new way of detecting problems on networks - so there's some value in that as a new product.'

'So, we have Burke dead from being in the house at the time of a gas explosion; but no evidence to confirm damage to the gas supply prior to the explosion. I'm not convinced about the Poole link chasing Haggely - they'd simply beat him up and dump him somewhere, unless you have anything to the contrary. Are we in a position to close off those avenues yet?'

'Not far off', replied Steve, 'if it weren't for the intelligence interest in Knollys, I'd be thinking he was simply paranoid too.'

'Not so sure about that', said Alan, 'Mark seems pretty convinced that there was equipment and a schematic diagram missing from the scene. And the new detector kit had gone, so perhaps there's the potential for someone stealing property and using the explosion to cover it up. I'm still looking into that as a possibility.

'Mark has recovered photographs of the schematic - Knollys had taken a few on his 'phone so he had a copy with him. These photo's show equipment that Knollys was building - we haven't found anything matching it.'

'You're thinking theft?', asked Dennis.

'Possibly - Knollys was away at a conference. No-one really knew that Haggely was at Knollys' house, and how could they have known that Burke would be inside. Take the kit, blow the house and move on - unfortunately, Burke happened to be inside at the time: intellectual property theft gone bad?'

'Well, I guess that's a possibility', said Steve, 'perhaps worth looking into the missing equipment. We have copies of the design - any ideas of who would want to get hold of it?'

'No. Not yet - it's something we've only just started looking into', replied Alan.

'Hmm.', Said Dennis, 'Still, that seems a little far-fetched. Let's see where it goes, but keep speculation down to a minimum.'

Dennis made a few notes and then looked at the team.

'Well, for information, our friends in the intelligence community asked us to maintain the protection around Knollys for the time being. I'm asking them to contribute to the costs on this - we're running with pretty hefty team as it is.'

'Strip!', shouted Jason as soon as the door had closed behind David.

Jason had already taken his sweatshirt off and dropped his pants.

'What?'

'Strip - DO IT', said Jason.

He marched forward and grabbed hold of Clive. Roughly, he turned Clive round and yanked his pants down. As Clive started to protest, Jason pushed Clive forward over the table.

'Shut up', Jason hissed.

A couple of seconds later the door opened and the PPS officer stopped in shock.

'Jesus Christ!', shouted Jason, 'can't we even have a moment's privacy.'

The PPS officer didn't know how to react and Jason made the most of the moment.

'Leave us alone for a few minutes. Just fuck off. Why don't you make yourself useful and stand at the end of the corridor - that way no-one's going to interrupt us! We'll open the door when we're done!'

Jason thrusted himself forward to make the point.

'Well?', he said.

Silently, the PPS officer retreated and the door closed again.

'What the …', started Clive.

'Shut up - for a bright guy you're fucking thick sometimes. Get dressed, quick. We'll only have a few minutes. We might get away with half an hour before he realises - might only get a couple of minutes. Come on.'

Jason pulled up his pants, grabbed his top, and then picked up the bags they kept with them in case they had to move.

'Ready?', he said, and walked towards the emergency exit

door at the back of the small conference room.

As Clive caught on, Jason opened the emergency exit and the pair stepped outside into the car-park at the back of the hotel. Jason closed the door behind them and they ran around to the front of the hotel.

'Let the adventure begin!', shouted Jason and picked up the pace, heading for the railway station. They crossed the road and Jason sent Clive up to the ticket office.

'Get two cheap tickets going anywhere - say Stoke or Manchester. Cheapest you can get!'

Clive bought two tickets for Stoke-on-Trent while Jason went to the bathroom with the bags. He came back a few minutes later.

'Now we'll have to get a move on. I'm not sure how long we've got before our protector realises we've gone. Follow me - and do as I say.'

For once, Clive was glad of Jason's dubious history. If anyone could get them away and to safety, it would be Jason.

They headed for the central platform, a train bound for London had just pulled in.

'Right', said Jason, 'in at this end. Drop the MI5 bag in a luggage rack and get out right at the back - beyond that camera - let's hope there's a tracker in the bag, they'll follow that!'

They ran to the train and, under the watchful eye of the camera, boarded it. Depositing the bag in the luggage rack of the carriage they entered, they moved quickly to the rear of the train.

'Leave that there - let's go and grab a coffee from the on-board shop', Jason said loudly enough to prevent anyone worrying about an abandoned bag being left on the train.

The pair exited from the train just as the doors started to close. Jason ducked under some stairs and checked out the location of the cameras on platform opposite.

'That was the London train - next stop for the bag is Milton Keynes. That's a good hour away - so, we get on that train', he said pointing to a train just arriving on the other platform.

'Chester: that works', he said reading the sign on the side of the train.

'We'll go from there to a friend's place in Wales - let's see them find us there. Keep to the left of the steps and we should just avoid the cameras.'

They settled on the train and it pulled out of the station.

'Shame about the black bag', said Clive, 'I liked that.'

'Yeah - but never mind - I transferred your computer stuff into these. We need to change. I've got a couple of hoodies in here - just in case they're looking for us when we get to Chester.'

A quick visit to the train toilets allowed both Jason and Clive to change their appearance. Jason chucked a black beanie hat at Clive.

'Put that on too - it might just work.'

As it was, the two didn't need to worry. The cameras at Chester station were poor at best, and today the platform cameras were being maintained.

At Chester, Jason and Clive boarded a train bound for Holyhead. Jason was pleased because the train was absolutely packed.

'I hate them when they're this busy', said Clive.

'Too full for a ticket inspection', said Jason quietly, 'so stop complaining.'

The train was a stopping train - it stopped at every station along the route. While slow, it did mean that it would stop at the smaller stations along the North Wales coast.

At Llanfairfechan, Jason and Clive left the train. Avoiding the station cameras, Jason led the way to the promenade.

'Give me your 'phone', said Jason.

Clive unlocked the burner and handed it over.

Jason dialled a number.

'Hi Mate, it's Jase. Look I need to lie low for a bit - shagged someone I shouldn't, so I'm staying quiet. You said you wanted me to do some work up at the holiday cottage at Ravenspoint. I was thinking you could provide paint, food and drink and I'll do it up for free.'

The conversation carried on a few minutes.

'I've got a friend to help out - come and get us if you don't mind. We're at The Beach Hut on the prom. See ya!'

He hung up and passed the 'phone back.

'Who's that then?', asked Clive.

'A mate: Trevor. I've known him for years - he runs a holiday cottage letting business - mostly a collection of late 70's bungalows, but he calls them cottages. Better for the website. Anyway, he's a really nice guy. I've done a few of the cottages up for him in return for holidays before now. It's off-season, so he won't mind.'

'How far is it from here?'

'Oh a good hour in the car - it's on Anglesey - far enough from any prying eyes. Just stay low when we go over the road bridge onto the island. They'll probably have cameras there - I doubt they'll pick you up, but just in case, keep your hat on!'

'But wasn't the train headed for Anglesey anyway?'

'Yes. But Holyhead's a major port, the cameras on the platform will show we never got off the train there. If we missed the cameras in Chester and on the trains, then they'll never find us. However, if one of the train or platform cameras get to us, then they'll track us to here. We need to get away from here - they won't be looking for a guy called Trevor who runs a holiday letting business on the Island!'

'Just one more question then', said Clive.

'Go on.'

'Which of us is Thelma, and which Louise?'

* * *

'Gone? Gone where?', shouted Steve into his mobile.

The office fell silent.

'What do you mean you don't know?'

The news about Clive and Jason's disappearance had landed with Steve White. Now they had two significant people, potentially vulnerable, either taken or escaped from the protection service.

Steve called Dennis Keeling, interrupting a strategy meeting. Dennis authorised the mobilisation of a large team: uniformed officers, detectives, and technical teams to start looking at all the obvious transport routes away from the Crewe Arms Hotel.

Unfortunately for Steve, the Crewe Arms Hotel sits on a major roundabout that links Crewe to the motorway network, as well as sitting directly opposite one of the key railway hubs. It was somewhat ironic that the very reasons for choosing this hotel - the ease of getting protected persons away from danger - made it ideal for spiriting people away should the protection lapse.

'So much for keeping costs down', muttered Steve to himself. Budget constraints had left him without sufficient money to keep more than a single officer on protection duty at all times. This decision was now coming back to bite him. He'd have to account for a massive hit on the bottom line for the investigation.

In the meantime, he called David Harswell.

'David, it's Steve - PPS has lost Knollys and Haggely. We have no idea what's happened to them …'

Within a few minutes, John Fitzpatrick had parked himself in Steve's office with his laptop.

'Ok, we've got a trace on the bag - it looks like they're heading towards London Euston. The train stops in about 5 minutes at Milton Keynes and then goes straight through to

Euston.

'We'll only have time to get a couple of officers to Milton Keynes at best, so seal the exits. Hopefully they'll stay on the train and we can pick them up at Euston.'

'Thanks', said Steve, and started making calls.

'In the meantime, I've got the schedules for all the other trains at Crewe around that time. There are quite a few. We're getting hold of the station CCTV and should have that quickly.'

Just as John finished talking, Theresa Higgins poked her head around the door.

'Sir - Crewe Station CCTV shows them both getting on the Euston train.'

'Do they get off again?', asked John.

'No Sir - they got on the train. None of the other cameras picked them up in the station after that. We've got officers checking the platforms, just in case. But we're pretty sure they boarded the train together.'

'Anyone with them?'

'I don't think so. They looked like they were on their own.'

Steve had been talking to the incident control room at Milton Keynes.

'Shit - the train's already left.'

Steve marched over to the door of his office.

'Alan', he shouted, 'can you pick up the liaison with Milton Keynes? I want you to see if you can find Knollys and Haggely. It looks like we missed a lock-down by a couple of minutes. We might have them on CCTV or still in the vicinity. We might need you to head down there or to London if they're still on the train.'

'Well', said John, 'we've picked up the bag again - it's still heading for London.'

'Let's hope it's more than just the bag', replied Steve grimly.

* * *

Despite the circumstances, the drive up the coast towards Anglesey was glorious. The sun broke through and nearly the entire journey followed the long sandy beaches and exquisite coastline that brings tourists to North Wales every year.

Trevor was good company - and, Clive admitted to himself, good eye-candy too. He was in his early thirties, born on Anglesey but then moved to London after attending Staffordshire University. He become a futures trader and made a reasonable amount of money. Gradually he realised that he actually hated the fake people, noise, and smell of London. He sold up his Whitehall apartment and bought 3 properties for the price of the tiny city apartment.

He now lived in one of them, and started renting the other two out as holiday lets. Within a couple of years, he had been able to buy another couple and intended to keep increasing his property portfolio.

'How did you two meet?', asked Clive.

'Ah - and imaginatively named dive called "The Club" in Stoke-on-Trent', Trevor replied.

'Closed now', added Jason.

'There was a drunken reprobate at the end of the bar. I think he'd managed to drink more than I had - and to me as a student, that was an impressive feat. Anyway he came back to mine - did you actually have anywhere else to go that night? I always wondered.'

'Nope', replied Jason, 'I needed a bed and you were it!'

'Classy', said Trevor, 'good to know you went for my sparkling personality and wit.'

'Nah, just your arse and somewhere to sober up after.'

Trevor aimed a good natured punch in Jason's general direction.

'So what have you got yourselves into?'

'Temporary trouble, but it turned nasty. We need to lay low

for a while', said Jason in a final tone. Clearly Trevor wasn't going to get any more out of Jason.

'What about you Clive, what do you do?', asked Trevor.

'Computers, networks, security, broadcast stuff - a geek.'

'Excellent - well, if Jason's doing the place up, would you mind sorting the net out for me? It's got an old PC and broadband connection, but I'd like to put wireless in - most people ask for it these days.'

'Sure.'

'Just don't laugh at the PC, it's only really used for guests web-browsing. Let me know what you need and I'll get it for you.'

Clive settled back and watched the coastline drift by. Despite the situation, this had been a fun day - it was great to get away from protection officers and the case. He thought about MKI and whether it would survive, and then thought about Bren.

'Priority one must be the recovery of Knollys. We need him.'

David Harswell looked at Steve and Dennis.

'This is a mess - and we need him back in our care. He's at risk.'

'What do you know that we don't?', asked Steve.

'Confidential information received from the FBI suggests that they suspect Knollys of providing a secure communications infrastructure to large-scale organised crime networks.'

'For fuck's sake!', exclaimed Steve, 'and you're telling us this only now?'

'Actually, we didn't know until this morning. The FBI had assumed that with Knollys dead, someone else would end up picking up the network administration and wanted to see how things panned out. They thought someone in the US would pick it up and hoped whomever ran with it would perhaps be a little less careful than Knollys.

'Part of me getting Knollys back online was to track what he was doing so that we could get a handle on things from this end. We didn't want the US calling the shots. We gave him a laptop, but the first thing he did was open it up and disconnect the blasted radio antennae - otherwise we'd have a copy of everything he did.'

David paused and then continued, 'Of course we thought he was cracking a criminal network, not inventing the damned thing.'

Dennis raised an eyebrow and asked how the FBI had found about about Clive's activities.

'We only received this from the FBI once my colleagues at Joint Intelligence requested the information gained from the work completed by the field unit in the USA. Almost immediately, we got a call from Bill Price - the Director of Digital Intelligence out there. He let me in on their investigation - so I'd like to suggest that we change the investigation priorities a little.'

'Go on', said Dennis.

'Firstly, we must get Knollys back. I don't care about Haggely, but if they're travelling together - well, that should make finding them slightly easier.

'Next, I need to know what's on those computers you recovered from the scene. If there's anything there that could provide us with enough background information to get on to this covert network, then we need to do it.

'You've got an analyst who's already been looking at the computer kit, I'd like to use him to provide a technical brief for the FBI so that they can continue to work the case from their end. I'll say now that there's a lot of pressure to leave this to the Americans as they have the experience and resources to throw at it.'

'So what of the explosion?'

'Personally, I think its safe to rule out both Haggely and Burke. Nothing suggests that Burke was in on the dark network, but I guess we should keep an eye out for anything that contradicts that view.

'The FBI think it highly likely that is was an attempt to get Knollys out of the picture. We all know he was at a major hacking convention and must have been seen talking with a guy called Whiteman - one of the FBI agents attending the same conference. Perhaps it's a trust issue - particularly if Knollys is running some of the more potent dark networks.'

'And MKI?'

'A safe shop-front for these activities - keeps him nicely in the loop with everything the security forces are up to. The oldest tactic in the world: know thy enemy', he shrugged, 'who knows?

'I'd like to send images of the servers over for analysis, although I doubt Knollys would have been stupid enough to use his own servers - but let's see.'

'Come on sleepy, let's get inside', said Jason gently.

Clive awoke. He almost never slept when travelling as it usually made him feel extremely travel sick.

'Sorry about that', he murmured to Trevor, 'must have been tired.'

'No worries mate', replied Trevor, 'we've just been talking about you.'

'It's all lies', replied Clive.

They climbed out of the car and looked out over a wonderful scene. Distant cliffs enclosed either side of a sandy bay with a small cluster of rocks making a tiny island in the middle. The sound of the gently crashing waves was music to Clive's ears.

The sun shone brightly, making the sand appear an almost perfect colour against a beautifully clean sea.

'Wow!', said Clive, 'what a place.'

'Well, the scenery's what they come for. Come on in', said Trevor as he walked to the front door of a somewhat small bungalow.

He let Jason and Clive in, then led them down a hallway.

'Ok - so - bedrooms either side, then the bathroom on the left, kitchen on the right, but …', he said as he walked to the end of the hallway. He opened a set of double doors.

'This, is what they pay for.'

Beyond the doors was a large lounge, well appointed but with obvious signs of building work around a set of new french doors overlooking a small garden. Beyond the garden was a cliff edge, and then nothing but the sea and sky.

'What a fantastic view', said Clive, 'I could die happily here!'

'It is', said Trevor, 'although the storms this year have been particularly severe. We had one after the next after the next - we survived the first few, but the second to last must have churned some rocks up and it took the patio doors out. We didn't know until after the last storm hit and a neighbour told us to check the place out.

'After that storm took the glass out, we ended up with a fair amount of sea and rain inside. So - we've put these French windows in to replace the old patio doors - if anything hits these, it should only smash a small pane instead of taking out half a wall, in effect.'

'You were lucky it didn't do more damage', said Jason, 'although they've done a good job with the doors.'

'Well - it all needs decorating now - so, that's the fee for staying here. The paint's over there, I've got a few basics in the car, but after that you're on your own.'

'Great, thanks lots'.

'Oh - and the computer's in the corner - no password, just start it up.'

While Clive and Jason admired the view, Trevor brought the shopping in from the car, handed a set of keys over to Jason and then left.

'That's one hell of a view', said Clive.

'Yep', said Jason removing his top, 'and while you look at that, I'm going to finish what I started in that hotel room.'

37

Steve was losing control of his case. Far from closing sections down, he was now having to lead a national man-hunt without being able to use the press.

At MI5's request, he had deferred Burke's inquest. While they family liaison team had complained about the decision, there was little else he could do.

'Ok, folks, let's kick this session off.

'Firstly, to make sure everyone's up to speed - we had a new PPS officer assigned to Knollys and Haggely. The two conspired to create an embarrassing situation for the officer, who left to give them some privacy.

'During this time, the two eloped via a fire escape at the rear of the premises. We believe they eloped as we subsequently saw Knollys and Haggely arriving at Crewe station. Knollys bought tickets for Stoke-on-Trent while Haggely used the public toilets as a place in which to transfer the contents of a GPS-tagged bag into their back-packs.

'We have CCTV from Crewe station showing that the two boarded a train bound for London Euston. We subsequently recovered CCTV footage from the train that shows that the two left the tagged bag on the train but had, in fact, departed from it at a position just beyond the platform cameras.

'At this stage, we lost both of them.

'As this occurred at Crewe Station, there were several trains within an hour window. So, two trains to Stoke, another to London, two to Manchester, two to Chester, one to Preston, then we have the local services - basically trains in all directions. A future lesson - never arrange a PPS meeting near to a major transport hub.

'Anyway - has anyone anything to add - do we know where the hell these two actually went?'

Alan stood up. He had already attended a previous meeting where the search coordinators had briefed him.

'We know it's definitely not Stoke, Milton Keynes, or London. We've been through the CCTV footage on those stations and had officers watching every arrival, just in case.

'We've checked the major routes, and are currently going through individual train CCTV recordings. Unfortunately, not all operators are as vigilant as they should be - so some of the cameras are worse than useless.'

'So', said Steve, 'two of our potential targets, or principal suspects, have escaped. We need to know why. Which brings me to the next little nugget: Information received, but as yet unattributed and subject to verification, suggests that Knollys might not be as clean as we initially thought.

'We need to go back through MKI's computer equipment and prioritise the analysis of all the computer equipment recovered to date. We need to check for hidden or covert services, dark-net access software, and so on.'

Mark raised his hand and then asked, 'Can I ask what we're looking for, specifically?'

'Not at the moment. Just look for hidden data or dark networks and see where that takes us - if anywhere.'

For March, it was unusually warm. Jason, in nothing but a pair of old shorts, had flung open the french windows and was painting over freshly dried plaster.

Clive, in the meantime, had spread the various bits and pieces of computer equipment across a sizeable area of the living room.

Once he was happy everything was working, he connected the equipment to the Internet and set up a connection to his private network. Once online, he sent a message to Whiteman.

Clive: "Ok, we got out. I think we're safe, but what do we do now? We can't stay here for ever."

Clive created a set of encrypted and hidden data vaults on the laptop. He had a lot of data he needed to retrieve from various servers around the world. He kicked off the data transfer process.

While waiting for Whiteman to respond and the transfer to complete, Clive sketched out few new design concepts. He wanted to create another honey-pot as he couldn't really use SeeZu or any of the existing projects. He was also unsure about whether Uncle Peter would track a 'normal' computer, or whether his computer had been targeted because of his work with the security services.

None of the designs really made sense, so he checked up on the data transfer process. The network connection, however, was painfully slow. It would take a while for the transfers to complete, so Clive decided to make a coffee before setting up the new environment.

'What a view', he commented as he brought two mugs of coffee back into the living room.

'I know', replied Jason, 'I could make it better but I've got to keep my shorts on while I'm painting the outside frame …'

'Shut it!'

'How's it going?', asked Jason, looking at the assorted boxes and cables lying around the room.

'Slow. Mainly down to the Internet connection - but, we'll

get there.'

'Good. Are you back up and running yet?'

'Pretty much. I've asked Whiteman what we do next - I mean that even though Trevor's a nice guy, I doubt we can stay here for any significant amount of time.'

'I wouldn't worry - I've been living like this for most of my life', replied Jason with a grin.

'Yes, but we'll have the police after us - and whoever this other lot are. I could do with talking with Whiteman. He told us to get out and we did - but I worry that it's just made things worse for us?'

'I wondered why he was telling us to get out too. Have you heard anything else?'

'No. I tried to find out this morning - I sent him a message. Anyway, I'll carry on with this for a few days, but if I don't hear anything, I'll contact DCI White and get us back in protection. We can always say we just needed to get away - other than travelling on the train without a valid ticket, I don't think we've broken any laws here …'

'Wasting police time, perhaps? But anyway, I doubt they'd go for it given the circumstances. What are you doing with all this lot?', asked Jason as he looked at the various wires and boxes lying on the floor.

'A few things - at the moment, I'm extracting as much data as I can from the various hidden services I run.'

'Hidden services?'

'Yeah - I host a whole series of hidden network services, no-one knows they're there unless they know what to look for. Nonetheless, there's a load of stuff out there that I need to get hold of - I've created encrypted data vaults on the laptop, so I can bring it back here and then remove it off the servers.'

'If no-one knows its there, why do you need to move it?'

'If someone starts digging really deeply, there's always the risk that I might have left a pointer or clue to its existence. If I clear it out, there's nothing for them to find. Also, if they take all the company servers down, I should be Ok, but have never tested it for real. I want to get it all before they close me down.

'Unfortunately, the connection here's bloody slow. It's taking an age to move it over. Once it's all here, I'll back it up on a removable drive in case I have to kill the laptop.'

'So, while it's all coming down, I'm creating a new honey-pot for Uncle Peter to look at, so that means me sitting down and creating a load of realistic looking junk!'

'Why?'

'Well, I can't use my old project. That would show I'm still alive for sure ...'

'Don't they know that already - I mean we're on the run from them, aren't we?'

'I don't know who we're running from at the moment. It's probably better to create something new than re-use anything they've seen before!'

'I'm glad I never understood all this crap', said Jason, 'I never thought you'd get killed for simply pushing a few buttons.'

Jason finished his coffee and returned to his painting.

Clive watched him for a few minutes, admiring the way Jason's muscles flexed and moved as he painted. He watched Jason dip a brush into the paint bucket and then saw the bristles spread out, spreading paint to the surface below.

That gave him the inspiration for his next project - a system to manage the distribution of vast amounts of data by spreading it over lots of parallel data connections: nothing significantly new, but probably enough to act as a hook for Uncle Peter, especially if he laced the documentation with enough references to security frameworks and encryption systems.

With a real sense of deja-vu, Clive set about creating his

new honey-pot. He called the project 'partition' - short for particle distribution. He then created a document: "Partition - A patent application defining methods and apparatus to distribute data securely while optimising network communications". If that didn't catch Uncle Peter's attention then nothing would.

It took a few hours to create the new environment, and at some point during that time, Uncle Peter had indeed latched on to the project. Clive was recording every interaction between the laptop and Uncle Peter.

Jason, meanwhile, had finished off one section of the room. He had showered and brought Clive another coffee.

'I could do with getting some food in', he said.

'Probably best to get it delivered - I've got Whiteman's credit-card number, so we could use that. It'll save using the cash up too - if I swap the network connections over, you could use Trevor's PC.'

'Won't that stop your downloads?'

'The software can cope with it. Once the network comes back, it'll just carry on. I'm about done for today anyway.'

Clive swapped the broadband connection back to Trevor's PC, leaving his local network running but disconnected from the Internet.

'There you go', he said, 'all yours.'

Jason created an account using the name and card details Whiteman had provided. Then, he ordered some food and drink for home delivery. After that, he surfed for a while.

The had a couple of hours before the delivery window, so the pair then headed for Trearddur Bay - the beach just beyond the cliffs at Ravenspoint. As the sun started setting they walked along the edge of the incoming tide.

'You know, if it weren't for the situation, this would be idyllic', said Clive.

'If I could get the work, I'd move here tomorrow - Trevor's

all well and good but I can't afford to stay here in the holiday season', replied Jason.

'Can't you start a property maintenance service? I mean, there must be loads of holiday homes here - start up a service to look after them?'

'Catch-22 - I'd need to have somewhere to stay while I build the business.'

'Oh well', said Clive, 'perhaps when all this is over, we can both move here - I can work from pretty much anywhere that has a net connection - and it'd give you the ability to make an honest buck for once!'

The couple returned to the bungalow. While Jason started making some food for dinner, Clive went into the living room.

'Shit!', he exclaimed loudly.

Jason ran into the living room.

'What?'

'Look', said Clive, 'my laptop's talking to Uncle Peter.'

'And? I thought that was the whole point?'

'But it can't - it's not plugged in to the Internet. I swapped the connection so that you could use Trevor's machine. How can it still talk?'

38

'Sir', said Mark Lockhurst, after gently knocking on the door frame to Steve's office, 'do you have a moment?'

'Sure', Steve looked up from his computer and waved Mark towards the empty chair facing him, 'sit down.'

Mark sat.

'So, what can I do for you?'

'Well, it's Knollys. I think we've found something.'

Jason had wanted to turn the laptop off immediately. Clive, following the FBI process of 'what was compromised is now a tactical asset', set about working out how the laptop was gaining access to Uncle Peter.

In the first instance, Clive simply pulled the broadband connection out of the wall socket. Immediately, the traffic indicators on the protocol analyser stopped flashing. When he plugged it back in, within a couple of minutes the LEDs started flashing again.

Clive turned off Trevor's PC and the traffic indicators stopped again.

'There's something on Trevor's PC as well', said Clive.

Clive restarted the PC. After a few minutes, the old machine had started back up and then the protocol analyser started showing traffic moving from the laptop to Uncle Peter.

'How's it doing that?', asked Jason.

'I don't know', replied Clive, 'the PC doesn't have wireless or bluetooth, and it's not connected to my network, so it's got to be communicating somehow ...'

Clive, looking at the ports at the back of the machine, could see there was nothing untoward plugged into the machine. Out of interest, he started unplugging devices.

As soon as he unplugged the microphone and speaker, the protocol analyser stopped flashing.

'No way!', he said.

'What?'

'I've heard of this being possible - I never thought they'd already got something like this working.'

'What? Stop talking in riddles - what have you got?', demanded Jason.

'It's an air-gap bridge', replied Clive.

'None the wiser.'

'Now', said Clive in his best teaching tone, 'in order for a computer to talk to other computers it will need something that can send data, and something to receive data.'

'Ok, so?'

'So - the network wire carries signals in both directions; on the laptop, the wireless systems use radio signals to do the same thing. To stop that and only allow communications to go through my recorder, I have unplugged the antennae on this machine, so it has no radio. When you wanted to order food, I had to unplug this entire network, so the laptop has no normal way of talking to the Internet, so how's it doing it?'

Jason looked blank, 'I don't know.'

'Well, when I unplugged the speaker and microphone cables on the PC, it stops talking. It means that Uncle Peter's capable of using the speakers and microphone to communicate.'

'Not sure I get what you mean.'

'Let me try another way - when you want to secure a computer so people outside can't get to it, you create a thing called an air-gap. It's literally air between the computers - you disconnect radios and make sure that there's nowhere to plug a network or communications cable in. That's how I've been protecting what I've done.

'However, it looks like this thing's using the microphone and speakers when nothing else is around. The microphone receives information, the speakers send it.'

'I couldn't hear anything', said Jason.

'Doesn't mean it's not there - if it's at a reasonably high frequency, the human ear can't hear it. Kids sometimes can hear a slight noise coming from the speakers, that must be what's happening. This is huge.'

'Why?'

'Nuclear installations, critical infrastructure, defence networks - they all use air-gaps. But this can create a bridge between all of these disconnected but networked computer systems and the open Internet. This has the potential to take control of every secure installation in the world.'

'Jesus', said Jason, 'so they can take control over anything?'

'Pretty much. I worked on designs for emergency police control rooms. They're absolutely banned from having any form of connection between the incident handling systems and the Internet. This ensures that nothing can interfere with the way say a major incident gets handled.

'The daft thing is that all these machines have microphones and speakers so the operators can deal with incoming calls. I'll bet that each control room now has at least one computer with an Internet connection - but to conform to the 'no connection to the Internet' rule, they'll have an air-gap between it and all the other machines there. That one

Internet-connected machine can create a sound-link that bridges the air-gap - it blows the whole thing open.

'Even more scary is that it doesn't have to be two computers here - it could be a computer and a mobile 'phone. Literally just bring a mobile 'phone near an air-gapped machine and you're done for.'

Clive sat back and looked at Jason.

'This just reinforces everything I had thought about it being created by a very well resourced government agency somewhere. It also explains why they're trying to get me out of the picture.'

'Go on, why?', said Jason.

'Because every nuclear power station, every defence system, every hospital, every bank or company. Any of these … hell … ALL of them could be at risk from this damned thing. Uncle Peter has the ability to terrorise entire nations. It's positively scary.'

'Are we now at risk again - do we know what they got while we were walking?'

'Give me a few minutes and I'll find out. Luckily, the recorder was working so we'll know a fair bit more. This thing should have given me a copy of the data they've collected. First things first though, let's just prove it is the audio system.'

Clive turned the laptop off and fetched his toolkit. A few minutes later and he'd taken the back off the machine.

'See', he said to Jason, 'there's the lead that goes to the speakers, and this to the microphone.'

He unclipped the two leads from the circuit board and re-assembled the computer.

He turned all the computer equipment back on. This time nothing showed up on the protocol analyser or recorder. It looked like Clive had managed to secure his development environment again.

Clive logged on to the protocol analyser while Jason dealt with the food delivery. Jason came back a few minutes later and chucked a can of lager to Clive.

'Well - did they get much?'

'By the look of it, no: I think they only got some of the new project I was working on. Luckily, the connection's really bad - the audio system must work extremely slowly compared to a normal network anyway. That, combined with this crappy broadband - oh, and me saturating it all with data from the covert network - I never thought I'd be grateful for a slow net connection. This time, however, it might just have saved us.'

39

'The worst deeds happen in the dark', said Mark, 'and this is no exception.'

Mark fired up the projector attached to his laptop to present his findings to Dennis Keeling, Steve White, and David Harswell.

'We started assessing the information stored on Knollys' computers. We created download exhibits of everything. However, we received information from the FBI that could potentially link Knollys to one of the online crime syndicates they've been watching for some time.

'The FBI provided us with a series of links into, what they believed to be, a potential dark network service, hosted on MKI's external servers. At the request of the FBI, we left the services running, but created a backup image of the entire disk array so that we could examine the storage offline.

'When you remove the MKI smoke-screen, we start to see a series of distributed data stores. It took us a while, but we were able to determine that these supported a large dark network - again, in line with the FBI's intelligence.'

Mark showed a pie-chart defining the storage breakdown.

'Here, you can see the total storage', he pointed to a green segment, 'this being the MKI data and this', pointing to a slightly larger red area, 'being that reserved and used by the dark network system.

'Now, as it's in a dark network, Knollys has encrypted most of the data stored here, but by gaining access to the servers themselves, we have been able to obtain the encryption keys used by the system to access the databases and configuration data.

'While it's early days, we seem to have a repository supporting several dark-net web services. These include credit card databases, payment cleansing services, and vast collection of indecent images. The data here seems to support a claim from the FBI that Knollys is directly involved in all sorts of covert stuff: peddling kiddie porn, acting as a money-laundering service, and hosting several very dubious sites that are selling everything - drugs, guns, identity data, bank details - you name it.'

Mark showed several slides in quick succession.

'These images show the configuration files that suggest that while Knollys would appear to own the indecent image side, others seem to own the other services. Knollys has merely provided a safe haven to host these services. No doubt he makes additional money from hosting these services - although we have yet to find any traces of the money.'

'How much material have we got?', asked Dennis.

'It looks pretty significant', replied Mark.

'Enough to warrant Knollys doing a runner?'

'More than enough for that. I think we're into hundreds of thousands of images - potentially twenty or thirty hosted services … it's quite a sizeable operation: it's taken a few days just to get a forensic image of it all.'

'So not something he can run on his own?'

'Actually, he can run them all easily: it's pretty simple to set up a new service - they just run themselves after that. He's probably got a remote administration console somewhere so that he can create new sites and manage them. It's not as if anyone would complain if their service went offline for a few hours either - so, you wouldn't need the type of support infrastructure you would for a regular hosting company.'

'Sir', interjected Steve, 'I'm running way over on this case already. If you're wanting me to look into this lot, we're going to need a major incident team here - God knows who else needs to get involved in this.'

'Yes', agreed Dennis, 'I think we should look at this in terms of it becoming a national operation. We don't have the capacity to deal with this - I'll contact the NCA. Do we know, whether Knollys is generating content or distributing it?'

'We don't know yet - there could be some first generation content in there, but we've not had the time to go through it all yet.'

'First generation?', asked David.

'If we found a modest amount of child pornography', replied Mark, 'then we'd assess it to see if it was created by Knollys or someone known to him - Haggely, for example. We do this for victim identification and protection, as well as prosecution. If it comes from him or someone close, then we call if first generation.

'However, in this case, there's a lot of material - and when you combine it with the credit card databases, we have potentially found a link to scores of paedophiles, some possibly being live contacts.

'We have large amounts of hi-tech stuff to examine, with connections to God knows how many other suspects. If we wanted to tackle this, we would have to set up a major incident operation on the scale of the ripper.'

'We're not doing that', said Dennis, 'it's for CEOP to run with it. They're part of the national crime agency anyway, so I'm inclined to tidy up the documentation and pass this over to the NCA, if they'll take it.'

'What about the dark-net services - they're still running?', asked Mark.

'Leave them running', replied Dennis. He looked up from his notes and continued, 'At least for the time being. Shutting them down might alert Knollys that we're on to him - we'll let the NCA decide whether to close it down. I presume we are now tracking everything happening on those machines?'

'Yes', replied Mark, 'well - we're working with the hosting company to put that in place as we speak.'

David sighed.

'You know', he said, 'if you put me up against the wall and threatened to shoot me, I'd have never thought Knollys was a paedo - just goes to show …'

Clive's burner buzzed. He had a message from Whiteman.

"Whiteman: Glad you got out - talk?"

Clive hit the call button.

'How are you doing?', asked Whiteman.

'Firstly, take a look at your display - what does it say?'

'Hold on', Whiteman looked at the display on his mobile, 'Final Potplant', he said.

'Great. Same here. We're secure. Sorry about that, it's just that we'll end up with different words if someone's in the middle. The digital equivalent of secret pass-phrases on the park-bench.'

Clive looked over towards Jason, who was applying gloss paint to the window frames.

'Anyway', he said, 'we got away cleanly enough - or at least I think we did. What now though? We can't stay here for ever.'

'We?'

'Yes - I have Jason with me - my partner, remember?'

'Whatever - it's always easier to slip into a crowd on your own though. Two together can end up being easier to find …'

'Well, there's no option on that - and anyway, he was the one that came up with the idea that got us out from under the protection service's watchful eye.'

'Oh, well - whatever - you're lying low though, right?'

'Yes - but I have had to use that credit card number you gave me.'

'That's what it was there for - I'll top it up again, you'll need some money to keep going, I guess.'

'Of course - that's one of the things that's been worrying me. At some point pretty soon I'm going to have to return back to normal life again. This is a crazy situation.'

'Don't worry about that right now. We've got to see where this Uncle Peter thing goes. I've got an investigation pot that I'm using to fund your stuff for the time being, so if you need anything, just use the card.'

'Thanks - but weren't you taken off the case? Weren't you booted out of the lab?'

'Bill Price is officially investigating this case from our end. The problem is that I'm the only one who really understands the honey-pots: more the psychology of the people behind them and how to communicate with them. So, I'm back in my old position with a suitable slap on the wrist', Whiteman paused.

'The official line was that the internal investigation into Paul's death can't hold me entirely responsible. While I may have allowed Paul to work to exhaustion, the workload for the department was such that I should have called for additional resources, or some crap. Anyway, as I wasn't responsible, they've put me back where they need me.

'Uncle Peter, however, is out of my hands. Price and his team should be looking into it all. I'm not convinced they're really doing a great deal with it yet and I don't want Paul's death to mean nothing. So crack Uncle Peter for Paul!'

'That sounds like a corporate slogan', laughed Clive.

'Yeah, sorry about that. Anyway, have you had a chance to get anywhere, or have you just been on the road?'

'Actually, I have some real news - Uncle Peter can bridge air-gaps.'

Clive went on to explain how he had discovered Uncle Peter's ability to use high-frequency sound to link computers when no network was available.

'Shit!', exclaimed Whiteman, 'That's a problem - I'll have to think about how we do the department's business in the future. We even take laptops into the supercomputer centre to act as local terminals', Whiteman drifted off.

'And', said Clive, 'I think I've got the whole of the initialisation sequence sorted now. Can I send you some data I captured - I can't seem to trace the end-point, but you might be able to trace it with your core network monitoring tools?'

'Sure, fire them over.'

'Thanks - so why did you tell me to get out?'

'Things aren't right. I looked into Paul's death and it all stinks. I won't go into the details, but I'm pretty convinced it was a professional hit. The way it's been handled this way only nods to "due process", but I actually think it's been a huge cover-up.'

'Really?'

'Yeah - not only that, but I've been asked a lot about what you knew. I played dumb - vague details, actually I diverted by asking more from them than they did from me. They gave up in the end.

'Anyway our internal reports suggested you had died in an explosion at your house. I have a friend - actually an old member of my inner circle here in my department - he's now in Price's empire. He let me know that Price had just received notification not only that you were in protective care, but also giving him the address.

'If he has it, then someone else potentially does too - if

Uncle Peter's tracking you and had attempted to take you out, then this was just careless handling. That single action put you straight back in danger. If they're that sloppy with your handling, then you're better out of it. I also have no idea why the FBI should have the details relating to your location - usually we have knowledge that you'd be in some form of protective care, and be given access via a single point of contact between the FBI and local services in the UK. Someone's leaking, and if Paul was as hit, then they may as well have pointed a gun at your head.'

'Thanks for the warning', said Clive thoughtfully, 'I was contemplating giving DCI White access to a secure communications channel. It wouldn't reveal where I was, but would perhaps stop them having to waste time searching for me - they can get in touch any time then.'

'No - daft idea', replied Whiteman immediately, 'stay dark for as long as you can. Keep working on Uncle Peter. By the sound of it you're nearly there with decoding it all. I'll take a look at the data when you get it over to me.'

'Ok', said Clive, 'You'll need to follow the compress and encryption processes, remember, it's a ball-ache, but Uncle Peter will probably delete it automatically otherwise.'

'Yeah - noted. I'll make sure I'm properly isolated too.'

'Worth considering that your mobile could also act as a bridge - I can't test that out, but you might be able to.'

'Damn - that's a good thought. Are we safe?'

'I think so', said Clive, 'they might be able to get the encrypted data - but the way we handle encryption means that if anyone's in the middle, we'd get different messages on the screens. Basically, authentication would fail - that's why I asked what words had appeared on your display.'

It took Clive a couple of hours to extract all the start-up sequence data, package it up, and then send it over to

Whiteman. Clive used every trick in the encryption book to protect the data and make sure that Uncle Peter had no way of accessing it. The mobile connections at Ravenspoint were decidedly poor, so Clive had to use the house broadband and this meant connecting the laptop back to the open net.

Clive moved everything he had into encrypted vaults, and then closed the vaults so that only the encrypted versions remained. If the system was leaking data, then Clive wanted to make sure Uncle Peter couldn't use it.

With the laptop tied up, Clive plugged one of the kit-computers into the house TV and called up the protocol analyser code. Over the next few hours, he lost himself in building a set of services to mimic Uncle Peter.

Once the upload to Whiteman finished, Clive swapped the machines around. He set the kit-computers running to finish off the covert network download - it didn't need a particularly powerful machine for that. The laptop being better suited to code development anyway.

Clive made himself and Jason cold drinks and then took the laptop outside. He sat on the cliff edge in the sun and started testing the services he'd written earlier.

Stage by stage, the Uncle Peter mimic was coming together. He could now get a new virtual machine to respond, authenticate itself, and set up an encrypted remote access pathway.

'How are you getting on?'

Clive jumped. He hadn't heard Jason coming up behind him.

'Ok - thanks. I've sent the trace data to the FBI - here's hoping that Whiteman can work out where all this stuff ends up. In the meantime, I'm creating something to work out how Uncle Peter communicates to the machine. I think I've got the initial bit working, but I need to work out the command and control protocol now.'

'In English?'

'Sorry - it's a bit like a 'phone call. I've got a nice secure connection to the switchboard now, but don't know what I should ask for - or in which language. If I can work out how that bit works, I will have pretty much cracked how Uncle Peter does what he does.'

'Ok', said Jason, 'I'm done for the day, so I was thinking we could go for another walk on the beach. Give you a bit of a break too.'

Just as Jason finished talking, Clive's burner buzzed.

Clive looked at the display.

'That was quick', he said.

'What?'

'Whiteman's looked at the data - give me a couple of minutes to deal with this, then we can go to the beach.'

Clive opened the message.

"Whiteman: Have you sent me the right data?"

"Clive: Yes. Why?"

"Whiteman: This is a series of software update requests."

Clive hit the call button.

'Orange Bathroom', said Whiteman immediately.

Clive grinned and looked at the display on his burner.

'Same here - now what's this about a software update?'

'That data - it terminates at the primary operating system update servers for your machines - there's a video CODEC update request from one vendor, and another for a generic printer driver … it's standard stuff, and all via the proper software update channels. That's why I asked whether you'd sent the right data.'

'Shit! Perhaps Uncle Peter's got into the transfer and trashed the data - hold on.'

Clive opened up the vault on the laptop and ran a command to calculate a hash of the data contained in it. Whiteman did the same - the hashes matched.

'In which case, has one of the software update servers been compromised?', asked Clive, 'if the hashes match, then you've got exactly the same data that I captured by recording traffic between my machine and Uncle Peter.'

'It's more than one server then', said Whiteman, 'this is going back to all the primary operating system development companies. If we're right then Uncle Peter has wriggled his way into all of the biggest software companies in the world.'

40

'Good morning everyone', started Steve.

'Things have taken something of a different direction with this case. It appears that Knollys has been running some kind of dark-network operation alongside the security company.

'The scale of the operation suggests that he's been the hub of an international dark market, selling anything and everything you would expect from this type of criminal online hub. However, the size of it takes it beyond our resources and we have sought external assistance. We're now talking to the NCA and CEOP teams to find a new home for the investigation - most likely within the NCA itself.'

There were a few murmurs around the room before Steve continued.

'We need to get everything in order and package it all up properly. It may well be that our friends in the NCA request ongoing support from some of you - but we'll cross that bridge as and when we get to it.'

Steve looked around the room.

'In the meantime, we want to continue with the technical analysis of the equipment, the lab work, and some of the current strands around MKI and its finances. Alan and Gary will be talking to each of you over the course of the next few days, and we will jointly continue to manage activities until such time as the NCA takes over formally.

'For now, please assume that someone else will have to pick up your work, so make sure it's in a suitable state for that - if you don't, I will see to it that it will be worse than a full-on rubber-gloved internal.'

Jason insisted on Clive taking some time over the weekend to relax. Clive wasn't too concerned as he wanted to give the machines enough time to download all the data stored on his covert servers. So, Clive rigged up his protocol analyser to block Uncle Peter's initialisation system, then the download could continue without any risk of Uncle Peter capturing the data.

By the end of the 24th March, the download completed.

41

Austerity drivers meant that all the analysts were in constant fear of redundancy. The introduction of publicly appointed commissioners had meant that more officers were required on the beat - visible policing - with forces then having to reduce the back-office capabilities and stop many of the longer-term intelligence-led investigations. Becoming instrumental in a case such as this could ensure that Mark had a future in the force - or possibly within the National Crime Agency.

Mark was starting to make some headway into the indecent image management system. There were a couple of primary services comprising of a messaging platform and a file share. Behind this was a payment processor that handled net-based currencies, used because they were extremely difficult to trace, but it could also deal with credit-card payments.

The system could handle pseudo-anonymous file uploads - any site member could upload files and make it available for free viewing or at a member-defined price. When someone purchased access to the uploaded files, the data was decoded, copied to a user-download management system, and then re-encrypted using the purchaser's keys. The purchaser then received the key to decode the data and could then download the encrypted content at their leisure, later decrypting it on their own computer using the provided key. This mechanism ensured that even though site users connected via an encrypted dark-network, in the extremely unlikely event that someone could listen in to the connection, the system still provided a level of protection for the data in transit.

It looked like anyone posting data could leave files on the system for others to view or purchase - and other options to set up rules for subsequent removal. Image retailers could make copies of images available for free - almost as loss leaders - with the rest of an image collection available for a fee.

Once purchased, each purchaser had a local copy of the material, subsequently transferred to the purchaser's computer.

For sellers, the platform offered 'removal after purchase' options that could reduce the perceived risk of arrest of the original poster. It also allowed people to post information and market it as limited edition 'premium content', and restrict the number of people that could download it.

Within the platform, Mark also noticed the ability to create small pay-to-join groups. Here, group members could exchange information freely, but paid a site membership fee, and then a recurring fee to the group owner. It looked like the site managers (presumably Knollys) could also take a percentage of the group membership fee. The site charged for the creation of these specialist groups.

It also managed an escrow mechanism: it took any payment immediately, but then held on to the payment until the purchaser downloaded the content, or marked a transaction as complete. All purchases were rated, so it gave both parties the confidence to deal with each other. In the event that something went wrong with a particular purchase, the escrow system would either refund the original purchaser (less an administration fee), or continue to hold funds until the retailer and purchaser could resolve the issue.

As with most organised crime systems, everything generated money for the site operators. Mark started drawing out how the various system components linked together, and drew in the money-generating items. He wanted to find the links in to the payment management systems so that he could follow the money. This might then lead him to covert accounts used by Knollys and any accomplices.

Part of the analysis of the system involved Mark looking at the configuration files - things it needed when starting up: location of databases, links to other platforms, security credentials, and so on. In amongst these, Mark saw a set of references to generate emails in the event of problems with the system. Each of these had exactly one entry, that of Knollys' personal email account.

'No, no', said Clive, 'it's not just a case of blocking traffic any more - I think we have to do better than that.'

'What do you mean?', asked Whiteman.

'Well, this thing's capable of connecting via anything - so, if we block only one channel, it may well find another route. Potentially one that we can't control directly.'

'Hmm', replied Whiteman, 'what are you thinking then?'

'Well, I've already worked out how the initial handshakes work. If we mimic Uncle Peter - we can, in effect, just send a 'nothing required' message back to the local network. The computers will see Uncle Peter, get told there's nothing to do and that should be that. A straight block might well make the machines here try every route until they find a connection.'

'Yeah, good point. Do you have enough information to do that?'

'I think so. It'll take a few days, but that should allow us to emulate more of Uncle Peter too, so there's an additional benefit. We could potentially mimic Uncle Peter and get to know how the other commands work.'

Whiteman paused for a moment.

'I was thinking about the air-gap. How old's the PC there?'

'It's not just old, it's ancient! Why?'

'Well, I've been trying to work out how long this thing's been around. You said it was an old machine and yet it was doing some pretty sophisticated stuff. That suggests this is a very mature system.

'Furthermore, it looks like whoever's behind this can deploy updates to a wide range of equipment. You think about the management of drivers for all the various ages of machines, different operating system versions, you name it. Version control and deployment alone would require significant resources.'

'Agreed', said Clive, 'I have seen the number 6.8 banded around in all the headers. I actually think that the software behind it keeps track of version numbers - perhaps it upgrades older instances automatically. 6.8 also suggests that it's been around for a fair while.'

'So, we're talking about something that has been around for a long time, requires individual device management, and probably also needs people to assess what it considers worthy of collection. Would that be fair?'

'Absolutely - that's why I said it has to be a major state-led initiative. It has the potential to do damage on a global scale. If I'd let it, it would terrify me.'

'Me too. Do you know what your intelligence lot are doing with the information you provided?'

'At the last count, we were passing everything over to Bill Price in the FBI. I think there's a joint tactical information group for this type of thing, but I have no idea whether this has any real priority - but it should do.'

'Ok, I'll have a dig from this end - let's see what comes up.

In the meantime, if you need anything from me, just shout.'

42

Mark plugged in the projector so that he could present the current findings more easily.

'While we wait for this lot to start up', he said, 'perhaps I could start off by saying that the indecent image side of things appears to be entirely within Knollys' domain. It looks like we've found a management console that allows him to set up and administer the various sites reasonably easily.

'Basically, ask for a hosted dark-net site and pay your fee. Knollys hits a few buttons and sends the entry point to the purchaser. So I think the other hosted services probably need more investigation to resolve questions like site ownership, management and service definitions.

'The FBI has asked that we keep our hands off these services for the time being as most seem to have originated from the US. I have to write up all the findings and will do that in due course.'

The projector had set itself up and the screen now showed Mark's title slide.

'I have concentrated mostly on the indecent image site. Don't worry though, I'm not showing the highlights here.'

Mark often resorted to dark humour when working with difficult or shocking material. His first slide showed an analysis of the covert site: it's most popular pages, sorted by traffic volumes by primary regions.

'We are seeing traffic, but perhaps not as much as we might think, given the number and type of images served by the system. It's either relatively new, or it's available only to a very select membership. I'm leaving it to the CEOP team to work out what's in the imagery, and to categorise it all. Suffice to say that initial indications are that the content covers all categories of indecent material.

'Interestingly, from a site perspective at least, we can see a lot of US dollar transaction records. Currently, we have seen no movements matching any of the payments in Knollys' accounts. Also, for an operation of this size, I would expect Knollys to have something more than a grotty house in the middle of a run-down estate in Crewe. So, I'm yet to find out where the money goes. Perhaps our friends in the FBI could help with tracing these payments. Whichever way, I can't find the money-route to Knollys yet.

He switched to the traffic analysis provided by the hosting company.

'Also, we've seen a massive ramp-up in the data transfers in and out of the hosting service since the explosion. There are numerous sizeable outbound movements - things possibly being transferred out of the hosting environment - over the past few days. Unfortunately, it's all encrypted traffic so I have no way of saying what that was. And, it would appear that whatever it was, it has now finished as the traffic has dropped.'

Mark moved on to another graph, this time showing historic traffic analysis data.

'From the historical analysis of the hosting provider, we can see that inbound traffic increased dramatically a couple of days after the explosion. Aligning roughly with when MI5 provided Knollys with his laptop.

'From a technical perspective, I'm beginning to wonder if Knollys avoided using MKI's servers unless something went catastrophically wrong with some other environment - perhaps one running from his own premises.'

'What do you mean?', asked David Harswell.

'Well, if I were running this type of system, I'd want to keep it reasonably close from a control perspective. But, I'd want to have a back-up ready at the drop of a hat. Perhaps a simple mechanism that kills the data in the event of a raid. If you have that kind of system, you'll need an offline backup somewhere so that you can either rebuild the system, or have it transferred somewhere else.

'Perhaps, therefore, Knollys had a method of kicking off a transfer to set it running on MKI's servers as a back-up for the ones destroyed during the explosion. By providing him with a laptop, he might have had access to equipment that would allow him to do a restore from the backup. That would explain the large data upload seen on the hosting company's network. The download could be another backup process to capture the new environment in case something goes wrong. This would also explain the apparent lack of any significant traffic prior to the explosion.'

'If he is controlling this lot, can we work out where he is?', asked David.

'No Unfortunately all access comes via various dark networks. I have asked for assistance in that regard as it requires a live intercept at a network level - something beyond our local resources. I wouldn't hold your breath on that one anyway - traffic could be coming via many hops through many countries - so, the likelihood of finding a specific location becomes something of a challenge.

'If we can get him to download one extremely large file, we might stand a chance - that generally requires the path to stay open for a reasonable time and we can inject data into the feed while it runs to see where it ends up - it's a long-shot and works but only if the data lands back in a friendly territory.'

Steve White looked at Mark and asked whether Mark had noticed anything unusual about the MKI-hosted dark network service.

'There are a few things that really don't make a great deal of sense.'

'Such as?'

'It's the daft things - why use MKI's servers? Knollys must have thought we would look at them as part of the investigation. If I'm right on the setup being run just after the explosion, then it would make more sense to hide them on servers in Russia, for example - or anywhere well away from anything we might investigate.'

'Perhaps', said David, 'he thought you had already taken forensic images of the servers. We mentioned that we had spoken to the staff …'

'Possibly, but there's also the lack of high traffic volumes - even with an address change, I would expect this type of site to have much more activity. Again I haven't gone through the content - and I really wouldn't want to either - so it could be that this site deals with original or extremely valuable content. In which case, Knollys might want to keep the number of visitors down to known trustworthy service users.'

'Could well be', replied David, 'anything else?'

'The money - where's the money?'

'We've got the FBI looking into that right now', said David, 'that's one of the reasons that they want us to leave everything running. Every new transaction increases the chances of them finding out where the money flows. Let's hope they can do it quickly - who knows, the money might actually give us a location for Knollys too - he has to live, so where's he getting his money from?'

43

Jason and Clive walked along the coast road. It had been a glorious day and Jason had suggested that they go for a walk at low-tide. As they approached the bungalow, Clive stiffened up.

'Look'

'What?', asked Jason.

'There's a car on the drive.'

Jason shrugged it off saying, 'it's probably just Trevor. He said he'd be calling through to see the paintwork.'

'What if it's the PPS or the police?', asked Clive nervously.

'Where's the police car?', said Jason looking round, 'seriously - do you think they'd just park a car on the drive if they wanted to surprise us?'

'Fair point.'

Nonetheless, the two approached the bungalow carefully. Jason opened the front door and stepped inside.

'Hello', he shouted.

'Hello', came a reply from the living room.

Clive saw Jason open the double doors and stiffen up.

'Who the hell are you?', asked Jason.

'FBI', said a familiar voice, 'and I presume you're Jason?'

'Whiteman?', asked Clive as he stepped into the hallway,

'is that you?'

'Sure is.'

'How did you find us?', asked Clive.

'Search engine cookies - you should be more careful: if I can find you, then so can they!'

'Oh', replied Clive, 'do we need to move again?'

'Probably. But leave that to me, I'll sort that out.'

'Hold on a minute', said Jason, 'what do you mean by "search engine cookies"?'

'Virtually every browser stores them', said Whiteman, 'it's what I do to trace people. Whenever you first search for something, the search engine creates a single magic pixel and stores a reference to it in your browser - nothing but a single tiny dot on your screen. Let's say it calls you "computer 1". It stores everything you search for as "Computer 1" using this and a thing called a cookie.

'At this point, it knows nothing about you, just that someone using "computer 1" did a search for, say, paint. A bit later, and a few more searches, it t knows that "computer 1" was also used to find underpants.

'A bit later, you visit a supermarket, and they use the same cookie - the thing calling you "computer 1" to see what you search for. That "computer 1" cookie allows the supermarket to show you things that interest you - so you start getting paint or DIY adverts and a few from leading underwear brands.

'So that cookie saying you're "computer 1" is used by loads of sites to target you for adverts for stuff that you might find interesting - because that's the stuff you searched for. Of course, as soon as you register for a site, or sign in, then we can start to link your identity to the "computer 1" cookie. Now I know you're most likely going to be Jason using "computer 1", and that Clive also uses "computer 1" - after that it's easy. If I find out where "computer 1" connects to the net, then trace that point I can come over and stand in your living room.

'Of course, I also had a fallback position - I know the credit card number I gave you, and could have used that to trace you. But I didn't need to in this case.'

'Scary', said Jason, 'and I was just beginning to like it here.'

'Sorry', said Whiteman, 'but I'll find you somewhere safe. Firstly though, I need a couple of photographs. I'll get some new identities sorted for you both, I'm an old hand at identity creation and management.'

He took a couple of photographs of both Clive and Jason against the white wall of the living room and then sent them to someone via his mobile.

'Why are you here?', asked Clive, 'not that it isn't great to see you.'

'Well', responded Whiteman, 'you got me thinking about Paul - working late was nothing new to him - and he often worked for longer periods than when with you. So I did a little digging and it looks like things weren't entirely right.'

'What do you mean?'

'Officially, Paul died by falling asleep at the wheel - so why did the FBI take over the roadside crash investigation? I visited the scene and there were no skid marks or anything indicating a crash at a speed sufficient to kill someone: why?

'Why, if it was just a crash, did the FBI conduct an autopsy instead of leaving it to the county coroner? Why, if it was just a crash, would the FBI go to great lengths to ensure that all his data went to Bill Price and the Digital Intelligence team immediately after Paul's death? And why have they done diddly-squat with all things to do with Uncle Peter since?

'Things just seemed a little odd. So I asked a few questions. Then there was you - an explosion at your house as soon as it was obvious you had continued working on Uncle Peter.

'I dug some more and found out that MI5 had contacted

Bill Price to ask about what you were doing in our labs. After that, I started seeing some developments over here that I want to check out before I say anything else. Suffice to say, I think things are being covered up and I don't like it - I think we're leaking information to Uncle Peter. So, I think you're at great risk so I wanted you somewhere safe.

'Officially, I'm here at the request of MI5 and NCA to help them trace a serious organised crime syndicate here in the UK. I'm going to lend a hand in tracking the users of the site, and work out how it all hangs together - especially as most of the traffic appears to terminate in US-hosted dark networks. The UK NCA wants to collaborate with the FBI on this case, and I'm the natural lead on this - especially if it takes me away from asking anything else about Paul.'

'And unofficially?', asked Jason.

'Unofficially, I want to get you both properly safe and then find out as much as I can about Uncle Peter. Clive's the only person I know of that has any knowledge in that regard. So while you make me a coffee and start packing, I want to find out what's new with Uncle Peter.'

While Jason went to the kitchen and made drinks, Clive started turning on all the various pieces of equipment littering the living room floor.

'How long have we got before we have to move on?', asked Clive as the equipment started up.

'A couple of days or so, I recon. I've taken the liberty of creating a few remote clones of your PC - scattered all over the UK- it should slow them down if they're using the same techniques as me. But, they might be able to trace things back to this address, so I think we need to assume they will - in which case it's just a question of time. I need a couple of days to sort out new identities for you both, then we can move safely.'

The machines had powered up and Clive logged on to the

protocol recorder.

'If you look at this', he said, 'I can now mimic Uncle Peter for the whole of the setup process. The initialisation bit all looks like a standard software update check. After that, I was able to work out that whenever I generate new data, the system sends a hash-code up to Uncle Peter. See …'

Clive opened up a file on one of the other machines and created some new data by typing randomly on the computer. After a few minutes, a short sequence of numbers and letters appeared on the protocol recorder.

'This looks like a unique identifier for this data and appears after what looks like a random delay. I can respond by entering what I think it a file retrieve command and the other computer then sends the entire file in encrypted form up to Uncle Peter. Interestingly, it splits the information into lots of small chunks and seems to send them as parts of pages next time the browser asks for a page. Look.'

Clive typed in a command on the recorder, followed by the sequence of numbers and letters he had shown Whiteman a few seconds earlier. Then Clive opened up a page on the computer browser.

'See - here's the normal page request. But look, here are encrypted things that look like advert requests and cookie data - actually, I can trap it all and it's actually the file I updated - but encrypted and split over lots of small requests. You'd never notice unless you were looking for it - and, they never appear in any network trace - if you log the network traffic, the traffic monitoring tools ignore this traffic.'

'Neat', said Whiteman, 'if you can find it, it's all hidden in plain sight!'

'Yes', replied Clive, 'although I can't connect to Uncle Peter directly yet - I want to sit in the middle of a live connection and decode it all in real-time. Then I can block it, so we stand a chance of running online without leaking data - or at least I think I can block it.'

'Have you managed to work out where in the operating system this lot runs?', asked Whiteman.

'Not yet - frustratingly, I have test tools I could use, but can't access them. Sometimes my security measures shoot me in the foot!'

'What do you mean?'

'I have some additional tools that are part of a secure backup I created. Unfortunately, it needs an image from either the memory card that was in my safe at home, or on my laptop, or on my mobile. The police have all of those devices, so I'm locked out of my own data!'

'If I could access them, what would you need?'

'The original memory card would be the best - not a copy, copies won't be an exact image - I hide the key in the unused space on a device so that if anyone tries to use a copy, it won't work.'

'Ok', said Whiteman, 'I'll see what I can do.'

'Mark, this is Paul Whiteman over from the FBI to assist with the Knollys data', said Steve.

Mark jumped, he was engrossed in working his way through some data contained in one of the MKI server downloads.

'Oh, Hi - good to meet you Paul', Mark extended a hand to Whiteman.

'Good to meet you too - I'm generally known as Whiteman - I got used to it after doing some work in the field in the US'

The two shook hands.

'Ok - well, I'm Mark Lockhurst - senior analyst and general dogsbody!'

'I hear you've uncovered some interesting data?', said Whiteman.

'Interesting - well - you could call it that!', replied Mark, 'we're still trying to work out exactly what we have.'

'Go on'

'Well, we appear to have some kind of dark network hosting facility here. There are a load of general drug, financial, identity exchange - all the usual stuff - but there's also a child pornography trading site: that's been our main focus. It looks like we have a few first generation images, and that means we could have kids in danger. So, that site has gone over to CEOP - the child exploitation and online protection side of the national crime agency. I'm just finalising the review of the site software.

'After that, I was going to look at the other dark-net services. I guess that's more your line though?'

'Yep', replied Whiteman, 'that's why I'm here - I've been involved in a few of these cases over the years. Happy to help - indeed it would make sense to go through sites so that I can work out if Knollys has set up anything we've not seen before.'

'Knollys has mentioned Whiteman before - are you the person he met in the US recently?', interrupted Steve.

'Yes, the agency has used Knollys and his network protection software in the past. That's one of the reasons I'm here - if he's been pulling the wool over our eyes, we want to know how he's done it and if he's compromised any of our services.'

Whiteman looked over to Steve.

'This could get quite messy for us if it turns out that we've been conned by someone masquerading as a security specialist and raping us for our techniques the whole time. It's something of a personal issue for me - I want to make sure we know what we're dealing with, and whether it's compromised any of our ongoing investigations. This could affect several cases we have, and probably a good few for you guys too. Actually, I'm taking it slightly personally - he's been inside our operation and knows how it works. I was responsible for that, so I want to make sure I'm doing all I can to ensure I've not introduced anything hostile, if you know what I mean.'

Steve nodded thoughtfully.

'Well, if you need anything - just ask', he said.

'Thanks - I appreciate it. Have we got any probes into the live systems? I assume they're still running?'

'Yes', replied Mark, 'we've got the hosting company involved, so we can put anything we like in-line with the MKI servers. We also have images of everything, if that helps.'

'No - in the first instance, I want to see how this stuff's running - and what software's behind it all.'

Steve coughed gently.

'Well, I shall leave you guys to your work', he said, 'but please keep me updated. I'm not sure how long we'll be involved as the NCA will probably take it off our hands within the next few days - but in the meantime, just ask if you need anything.'

'Thanks', replied Whiteman and pulled a laptop out of his bag, 'for now, I just need access to your man here and a few minutes to assess the servers - then perhaps a copy of some of the recovered data, if that's Ok?'

'Who do we trust in all of this?', asked Jason nuzzling into Clive's neck.

Clive groaned gently.

'Oh, I don't know - it's all such a mess.'

'This FBI guy - how well do you know him?'

'Why?'

'Well, we're about to put ourselves entirely in his hands. I just worry about who's hands they are.'

'What do you mean?', asked Clive, turning round and

looking at Jason's concerned face.

'Is he here on behalf of the FBI, MI5, the police … himself?'

'I don't know. Does it matter at the moment.'

'Sure it does - have we just handed our backsides to the FBI by running from the police here? Should we just hand ourselves over and be done with it?'

'Why should we hand ourselves over? This is way better than sitting in some grotty hotel room or grim flat - at least we have some privacy here. You can have your wicked way with me anytime you like!', said Clive with a grin, trying to ease Jason's concern.

'Never stopped me', responded Jason, 'do you trust Whiteman? Should *we* trust Whiteman?'

'I think so. He's played it straight down the line so far', Clive paused, 'but you're right: we're really on our own here, so I think we look out for us. Above and beyond anything else, we protect us. Ok?'

'This is a big set-up', said Whiteman to Mark.

'It is - that's why we got the NCA involved. It goes beyond anything the local force could afford to pursue, if I'm totally honest. It needs deeper pockets, and a lot more manpower than we can spare.'

'There's something about this that doesn't quite fit though', said Whiteman.

'Oh?'

'Look at this lot', said Whiteman as he pointed at his screen, 'this is a configuration file for one of the hosted services.'

'Yes', agreed Mark, 'what am I looking for?'

'If we've got a guy like Knollys - who's an absolute expert in all things security - then why would he put a traceable email address in the configuration files for the server? It pins him directly to the system - he'd use a covert email service, surely?'

'I would have thought so', replied Mark slowly.

'But he's got his personal email address here - and here. The system's configured to send service messages if and when problems occur. I'd have gone for something a little more sophisticated - even tying it in to one of the many secure messaging systems available. That way you get an instant notification if something goes wrong.'

Mark looked at Whiteman.

'Yes, it's a little odd - but perhaps he was in a rush to get things up and running. We still haven't started to assess more than a tiny fraction of the data - I don't know how many services he's got on this lot, so perhaps that's one that is still in development?'

'Could be', said Whiteman, 'where are the clients?'

'In which context - clients using the site, clients paying for hosting …?'

'No, sorry, the client devices Knollys used - a mobile, laptop - did he give you any memory cards? He seemed quite attached to them when he was in my office?'

'Yes - we've got all of them imaged. I can point you to the images on the server if you'd like to access them.'

'Actually, I'm wondering if I could look at the devices themselves - there's something here I'm not seeing, and I'd like to check the devices themselves, just in case.'

'Ok, I'll pull them from evidence - although we will have to maintain control, so I can't give you access to them without me being present.'

'That's Ok', said Whiteman, 'it should only take a few minutes to look anyway'.

Having secured access to the memory card, Whiteman moved on to discuss Mark's view of Knollys and Jason.

'What do you make of Knollys?'

'Smark cookie', replied Mark immediately, 'really knows

his stuff.'

'What made him run, do you think?'

'It was only a question of time before we found this lot - perhaps he got wind of us taking images of all the MKI servers. It's a strange coincidence that as soon as we start looking into the equipment, he disappears.'

'Any idea where he went?'

'No. We've chased down as many links as we can. Unfortunately, surveillance on the rail network isn't as robust as people seem to think - we have a few grainy images that could be them heading to Manchester, and a few more towards Chester - but nothing concrete.'

'Didn't MI5 put tracers in the equipment?'

'Oh yes, but Knollys hasn't put the batteries into his shiny new MI5 wireless router, and the trackers in the bags went on holiday to London without him. He knew - well, either he knew, or he guessed that there was something in the baggage. Whichever way, it went one way and they went the other.'

'You couldn't write this stuff.'

'Yeah - I had a quiet giggle, but don't tell anyone!'

'Had it been my choice, we'd have kept Knollys in the states.'

'Really?'

'Yeah - we got some pressure from MI5 over here to let him come back. We wanted to keep him occupied for a while so we could see which side of the fence he worked on. Looks like we should have pushed a little harder.'

'Perhaps', said Mark, 'but then we might not have found out what he was really up to.'

44

'Well, it's been an interesting few days', said Whiteman as he sat down with his coffee.

'Oh?', replied Clive.

'I have a few small tokens of the FBI's appreciation for the work you do …'

Whiteman handed a manilla envelope over to Clive. Clive opened the envelope and saw a couple of US passports, driving licences, identity cards, and two debit cards.

'Thanks, I think - passports?'

'Yes', said Whiteman, 'things are hotting up a little here. I thought that since you were this close to the ferry port at Holyhead, we could get you over to Ireland and away from immediate danger. Your passport won't be tremendously useful in that respect.'

'Ireland?'

'Yes, we have numerous safe-houses there. It's our outpost when we need to do operations in the UK that are, shall we say, less favourable in the eyes of the UK services.'

'But these are US passports - I think we'd struggle to sound American.'

'And', chipped in Jason, 'if they ask me a single thing about America, we'd be screwed!'

'Stop worrying guys', replied Whiteman, 'nothing says you had to live in the US for a while, merely that you were born there.'

White sensed Clive and Jason's unease.

'Look - there's probably an all ports bulletin out on you two right now - if we get you out of the country, then there's a much better chance of you staying under the radar for the time being. You also need me to help create proper untraceable identities for you both. The only way I can do that with any degree of confidence is to use the systems I used in the past. I know they work because much harder eyes than the security services have tried and failed to find me in the past.'

'Much harder eyes?'

'The Russian mafia; Chinese government; Koreans … they command much bigger resources than you could ever imagine. If they want to find you, they probably will - but with me on your side, it'll take them a lot longer, if at all.'

Jason sighed.

'So', he said, 'you're talking about us continually hiding, changing identities every few months and so on. Does this apply for the rest of our lives?'

'Depends on what Uncle Peter turns out to be', replied Whiteman, 'If it is one of the big criminal groups then we need to stop this system from working - then we've just added a massive barrier to them discovering you both.'

Whiteman looked at Clive.

'You started off on this journey - and I'm very much afraid that you'll have to finish it. There's probably a time limit to you finishing it too.'

'And if we don't finish it?', asked Jason, 'if we just stopped now, for example?'

'I don't think that's an option: you started a journey that you have to finish - or they will most likely finish you. If for no other reason than to stop anyone else following in your footsteps.'

'Shit!', exclaimed Jason. He looked at Clive, 'In that case, I'm going to chain you to the computer kit - the faster we can clear this lot, the better.'

'At least you're used to a semi-nomadic lifestyle', joked Clive, 'you're going to have to teach me how you do it.'

'Nomadic lifestyle's ok, but I was hoping we'd settle down soon. You can get really tired of moving, let alone having to remember where you are - and who you are this week. It's too easy to fuck up and answer to your original name - been there, done that.'

'Or', said Whiteman, 'not answering to your new name. That takes a bit of practice. That's why I use Whiteman and insist on everyone calling me that - it means the underlying name can change as often as I need, but the nickname can float nicely between any identities. In some ways using a nickname tied to several 'real world' names helps as it adds a little confusion to the mix.'

'What do you mean?', asked Clive.

'Well, if you want to find Whiteman, and Whiteman points to several different people, which do you mean? It would take a lot more digging to work out that all of these identities used by Whiteman are one and the same person … especially if you have official real-world documents to back you up, and they cover several nationalities. Whiteman links to a Fred Smith in England, or Francois Girauld in Paris and so on.'

'So we need nicknames …'

'Worth thinking about. In the meantime, I used the same forenames - so if we stick to "Whiteman", "Clive" and "Jase", we should be fine.'

Whiteman finished his coffee.

'Anyway, we need to check we have everything packed - I've booked tickets for us in the morning. I'd suggest you think about how you want to respond to any questions you might get asked. Rather than attempting a phoney accent, you simply go with your parents working for the US military or a US corporate and bringing you to the UK as young kids. Should make life easier as you can then draw on local knowledge as if you were UK citizens. If you got here when you were say 3, or 4, then you'd have no real memories of the US, and no discernible accent.'

'Ok', said Clive.

'And, you've got me coming with you. So I'll do most of the talking.

'Oh, and don't use the MI5 router, it's got a GPS locator', finished Whiteman, taking his mug through to the kitchen before walking into the bathroom.'

'You wanted me?', asked Mark while simultaneously knocking gently on Steve's door.

'Yes, thanks, come in and join us', Steve motioned that Mark should sit at the circular table. David Harswell sat opposite Steve and nodded in response to a 'morning' from Mark.

'How can I help?'

'Well, we're nearly done with handing everything over to the NCA now. Your section has proven somewhat more complex than we originally thought, so before we pitch it over the fence, David asked if you could go through our thoughts to make sure there's nothing else from our side that warrants special attention', said Steve.

'Ok', replied Mark, 'we've definitely captured a load of data in relation to approximately 20 sites - I'm not sure of the exact number as some seem to split out into segments or rely on other services, so we could do with tracing each of those too.

'With regard to the indecent images - well, it looks like we have a collection of first generation images along with credit card details. The data suggests that Knollys has acted as a payment gateway to those generating the content, and either taking a cut or trading directly.'

'So that's that?', asked David, 'What of this secret data acquisition system, this Uncle Peter - any evidence of that?'

'Not so far', said Mark, 'but I've not looked at that. So far we were swamped with data from the MKI servers and Knollys' laptop. I'm an analyst, not a coder, so I can't comment on what Knollys' code does without expert assistance.'

'Ok, let me ask that in a different way: do you consider that this whole Uncle Peter thing is a smoke-screen to keep us away from what he was doing with the dark networks?'

'To be honest, that's outside my area of expertise. It seems a little elaborate for a smoke-screen.'

'But it's possible?'

'Sure, it's possible', replied Mark and looked at Steve for guidance.

Steve shrugged.

'I'm told that, with technology, virtually anything's possible', said Steve, 'although I'm with Mark on this - it all seems a little over the top as an exercise in throwing us off the scent. Anyway, I think that's for the NCA to resolve now

'Have you noticed anything unusual about any of the sites - or anything that gives us a clue to where Knollys might have gone?', asked David.

'On where he is - no. And on the 'anything odd' question, only that it all seems a little clumsy', replied Mark, 'Whiteman from the FBI mentioned it too.'

'In what way?'

'Well, if Knollys is this great security expert, then why would he set the sites up sloppily?'

'Sloppily?'

'Yeah - things like using a directly attributable email address, for example. It doesn't make sense - he'd use an alias, surely?'

'Unless he didn't think he'd get caught. Perhaps he has a remote wipe capability on his 'phone or laptop. I'll bet he didn't expect to lose all his personal mobile tech in one go. So, perhaps he didn't need to worry?'

'All speculation', said Steve, 'we need to ask Knollys that - when we finally get hold of him. Anything else?'

'No', said Mark, 'I just thought it was worth mentioning.'

'Ok, thanks', replied Steve, 'well, carry on with closing things down from our side. Make sure everything's documented - other eyes will be looking at this, and all of us would benefit if it all looks tidy.'

'Yes, thanks for popping over', said David, 'perhaps it's worth leaving the speculative bits out of any report - just hand the facts over and let the NCA team come to their own conclusions - particularly about the security stuff: it's better they look at it completely independently.'

'Surely it's worth mentioning though - even if only in the covering note?'

'No', said David, 'if both you and Whiteman picked up on it, then they will too. They know what these sites look like as a rule, so they would highlight anything unusual. If you colour their analysis before it starts, we could end up tainting the whole investigation. Best to keep speculation to yourself!'

'Indeed', agreed Steve, 'just stick to the evidence'.

45

'Well, that was easier than expected', said Clive as he settled into one of the big leather seats on the Holyhead to Dublin ferry, 'I was expecting more than a disinterested nod!'

'Told you', replied Whiteman.

Clive had upgraded the seats so that they had access to the upper deck on the ferry. There was only one other passenger on this level, so it meant that they had relative privacy and less chance of being seen.

The ferry slipped gently out of Holyhead and past North and South Stacks before turning towards Ireland.

For Jason, this was the first time he'd left the UK and he was both excited at seeing a different country, and slightly depressed due to the circumstances forcing his departure.

'It moves at a fair old speed', said Jason. Getting no response from Clive and Whiteman, he went for a walk on the decks. He watched as Anglesey slowly disappeared behind them and stayed on-deck until the sea breeze made him shiver. He went back inside and ordered a coffee.

It was obvious to Jason that Clive would need some support and assistance if they were to stand any chance of regaining any semblance of normality. He didn't particularly trust Whiteman, there was something about him that made

Jason think that Whiteman was merely using Clive.

'Why', he thought, 'has he taken us out of the protected person network, and then out of the country?'

'Coffee?', asked Clive, 'are you ill?'

'No', replied Jason with a broad grin, 'just wondered what you look like when I'm sober!'

He made a big show of looking at Clive.

'And?'

'You're an ugly fucker!'

'Love is in the air, every sight and every sound', sang Whiteman gently.

Clive looked at Jason.

'Thanks bitch! We were just talking about you.'

'Yeah?'

'Yep. You've got friends all over the place - did you say you knew some people over in Ireland too?'

'Yes. Actually, they're family - distant family, but still family. Why?'

'Just in case', replied Clive, 'it things go tits-up in Dublin then we still have somewhere to go.'

'I guess so.'

Whiteman looked relieved.

'Good', he said, 'this was really a one-shot option for me. I don't have a fall-back plan if we get discovered out here. So I'm hoping we can close this down quickly. I'm intending to check you guys into Le Hotel De EffBeeEye and then head back to the UK to spend a little time with our friends in London.

'Once I've got things in London clear, then we can reconvene. In the meantime, I need you to keep working on Uncle Peter. We have to know what's really going on - I get the distinct impression that we're being kept in the dark.

'In the meantime though, it's better that you're both out of the UK for a while.'

'Why the rush to get us away?', asked Jason quietly and then almost whispered, 'couldn't the protected person service keep us safe?'

'No. It's worse than that. Much worse. You were about to disappear for a while - and not in a good way.'

Whiteman suddenly looked very grave.

'Clive', he said, 'I have to ask you something. Do you have dark networks running on the MKI servers?'

'Oh', replied Clive, 'they found them?'

Mark carried on filling flight cases with DVD's, each labelled with a unique evidential reference tag. As he worked methodically through the piles of discs, his mind kept returning to the case. Things didn't add up, and that annoyed him.

Generally, security conscious people would run this type of service from a remotely hosted environment: something overseas, most likely in Russia. Russia, in Mark's opinion, didn't really care about attacks on westerners: as long as they only attacked people outside of Russia, then who gave a damn.

Why, then, was a world-renowned security expert running dark networks in such an easily discovered way? Mark felt that this was simply too obvious - perhaps someone wanted to frame Clive - to get him out of the way, perhaps. Perhaps this could have something to do with the covert command and control system Clive had mentioned.

Mark stopped and stared into space.

'Right', he said to the otherwise empty room, 'let's do this!'

He left the boxes and left the room, locking the door behind him. He walked up to Steve's office and knocked on the door frame.

'Can I have a minute?', he asked Steve.

'Sure, come on in. Sit down.'

Mark sat.

'How can I help?'

'There's something not right here', started Mark, 'something has been niggling away at the back of my mind for a while - and the more I think of it, the more I think we've been misled with this Knollys case.'

'Go on'

'Well. Take this dark network stuff. If I wanted to set one up, I'd do it using servers hosted overseas; I'd ensure that I had suitable aliases so I never revealed my true identity; I'd set it up with arms-length controls so that I never needed to access the servers directly, let alone have them in my own data centre. It doesn't add up.

'Knollys knows everything there is to know about how people run dark networks, he knows how to find them and to hack them. He's designed systems that can use them to help intelligence services remain completely covert, and conversely how to break them to help international agencies work out how they're used.'

'Ok, so he knows about criminal networks - so what?'

'The "so what" bit means that he would never set up anything in this way. This is almost an amateur system. Perhaps it was state of the art a few years ago, but this has to be one of the crudest designs I have ever seen.'

'Perhaps he didn't have the time to do it properly.'

'I was looking at the design of the image network. Knollys knows how to hide things. Knollys knows how to design extremely elegant systems - and this … well, this is way beneath him. Too far beneath him for it to be him.'

'So what are you suggesting?'

'I'm not sure yet. But it's not right.'

'Listen', said Steve, 'we're done with this case. I've asked you to package everything up and send it over to the NCA. I'm pretty sure that they'll take it all into account - just as you have done. It's out of our hands now.'

'Even if we think it's wrong?'

'Look', said Steve in an exasperated tone, 'I've got pressure from MI5 and the powers that be to release this case as soon as physically possible - and in order to do that, I need you to finish up packaging all the data and sending it to the NCA. So, focus on that because then we can all get on to the next case. Hopefully that might prove a little less political and give us a conviction. I'm over budget on this one, and the stats are all way out because of it.

'I need it gone, sharpish. Ok?'

'So what exactly', started Clive, 'did they find?'

Whiteman paused and thought for a moment.

'Why don't you tell me what you put on the MKI servers?'

'Well - all sorts of stuff really. It's an entire lifetime of general notes, diary entries, current and future designs - ideas for other businesses, source code for loads of prototype ideas …', he trailed off.

'What about the other servers?', asked Whiteman, he watched Clive very intently.

'What other servers?', Clive look confused.

'The, shall we say, more commercial services?'

'I don't know what you mean.'

'You're telling me that you have dark network services running on MKI's servers. What services?'

'Well, they're not dark net in that sense. I have a hidden filesystem and access to it - that's about it.'

'A hidden filesystem?'

'Yes - that's why I need one of the original access keys - without any of those I can't access the full filesystem. I have all my personal notes, source code, designs … all the stuff I mentioned a minute ago.'

'And nothing else?'

'No - why?'

'That's Ok', said Whiteman, 'I thought as much.'

Whiteman sighed and passed Clive his memory card.

'Oh, thank God for that', said Clive, 'Thank you. Is it the original?'

'Yes', Whiteman replied, 'I had to do a little nifty slight of hand to break it out of the evidence chain - so if anyone asks, you had this all along.'

'Ok, understood, thank you. I thought you were saying the police had found all my original data - it's got some pretty sensitive material on there - all the next generation design backups and everything. Some of the code there will really save us some time in getting under Uncle Peter's skin!'

'Clive', said Whiteman, 'you need to be aware of what the police found on MKI's servers. I'm telling you this because you need to know - and I think you're being set up.'

'Set up?'

'Just listen for a moment.

'I'm here on official business as well as to support you as a friend. MI5 advised that the police had found a significant amount of dark network materials on your servers at MKI. There are numerous sites peddling all the usual suspects - drugs, guns, you name it.'

'That's nothing to do with me though', said Clive turning white.

'Shut up for a moment. Listen …

'There's also a kiddie porn site on there. It's a big site with lots of what they call first generation material: stuff generated or put on this site first - not stuff copied from other sites. This makes the site a high priority for investigators as it suggests that the images relate to ongoing and current abuses …'

Jason pointed at Clive.

'He doesn't do that kind of thing - he's helped put systems in place to track and stop Internet abuse. What the fuck are they talking about?'

'Enough', said Whiteman, 'I know that! Let me finish.'

Jason sat forward.

'This is a big site - the other sites also peddle all kinds of illegal content. But the kiddie porn has pushed this right up so that it's now a serious and organised crime investigation. You, my friend, are slap bang in the middle of it. This is why I had to get you out. Someone has access to your servers and has started to get you framed - I'm guessing that it all started around the time you went into the protected person service's care.

'The serious crime guys flagged a major dark net site to us. I had a look and recognised certain elements of it - and this is where things get a little weird.'

'Only now it gets weird?', said Clive.

'Yeah, yeah. Ok. Let me finish.'

'Ok, sorry.'

'So - when I first set up the unit back in the states, I brought Paul on board. Now Paul is an amazing analyst. Or was, sorry. The thing was that Paul, back then, wasn't a great software engineer. He knew how to find patterns but we were building something very different - we were building sites to trap people based on the profiles the Paul created.

'In other words, Paul could tell me what would appeal to criminal groups - from terrorists to small-time drug dealers - based on the way that they used other sites we had managed to monitor or infiltrate.

'We built our honeypots based on Paul's data'.

'Ok, got it', said Clive, 'but what does that have to do with me?'

'Well, the services we set up in the early days ended up being a hybrid of my code and Pauls knowledge. Later on, Paul had the skills to do it all himself. In the unit's early days, however, I wrote a lot of the code for Paul - and labeled it as his - so that I could warrant him remaining in the unit.

'You have to think that we were creating a new way of dealing with cybercrime. I didn't have the space back then for an analyst - I did have a space for a coder.

'Now, that early code went over to Bill Price and his team when they took everything belonging to Paul out of the unit.

'When I came over, I came at the invitation of the UK's National Crime Agency - they wanted an independent assessment of the sites found of MKI's servers based on the knowledge we have in the FBI.

'As soon as I saw the code, I recognised it as the stuff I'd written. It was early code and very rough. The configuration was all crude back then too - I hadn't met you, so security wasn't as strong as it was later on.'

'What are you saying?', asked Jason, 'someone in the FBI is setting Clive up as a paedo?'

'It looks that way', said Whiteman, 'but there's a lot of evidence on those servers that tie you to shed-loads of illegal content.'

'But why?', asked Clive.

'The only thing I can assume', replied Whiteman, 'is we've got an insider - someone from Uncle Peter's side - that someone must sit in Bill Price's team and wants you either dead or permanently removed. Whoever it is can pull the department's strings, so we're talking senior management levels.

'I'm guessing that there's a fallback position in the event that they can't eradicate their problem: you're locked up as some dirty SOB. If you played at being a security consultant to find out how to run dark networks and peddle kiddie porn, then no-one will believe this cock and bull conspiracy theory of yours. It will bury you and Uncle Peter for as long as they can keep you in prison.

'Meanwhile, it buys them time to change the protocols and

work out how to evade your protocol analysis tools. Win-win!'

'Fuck', said Jason, 'the bastards!'

'What do we do?', asked Clive.

'I need time to assess the rest of the material on those servers. I've already seeded some doubts with Mark Lockhurst - the analyst - I want to get him to really look properly at this. If he does, then it will become clear that this is all too convenient and very wrong. He can then throw the whole thing into dispute - in which case we stand a reasonable chance of keeping you and your reputation intact.

'By getting you out of the UK, I'm hoping to buy enough time for you to sort out what this Uncle Peter system does, and for me to go back to the UK and cast a lot of doubt over the dark servers. I can't think of anything else we can do at this stage …'

'Ok', said Clive thoughtfully.

'Sort out Uncle Peter, but for fuck's sake keep your wits about you. If whoever's behind this finds you, then the same could happen to you as happened to Paul: this whole thing will die with you.'

'Right', said Clive, 'as soon as we get to Ireland, I'll set up a local secure communications server. I'll send you the link so you can connect to it - I'll keep it updated with all the latest information and source code as I go - that way, if something does happen to me then you'll have access to everything up to that point.'

'Great, thanks', said Whiteman.

'What about Jason though?', asked Clive, 'I want him out of all of this - can he go somewhere safe?'

'Fuck that', replied Jason immediately, 'you need someone to watch your back, If someone's coming after you, then they come through me first.'

'No', said Clive, 'that's not right - you shouldn't be

involved in this. There's no way you should …'

Jason held up his hands.

'Not up for debate', he interrupted, 'we're in this together - whatever it ends up being.'

46

'I need to level with you', said Whiteman.

'Ok', replied Mark, 'I'm listening.'

Whiteman and Mark collected their coffees and walked out of coffee shop. Whiteman had thought it better to get Mark out of his office, and reduce the risk of them being interrupted.

'I'm going to tell you some things about the dark services you discovered - but - there's a catch. If I tell you, it will break your investigation wide open.'

'Oh?'

'Once it's out, I can't put it back. I do, however, think that we have a problem about reporting lines and who we can trust to handle this stuff sensibly. This will become political and very difficult to contain unless we agree to work together.'

'I can't promise anything', replied Mark, 'but it certainly sounds intriguing.'

'Before I say anything more, can I ask how Steve White has handled the intelligence gathering side of things?'

'I'm not sure what you mean by that - it started out as a potential murder investigation. The stuff we uncovered has taken it up to much higher powers and up to the metropolitan police - there's talk of promotion for Steve, so he's wanting to clear this out of the way and move on. I'm officially off the case within the next few days - I'm just tidying up the paperwork and I'm done.

'All I can say is that he's handled everything pretty much by the book - calling in specialists as required - everything changed when we heard this cock and bull story from Knollys and then our friends from the UK agencies and your good self brought some credibility to the whole thing.'

'Who asked the FBI to get involved?'

'I think it must have been the UK intelligence guys - the first I knew about it was you turning up at the office.'

'So you didn't formally seek our assistance?'

'Nope.'

'Ok. That's interesting', said Whiteman thoughtfully.

They walked to a small park and past a group of teenagers. Once they cleared them, Whiteman started.

'Right - the stuff you've found is very unlikely to have come from Knollys. I've seen that code before - believe me, I know it very well. Knollys wouldn't have had access to it, nor would he set something up that crudely. Didn't you think it odd that everything should have been so convenient? Didn't you question why someone with Knollys' pedigree would make so many basic errors?'

'Well' said Mark, 'I said it was odd …'

'That code comes from a source within in the intelligence community', said Whiteman.

'A source within the intelligence community?' repeated Mark.

'Yes. Knollys didn't put that there.'

'You seem very sure of that.'

'I am.'

Mark stopped walking and looked at Whiteman.

'If Knollys didn't, then who?'

'Now, that's the right question', said Whiteman.

They had walked to the other end of the footpath and were about to leave the park.

'That's why I'm here and that's why I need your help.'

'As I said', replied Mark, 'I'm virtually off the case. And really', he paused, 'you should be having this conversation with Steve, not me.'

'No', said Whiteman, 'you're exactly who needed to know this. You're the only one that can introduce doubts into the technical data. You can question the integrity of the evidence. Steve has his promotion to think of - he's already moved on to bigger things in his mind. You, however, need to do the right thing.'

'Hmm - but what proof do we have that Knollys didn't put that lot there. It will seem quite compelling to a jury.'

'I can tell you - but I need your word that it goes no further. I can not be the source of this information.'

'Ok. I'm not listening, so anything you say now never happened …'

Whiteman looked very intently at Mark.

'I'm serious. You can never tell anyone that I told you this.'

Mark raised his eyebrows and returned Whiteman's gaze.

'I know nothing!'

'Ok - I wrote that code.'

'What?'

'I run a department that creates fake dark networks. We want to get the dealers and the traders - what better way than to run the services ourselves.'

'That's one way of doing it, I suppose. Evidentially, I suppose you second source everything?'

'Yes. Anything coming from the honeypots becomes formal evidence via other means.

'The point is though, that when I first set up the department, I created a proof of concept. What you're seeing there is the proof of concept code: it was never released and never went online - it was full of holes and too easy to break. It was was my learning tool - I learned how to build things properly after the security boffins tore that code - and me - to shreds.

'Knollys never had access to it, so how did FBI internal proof of concepts end up on hosted servers for a tinpot company here in the UK?'

The apartment in Bray wasn't too bad. It was a Victorian 3-story end-terrace with broad double-fronted steps leading to solid outer doors on the middle floor. This particular apartment was on the ground floor and had an additional set of french windows with a view over the Irish Sea.

Clive had reverted to his obsessive self again: he needed to get everything off the covert servers. He worried that the UK police or combined intelligence services would take them all off-line. As a result, he had set the transfer processes running as soon as they arrived at the apartment.

Before Whiteman travelled back to the UK, Clive had set up a private server that could host a new instance of the secure messaging systems. Again, with the imminent risk of discovery, he moved all the secure services over to other systems and then set about deleting the covert framework from the MKI server array.

The memory card Whiteman had recovered from the UK police gave Clive access to all of his old data and a host of tools he could use to help trace Uncle Peter.

'There's something I don't understand about this lot', said Jason bringing Clive his fourth coffee of the morning.

'What's that?', asked Clive.

'Why didn't the police find all this stuff you're downloading now?'

'Ahh - a variation of steganography!'

'And the same to you …'

'It's a way of hiding information inside other information. Think of hiding data inside a picture, you look at the picture and don't see the other data.

'Anyway, when Whiteman said they'd found hidden stuff on the MKI servers, I thought that they had somehow managed to break into my system. I was nearly impressed at the intelligence community's analysis capabilities.

'The problem I had was that I stored the sequence required to access the data on another device so without the other device, no-one can recover the data on the servers - including me. I had my mobile, my laptop and the memory card in my safe to make sure I always had access to something that would allow me to use my data. With the explosion and subsequent removal of all my devices, I had nothing left that would let me get at my own tools and data - it was really slowing me down.'

'Why did you need that level of security? I mean, who needs it?'

'I invent security tools - if the source leaks into any hacker's hands, then they can build stuff that works around my tools. If I can keep it safely out of the way, then no-one can do that. You have to bear in mind that by creating tools used by intelligence services, I become a target for every other intelligence service. I make sure that each of the developers in my team never has access or sees the entire system - that way none of them can become targets. It will, however, be giving them all serious problems at the moment as they'll have to work in a different way without me there.

'Anyway, some of my tools break into networks too - they're hackers tools on steroids. Again, if I want to secure a system from attack, I need to understand all the attacks. I have a fair old arsenal of hacking tools now. If these were physical objects, I could open a hacking museum with this lot!'

Jason had glazed over. Clive realised he was now just talking for talking's sake and stopped. After a few moments Jason drifted back from wherever his mind had taken him.

'Ok', he said.

'All you need to know is that it will, finally, make things easier - and hopefully - get us out of this mess faster.'

47

'We called the NCA in on the basis of you finding this stuff on MKI's servers. We can't go back on it now - your concerns do not match the evidence. Bear in mind that you're responsible for so many people crawling over this - right now, I'm not minded to provide anything other than the evidence you collected. Let the experts form their own conclusions eh?'

Steve White was clearly not going to mention Mark's strongly worded doubts about the MKI-hosted dark networks. Mark, slightly annoyed at the suggestion that he was inexpert, thought he'd give it one last shot.

'Surely it makes sense to highlight the ....'

Steve cut him off.

'Just hand over the fucking evidence. If you're having a problem with that, then perhaps I could ask someone else to package everything up and send it over. We're not part of this investigation any more. Package it, send it, move on. Ok?'

Mark was furious but couldn't really say anything. He stomped out of Steve's office and back to the lab.

'Not bloody minded to provide anything other than the evidence eh?', he muttered to himself, 'well if you won't, then I will.'

He picked up his mobile, fished a card out of his coat

pocket and dialled a number.

'Hello', said Whiteman.

'Whiteman, it's Mark - I need to talk.'

'By George, I think she's got it!', shouted Clive excitedly.

Jason came into the front room. It now looked like a mad-professor's study: paper designs had been stuck onto the walls, process sequence diagrams littered the floor around several pieces of computer hardware.

'Got what?', yawned Jason.

'I think we're just about ready to take on Uncle Peter. I've got this machine believing it's actually talking to Uncle Peter, when in reality it's talking to my FreeBee box. I think I've got the whole thing mapped out.'

'About bloody time too!'

'Now', grinned Clive, 'I think we're ready to build an Uncle Peter tracking system: let's find out where this lot ends up ...'

48

'What convinced you?', asked Whiteman.

'Well', replied Mark, 'I had a really good dig into the systems - as they appeared on the surface - but then really started digging into the services. We had Knollys' email addresses in the configuration files, the hosting company reports showed a distinct lack of traffic for a site of that size, the whole thing was just clumsy. When I looked at the backend, I could see why it wasn't really fit for purpose - and the biggest thing of all: I couldn't find any payment traffic. It was almost as if the site suddenly appeared, along with a big customer base and trading history.

'When I looked at the hosting company's records, I couldn't see anything suggesting an organisation of that size. On the face of it, we have an organised crime network, it has network logs and all kinds of supporting materials to make it look like it has existed for some time. But if you correlate that with the hosting company records, they don't match properly. I agree with you - someone is trying to set Knollys up.'

'Told you!', said Whiteman.

'However, I can't do anything about it because I have to leave it to "the experts" in the NCA to resolve.'

'Ouch!', said Whiteman, 'that must have stung.'

'Yes. It did', replied Mark, 'I'm not a software expert, but I do know how to look at data and fit it all together. If you merely take the data at face value, then Knollys has been running a pretty comprehensive set of dark networks. Dig a little deeper, and it appears that the entire thing appeared overnight.'

'Any idea where it came from?'

'None at all. I can't find a single audit trail - I think the data came via a covert channel - perhaps the very thing Knollys was looking for.'

'Well, let's ask him?'

'You know where he is?'

'I can contact him', said Whiteman, evading the question.

Whiteman fished out his burner and sent Clive a message.

"Whiteman: Call - need to talk"

"Clive: Setting up now"

A few seconds later Whiteman's 'phone rang. Whiteman answered and then put the device on speaker. They exchanged the now customary code-word to ensure no-one had intercepted the call.

'Clive, I have Mark Lockhurst with me - the senior analyst that was assessing MKI's servers. He and I both agree that you had nothing to do with the dark network systems, but Mark is having difficulties convincing the investigation team that this is the case. How could those servers have been loaded up without anyone seeing it?'

'Hi both', said Clive, 'Easy - Uncle Peter.'

'Expand on that please', said Whiteman.

'Sure. Uncle Peter's not just one piece of code. It's actually a very comprehensive and very low-level command and control system. Anyone using Uncle Peter's control system can take full control of the target machine. Software installation, service manipulation, database management - it looks like it's all there.

'From what I can determine, Uncle Peter has its own mini-operating system within its host. It looks like a tiny kernel - a really small block of code that runs other modules. The protocol looks like it fires off a particular tool that runs inside that kernel - the data for that comes via the network or is generated by the tool itself.

'Basically, the computer side of Uncle Peter runs within a tiny footprint but because it's tied in to the operating system itself, it has immense power. It's a clever system.'

'So to install something on your servers …'

'Easy. I send an instruction to download an installer from one of Uncle Peter's servers. In time, the target machine will receive that instruction and then download the installer. Because Uncle Peter runs its own mini-operating system, I only need to write the installer once - it will run on anything with a processor and some way of communicating. So, the installer will then go and fetch the relevant files, install them on the host and then delete itself along with any history that it was ever there.'

'That explains how the code got there', said Mark.

'Yes', replied Clive, 'but the neat thing is that this core code for Uncle Peter only occupies a tiny amount of space. It downloads and then executes anything it needs to do - if you were to look for anything on the host computer, it doesn't exist for any longer than it absolutely needs to … and each module removes its own tracks as it goes.

'I actually think - although I can't prove it yet - that the core code tracks whatever changes on the filesystem and automatically cleans up after the code finishes.'

'So', said Mark, 'just so we're absolutely on the same page. You're suggesting that the people that you claimed tried to kill you are also responsible for putting this code on your servers.'

'I have no proof of that', said Clive, 'but I would imagine

so. I only found out about the servers a couple of days ago: I've been dissecting Uncle Peter!'

'But …?', said Mark.

'But yes. Yes, I think it probably is the same group - and as I've said before, I think it's all run by a government-funded operation. It requires a vast amount of resources to manage all of these computers and their associated operating systems, software conflicts and so on', replied Clive.

'How do we take this forward then?', asked Mark.

'Might I suggest', started Whiteman, 'that we give Clive all the support he needs to complete his analysis of Uncle Peter's activities. If he were to share some of that information with you, Mark, then you could check out whether anything similar exits on MKI's servers. If it does, then there's your answer.'

'Ok', said Mark, 'but be aware that I'm now off the investigation. This will have to be completely off-book.'

Whiteman nodded.

'Out of interest', said Mark, 'could they have installed Uncle Peter on our PC's in the labs?'

'Absolutely', replied Clive, 'It's actually worse than that. I think - although we have yet to prove it - that any computers associated with intelligence activities will have Uncle Peter's beady eye on them.'

'Shit!', said Mark, 'so much for secrecy, integrity and protecting the chain of evidence. Aside from the commercial and criminal implications, this could also blow every case based on the analysis of data. No wonder MI5 and the NCA are all over it. I can't think of a single cyber case that would stand in court if this got out.'

'Indeed', said Whiteman, 'it's a nightmare for every law enforcement agency globally. How do we otherwise prove that the data didn't come from an unknown source unless we catch the perpetrators at the scene at the time and actually doing the deed as it were?'

49

Detective Superintendent White was finalising the transfer of the Knollys case over to the NCA. His local force had done quite well out of the discovery of the dark network sites hosted on the MKI servers. From funding to inter-force PR, the senior management had made much of the technical and deductive powers of the investigation team.

Mark, therefore, had presented him with a few doubts about the dark network servers - had Knollys really been stupid enough to run systems that would directly tie him to criminal activities. Steve called up the investigation record on his computer and edited his notes to include:

"The senior investigation team raised concerns about why Knollys used his own email address and other associated data, rather than using more covert methods. At this point in the investigation, however, the technical team had established a significant amount of indecent material, most likely first generation, and immediately passed this information to the National Crime Agency."

With this single paragraph, Steve had inserted something that he could later refer to in the event that the NCA came to the same conclusions as Mark. He had, in effect, covered bis backside and protected the force from any come-backs from the NCA in the future.

Mark, however, had carried on digging. Immediately after the explosion, Mark had made DVD copies of all the data on all the MKI servers. He had also, as a precaution, taken copies of the hosting company logs so that he could prove whether someone had attempted to delete or access information remotely.

'Look', said Clive triumphantly, 'that's my machine responding to Uncle Peter'

Jason looked confused.

'And?'

'But it isn't Uncle Peter - it's my box. I've finally sorted out how Uncle Peter works.'

'About time too', replied Jason.

'It's a pretty simple thing - I found a small block of code that runs in the background, all the time. It's tiny and provides its own software version of a computer - a very small one. It almost looks like the old home computer systems where everything could run on a very low powered processor with virtually no memory.

'So this little tiny computer only does a few things. When it starts up, it sends a request that looks like a software update check. If the check comes back with nothing, the code sleeps and periodically sends another check message.

'If, however, the software update check comes back with something, then the code downloads whatever program code and data it needs, runs it, then removes itself again, leaving just the tiny bit of code again. However, it looks like it can keep its own library of code in its own encrypted file system. This means that when Uncle Peter sends something that it wants to run on a regular basis, this tiny computer can do it without having to download or contact Uncle Peter in the meantime.

'By doing it this way, the code itself stays tiny and is very difficult to find. However, it makes it incredibly flexible - you can send anything to the computer to make it do anything.

'It could also explain why computers inexplicably go wrong - you changed nothing yet the whole thing crashes and then starts up again normally - they sent something that broke the machine - as there's no permanent copy of it, it doesn't run again and you can't find out what happened.

'If this exists on mobile 'phones too, it could also explain why the battery suddenly tanks. You've done nothing on the device - but if it was told to act as a gateway to access other computers either by sound or by creating a local network, then it will kill the battery and again, leave no trace.'

'So how does Uncle Peter know what your computer is? I mean wouldn't it have to know about every computer and every device connected to it surely?'

'Not at all: if every computer has this tiny virtual computer installed inside it, then you can make it the same everywhere.'

'Not sure what you mean', said Jason.

'It's a bit like using an interpreter - we speak English, so we use an interpreter to allow us to communicate with someone in Spain or France. So if these various computers all speak different languages, why not provide a very small piece of code that runs my 'English' code and relies on a simple interpreter to allow a Spanish computer to understand what I want.

'Uncle Peter could then send an instruction that says "has anything changed in the computer" in English and that would then get interpreted by the Uncle Peter code into the same thing but in French, or Spanish.'

'How do they get that on the machine in the first place?', asked Jason.

'Good question', replied Clive, 'and I have no idea. I

haven't worked that bit out yet.'

'Can't you just stop that bit of code from running?'

'If I could find it, then I would - but even the software debugging tools don't show it. When I step through code, the debugger should show me everything step by step - but it doesn't go through anything that Uncle Peter does - it's almost like it has a stealth mode or something.'

'Stealth mode?'

'Yes. It's hidden from everything. I might even suggest it has buried itself in the computer firmware - the chips inside the computer. If it runs in there, then the operating system might not even know it's running this code.'

'So what are you doing now?'

'Well, I have been able to trace everything - and I'm able to trap the communications. All of this lot', said Clive as he pointed at the papers strewn around the room, 'show how the system works. Now I'm going to send Uncle Peter something off FreeBee and see if my code can get a load of instructions of Uncle Peter. If I can send something to him, perhaps I can trace where it ends up - then we know who we're dealing with.'

'How do you intend to do that?'

'I have created a document that opens up a link back to one of my servers. The second it connects, I will have that computer's address. I can trace that then - or at least I can in theory. Worth a try!'

Clive connected everything back to the Internet and then started up his computer emulator. After a few minutes, Uncle Peter had visited. Clive entered a few commands and then prepared to send his booby-trapped file.

'Ok', he said, 'here goes!'

He sent the file. Almost immediately, Uncle Peter closed the connection.

'Shit', said Clive loudly.

'What?'
'I don't think they liked that. They shut me out.'

50

'This coffee tastes like shit!', said Whiteman.

'It's the best we'll get round here', replied Mark, 'let's take a different route today'.

They stepped out of the coffee shop and walked away from the park.

'So where are we?', asked Whiteman.

'You're right - you're dead right. I can't find any trace of the dark networks before the explosion. As soon as Clive went into the care of the PPS things started changing on the servers.'

'Can we prove that?'

'Oh yes. I managed to retrieve the hosting company's backup tapes. I've spent the past few days going through and rebuilding the servers as they were at the time of the explosion at Clive's place.'

'I didn't think you had a pile of servers lying around.'

'Ahh - we can use those seized from other cases. We often find that the criminals have better kit than us: they can afford it. Once we have secured a prosecution, we have access to the machines for a while. Eventually, they get sold off or destroyed.'

'Good idea', replied Whiteman, 'keeps the technology bills

down'

'Anyway', said Mark, 'the backups came from the hosting company, not MKI. These are backups of the entire group. It's a good job the technical team aren't quite as bright as the company literature suggests - they were told to give me whatever I wanted under the terms of the original investigation. I went back to them and asked about their backup processes and then obtained one of their offsite backups. Luckily, they do a complete backup overnight and keep all of the last 7 days, then a weekly backup for the month preceding, then a monthly backup for the past 2 years.

'I was able to get backups that showed the server state 2 weeks before the explosion. None of the dark network code appeared on that backup. The backup schedule meant that the next one came a couple of days after the explosion. That's when the code existed.

'Also, the MKI server logs would suggest a level of traffic between the dark network servers and its apparent users that I can't find when I look at the hosting company logs. That level of traffic just wasn't there.'

They reached the end of the block and turned left.

'So', said Mark, 'I think the whole dark network stuff's a load of crap.'

'Told you', agreed Whiteman.

'I am going to have to raise this with Steve.'

'Ahh, our new Detective Superintendent', replied Whiteman, 'I'm not convinced you'll get a great deal of support for your latest research. Hasn't he been promoted on the back of finding this lot?'

'I know. But I am sort of duty-bound to tell him. I have a worry that someone's inside the case too - some evidence has changed.'

That alarmed Whiteman. He had swapped the memory card to allow Clive to access his data. Surely Mark hadn't noticed.

'Oh?'

'I printed a copy of everything stored on Clive's handset as soon as it came in. The thing is, now it doesn't tally with the electronic copy, nor the handset. If I hadn't printed it all, I wouldn't have known.'

Whiteman gave a silent sigh of relief. Mark had, however, confirmed Whiteman's suspicions - someone else had been working to set up Clive.

'I'd suggest we don't tell Clive about this lot yet', said Whiteman.

'Oh? Surely he'd like to know that we have evidence to prove he had nothing on the servers ...'

'Perhaps', replied Whiteman, 'but at the moment, he's entirely focussed on sorting this mess out. For the time being, at least, I think we should keep him motivated and concentrating on the task in hand, don't you?'

'That's a bit mercenary', started Mark.

'Look', interrupted Whiteman, 'we're on a tight schedule with some very well connected people. Think about it - they knew Clive wasn't in the explosion; they had enough knowledge to infect MKI's servers just ahead of the main investigation team - pure serendipity for us that MKI uses hosted services and that the hosting company does a proper job of backing up their data centre.

'So, let's just assume the worst for a moment and say that Uncle Peter's all over this. It's only a question of how long we've got before they find Clive, or until they work out that he's still trying to crack this lot. For all I know, they could be on to me too. This is big, most likely a foreign power or a major organised crime syndicate with significant resources. How else did they get inside your investigation?'

'I guess that's me in the spotlight too then.'

'Yes - which is why I was suggesting you keep things

relatively quiet and between us. You won't get any support from Steve White in all of this: he has his promotion and has all but moved on already. That means that you have to keep hard copies of everything and keep it all off the networks at the moment.

'The bottom line is that I think they would probably kill Clive to shut him up. Perhaps that means that both you and I end up in the same hit-list if we become to vocal. My recommendation is that you keep your head down and collect as much evidence as you can behind the scenes.

'If this ever hits a court of law, and I doubt it will, then your evidence will provide enough doubt to clear Clive. For what it's worth, I think they will want to know how Clive found Uncle Peter so that they can modify it enough to evade similar exposure in the future.

'Until then, Clive could be an asset. Once he has the system cracked, then he becomes either their greatest ally by designing a better version and exposing their weaknesses; or, their greatest threat and they'll need to silence him as soon as he can prove that Uncle Peter exists. The problem is, I'm not sure whether I can protect him in either scenario - and somehow I don't think there's much room for negotiation.'

51

'Right', said Clive, 'I think we're about ready. Are you both there?'

Both Whiteman and Mark confirmed that they were available via their secured lines.

'Great. In that case I can bring you up to date.'

'Before we do', interrupted Mark, 'do we have a time limit on this connection?'

'What do you mean?'

'Well, do we have a traceable connection - and if so, how long do we have before we have to clear the line.'

'Oh', replied Clive, 'that's not really a problem from this end - the secure messenger uses the dark network. In effect, we hop between thousands of servers globally. We change our connection, and therefore our location, every couple of minutes.'

'Yeah', chipped in Whiteman, 'it's the bane of our lives sometimes. However, we should only really use anonymised fixed line VPN or public WiFi with Clive's security code for anything serious.'

'Oh?'

'Put it this way - we have access to every piece of data on the mobile networks. We even have historical data analysis capabilities.'

'What do you mean?'

'We have access to the core mobile networks, so we record everything that comes off every mobile device. Then we use deep packet inspection to find anything of interest - basically, it delves into the data to find anything we might want to analyse further.'

'Isn't that encrypted?', asked Clive.

'Oh yes, but that doesn't matter.'

'How so?'

'Deep packet inspection can look at data, even if encrypted. That's how the big cloud services were able to intercept child pornography on their so-called encrypted platforms and tip off the authorities.'

'Yep', said Clive, 'there's no such thing as a secure cloud!'

'Anyway, deep packet inspection gives us a probability value - how likely is it that any given packet of information contains a word or phrase of interest? Once we find something of potential interest, then, as we have copies of all the mobile SIM encryption keys, we simply use that to decrypt the suspect packets.'

'Hold on - you have access to all the SIM keys - that's like open access to every mobile device in the world.'

'Oh yes', said Whiteman, 'and we can update or modify the subscription records if we need to. People forget or simply don't know that they're using a cellular radio network built on second world war technology. At the end of the day, we simply grab all the transmissions in the same way as you would record a programme off the radio. Once we've recorded it, we can replay it at our leisure - with the SIM keys, all the encryption simply disappears.'

'But if you have access to the SIM data, doesn't that mean that you can spoof anyone's identity?'

'Yes'

'So you could inject data into the network - fake text messages and the like?'

'Of course.'

'So what of the terrorist cases where mobile data was one of the primary pieces of evidence', asked Mark, 'are you saying the intelligence community can spoof that?'

'If necessary', replied Whiteman, 'along with location data too. We can inject content from any location - sometimes we only need to show that a person was at a specific location at a given time in order to secure a prosecution …'

'But that undermines …'

'Stop!', said Whiteman, 'We're talking about intelligence here. Sometimes the end justifies the means - it's the way of the world. Rules don't exist in the war against terror. Anyway - it's just a tool I have access to - mobile is radio; anyone can listen to a radio. Anonymised VPN and public WiFi communications all present something of a challenge for the services, so I prefer to use those services with encryption over the top of that.

'Anyway - let's assume they'll find the link eventually, and then I'm hoping one of us will find out and alert the others. In the meantime, where are we?'

'Ok', said Clive, 'I think I've got everything I need now. I've spent the past few days analysing all the services.

'I can now conform that we have a small kernel and that it lives in the firmware in all the machines here. In other words, whatever infected these devices either did it during manufacture, or as an update to the computer. Because it's in firmware, the operating system and any software doesn't see it, it just works. I've seen things looking like software updates already, so I'm working on the assumption that Uncle Peter delivers code and instructions via compromised software update services.

'Because it puts itself into the firmware - the chips inside the computer - if you subsequently reformat the machine or replace the operating system, it doesn't matter. The code's still there, so it just downloads any appropriate components for the new operating system as it needs it.

'This code runs in a tiny space - it's less than 16K in total and all it really does is provide a communications system and area where downloaded code can run. As far as I can work out, it uses any device as a communications tool - so if there's a network card, it can use that; wireless onboard, then it uses that; audio systems as a fall-back. I've also seen a segment of code that I think uses any connected devices - so, if you plug something into a connected computer then Uncle Peter can see it, and potentially infect it too.'

Whiteman interrupted, 'Can you explain that point again? I just want to understand the implications of that.'

'Anything you plug into an infected computer, say a scanner, printer or a hard disk - anything at all - well, Uncle Peter will update that device so it spreads the infection. Install Uncle Peter's code onto the printer as a firmware update to the printer. Later, you connect that to another machine or network and that machine or network then gets infected. Uncle Peter can then install the same code on all the connected machines - most likely via the same firmware or operating system updates for those machines.

'This makes a mockery of all the systems where we have no conventional network wiring as a security measure. Lets say you have a wired network that's locked down so there's no external connection, you take an infected mobile 'phone into the data centre, Then you take a document into the data centre on a memory card. You plug it in, and just by doing that, Uncle Peter has installed itself on an internal machine. If that machine has speakers and a microphone, Uncle Peter can use high-frequency audio to connect to your 'phone and then uses your 'phone's network connection to talk to the

Internet.'

'Ouch', said Mark.

'It gets worse', said Clive, 'Uncle Peter has an offline mode - or appears to. Here it can accept a set of instructions via these plugged in devices - let's say you use a camera on both networked and non-networked computers. Uncle Peter can store data on the camera memory card that, when you plug it into your non-networked computers, Uncle Peter downloads the code from the camera, runs whatever that code does and then puts the result back on the memory card. You take the memory card out and put it back into a connected computer, or mobile device, anything with a network connection and those results go back to Uncle Peter.'

'That's some system', said Whiteman.

'It is - and it's actually very simple. It's a tiny virtual computer kernel. Once it's installed on a device, then it simply waits for instructions in the form of downloaded data from any available network. Until it gets something it sleeps - the ultimate sleeper code.'

'And you've got proof of this?', asked Whiteman.

'Yes - I managed to print out the code. It's clever in that as soon as you try to access the firmware where it lives, it hides itself so you can't find it via normal means. Access a memory address containing Uncle Peter, and it gives you the contents of something somewhere else.

'However, I managed to grab and encrypt the real code by stalling the computer as it ran. And once I had the code, I could get it, decode it and print it character by character. I inserted additional lines of junk in case the printer was looking for some form of signature in the code that would then trigger a change in the code before printing it.'

'Shadow code', said Whiteman, 'I've heard of it, but never come across an instance of it.'

'Shadow code?', asked Mark.

'Yes', replied Whiteman, 'many years ago, we had a project in the agency that set out to create code that had a shadow. If anyone looked at memory in the shadow, they only ever saw the thing placed in front of it. We could hide anything in the shadows. It looks like someone got hold of it.'

'Interesting', said Clive, 'well - I think they got it working alright. Either it's your code, someone else developed the same concept, or some other agency got hold of it and deployed it in the wild.'

'Perhaps Uncle Peter had a previous version installed on our development computers back then!', replied Whiteman, 'And if someone had access to that covert project, then it's probably right to assume that that entity has access to every covert project …'

'Well', said Clive, 'it presents itself as version 6.8 of the protocol, so it looks like it's been around for a while.'

After a few seconds of thoughtful silence, Whiteman asked what Clive wanted to do next.

'Well, I have the code printed out. I have a complete copy of Uncle Peter and I have managed to build a version into FreeBee that will act as a decoder and blocker. I want to combine resources to create a honeypot - something so interesting that Uncle Peter will want it. Then we use my new FreeBee code to trap the lot. I'll print it so that we have a copy of everything - in a form that Uncle Peter can't modify after the event.

'If we have a few larger files - things that take some time for Uncle Peter to process - perhaps we can get lucky and find out where it ends up.'

'Slow the transmission down', suggested Whiteman, 'that way it will take longer to transfer stuff. I can set up network traces back at the office once we know what we're looking for.'

'Great', replied Clive, 'And, perhaps we could install a few trojan horses of our own - anything to give us an end-point that reveals either Uncle Peter's true identity, or at least his location.'

'I have an idea for a project', continued Clive, 'but I need to send you both a copy of the code that will protect you from Uncle Peter first. You'll need to get a small machine - something like a Raspberry Pi and I'll send you both memory cards with the detector and blocker on it.'

'Can you send us copies of the print-outs too?', asked Mark, 'It's the evidence we would need to effect a prosecution and it makes sense for us all to have independent copies of everything. Just in case anything happens to any one of us.'

52

'Ready', said Clive.

'And in 3, 2, 1', he pressed return on the keyboard.

'And we're live. Let's see how long it takes for Uncle Peter to take the bait.'

Jason massaged Clive's shoulders as Clive called up Mark and Whiteman.

Once they confirmed the words on their respective screens, Clive started talking.

'Ok chaps', he said in his best English war-time newsreel voice, 'we have launched the honeypot.'

'Excellent', replied Mark, 'do we take bets on how long before Uncle Peter starts sniffing?'

It had taken the team a few days to create a set of machines that would look like a new server installation. As Clive was now aware that Uncle Peter used the real hardware, he had taken great care to keep Uncle Peter's prying eyes away from the laptop. By making use of the hardware to hide Uncle Peter's activities, Clive was now aware that some of his earlier precaution of running everything within a virtual machine had done little to protect his machines from leaking data. Luckily, the earlier versions of FreeBee would have blocked data at a network level. If nothing else, Clive had created a product that could protect entire networks from the current version of Uncle Peter.

'Now to create the poisoned chalice', said Clive, after a few moments during which he added Mark and Whiteman's contributions to the newly visible honey-pot.

'What's the poisoned chalice?', asked Jason after Clive had hung up.

'Good question', replied Clive.

'We want to get something interesting for the Uncle Peter team, something that will let them download large files. The longer it takes for them to download something, the greater the chances we have of tracing the connection.

'The honeypot attracts Uncle Peter to it. Inside the honeypot, we make reference to a system of hiding files within files and then provide some examples. The best example being one of some considerable size - meaning that when they grab it, I slow the network connection down - a lot - so much so, that the computer will send one piece of information and literally at the moment that the other computer hangs up, thinking we've gone offline, we send the next bit. We keep doing that so that each piece of information takes an age to get there, with a connection open the whole time.

'When we notice that Uncle Peter has started downloading the files, Whiteman can use his FBI toolkit to trace the data path and then we know where Uncle Peter keeps his data.

'The poison part comes from the way that we encode our information. So, when you save a file on a computer, it's stupid - it has no idea what type of file you have just saved. These days, the computer uses a thing called a file extension - a full stop followed by a few characters that lets the computer know what type of information the file contains.'

'Oh, like JPG or PNG for images?', asked Jason.

'Yep. Exactly. So, if you end a file with .JPG then the

computer will try to open the file with an image processor. End it with .DOC and the computer will open it as a word-processed document and so on.

'So, if you look at how we encode information in these various files, we can find ways of exploiting them to do lots of different things.'

'Like?'

'So, a .GIF graphics file ignores comments and things at the start of a file; .JPG ignores all the stuff at the end of the file. So, we could store two different images in the one file - one will load as a GIF, the other as a JPG - and the computer decides which one to open based on the file name extension.

'We've taken that a step further and created a tool that will also allow you to embed a word processor document and within the document, we store a compressed and encrypted file. Within that, we store a whole directory of pictures and a small program that says 'Hello, World' when run inside a browser.

'We're hoping that whoever reads the file will get interested and amused enough to go through all the steps and then click on a link to run a small script that says 'Hello, World'.

'And, if they do, they'll also open another connection straight back to us. That connection contains a load of information captured from the computer opening the file. We should know exactly what machine, on what network, in which location, and even which user - or at least the login name of the user - is at the other end.

'We've made it all look innocuous - including the end data connection, which appears simply to reflect the information captured to demonstrate a point. If Uncle Peter comes after that server, then we've used the same shadow coding principles to hide what the services really do - trace Uncle Peter back to its source.

'Now we have to wait until Uncle Peter takes the bait - then it's up to Whiteman to do his stuff.'

'Wow!', said Jason, 'I'm impressed. This is proper spy stuff.'

'Oh yes', replied Clive.

'So does this mean I'm an agent too?'

'I guess so - why?'

'Well, if I'm the agent, I guess we've finally got some time to cut to the shagging scene.'

53

At 3AM, Clive's 'phone beeped.

Clive turned over and gently removed Jason's arm from around him. Still naked, Clive crept out of the room and hit the answer button.

'Battered Buttocks', said Whiteman at the other end, followed by, 'are all these check-words innuendos?'

Clive checked the screen. Sure enough, 'Battered Buttocks' appeared on his screen. They had a secure connection.

'Yeah, sorry. I let Jason edit the keyword file - he was bored.'

'Figures', said Whiteman, 'just waiting for Mark'

As he finished speaking, a rather tired sounding Mark joined the call.

'Battered Buttocks', he said.

'Ok, now we're all here', said Whiteman, 'I'm running a trace. Uncle Peter started fishing a few minutes ago, so I'm holding an incoming request for a directory listing. When I release this - and if he does as we expect - then Uncle Peter will start grabbing files. I thought you guys would like to share the moment.'

'Yes indeed', replied Mark.

'Thanks', Clive yawned.

'Ok, here goes nothing!', said Whiteman and released the hold on Uncle Peter traffic.

Almost immediately FreeBee's LEDs flashed to indicate that it was monitoring Uncle Peter. Then everything stopped.

'Shit', said Whiteman, 'have we screwed it?'

'Not necessarily', replied Clive, 'I've seen this before. Someone will need to assess the information and work out if it's worth accessing more. It can take a while.'

'Ok', said Whiteman, 'so we're still good?'

'I think so', said Clive.

For the next half hour or so, the three chatted generally and speculated about the likely endpoint for Uncle Peter. All agreed that it was most likely China or Russia, but wouldn't like to bet on either.

FreeBee's LEDs started flashing.

'Guys, the game's afoot!', declared Whiteman, 'God, I've always wanted to say that.'

Whiteman started tracing the network traffic. After several attempts, he stopped.

'This is stupid', he said, 'every time I start the trace, the connection hops. I'm going to wait until we get the bigger files in place. By the look of it, they're going for the documentation first. Perhaps someone will need to assess it.'

Uncle Peter disappeared again. After a while, the team hung up and Clive lay down on the sofa, so he could watch to see if the LEDs flashed again. Within a few minutes, he had fallen asleep.

He awoke to the sound of his 'phone ringing again. Jason must have covered him up as he now had a duvet wrapped around him.

'Morning!', said Whiteman, 'Blubbery Fart, lovely'.

Clive confirmed the words shown on his screen. Mark had already joined the call.

'Well?', asked Clive, 'what's happening?'

'I have a data request for the poisoned chalice. Do we let it go?'

'Hold on', Clive checked the status of the servers and made sure FreeBee was running properly, 'let's go for it!'

Whiteman hit the return key and Uncle Peter's request went through.

Slowly, the file started uploading and Whiteman started tracing the path again. Slowly, hop by hop, he worked his way through the various network nodes until he came to a stop. He looked at the address of the computer at the other end and then started another program to look up the registration address for it.

'Fuck!', he said.

'What?'

'Well, we've got an endpoint - but it's not where I was expecting it to end up.'

'Get on with it', said Clive.

'It's in the OS-Futures data centre.'

'What!', exclaimed Mark, 'that's one of the biggest software companies in the world.'

'Well, if they want it to look like an operating update then it'll have to at least look like it ends up somewhere legitimate, surely?', asked Clive.

'No, no - this isn't a spoofed address. This is the real end-point. It ends up in OS-Futures. Slap bang in the middle of their biggest data centre.'

'All the traffic's stopped again', observed Clive.

'Do you think they've worked out it's a honeypot?', asked Mark.

'Unlikely', replied Whiteman, 'I've been checking the honeypot logs. I've seen a few probes and other pretty standard scans to see if we've left any ports open - pretty much standard for the net these days. Opportunists scanning server address ranges until they find something, then scanning to see if there's any way in.

'Bear in mind, I'm using the FBI's most up to date model for the honeypot. Our NSA guys gave it a clean bill of health, so that's pretty much as robust as we can get it!'

'Apart from Uncle Peter', chipped in Clive.

'Yeah, yeah, yeah', replied Whiteman, 'there's nothing unusual there. I'm pretty sure of it. It's just a waiting game again. They've taken the poisoned chalice, so lets hope we've got some idiot who will get engrossed in the layer by layer reveal and just click the link at the end.'

Clive set up a few more controls on FreeBee.

'Right', he said, 'it's pointless us all sitting here waiting. I've set FreeBee up so it'll send a message to us all as soon as anyone hits the link at their end.'

54

At 3PM on Monday the 2nd of June Clive, Whiteman, and Mark all received an alert from the Uncle Peter link. Someone had finally clicked on the link in the honeypot document.

All three sprung into action, firing up respective communications systems and laptops.

'Right', said Whiteman, 'I'm on the trace; Clive what have we got from the link?'

'It's still active, and there are several links off the original site - whoever's at the other end is clicking away quite happily.

'Theory suggests that the machine at the other end will run the embedded code so we should have a portal back into that machine. It looks like our poisoned chalice has done the trick.'

'Ok, we've got it', said Whiteman, and then stopped.

'What?', asked Clive.

Whiteman remained silent for a couple of minutes.

'I need to run the trace again. Give me a minute.'

Mark and Clive could hear Whiteman tapping away on his keyboard. After a moment or two, Whiteman whistled.

'Jesus Christ!', he said.

'Stop keeping us in suspense!', responded Mark.

'You guys - I'm not entirely sure what we have here now.'

'Why?', asked Clive, 'Come on what have you got?'

'The trace ends up back at Quantico - the Operational Technology Division of the FBI by the look of it.'

'This is an FBI hack?', asked Mark.

'I've run it twice and it certainly looks like it.'

'So, we have a compromised software update mechanism that grabs data and stores it inside the cloud services provided by the operating system companies, that is then assessed by FBI staff? Is that what we're saying? This whole thing is an FBI operation?'

'It looks like it', said Whiteman.

'What do we do now?', asked Clive, 'I mean, we all thought that this was some foreign superpower - well, ironically, it is - it's just the wrong superpower.'

'Well', said Mark, 'clearly we have a conflict of interests here. I mean, does this mean that the US Federal Government has installed spyware on every computer system used with Federal systems, or does it go wider than that - is the US, for example, spying on all intelligence agencies, contractors, suppliers … where does it stop?'

'I need to think', said Whiteman.

'It would explain why Paul had to disappear, and why they tried it on with me too!', said Clive, 'I mean, if Paul found a link back then he had to go. I have to ask whether I'm now in danger - who in the FBI knows I'm shacked up here? Does anyone else know Mark's involved - is he in danger too?'

'I moved you on my own', said Whiteman, 'I wasn't sure if we had a leak somewhere in the intelligence chain, so I wanted you safe and out of the way. Mark, I've never mentioned you and I'm assuming you've gone off-book on this?'

'Totally', replied Mark grimly.

'Right, so we three are the only ones that know about this - and that's both good and bad. If anyone finds out that we know, then we're likely to end up going the same way as Paul. So, the genie's out of the bottle, and we're most likely targets now - we know Clive is. Mark, you're probably safe.'

'I can't live in exile for the rest of my life - they will find me eventually, and you can't continue to support me from FBI funds', said Clive.

'No, I know', replied Whiteman.

'What', started Mark, 'is the right thing to do? Forget for a moment that we are talking about the US. What were we going to do?'

'Expose the whole damned thing', replied Clive.

'So we stick to the plan', said Mark.

'Turn whistleblower?', asked Whiteman.

'What choice do we have?'

'No, we can't - at least not yet - perhaps we need a little more proof', said Whiteman, 'I'll package up the trace data and get that copied over to both of you. I'm not sure that we can use the FBI resources for too long - the team might notice a trace coming from inside my department to Quantico so I'm going to have to be very careful.'

'I'll work on a reverse hack', said Clive, 'see if we can't use Uncle Peter back on them. We'll feed them another document embedded within a document - perhaps do it with a video stream this time. It's a big file and should keep them amused while we infect their machines behind their own shadow.'

55

'Right', said Clive, 'I think we're about ready to deploy.'

Whiteman and Mark set up their respective machines to trace the various systems and to record a log of all the events.

Clive hit the 'deploy' button on his screen.

'Now it's a waiting game', he said, 'let's see whether they want the video file.'

The three hung up and each sat by their machines waiting for Uncle Peter to visit.

'What are you waiting for now?', asked Jason.

'We know how Uncle Peter works now', replied Clive, 'so we have set up a video file that, if you change how the computer looks at it, becomes a massive spreadsheet - and within the spreadsheet, we've embedded a few links to other pieces of data.

'We're hoping that whoever looks at the data chooses to go through the steps of changing the type to a spreadsheet and then clicks on a few of the links inside it. If they do, then we install our own Uncle Peter code on that computer.

'If that machine responds, then we have set up our own mini-Uncle Peter, where we can then monitor what that user does on that machine. Perhaps we can get a few machines that share the network. It uses their own system against them.'

'What are you hoping to get from that?''

'If we record everything from that machine, then we can see what happens to our data. Where it ends up, who uses it, and so on. We're going to blow the lid of this, so we need to prove everything, every step of the way. We already know how it works when it's on the machine, but why are they doing this? How do they install it in the first place? Who is really behind it all?

'There's a bit of psychology here - if you're sitting watching stuff all day, you'll get bored senseless. If something comes along that requires a bit of thought, and that takes you part way down a path, you're likely to carry on down the path, even if you know you shouldn't.

'Intelligence training should say "never click on an active link", in this sort of scenario. But they did last time, and I'm betting they will again this time. If they do - then we have them. If not, we still get another trace back to the FBI and while it really only confirms what we already know, it might help us convince someone else that we're not all barking mad!'

Clive received an alert on his mobile. He called up Mark and Whiteman.

'Ok, they're pulling down the video', said Mark as he watched the log files.

'Trace running', chipped in Whiteman.

'Keep everything crossed that they follow the instructions in the video and change the file extension.'

'Ok, got them', said Whiteman a few minutes later.

'Wow - it's the same machine. It looks like we're allocated our own agent!'

'Good - that increases the chances that we'll get a click on the embedded links.'

After a few painful minutes, Clive's display showed a live

connection.

'Gotcha!', he said.

'Is it working?', said Whiteman.

'It's deployed and giving me a connection, so let's see if I can do anything with it', replied Clive.

'I'm sending a profile request - this should give me the user credentials and login data, if I got it right …'

Clive hit return after assembling a sequence of commands he'd seen issued to his own machines in the past.

Nothing happened.

'Shit', said Clive.

'Can't see anything on our Uncle Peter emulator.'

'Nothing on the network either', said Whiteman.

'Wait', replied Mark, 'doesn't Uncle Peter create several routes to the data - we might have just sent a load of data to OS-Futures' cloud'

'No', said Clive, 'part of the request defines where the result should end up - I set the addresses to our virtual server. I can't see anything at all yet. I must have misread the code. Here's hoping it hasn't screwed up the connection, I'm not sure we can assemble that many more documents to amuse our friendly agent.'

'Well', said Whiteman, 'let's exchange the log data amongst ourselves anyway, it goes to prove it wasn't a one off. Interesting that it ends up on the same desk nonetheless. It does suggest that they need some form of continuity at the agency and that kind of makes sense. It means they're not just looking at abstract data.'

Late that night, Clive received an alert from his Uncle Peter emulator. He logged onto the machine and checked what had come back. He saw a complete machine and user profile for the agent in Quantico.

As it was late, Clive sent copies of the data to Mark and

Whiteman. Then he set about deploying a small module that would record everything the agent did for a period of 24 hours. This would show what information that machine captured, and what happened to the data during that time.

Mark had generated more documentation, so Clive inserted that into the honeypot. New data in the honeypot should guarantee that the agent received something to review.

Clive then deployed a second module to the agent's computer. This would send the log file back to Clive, then delete itself from the agent's computer. Now, it was a waiting game - clearly Uncle Peter used a fire and forget model - it was just a case of waiting for the results to come back.

56

'Right guys - let's go round each of us in turn', said Whiteman at the start of the call.

He continued, 'I've got from around 8:45 through until lunch-time by the look of it.

'The headline: I've got another machine. The data comes in and goes through a triage process by the look of it. What we see here is an agent reviewing information and then categorising it. Anything of interest gets flagged to a more senior agent. The rest returns to OS-Futures and I'm now mid-way through the process or tracing that environment. It has to be one of the most mind-numbing jobs in the world as most of the data seems to include emails, word processor documents and so on.

'From this, it looks like each agent has a set of machines to monitor. All our traffic has gone to the same computer so far, so the unique identifier must somehow map to a specific machine or agent. I'm still digging, but it also appears to cover information from a wide range of users - I think some are domestic users and I'm tracing the connections back to find out where each is located.

'That's about as far as I've got - there's a lot in there!'

Mark picked up the conversation from there.

'I have the rest of the working day in that case. I, too, have seen a wide range of topics, suggesting that it's not just commercial or government machines that have made the watch-list.

'Looking at the agent's response times, they read remarkably quickly - so perhaps this is literally a case of scanning for anything that might look interesting and flagging it to someone else. The flagging process seems to involve several others, I have broken those down into a spreadsheet and will circulate them at the end of the call.'

'I'll look at them', chipped in Whiteman, 'I can use our tracer to find out who's involved.'

'Great thanks. I've also constructed a relationship chart. If we can piece together the network behind this - and I'm meaning people or types of data - then we can build a picture of what they're looking for, and what they do with our data. Clive?'

'Good work chaps. Now, I've worked on a couple more services. There's a network discovery routine that recurses through all the machines connected to the target machine. This propagates our code through their department, all still in the shadow code. I deployed it last night, so we should start seeing data coming back from those machines in the next few days.

'With the second link, well, that could be interesting already - Whiteman, did the second machine come via the link embedded in the document files?'

'Yes'

'Excellent', said Clive, 'that means I should have another compromised machine - somewhere higher up the tree.'

'Surely they must check they're not leaving a trail behind them?', asked Mark.

'I think they're bored. This is a little light entertainment for them! It looks innocuous enough - after all, it's just a document hidden within a document and so on. It's such a simple thing, they just change the filename, click on the new file, see it open in something else. By the time you've done that a few times and seen no alarm bells, you'd just keep clicking', replied Whiteman.

'I agree', said Clive, 'but in the meantime, we're getting a few more targets to process. So, I'll now deploy our logging code to the other machines, and lets see what we get. This time though, I'll reduce the capture window, otherwise we're going to get swamped with data. I'll also stop logging our initial agent's actions - I think we've seen enough to understand the process'.

57

The three worked almost around the clock. By sheer fluke, the poisoned chalice seemed to attract the attention of several people both in the FBI and within OS-Futures. Clearly there was a data sharing arrangement between the FBI and OS-Futures.

Whiteman and Mark were both experienced analysts. They had very similar methods but applied the skills in very different ways.

Clive kept planting more and more pieces of shadow code, using previously compromised machines as gateways into the various organisations. He was sure he could now take control of enough machines to deploy his version of Uncle Peter to all the machines in the department, but chose to limit his activities to those machines accessing the poisoned chalice. Compromising more machines may provide some academic entertainment, but they really wanted to know where the data ended up, and who was involved in handling it.

Whiteman was quite excited on the afternoon of June 10th.

'Guys, we have enough now to show how this lot hangs together. It looks like you've been able to work out the whole system. I doubt the teams inside the FBI actually know what they're assessing - from what I can glean from our internal structure documents, it looks like it's all ending up inside something badged as a homeland security support unit.

'If they keep each of the agents employed with a specific set of machines and users, then they may well think they're looking for terrorism references or covert technologies within terror cells. They then ping anything interesting up the chain. I would imagine that they move the targets around a little so that the monitoring agents don't start to suspect that this is mass surveillance.'

'You could be right - it's one hell of a smooth operation', replied Clive.

'Anyway, I'm going to send you both the network map and data distribution path - I think I have a fair few of the processes mapped out too'

Whiteman hit the transfer button on the messaging application and both Clive and Mark accepted the compressed archive. They waited while the transfer counted up.

10% .. 20% ..

'God', said Clive, 'this is painful'

'Yeah', replied Mark, 'I guess that's the problem with using layers of relays'

40%

In the background, Clive and Mark could hear a knock at Whiteman's door.

50%

They heard Whiteman move things around his desk, probably hiding the assorted evidence from prying eyes. Another knock at the door.

70%

'Ok, coming', said Whiteman.

80%

There was a huge thump followed by a couple of muted bangs.

90%

A voice said 'Grab that lot and let's get out of here.'

The line went dead.

96%.

58

'Mark, I'm sending the last block now', said Clive, 'it's as much as I can recover'

Sombrely Mark replied, 'Ok, thanks. I think we've got enough to cause some serious waves. I need to work on how we present this lot though - it's a lot for someone to understand.'

'Yeah - but you're good at that kind of thing!'

'I've presented worse for jurors before, so I can get this into some kind of sensible order. Where are we with the honeypot?'

'I've shut it down. I can't take the chance that it compromises us. I keep getting reports from the poisoned chalice though - it's going through a few departments, by the look of it, although I'm struggling to trace them all - I haven't got access to Whiteman's resources!'

The last block finished transferring. Clive had spent some time recovering most of the file - even though the last few blocks were missing, he had managed to obtain most of the network data Whiteman had mentioned before …

Clive tried not to think about what had just happened to Whiteman. He also tried to avoid playing "what if" in his mind. What if his credit cards no longer worked? What if

Whiteman had left references to the current address or to Mark? What if, right now, someone was heading for Clive.

Mark had said something.

'Sorry, missed that', he said.

'It's Ok, I think I can see everything I need anyway. Look, I'm going to start documenting this lot properly. If we're going to expose it, we need to have it in a form ready for a journalist to take on. I'll start writing - I could do with you drawing out how the network operates, if that's Ok?'

'Sure', replied Clive, 'I'll get on it'.

He hung up.

Jason had walked into the room with their back-packs.

'I'm ready', he said.

'Ok, thanks', replied Clive, 'we need to be ready to move at any time - I'm not even sure we should be here now'.

'Where do we go?'

'I have no idea. I don't even know if these cards will keep working - we're stuffed!'

'Never', replied Jason with a grin, 'we'll get through'

Clive sat down and started sketching out the top level of the systems based on the data obtained from Whiteman and the poisoned chalice. Part way through, the 'phone went. Absent-mindedly, he picked it up and looked at the display - it was Whiteman.

Clive hit the 'answer' button and saw the words "butt flaps" - however, the caller at the other end said entirely the wrong thing:

'Knollys?'

Clive hung up.

'Jason, JASON', he shouted.

Clive unplugged the power and network leads from the equipment and shoved it into his bag.

Jason came running through.

'What?'

"We're leaving. Right now. Come on, move!'

Clive struggled to get his coat on and realised he was still holding the 'phone. He spent a moment starting it off on a factory reset and then threw it onto the sofa - it was compromised now anyway.

Jason scooped up his bag, grabbed his coat and the pair left, slamming the door behind them.

The pair crossed the road and seeing a bus starting to work its way down the road, jogged towards a covered bus stop. They ducked inside - it was an enclosed structure: the bottom half made from brick, the top half glass.

Two cars, an Audi and a BMW sped along the front and stopped outside the house. 6 men leapt from the cars and ran inside. 1 man remained and was looking towards the bus. It stopped at the far end of the road to let a passenger off.

Clive and Jason hid below the half-solid partition and Jason held his 'phone against the glass top-half and hit record. Though hidden from view, Jason and Clive could see the men working through the house.

A couple of minutes later, they emerged: one holding Clive's burner 'phone, another talking rapidly on his own 'phone.

Further down the street, a young lad with his girlfriend was about to receive the shock of his life: endeavouring to impress his potential bride to be, he floored the accelerator on his VW Golf and wheel-spun his way up the road and out of sight. The men, assuming that this was Clive and Jason taking flight jumped into the cars and set off in hot pursuit.

Clive let out a huge sigh.

'Thank fuck for that', said Jason.

'A bit too close for comfort, that one', said Clive, 'can I borrow your phone?'

Clive used the secure messenger application on Jason's 'phone to send a message to Mark.

"Clive: Dublin raided. We're safe for now but on the run. Will contact you soon. Keep your eyes open."

"Mark: Ok - do they have a link to me?"

"Clive: Not as far as I know. Phone reset, secure app = no audit. Going now. Chat later."

With that, he closed the messenger application and passed the 'phone back to Jason.

'Thanks'

The bus had made its way down the road and stopped for them. Clive and Jason didn't really care where it was going, they just knew they had to get out of the area as quickly and quietly as they could. Seeing a taxi rank, the couple left the bus and hopped into a taxi, just in case the men came after the bus when they realised that they had missed their prey.

59

Clive looked at the pile of cash on the bed.

'We're stuffed - we'll get another load tomorrow, but I'm not sure how long we can keep going without Whiteman topping the cards up in the background. I'm really not sure what we are going to do.'

'We'll be Ok', replied Jason, 'there's more cash here than I've lived on for the past 6 months.'

'Pass me the 'phone, I want to call Mark.'

'Is that wise? I mean didn't they track Whiteman's 'phone?'

'I'm not worried about that - they had access to a known 'phone and an entire network to play with. But ...', he assembled all the various pieces of computer equipment and looked out of the B&B window, '... if it's not Mark at the other end, we move. Ok?'

'Ok'.

Clive set up the secure call using a new 'phone they'd bought for cash earlier in the day.

'Hi Mark - how are the orange buttcheeks?' asked Clive, looking at the screen.

'Yes', replied Mark's familiar tones at the other end, 'they're orange buttcheeks here too.'

'Great. Now, we managed to get out - they turned the

house over as soon as we connected, so they managed to get hold of the operator logs for Whiteman's 'phone to my burner. I've not used this one to call you before, so this end should be ok. Did you ever speak to Whiteman directly?'

'Yes, of course. But that's probably Ok because it was all part of the investigation. I had to call him.'

'Hmm. Keep an eye out though. Best to assume they'll track your number at some point.'

'I'm already paranoid enough without you adding to it!'

'I'm holed up in Dublin at the moment - and we need to get back to the UK. Here we'll struggle to blend in. So, I'm thinking that I'll put the documentation together on how Uncle Peter works, and where the traffic ends up. At that point, I'll send it all over to you. If you can print it, perhaps we can present it back to Steve White and his lot?'

'Not a good idea. I mean do the first bit - I think we need a copy of everything. We need to have several copies of everything, in several places. Leave that with me. However, Whiteman was pretty adamant that we had a leak from someone reasonably high up in the investigative team. We might be better going directly to MI5 with this - get hold of David Harswell - he might even help pull you out of Dublin.'

'Ok', said Clive, 'but let me complete this lot first.'

'It might also prove useful to split up for a while. Two's always easier to track than one.'

'I know - I just don't want to. Neither of us really want that at the moment.'

'Just saying …'

'I'll think about it.'

Clive hung up and looked at Jason.

'He's right, you know.'

'What?', asked Jason.

'We need to split up for a few days. Does Trevor have any other lets on Anglesey?'

'Yes, several - I can ask if you want. Why?'

'Well, I'm thinking that you go to one of those. Today. Get on the ferry and head back. I'll come and find you as soon as I've handed everything over to MI5.'

'But what if MI5 are in on it?'

'That's a risk we'll have to take.'

Jason shook his head.

'Isn't there any way we can find out for sure, before you call?'

'No - I can only say he's been supportive so far - if he's in on this, then at least Mark has sufficient data to prove that I've been set up. So the dark network bit wouldn't stand up in a court of law.'

'Couldn't they just add some terrorist data and say that they'd missed that in the mean time. They could lock you up for ever if they could prove some connection to one of the big terror groups - in those cases, they can hold you pretty much indefinitely - or even send you over to the US.'

'Look - we can't stay here forever. We will run out of money and we can't survive on the run with US passports for any reasonable amount of time. If we're in the UK, we stand a better chance. You have people and places that you know - and if I can get this lot cleared through MI5 or whatever other route we can find, then we're back to a normal life. This isn't normal. If we split up and head back via different routes, we stand a chance of surviving. Who knows, we might even be able to lead a sensible life again. After all, the house was insured - hey we could even end up at that beach on Anglesey!'

'Ok', said Jason after a few thoughtful moments. 'If I get the next ferry, will you be on the one after that?'

'I don't know. I'll let MI5 know where I am and then we'll see how it goes from there.'

Jason picked up his 'phone and called Trevor.

'Hi mate, can I stay in the Watertower for a week or so?'

While Jason organised his trip back to Anglesey, Clive started to assemble everything. He wanted to send Mark traces off every component - enough to prove that Uncle Peter existed, and show how the system worked.

'Right', said Jason, 'that's sorted. I gather a few people have been to the house at Ravenspoint and asked around. It looks like we got out just in time.'

Jason handed Clive an address.

'This is the most stunning place to stay', he said, 'it's an old water-tower I worked on. It's in the grounds of a private school, but is a good way away from it, and very secluded. It's just up from Menai Bridge - so easy enough to get to.'

'When are you heading back?'

'Tomorrow morning, bright and early.'

60

Clive hugged Jason and then watched from the window as Jason climbed into the taxi.

'Bugger', he said quietly to himself.

Over the next few hours, Clive busied himself with tracing more of Uncle Peter's activities. He photographed his images defining how Uncle Peter worked. Then, he photographed all of his meticulous notes before packaging the whole lot into an encrypted digital archive that he sent to Mark.

He sat back and sipped a coffee while he waited for the transfer to finish. His 'phone beeped and the display showed an incoming message from Jason.

'Arrived in one piece. I can see you on the GPS tracker app, can you see me?'

Clive called up the tracker and could see the location of Jason's 'phone on the map.

'Yes - but technically, you're seeing my 'phone, not me …'

'Yeah, yeah, yeah.'

With Jason safely ensconced in the Watertower and all the data copied over to Mark, Clive looked at the mobile network unit that MI5 had provided.

'Well', he said to himself, 'here goes nothing.'

He inserted the battery and turned the device on. Soon it

had found a mobile network, and Clive waited. After a few seconds, it beeped - Clive logged on to it and read a welcome message from the Irish Network Operator.

Nearly an hour passed while Clive packed everything. The device beeped again.

An apparently old text message had arrived from a mobile number - it was sent on the day Clive and Jason had run from Crewe:

"Clive, please call on this number. We need to speak urgently. David."

Clive walked down to a nearby mobile 'phone shop and bought a cheap 'phone. He only intended to use it once, so he bought the cheapest he could find.

After that, he walked to Askel McThurkels, a pub where Clive and Jason had discovered Irish Guinness and eaten several huge meals. Clive ordered lunch and went to collect his food.

After that, he sat down and looked at the 'phone. He spent a long time just gazing at the screen before muttering 'fuck it'. He dialled David's number.

'David Harswell'

'Hi David - It's Clive, Clive Knollys'

'Well, good afternoon - I see you're in Ireland!'

Clive was slightly taken aback.

'How do you know?', he asked.

'International number on the screen: plus 353 - is that Dublin?'

'Yeah, it is. I wanted to get out of the way so I could concentrate on getting the job done.'

'Is Jason with you?'

'No - we split. The pressure's a little too much, so I think he's gone back to his family in Stoke. These things take their toll. Have you heard from Whiteman?'

'Did he help you get over to Dublin?'

'There was a little help from the FBI', replied Clive carefully.

'Ok', replied David, 'I thought as much. You said you wanted to get the job done - presumably you mean with Uncle Peter - have you?'

'I think so'

There was a pause.

'Right. We need to get you back to the UK', said David.

'There's some bull about me being involved in some, shall we say, dodgy activities online.'

'All bollocks', replied David quickly, 'we know that. I'll arrange a flight to Liverpool for you - are you on your own passport?'

'No. Don't worry, I'll book something and send you the details.'

'Ok, has anyone else approached you?'

'Anyone else?'

'You know - other interested parties. People trying to find out what you do etc.?'

'No, why?'

'And is anyone else, other than Jason, aware of Uncle Peter or what you've done with it?'

'I don't think so', lied Clive, 'and even Jason couldn't string two lines of code together, so I'd hardly consider him any form of expert. He got bored of Uncle Peter as soon as he realised it wasn't a real person!'

David laughed.

'Ok', he said, 'I'll collect you in person from the airport.'

'No, it's Ok, I'll arrange an hotel and send you the details.'

Clive wanted to keep things under his control as much as he could.

After hanging up, Clive ate his lunch and then left the pub.

61

There was knock on the door. Clive jumped.

'Fuck', he thought, 'he's early.'

'Hold on', he shouted from the bathroom, 'be right with you.'

He grabbed his 'phone and set up a call to Mark.

'He's early', he whispered into the handset as soon as Mark answered, 'hit record and patch Jason in so he can do the same.'

Clive walked back into the hotel room and slid the 'phone under the bed. He hoped it would pick up everything.

He had a quick look around the room and then opened the door.

Whiteman stood outside.

Clive froze.

'Whiteman?'

'Hi Clive, good to see you.'

'What the hell?'

'Aren't you going to invite me in?'

Clive stepped aside.

'Yes, of course - I thought you … they … I heard them …'

'I had a slightly unfortunate experience with MI5 - I think they thought you were with me.'

Whiteman came in and sat on the edge of the bed. Clive closed the door.

'I'm expecting David soon.'

'Yes, I know. That's why I came here first. I need to know what you know about Uncle Peter before MI5 turn up.'

'Well, I think you know most of it …'

'Oh?'

Whiteman's tone had changed.

Clive looked at Whiteman.

'… Possibly all of it. Are you here to kill me?'

Whiteman looked at Clive with a resigned look on his face.

'What do you think you know?'

'Something you didn't consider. Something I found in the data.'

Whiteman look confused.

'What do you mean?'

Clive walked over to the hotel-room table and pointed to FreeBee.

'As you know, I created an emulator that could pretend to be Uncle Peter.'

'Ok'

'The thing is, that shadow code finds the easiest and quickest route to Uncle Peter: it wants to do things as quickly as possibly to avoid detection. With me so far?'

'Yes …'

'So', continued Clive, 'when I created my instance of Uncle Peter, all of your computers suddenly found a very quick and easy route to FreeBee instead - all of them thought they were talking to the real Uncle Peter. In that aborted download, as a by-product, I had a copy of all your email, messages, and some very interesting notes.

'I was intending to share them with David Harswell - and I'm guessing you're here to stop that from happening?'

Whiteman didn't reply.

Mike Hawkes

'But I warn you - I have protected myself.'

'Oh?'

'I'm intending to let Uncle Peter to announce his own retirement.'

'What do you mean?'

Clive walked back from the equipment laid out over the desk.

'Well, the problem with creating a global command and control network is that you have to maintain control over every aspect of your network. Everything's fine as long as no-one can insert themselves into the command and control chain. Like most weapons, however, once you give someone else access to the targeting system, ammunition and trigger, nothing stops them from using your own weapon against you.

'So in my case, I thought that the FBI might have a pressing need to stop me from talking to anyone. When I read your notes, it became clear that you've been instrumental in keeping me isolated - well away from MI5 and the UK government.

'After Bren, Paul, the explosion at my house, and your apparent death. I thought that someone might want to keep me quiet - so I slipped in a few commands of my own. My shadow code is better hidden than yours - and even now it's now distributing itself around the world, courtesy of Uncle Peter.

'If I die, then every computer attaches itself to a new data distribution network within Uncle Peter - I've created the largest broadcasting system in the world.

'Every person receives a copy of all the data you've collected about that person: a copy of the searches run on their data, and which companies received their information - a complete history of everything the FBI has done with that individual's data. Oh, and of course, it also sends a complete breakdown of how the system works to every media outlet in the world too.

'At that point, I reveal the truth behind each and every one of those technology companies, every operating system manufacturer, every software and hardware company - it will expose the whole US computer industry for what it is. Let's see how the USA fares after that.

'It appears that I have a little leverage here, but I also wanted to make sure there's a little extra protection - so I'm not the only one with the trigger.'

'What do you mean?'

'Well, if I suspect that the FBI has messed with me, or any of those around me, then I hit the trigger. I have both systems and friends that can hit the trigger if anything happens to me. Simple huh?

'So, if you intend to kill me before David arrives, do it - but rest assured, all hell will break loose.'

A soft knock on the door announced David's arrival.

'Well, it looks like I'm still alive. Time to sing!', said Clive and opened the door.

'Welcome', he said, 'come and join the party!'

'Hi Clive, Whiteman. I see we have another cosy hotel room.'

David sat on the bed next to Whiteman.

'So, have you completed your research?', he asked.

'Yes', replied Clive, 'but I don't know how the UK Government will respond to it. This is the biggest system I have ever seen ...'

'I'm sure we'll cope - I'm all ears.'

Clive stood next to the equipment laid out on the desk.

'As we thought, Uncle Peter is a system that captures every single piece of new information created on an infected machine. So far, every device I have seen appears to be infected.

'It runs as shadow-code - a program that hides itself inside other pieces of code. If you look for it, it moves into another shadow. It can adapt itself to hide in the lowest possible level of a computer - usually the operating system or firmware - the stuff that controls how the computer works. I suspect that some elements actually exist in the fabric of the chips themselves.

'Shadow code distributes itself beyond just computers - it targets mobiles, memory cards, disk drives, printers, cameras - in fact anything you connect to an infected computer. Then it transfers itself to all of the devices connected to the new host. It can bypass air-gaps because when the computer trusts something that you plug into it, there's an open pathway for shadow code to install itself anywhere and everywhere.

'Once the shadow code starts up, it tries to connect to a command-and-control network. This connection looks like a software update request, but it actually registers the computer on the system and establishes a route back to Uncle Peter.

'It makes each new device part of the network, so it increases Uncle Peter's reach - more importantly, it also adds additional processing power and memory. Uncle Peter can use all of the spare capacity across all of the infected computers to act as one big super-computer. This is how it can process all of the data it captures so quickly.

'Anything of interest gets sent to a human operator to review. That operator can then forward it to other operators or set a marker such that any changes to the original material go back to that same operator in the future.

'All of these computers make this the biggest search tool in the world. The neat part isn't necessarily the collection and networking processes, it's how it uses all this combined processing power to search through and categorise data.

Shadow code isn't merely a collector, it can use every computer, every mobile phone - even the spare capacity in your TV processor to help analyse, categorise and extract information. Ever wondered why your 'phone suddenly chews its way through its battery, or your TV flickers? Perhaps Uncle Peter needed a little extra grunt that day.

'Shadow code uses Uncle Peter to work out new ways to communicate - every device you buy becomes part of the network, part of this global computer. As consumers, we add more and more power to Uncle Peter's systems every day.

'The really scary bit is that this connection can exist via virtually any route - if you have a sound card, it can use the microphone and speakers to set up a network; a web-cam and display gives you a high-frequency flicker to talk to the network. It can use any wireless system, any wired network - even transferring instructions via memory cards, printers, in fact anything you connect to a machine.

'So, you have an omnipresent network connection to a command and control system. This command and control system can then install components to monitor, record, search through or control every piece of equipment.

'In theory, if you have a TV set in the room, then that can be used to send commands to the webcam on your laptop or mobile 'phone so that it assembles information for the next time you connect to a better network.

'All of it terminates at the FBI's offices in Quantico - Paul's data proved it. At the time though I didn't see that and he died before he could tell me. I think that's why he died - Paul had managed to trace it to one of the FBI's own departments. They manage shadow code to collect any, or possibly every piece of information on every piece of technology around the world.

Clive paused for effect. Seeing no reaction, he continued.

'I managed to create a copycat service: the kit on the table mimics Uncle Peter. I have copies distributed elsewhere now too.

'We then created a honeypot - one of Whiteman's specialities of course. But my honeypot delivered a poisoned chalice, something that a human operator would find interesting. We needed a concept that would intrigue an operator enough to take a look at it - something that created a link back to that box on the table. As soon as the operator opened the chalice, I used my own shadow code against the connected machine - a shadow in the shadows.

'I installed a tool to log everything that operator did. By the time I'd done that, I also managed to control a few other machines in the same department - shadow code's good, but it's dumb: it never knew I wasn't the real command and control system. So I managed to create a virtual map of the department, its network and how it works - and it's a huge operation.

'Anyway, like the real Uncle Peter, this lot collected all the information from every compromised machine. OSFutures, an FBI cover-company by the look of it, maintains shadow code. They're into pretty much everything and get it installed on virtually every machine - even those manufactured outside of the USA.'

'How?', asked David.

'They make their code available for free - licence free software. Looking at it now, I think the US Government created the whole open-source movement to install shadow code on technology developed elsewhere in the world. Anyway, we're on version 6.8 at the moment, and OSFutures has existed since the dawn of the personal computer. As I said, it's been around for a long time.'

'Where do you suspect the data ends up - surely an operation like this would require massive data centres', said David.

'Yes, it does - although the distributed nature of the network helps relieve some of the pressure there. I think it's actually handled thanks to collaboration between the US government and the big tech giants. It looks like our honeypot data eventually ended up in a couple of the large corporates - we saw hits from their R&D divisions.

'The FBI receives the initial data and then sends it to the corporates that have big enough data centres to provide these vast repositories. It could explain why they're all so keen to adopt cloud computing services. In actuality, cloud makes it easier to snoop - and it will reduce the risk of someone like me finding Uncle Peter. You only need to fire up Uncle Peter if you can't access things through the cloud - and most people are stupid enough to supply cloud data voluntarily of course.'

'Can you stop it?', asked David after a few moments of thoughtful silence.

'Yes. That's what my protocol analyser/blocker does.'

'Can we see it all working?'

Clive stood and walked over to the table in the corner of the room.

'It's here - I'll talk you through it.'

With Whiteman and David watching, Clive connected his laptop to the network. Almost immediately, the LEDs on the protocol analyser started flashing.

'See, we're already capturing traffic from Uncle Peter, but it's not going any further than my analyser at the moment. Now', Clive connected to the protocol analyser, 'let's see what we have.'

After logging in to the analyser, he called up the control screen and then navigated through his system to something that showed the data logs.

'This is the main bit of interest - as you can see, we've captured all that traffic. At this stage, it's not gone beyond this box. If I press this though', Clive clicked on a button marked "Allow".

'You can see the traffic goes through, and then Uncle Peter will respond in a moment or two … there you go. A response from Uncle Peter, in this case acknowledging receipt of that data. If he wanted, he could now send another series of commands, a small program, or simply ask for data from the machine.'

'And you can stop it all?', asked David.

'I think so - at least for as long as they follow the current shadow code protocols - I've mapped them all out here.'

He pointed to a set of diagrams stacked up on the desk.

'And it looks like it all ends up in Whiteman's domain - perhaps even on your desk.'

'Well', said Whiteman ominously, 'You're nearly there'.

'What do you mean, "nearly there"?'

'Sit down, and I'll talk you through it. You know this much, you might as well know the rest.'

Clive sat back down, Whiteman remained standing up, looking at FreeBee and the associated tools spread out over the table.

'Back in the 1980's, we saw an explosion of home computing. We had MILNET and ARPANET and JANET, in the UK there was Prestel, France had Mintel - who knows what other networks existed around the world. These all eventually combined to form the Internet that we know today. It was becoming very clear that people would start to use this network as a tool to research and develop new technologies - in fact we encouraged it.'

Whiteman walked over and sat down next to Clive.

'It also became very clear that criminals and terrorists would use these systems to ply their trade. The cold war was still in full swing too. So, the US Government, in association with the Israeli and UK intelligence services, set up a development project to allow us to monitor Internet communications.

'Unfortunately, not every machine was connected to a public network. People could buy modems and create small networks of their own - not actually connecting them to the Internet itself. We wanted to find out what people were doing on those networks. For defence purposes, we might also need to take control of one for a while: if, for example, we wanted to disable a nuclear or oil facility in hostile territory, or intercept everything that a hostile foreign power was sending over private networks. It was clear that we needed something more sophisticated.

'We had a simple solution - we made the Internet open: basing it on open standards and lots of free software. People like free stuff - so they stopped creating their own networks and connected to the Internet instead. Of course that also allowed us to insert shadow code into the vast amount of software people downloaded. We only needed to do that in the early versions; now it's so prolific that we don't need to have that early code in the source any more. People who did discover parts of it merely assumed that they had found bugs in the code - they closed them, but we'd already gained enough traction to be able to deploy it to any connected device.

'The shadow code commercial model works really well: it's deceptively simple. We approached chip manufacturers and the major US software vendors and gave them early access to a few defence projects in return for their co-operation. They jumped at the chance to gain market advantage, and of course we lined their palms for making our life easier.

'Back then, it was relatively easy to work with them. We installed back doors that allowed us to distribute sleeping shadow code throughout the world. Every chip-set includes the ability to run a section of code completely securely. We hid the shadow code inside that.

'Once the world-wide-web became available, it was clear that we would need significantly better resources - more storage, more people, the development of systems to deal with "big data" along with the tools to interrogate and mine that data. So we struck a deal with the device manufacturers and software companies: in return for harvested intellectual property they would install and maintain the command-and-control systems - and provide storage for the second tier of analysis of all the data collected.'

'Second tier?'

'Yes - the FBI sees everything first, just in case a company tries to play hardball.

'Anyway, it worked so well that we extended this framework to allow companies that became involved in storing the data to access and use any intellectual property they discovered within it - in return for allowing the FBI to access and analyse all of that recorded content at its leisure.

'Back then, we couldn't store all everything generated all the time, so we use a series of tools to analyse and find anything of interest. Early search engine technology came out of this research.'

Clive was flabbergasted.

'So you're saying that the FBI has stolen all the intellectual property from every piece of research around the world and given it to companies that are prepared to help develop or run shadow code? What of the computer manufacturers that didn't agree to being part of the scheme?'

'We always need new ideas', said Whiteman flatly, 'This is a new battleground. It's an intelligence led digital war. If we know what's out there, then we know how to counter it. The companies that worked with us gained access to new ideas, technologies, working methods - new development techniques. With our help, they can file patents and generate technology faster than most individual inventors or small companies.

'This let them become the dominant technology providers and kept us ahead of the market in intelligence terms. Those that didn't play - well - we could ensure that they could never compete against those that did. And anyway bringing things down to a handful of large companies minimised the risk of discovery - particularly back then. The FBI provided some great incentives to provide friends with access to development funds and global distribution deals.'

'This is crazy! What if a company found out, or refused to play ball?'

'Easy - we have the ability to destabilise or remote wipe every device they make - as long as they conform to industry standards or use open source libraries! You know about the open source stuff, but we also skewed the industry standards. We provided funds for the trade associations in return for presence on the board. Usually done by placing a major corporate in there, rather that the US Government per se, of course.

'Those that don't play our way suffer from a few technical problems - they get a terrible reputation for reliability. We have introduced a few pretty neat bugs into systems via the shadow-code framework.'

'That's commercial blackmail, said Clive, 'Is that what you're expecting to do with me and my company?'

'Oh no. You're the first one that managed to find shadow code and prevent it from working. We knew it was only a matter of time before someone did.

'We needed to give you time to complete your analysis. We also needed to stay close so that none of this would leak out. Now we know the techniques you employed, we can work out new shadow images that will give us immunity from this type of analysis in the future.'

'You can't be serious', said Clive, 'surely the UK government wouldn't agree to this?'

'Come on. Wake up. We work together!'

'What do you mean?'

'Look', said David, 'all allies have a version of Uncle Peter. The US made it available to the "Five Eyes" many years ago.'

'Five eyes?'

'Sorry, yes - you might have seen it as FVEY - Australia, Canada, New Zealand, US and UK. It's a framework for sharing intelligence - including data gained from Uncle Peter. In fact the whole principle of Uncle Peter came out of the ECHELON surveillance system we created during the cold war. It's an invaluable resource. It lets us circumvent some of the more difficult privacy laws - and there's a whole information economy that allows us to trade information between intelligence communities and the corporates that need to know.'

'You can't just spy on UK citizens', said Clive.

'Oh but we can', replied Whiteman, 'that's what Five Eyes does. For example, we can spy on the UK - it's perfectly legal; the UK can spy on the US - that's all legal too. Then we have global information sharing agreements that allow the intelligence communities to collaborate. It's a legal way of obtaining intelligence data: "can you spy on so-and-so on our behalf?" - with nothing appearing in the local courts or police records.'

'Initially', continued Whiteman, '"the powers that be" didn't see the big picture. We convinced a few of those in, shall we say, the more senior positions, that we could jointly benefit from the intelligence gained by deploying shadow code.'

'How?'

'We have information on everyone. Sometimes that

information can prove useful to help us get what we need ... more often than not these days, we simply suggest that they help us.'

'You blackmail people?'

'Blackmail's such an ugly word, don't you think? But there are times when it might not be in the national interest for certain individuals with interesting personal lives to stand for election, or to make too much noise ... Sometimes it helps us place particular people on the board of a company or organisation ...'

'So this is how the tech companies grew so quickly', said Clive bitterly, 'what of the UK computer manufacturers - didn't they qualify for intellectual property gifts or something - were you keeping the best for the USA?'

'Many of the UK computer manufacturers wouldn't play with us - and we didn't have enough information to influence support in the early days. We just had to take them out - we gave them free access to shadow-coded operating systems so we could acquire new system designs. Then we passed these over to well funded companies that could implement them better and more quickly - and that put them out of business. It was their choice at the end of the day.'

David looked at Clive.

'It was an unforeseen consequence of compliance by the UK. By the time we realised what the shadow code could do, we'd lost control of it. We had to go along or run the risk of being locked out of our own intelligence data', said David.

'If you think about it, the US could shut down every computer and communications system in the UK. It would reduce us to a third-world country overnight. As a result, we came to the conclusion that collaboration and information sharing is very important to us as a nation. Your tools compromise that entire model - in effect, you have the UK's future in your hands.'

David looked very intently at Clive.

'We would like you to think about sharing your work with us. Perhaps even working on the next generation of shadow code. You might win a tender from the US DOD - or any other government agency of your choosing. MKI receives a multi-million dollar contract to keep doing what it does, while you work on the next generation of shadow code.'

Clive shook his head in disbelief.

'I've spent almost my entire career preventing this type of thing - and the whole time it's been worthless. This undermines every security system in the world. I can't support this - it's … it's just wrong. You're using personal data against people to control what they do - where does it stop?'

'What do you mean?'

'You can close companies or blackmail people to prevent them protesting, or capture enough personal data to discredit them should they start becoming a problem. This is the US potentially taking control of every individual with a computer - do what we say or we compromise you. They've already got the UK. Where does it end?'

Clive sat bolt upright.

'Wait a minute - that means that you can also fabricate anything too. Is that where all that dark network crap came from - were you trying to frame me?'

'Not at all', said Whiteman, 'We needed to stop the police from digging too deep. We wanted to bring the investigation into the NCA and from there to the FBI. Give the police a hot potato, hint at promotion if the lead investigator throws it over the fence - it's a proven formula. It was nothing personal, we just needed the police out of the way.'

'Nothing personal! I could have ended up locked away for years - silenced because you can fabricate a complete lie! You turned me into a fucking paedophile - why?'

'Easy target, sorry. You're gay - mix some additional smut in there and no-one will touch you. Easy link between the two: mud sticks! I told you, it's war and we use whatever tools we have. In my case a little social engineering and technology.'

'But it's a complete fabrication!'

'Who cares? It worked, didn't it?'

'Do you do this to suspected terrorists? If you can't get any evidence then just invent it? It's just wrong …'

David sighed.

'It may be wrong, but sometimes we need to do things we would never otherwise consider. What's done is done - so I might suggest we look at how we move forward from here.

'I hear you like music and painting. What would it take for you to consider retiring?'

'Are you serious? This shit is capable of wiping out every business, every communication system, every weapon we have - and you're happy with that? You're happy for the UK to remain entirely under the control of the USA? You can pretty much control anyone, anywhere - and that makes this the biggest global threat to democracy.'

Clive stood up and walked towards the equipment on the table.

'It's not right - and if I can stop it, then so can someone else. Then what?'

Clive paused. David shrugged in a 'what can we do' sort of way.

Clive continued, 'I don't understand why the technology companies still agree to this - if it ever came out …'

'They have no choice - and they wouldn't dare!', Whiteman interrupted, 'As I said: we turn them off if they don't play ball. We can turn an entire country off or a whole technology platform: "click", it's gone.

'For companies, we often use system instability as a

weapon - if your system crashes often enough, then people stop buying. We could have done this with your systems of course - but we didn't.'

'I guess it's still an option', replied Clive bitterly, 'either that or wipe us!'

'Shadow code, remote wipe and remote lock are the biggest and best threats in the world - and we have the switch. The digital nuke: mess with us or stop playing ball and you're gone.

'Why do you think we've had it written into law that mobile devices must support remote lock and wipe? Mobile platforms were starting to emerge from Asia - by mandating the provision of remote locking or wipe tools, we can finally exercise control over those too.'

Whiteman stood up and looked again at the assembled equipment on the table.

'Let's stay friendly here - as David said, we'd like to invite you onto the team that has already started developing the next generation of shadow code. Or perhaps you'd prefer to sell your company to one of our big software allies so that you can concentrate on your music or painting. Which is it?'

Clive looked at Whiteman and scowled.

'Did you offer this deal to Paul?'

'Paul was already talking to too many people. He was practically broadcasting that he'd found the link back to Quantico. Let's just say that his principles got in the way of rationality. In war, casualties are unavoidable.'

'Even our own?'

'Even our own.'

'You're not really making me an offer, are you?', asked Clive.

'There's an offer there', said David, 'but you only have two choices - join us or retire - I will of course remind you that you have signed the official secrets act.'

'It's a strange thing that your national security strategy is the biggest threat to national security. And I don't think you can use the official secret line here: it's there, in plain view if you know where to look', replied Clive grimly.

'I told you his principles would get in the way', said Whiteman to David.

'I can't believe I was so stupid', said Clive.

'You groomed me - it's a classic case of grooming. Isolate me, get me too paranoid to talk to anyone else, make me believe you're my friend in all of this? Why fake your death?'

'I didn't', replied Whiteman, 'MI5 thought we were going to arrange for rendition so that we could gain exclusive access to your skills. They thought you were with me and sent a team to recover you before that could happen. They confiscated the kit as part of the raid.'

'But why, if you're working together?'

David looked at Whiteman, 'Clive, you know how Uncle Peter really works. You know how to find out what's actually happening under the covers - that information might come in very useful if anyone compromises the shadow code framework. We need to keep control of your knowledge, preferably within easy reach of our own agencies.'

'Anyway, it's something of a rolling bet between the FBI and MI5 - could we really extract someone under the joint protection of the PPS, police, and MI5 tracking systems? I told you, I specialise in social engineering, A little isolation and a few choice words and I got you as far as Ireland on a US passport - I could have offered you permanent safe residency back home. You were paranoid enough to have taken it too - had MI5 not tried to recover you from Bray.'

'That was MI5?'

'Yeah - I told them where you were. But you'd already got away.'

There were a few moments of uncomfortable silence.

'Where do we go from here then?', asked Whiteman, 'You say you've distributed your own shadow code via Uncle Peter to expose the system ... surely you now understand the implications and why we can't allow that to happen ...'

'You've done what?', asked David turning pale.

'I needed to protect myself - and everyone else I know too. If any harm comes to me or anyone else for that matter, then this little secret gets out.

'You have no choice about whether it happens: if I so much as catch a whiff of you lot messing around then I send a copy of the information collected and everything done with it, to the person that originally generated it. Each individual gets to see your dirty little secret!'

'Shit', said David, 'so what do you want?'

'I AM going to whistle-blow - it's just the way and the scale of the disclosure that you can influence here today', said Clive.

'You can't - this is national security. You've signed the official secrets act ...', started David.

'Fuck that!' shouted Clive, 'You can't do this. You just can't. I think it's my turn to offer difficult choices.'

'We're listening'

'I am going to tell the media and you will not stop me. If you try, or if you remove me, then every piece of data gets exposed - all of it. But ... if you stay out of my life - our lives - then I shall only reveal the fact that you're doing this, I won't supply the proof.

'You then have a chance to manipulate the media and public perception to try and make this look like just another conspiracy theory. Let's face it, once this gets out, the media will become the judge, jury and executioner. Public perception is the real threat to you now. I'll give you six months and then I go public.'

Clive reached under the bed and pulled out the mobile

'phone.

'Mark, Jason, did you get all that?', he asked.

David and Whiteman head Mark's voice at the other end.

'Yes, we recorded it all.'

'Good. I think you can upload that to the repository now - we're pretty much done here.'

He looked at the two agents.

'I think, gentlemen, you have some disclaimers to write. I also suggest you look at remote wiping the shadow code - wiping yours will wipe mine. It would never do for someone to find a copy in the wild once this goes public.

'Six months gentlemen, you have six months.'

62

Clive sat and looked at the constantly moving tide from the headland above Trearddur Bay. The sun was shining and small white clouds scuttled along. A few seconds earlier he, Jason and Mark had simultaneously hit 'send' on their respective mobiles. They had started distributing the Shadow Code book to news agencies around the world.

'Penny for them?', asked Jason.

'It's out now', replied Clive, 'I think I've done the right thing. I hope I have - I mean I've killed one of the biggest spying tools in the world. I just hope it's levelled the playing field a little. Tell me I've not just helped a master-criminal or enabled a new level of global terrorism in the name of privacy?'

'Meh! It's for the public to decide and debate - openly. How much privacy do they need to stay free. The second that 'suits in dark rooms' start to make decisions about civilisation as a whole, then we're all lost! You need privacy for democracy to work.'

'That's deep for you!'

Jason slapped Clive playfully.

'Tell me something'

'Go on'

'In that meeting, you said you'd a created a broadcast system to send all the data gathered against someone back to that person. With access to all that data, weren't you tempted to look at your own records, or mine?'

'No', grinned Clive, 'I couldn't see any records: it was all bullshit!'

'What?'

'Look - I thought they'd killed Whiteman. I needed something up my sleeve to stop them killing me - or Mark, or you ... '

'So you didn't have a way to leak it all?'

'Hell no - have you any idea how long it would have taken me to write the software to do that - and hide it?'

Jason whistled.

'Crafty bastard'

'Let's just keep it between us, eh?'

Lightning Source UK Ltd.
Milton Keynes UK
UKHW02f1959050618
323782UK00009B/287/P